Praise for A

'A nuanced tragedy as wel...
Six Strikes explores the min...
who only wants to...
Marie Tierney, aut...

'Antonia Grave has the knack of being able to sweep you up in the story and make you really feel for the characters . . . Thrilling and moving. A must read!'
Jane Renshaw, author of *The Stepson*

'From the emotional jolt of the prologue to the gut-punch ending, *Six Strikes* grabs attention and does not let go. An utterly enthralling portrayal of a good woman damaged by very bad things.' **Frances Crawford, author of *A Bad, Bad Place***

'Antonia Grave has created something remarkable: an entirely relatable serial killer. I couldn't put *Six Strikes* down until long after I was meant to be asleep and I couldn't wait to pick it up again in the morning – the pages practically turned themselves!'
Alison Belsham, author of *The Girls on Chalk Hill*

'Perfectly plotted and masterfully executed, *Six Strikes* is an exceptionally gripping and suspenseful debut novel.'
Julie Lancaster, author of *Remember Where You've Buried the Bodies*

'A firecracker of a novel. Compelling, twisted and deliciously dark. I was hooked from the first page – and I've never rooted for a serial killer like I was rooting for Maddie Reid.'
Hannah Brennan, author of *No Safe Place*

'A dark, twisted journey of serial killers that exposes the pink underbelly of today's gender battles.'
N V Peacock, author of *Little Bones*

Antonia Grave writes in a small room just outside of Manchester, England. She is the author of dark thrillers with characters who believe two wrongs can make a right.

When she isn't writing you'll find her drinking too much coffee, reading, playing computer games, and spending time with her pets.

SIX STRIKES

ANTONIA GRAVE

avon.

Published by AVON
A division of HarperCollins*Publishers* Ltd
1 London Bridge Street
London SE1 9GF

www.harpercollins.co.uk

HarperCollins*Publishers*
Macken House, 39/40 Mayor Street Upper
Dublin 1, D01 C9W8, Ireland

A Paperback Original 2026
1

First published in Great Britain by HarperCollins*Publishers* 2026
Copyright © Antonia Grave 2026

Antonia Grave asserts the moral right to
be identified as the author of this work.

A catalogue record for this book is available from the British Library.

ISBN: 978-0-00-876944-4

This novel is entirely a work of fiction. The names, characters and incidents portrayed in it are the work of the author's imagination. Any resemblance to actual persons, living or dead, events or localities is entirely coincidental.

Typeset in Sabon Lt Std by HarperCollins*Publishers* India

Printed and bound in the UK using 100%
Renewable Electricity at CPI Group (UK) Ltd

All rights reserved. No part of this publication may be reproduced, stored in a retrieval system, or transmitted, in any form or by any means, electronic, mechanical, photocopying, recording or otherwise, without the prior written permission of the publishers.

Without limiting the exclusive rights of any author, contributor or the publisher of this publication, any unauthorised use of this publication to train generative artificial intelligence (AI) technologies is expressly prohibited. HarperCollins also exercise their rights under Article 4(3) of the Digital Single Market Directive 2019/790 and expressly reserve this publication from the text and data mining exception.

For Tallulah

Prologue

1999 – Ben's House

'You wouldn't understand.'

His words merge, making his sentence vowel heavy: yoooooouuwooooouuuldn'tuuuuunderstaaannd. Red wine drips from the coffee table, his last gulp sloshing out of the glass as he lifts it. Drops of liquid queue at the edge, waiting for their turn to fall and disappear. What pleasure it would be to fall. To disappear.

'The offside rule, okay?' He glances in my direction, and I nod. 'Females. They just don't understand it. You don't understand it.'

The closing credits to *Match of the Day* fill the small room. It's a two-up, two-down. I can't remember if it's average-looking on the outside, but I suspect it is. I remember being able to see out of the windows in other houses. Faint memories. Here blackout curtains are nailed to the walls concealing the windows. Sometimes they betray him, allow slivers of light to cascade into the house. I find them. I bathe in them. I worship them. Not tonight, the only light is a dim lamp in the far corner, veiled in a dusty, fabric shade.

'Now, I'm a patient man.' Lie. He's lying again. 'But even my patience would be tested attempting to explain footie to a girl.'

He places the empty wine glass on the edge of the coffee table, and I sweep it up. He's flicking through television channels as I approach the kitchen door. I pause at the threshold. Three knocks for permission to leave a room he is in. Hollow bangs greet my fist.

'Proceed,' he shouts from behind me.

The house is small enough to make this act redundant. I've never pointed this out. I don't desire fist-shaped gifts or broken ribs, with the only medical attention being kisses.

Three bottles of wine are lined up on the kitchen counter. The first bottle of wine is empty. It hits the bottom of the bin with a thud. I fill his glass. Halfway. How he likes it. He's not an alcoholic and only someone with an alcohol problem would want their glass filling to the brim, or so he tells me. I eye the two remaining bottles on the kitchen countertop, their corks removed, so they can breathe. My suffocation comes as they empty.

Three knocks to enter a room he is in. I pause at the doorway of the living room. The fat on his neck wrinkles as he looks over his shoulder at me.

'Proceed,' he says with a bored air.

He flicks through the television channels.

'Look at the state of him,' he says, nodding at a tanned man advertising perfume on the television. He shakes his head and I mirror him as he reaches for the glass. Our fingers graze one another's as I hand it to him. Bile creeps up my throat.

'Metrosexuals.' There is a note of disgust in his tone. 'There's a man at work who is like that. What's his name?' His eyes narrow. 'He goes to the tanning booth. Can you believe that? A man in a tanning salon?' He stares at me hard. 'Men aren't made to be chiselled and lusted over. We're the protectors. It's all a bit topsy-turvy if you ask me.' I nod my head to agree with him. 'You're too young for this,' he says as he flicks to another channel with more adverts. I'm too young for many things, but that has never stopped Ben. 'Peter, that's his name,' he mutters, shaking his head.

Peter from the office likes to go to the tanning salon. I cling on to details from the outside world, these accidental snippets he feeds me. I've spent hours imagining I'm someone else: a woman who wanders freely in the world. Perhaps, in a couple of years, I could have a job? When I'm a bit older. I picture myself wandering around an office with an armful of paper. I fantasize about day-to-day activities – filing, scanning and what I would pack for my lunch. I suspect even the pretty men are not to be trusted but, if I'm feeling generous, I might compliment a man's tan. I know there are more men outside of this house. I know they are there. Lurking.

He pulls a cigarette from his packet and reaches for a disposable lighter on the coffee table. His thumb hits the flint wheel. Nothing. He shakes it and repeats. Another common fantasy enters my head – Ben on fire. I feel a warmth engulf me as I imagine his screams, and a smile spreads across my face like the flames would in this house.

One knock. It pulls me straight from my daydream and Ben stares at me, irritated. He repeats one knock against the table, which vibrates through me, leaving a thrum under my skin as I realize I have missed his cue. He holds the empty lighter up.

'Jacket pocket,' he sighs, as if I should know this.

On my feet. I make my way to the hat stand and rifle through a dozen coats to find the only one he wears. I don't have any coats. My eyes flicker to the door, guarded by metal mesh, as if he housed a wily cat obsessed with escape. Every day he steps into this metal cage, locks it, and then opens the many, many locks on the door. He overestimates me.

At arm's length I hand him the jacket; he grabs it and with his spare hand pats on the sofa beside him. As if there is anywhere else for me to go. A nature documentary replaces the television adverts and the narrator's voice is low and deep. Ben takes another gulp of his cheap wine. The whole house will have a vinegary stink all weekend. He won't notice but I will. I'll notice the way it sweats from him, how it lingers in the kitchen, how it clings to the coffee table. It won't leave until Monday, like an unwanted weekend guest.

He rummages through his pockets until he pulls out another disposable lighter. I make a mental note. I've checked his pockets before to be greeted by nothing but lint.

He brushes a strand of hair off my face, his now lit cigarette hanging from his mouth, and I fight off a shudder. He stares into my eyes and I picture nothing but a pitch-black void. He breaks eye contact and knocks once on the table. My brain scrambles for what he wants: his glass is full, his cigarette is lit, and the lighting is dim – how he likes it. I swallow a sigh.

'I love you,' I lie, as the dress he insists I wear on Saturdays scratches at my skin.

He nods with approval. The nature documentary turns gory, with a lion chasing a gazelle across an arid landscape. It catches Ben's attention, affording me a reprieve. Ben grunts as the lion catches the gazelle, ripping it to shreds. He leans forward in his chair, as if he wants to join the lion feasting on raw flesh.

'I reckon I'd make a cracking lion,' he says, as ash from his cigarette tumbles down his T-shirt.

My mind fills with white noise as entrails splatter across the television screen and I am transported to another life: I'm a gazelle racing across a Saharan desert, my limbs stretching as I bask in vast swathes of freedom. I close my eyes taking in a landscape where I am master. My body hums with joy.

Ben places a hand on my thigh.

I'm jolted from my imaginary world and when I rejoin it, I'm no longer alone, a lion nips at my ankles, its face morphing into Ben's. I pinch the skin between my forefinger and thumb. The lion vanishes and I become a lamb frolicking in a field. The stars are exclamation points in the night sky.

Ben's hand moves higher up my leg.

I focus my mind's eye on the lamb I have become, dancing in the air as I vault wooden fences.

Ben's voice: *maybe it's time for bed.*

The lamb in my imagination tumbles to the ground, mud sticking to its wool, and my brain zooms into a small shaven patch on the neck of my make-believe lamb. A flea. Somewhere in the distance, a lamb squeals for help as the flea drains its blood. My eyes flicker open.

Ben takes a deep inhale on his cigarette and for a second his full cheeks become hollow. His hand curled around his wine glass is pincer-shaped. My head tilts as I picture him shrinking so small I could squash him between finger and thumb.

I look around the room at the wire mesh that guards the front door, the curtains nailed to walls, hiding the painted-shut windows and the soundproofed walls.

Ben is not a lion. Ben is a flea.

1

2007 – Leicester

He's following me.

I've picked up a flea somewhere between the war memorial and the university. About a quarter of a mile back. I've caught his reflection in the angles of bay windows jutting from the front of darkened Edwardian houses. In the window screens of cars parked for the night. A hazy image of a man, dressed in black, with a baseball cap worn low.

I like to walk alone at night. The stars are brilliant listeners, and they never have a bad word to say about anyone. Ten-out-of-ten company. And it means I don't have to hear the other women at the refuge crying themselves to sleep. The walls are too thin. I have learnt crying comes without accent, a Scouse woman and a Welsh woman sound the same as they sob. The night sky was impressed by this factoid. I bet the man behind me knew this fact before I did.

He's fifteen feet behind me. For now. His footsteps don't echo. His tracksuit doesn't rustle. His head is down but his eyes are up, watching, steady, focused. I am certain he is following me.

Dirty water from a shallow puddle soaks into the bottom of my jeans as I pause at the corner of the road. Wet denim sticks against my skin. I look left and right. One might be forgiven for thinking I am looking for traffic, but no, there are no moving cars on this street at this time. He looks at the ground, his pace slowing as I cast my eyes over him. I will him to look up. Let our eyes meet.

I cross the road and a cat appears from underneath a car and races away. I cut down a residential street filled with squat terraced houses. Their flattened fronts offer no reflections. If I ask nicely, do you think he will give me until ten to hide?

I wonder what the headline will be if they find my body in a few days? Body found by dog walker. No, woman found dead by dog walker. I can see the elation on the journalist's face when she discovers I'm not 'just' any woman. When they discover who I am, what my past is, I'll be reduced to clickbait. I can almost hear the frenzied taps on smartphones. My face among adverts for lotteries, weight-loss drugs and celebrity tattle.

The street comes to an end, and I join a busy stretch of road. Traffic lights shine in the distance, and I picture council-funded CCTV trailing me as I walk alone with a stranger in my shadows. They'll see a twenty-four-year-old bag of bones in a hoody and jeans.

Ben told me in the past, they would re-enact someone's final movements on television, employ an actress who was eerily similar in looks to the victim, but now they don't need to. They can just hit rewind and watch someone's final moments. You know, the hours, maybe the minutes before it happens. I picture myself walking down the road with the terraced houses, jumping from domestic camera to domestic camera, as if each house is capturing a different scene. Then onto the busy road, one long shot of me looking oblivious, never looking back, as though I didn't realize what I was close to. They'll assume, in the quiet parts of their mind, that I am an idiot. Then the grainy video will stop, a woman's voice will explain what happens next, off camera, she will describe my murder with the goriest of details media regulations will allow. Then, if they can, they will show the after. The suspect dragging a suitcase or a bin bag. Struggling to lift literal dead weight into the boot of a car.

I stop at a pedestrian crossing. Hit the button, despite the traffic being light. I take a natural look to the left and then to the right. For a second I don't breathe, like a balloon is in my throat, its plastic edge cloying at the sides. Maybe I'm an idiot. He's closer. He's narrowing the gap. The green man flashes, no beeping.

If I was smart, I would wait for the right moment and scream bloody murder from the top of my lungs. And if I did that, what then? Another girl on another day. I need to confirm this man is who I think he is.

Police patrols will increase. After they have found my body. It will be a futile attempt to reassure the local community. It won't just be women who will carry suspicion, men will too. They'll wear it differently though, defensively: *it's not me, it's no one I know, it's not all men.* As a symbol of their innocence, they will offer to walk female friends and colleagues to their destinations. At least until the initial horror has waned.

They won't remember me forever but monsters who slay women aren't forgotten. They write books and films about them. The once scared, suspicious women will become admirers who pen love letters to their incarcerated, misunderstood Romeo.

Up ahead, buildings sunk in darkness block out an industrial skyline, a silhouette of industry. There is no innocent reason to be here at this time of night, and if he comes with me it's the confirmation I need. I pass the first empty factory and head deeper into a maze of units and warehouses. I pass a darkened factory window and his reflection stares hard in my direction.

If he succeeds and I fail, questions will be asked from the outset. Not the right questions. They will rally the pitchforked mobs – look at her clothes, she was alone, it was the middle of the night, she should have known better. She was asking for it. As if my existence equates to consent.

In quieter corners, around water coolers, they'll speculate that I have taken many lovers, and it is no surprise a woman like me would end up a naked corpse disposed of in a gutter, in a field, in the woods. If we don't play by the rules men set us, then we are fair game. The media will follow suit. No apologies or corrections will be issued when they establish the facts. Nonetheless, it will be inferred that I must carry some of the blame for the events of this evening because I made a poor decision. Because I didn't follow the rules.

The gaps between the streetlights widen the deeper I submerge myself into the industrial estate. An errant HGV is parked on the side of the road. Grey curtains are pulled across the windscreen. A trucker bedded down for the night? I make a note in case things go wrong, and I stop the laughter bubbling in my mouth. The trucker is likely a flea too, and here I am planning to serve myself up with a side of mint sauce.

Footsteps. He's closing the gap. He doesn't care whether I hear him. I freeze. Adrenaline courses through me, shattering the ice holding me to the spot, and again I up my pace, refusing to sprint, refusing to release his primal instincts to chase. That's what they all want – a chase. Boys will be boys.

This location is the type of place safety leaflets suggest women avoid, alongside dark car parks, lifts, and shortcuts of any sort. Avoid wearing your hair in a ponytail – too easy to grab. Place your keys between your fingers. Fight your attacker. Don't fight your attacker. Tell your attacker about your family – humanize yourself. Keep your mouth shut. Cry. Don't cry. We must, they tell us, as they hand us rape alarms, stay in brightly lit, well-populated areas. Of course, I have read all the safety tips. I have watched the videos. I have heard the call to arms.

I take a shortcut through an alleyway between two buildings, our footsteps echoing in sync. I smile as my ponytail bobs up and down in the night. I enter the empty parking lot; he must be thinking this is it, now is the time. What he doesn't know is at the back of this car park is a shortcut that leads back to the main road. I've taken him in a big circle.

There is one flickering streetlamp at the far end of the car park. It buzzes as a dewy glow comes and goes. Footsteps. Louder. He's narrowed the gap. Any second now, a hand will wrap around my mouth. I pull my hood up. A starter's pistol fires in my mind's eye and I break into a sprint towards the footpath. His commando boots hammer against the ground as he pursues me. Tree branches slap against my face. I can almost feel his fingertips reaching out for me as we navigate the darkness. My head is telling me to keep moving. Be strategic. My heart tells another story and begs for him to catch me. Force me to kill him now. To clean the sweat breaking through my forehead with his blood. When I burst into the main street, I turn and grin. My smugness oozes through my skin, but nothing greets me.

Darkness. He's disappeared.

I stand at a bus stop. Panting for breath. A group of students wander towards me. One cackles at another, pushing her glasses from the tip of her nose to the bridge, delighted at the comment the other has made. I want to join in. Ask what's so funny. I picture myself in corduroy with a satchel and knock-off Doc Martens.

'I'm so glad I didn't end up at Manchester Uni now. Devo'd at the time,' says a student with plaits either side of her neck. I shuffle a little closer. Manchester is where I killed my second flea.

'I know, right? Imagine,' replies the student with glasses.

I'm trying to imagine, but these women are maybe only four or five years younger than me, and I have no idea what they're saying. The one with the plaits holds up her phone to glasses and a third student in a pleated skirt.

'Another woman has gone missing.'

They both gasp.

'It'll be him,' they reply in unison.

And for a second, I'm so absorbed in wondering who 'him' is and what's happening in Manchester, I'm half surprised as my flea emerges from the footpath. Casual as you like. As if he hadn't spent the last twenty minutes stalking me.

He wanders right up to the bus stop. The audacity. He leans against the glass next to the students and stares at the floor. His cologne. It's thick. The students giggle. Whatever is happening in Manchester is forgotten. Unaware of the danger so close to them. He's handsome – his jaw is strong, clean shaven, and his eyes a sparkling blue; it's hard to see the monster when its smile dazzles. I wonder what his weapon of choice is – a hammer, a knife, brute strength? I take comfort knowing he can't do anything here, with the CCTV looming and the cars passing. I have made him impotent. At least for now.

Then his voice appears. Low and steady.

'What's your name?'

I look behind me. He's talking to one of the students, the blonde one with the plaits. She blushes. Her friends giggle. I want to scream. To warn them. I don't hear her reply, but it doesn't matter. We are all Emma, Lucy, Stacey, Gillian, Hayley, Becky, Taylor, Denise, Anna. It doesn't matter. To him, to them, we don't matter. Their politeness is trickery.

He nods to her reply. His head rises and – just as my eyes are about to meet his – a bus screeches to a halt. The doors open with a gasp and drunks tumble off. He doesn't look back as he boards the 111.

'You getting on or not?' the bus driver shouts in our direction.

I nod and board the bus. The students hang back, waiting for another bus going in another direction. And they will never know how close they came to danger.

The bus is damp from rain and sweat. This time of night should be reserved for sleeping, but instead the bus is crammed with bodies. In the corner, a couple kiss. A small group of young women sing along to a song. I want to join in and allow my voice to crack on the high notes with abandon, but I don't know the words. Worst of all, the bus is bright. Illuminated. Amongst the mess of bodies, I've lost him. There's no seats and I stand amongst rowdy passengers with one arm in the air clinging on to a plastic strap.

I scan for his face, but as the seconds pass it becomes pixelated in my mind's eye. Sweat makes my hand slip away from the strap. I grasp tighter, trying to regain my balance. This is not how I planned it. Regardless, I am armed with the confirmation, he is a flea.

Around me everyone is drunk, slurred words float around my head as I try to decipher what is being discussed. I stand, my body unsteady as the bus trundles along. My knuckles white as I cling to a plastic strap. All these women who surround me, travelling home, are the other girls on another night. Any woman can be the other girl on another night.

Where is he? He appears as the bell rings, alerting the driver to stop. He was standing on the stairs to the top deck. Concealed from me, yet I was within his sight. Was he watching me?

A young woman, blonde, slender, in a sparkly dress and carrying a clutch bag, stumbles to the front of the bus. He looks away from me. A couple of sequins have fallen from her dress, leaving parts bald.

'Thank you,' she slurs to the driver as she disembarks.

He follows. I breathe out, realizing I have shaken the flea, but his attention has been stolen by the woman in the sequined dress. She is the other girl on another night. The bus rumbles to life.

'Wait,' I shout.

I step over people and force my way through the crowd towards the front of the bus.

'This is my stop,' I say to the driver, and he rolls his eyes as the doors open once again.

The cold hits me on the street, but neither the woman in the sequined dress or her follower turn to see me get off the bus. The doors close. Passengers chant a football anthem which fades as the bus drives into the distance. Goosebumps prick across my body. Ben's voice appears in my mind – *you won't last a day in the real world.*

I'm following the follower. Nausea hits me. Instead, I keep a distance between me and him. My footsteps change, from stomping into the night to delicate light steps, afraid an echo or a splash in a puddle will give me away.

In the distance, her dress sparkles from the light from the streetlamps. No wonder his attention was caught: she's sparkly and golden, ethereal in the night. Her high heels punctuate her every step. When her body is found, they will suggest the clothes she wore made her vulnerable. His pace quickens. She staggers towards a darkened park. A shortcut? He begins to jog. I'm shaking. This isn't my plan.

I break out into a sprint. As I pass him, our shoulders graze; the surprise knocks him and for a moment he holds still. I hook my arm through the woman's and her head snaps in my direction.

'I thought it was you,' I say loudly, allowing my voice to take up all the empty space around us as we enter the park. 'How long has it been? Must be six months?' Confusion is etched across her face as her eyebrows furrow, and she frowns. 'You're being followed,' I whisper, and my words hang on the still night air. She glances over her shoulder. My once-drunk party girl sobers as she spots him.

'Oh fuck,' she whispers, taking her shoes off. 'My boyfriend is waiting for me on the other side of the park.'

Barefoot, she keeps pace with me. The bushes rustle and shadows move as we walk. Every so often she winces, as if she has walked across a sharp stone, but it doesn't stop her.

'He still there?' she whispers.

I look back over my shoulder and he is. Two of us together has slowed him, but it hasn't stopped his pursuit. In the distance the silhouette of a male stands near the park gate; his shadow is long.

'Mark, Mark.' My sequined friend shouts and the male walks forwards towards us, waving hello. I look back. Our follower has turned; he is walking out of the park and back in the opposite direction. The woman's boyfriend approaches. She feels safe now she has a man to protect her from another man. It's akin to taking poison to treat poisoning. At some point we need to stop drinking the poison.

I feel a statistic wriggling on the tip of my tongue. A maggot of a fact created to repulse and shock. It doesn't quite emerge, but I am telling you, the men we know should be the men we fear. My flea, the stranger in the night, is quite the rarity. A fine addition to my collection.

Said flea is outside of the park, walking away without a care in the world. I give chase. He's a danger to me and to all women.

'What are you doing?' she shouts, but I don't look back and I don't break my stride until I see my flea heading towards the main roads.

He enters an alleyway. He doesn't fear shortcuts. I run down the street and he emerges from the top of the alleyway, walking at pace and without a glance in my direction.

I catch a couple of grunts as I keep a safe distance on the other side of the road. We walk. Half a mile, maybe three quarters before he stops and pauses at a house. A two-up, two-down. He reaches up to a hanging basket and fiddles with it. Then unlocks the front door and disappears into the darkness of the house.

A light from within the home flickers on. It illuminates the street and our follower is now in his very own goldfish bowl. He chucks his baseball cap against a wall. The TV switches on. A blonde woman bent over a bed. A skinheaded male bites into her shoulder as he thrusts roughly.

I wonder what made my little flea like this. Every villain has an origin story, but so does every hero.

'I'm coming back for you, flea,' I whisper.

2

2027 – HMP Bronzefield

Today is a special day. I have a visitor. No, a guest. Visitors are people you don't want, a clinical term for those who burden us with their presence. Guests are welcomed. I'm here. Arms open wide. Today is a special day.

The prison guard squeaks along the corridor behind me, her shiny boots making the concrete floor an off-key musical instrument. I know my guest requested to see me alone, but the governor refused; she feared I might murder them. They overestimate me.

A door swings open to a small room off B wing. The walls are green. Not mint, or lime, more baby vomit. Green is meant to calm. But right now, I'd do anything for a cigarette. My mind flickers back to old black-and-white movies with a prisoner being questioned with a burning cigarette in an unattended ashtray. Smoke swirling upwards.

I look towards the centre of the room. On a foldable chair behind a table, my guest sits. I feel old next to the young prison guard in her crisp uniform. I wonder if my guest has noticed the way the grey tracksuit washes me out? They look up. I smile.

'Hello, old friend,' I say.

I attempt a relaxed smile, as if this whole situation is normal. As if years haven't passed with a blink of an eye; as if we are, like I say, old friends. I never would have believed I would see them again, to have my eyes meet with theirs; and yet here they are. They want to relive the past. I suppose my journey was theirs too. They said they would write a book. I guess neither of us knew that I would be the focus.

They extend their hand out of instinct to shake mine. I raise my wrists; the sunlight, catching in the metal of the handcuffs, dazzles them for a second. Heat rises in their cheeks. I feel their embarrassment second-hand; they are my guest and thirty seconds into my presence, I have caused them discomfort.

'Are the handcuffs really necessary?' I bark at the guard. She remains silent, ever alert at the door in case I, Maddie Reid, might dare to escape and make the world right. I'm not sure who it is they think they're protecting.

'I'm sorry,' I whisper under my breath. 'They're always like this.'

'That's okay,' they reply.

I sit in the seat opposite, resting my wrists on the table. They glance at them, every so often; stolen looks, like a child seeing something they shouldn't for the first time. I came here clear-headed, but now my thoughts are jumbled in my brain like a wasps' nest.

'I need to be up front with you, Maddie,' they say. 'I've drawn a lot of public attention over the years.'

I try not to frown or stare, or show my contempt for their good fortune born from my demise. I've tried to follow their career, but it isn't easy when you're locked in a cage. My flames left me in a pile of ash, but they arose like a phoenix.

'So, I'm writing a book. I've read the case notes, but I'm afraid they don't tell the whole story and I want us to talk. I want to hear your side of the story, not interrogate a pile of exhibits. I want us to simply chat. Like friends. Like the old days. My intention is to present the facts and not change the narrative in a way that might benefit anyone.'

'Presenting the facts would be changing the narrative. I'm not the monster they say I am.'

They nod. I can't tell if they're placating me or agreeing. I want to ask, but it would be rude to put my guest on the spot. If they think I am a monster, then maybe I am.

I'm not the only one who has aged. They have too. Grey in their hair. Laughter lines at their eyes. I bet their life has been joyful whilst I've been rotting away. I'm not bitter. We play the cards we're dealt. It's just sometimes it feels my hand was dealt from a pack filled with jokers.

'I'm not trying to sway public opinion,' I say.

I'm a cliché with a few confessions to make before I run out of time.

'Good, because I can't make promises like that. What I can say is a publisher is interested. The book will happen. First question: you have turned down every opportunity to explain your actions. Why now?'

'Well,' I tap my fingers against my skull. 'Turns out, I have a brain tumour. So, congratulations, you get to scribe my deathbed confession.' They pause and I watch them absorb what I'm saying. 'I'm not looking for sympathy. I want to focus on telling my story.'

'I'm sorry . . .' they say. I shake my head no and they stop.

This book, it was destined from the very beginning. I wonder what took them so long. I was beginning to think they would never come at all. I bet it was an easy sell once the notorious Maddie Reid was on board. Even easier if they explained our personal connection. Did my guest have publishers chomping at the bit? I hope it left them feeling grubby.

'How would you feel talking about your victims?'

I want to ask the questions. My entire life, I have never been the one who gets to ask the questions. I want to know what their life is like now. Are they married? Do they have children? What car do they drive? What colour is their living-room wall? I want them to tell me every banal detail of their life.

'I don't have any victims.'

Where are they planning to go on holiday? What's their morning routine? How do they take their coffee? Is it still milk and one sugar? Or have they cut out sugar, cut out the caffeine? Taken up golf? What's their handicap? I want to soak in mundanity.

'Maddie, why do you think you're in prison?'

I turn to look at the prison guard. She is doing her statue impression. I prefer it when they send me the unprofessional types. Either way, I never learn their names. Unlike me, they can leave when they want, and often do.

'I wouldn't call those men victims.'

My guest picks up a notepad and scribbles something.

'What would you call them?'

I lean back into my chair, allowing my hands to fall heavy into my lap, the edges of the handcuffs press into my flesh. I close my eyes. Faces appear one at a time. I lean forward, and my guest is watching as my eyelids flicker open. I smile.

'I'd call them filthy little fleas.'

A shadow crosses their face. I note the blinds are closed

in the room; only a couple of slivers of sunlight make their way through the gaps. I wonder who made that decision. The prison? My guest? Who thought it was best I didn't get a room with a view?

'All of them?' they say.

'In a world made for men, I carved out a place for women to be safe.'

They know I'm right. How many lambs have they witnessed drained of their blood, their essence, because a flea attached themselves to them? I was levelling the playing field. Nothing more.

They tap the end of their pen against their notebook. Did they expect me to be all apologies? To have found God and redemption? Is this not working out the way they expected? The way they wanted?

'Can we open the blinds?' I ask.

My guest shakes their head and casts their eyes towards the floor.

'The governor has said they must remain closed. I'm sorry.'

I'm not sure what they think a woman of my size could reasonably do. Throw myself out of the window. I'm small. The sort of person a good mother would want to feed. My size was a point of discussion during my trial. As if the fragility of my frame pointed towards my innocence against all those big men. They merely lingered on the fragility of my mind. How could I claim to be insane when it was those around me who were mad.

'Shall we talk about Ben Starr?'

'No,' I say, sounding more abrupt than I'd like.

Why does everybody want to talk about Ben? Ben this. Ben that. They shift in their chair. That would be an easy place to start. Get my excuses in quick.

'Where would you like to start?'
'Robbie Jones.'
'Robert Jones?'
'Is that a problem?'

They remove another notepad from their bag. I want to laugh at how old-fashioned they are, running around with notepads rather than electronics like every other person. Maybe this is why they are the only person I have agreed to meet. They are pure nostalgia. They take me back to the only time in my life I was free. Their papers rustle as they flick to a page in the middle.

'Robert Jones was a serial rapist who the police were struggling to catch at the time. Leicester is a city with a population of 350,000. The one person the police were struggling to find, and you managed to stumble across them.'

'He found me. They always find me.' I laugh. 'That's a lie. I found him, looking for me; well, looking for any lamb with their throat on display. I suppose we found each other. Isn't it funny how life works out?'

They obsess over my victims, how did I find them? Where did I find them? You know what question comes next . . .

'And what made you pick him?'

Bingo. Every time. What made you pick him? I would have thought the answer obvious.

'Robbie Jones was my equivalent to a perky, blonde seventeen-year-old. I'm a serial killer.' I shrug. 'We tend to stick to type.'

3

2007 – Leicester

Daisy Parker sits amongst the greys and blacks of the refuge's kitchen. No doubt she spotted me sliding the ground-floor window open, my two small hands, white-knuckled, clinging onto the window sill, a small groan. A grunt as I swing my second leg to join my first.

Daisy has a baby attached to her nipple. Stone-cold tea stagnates in a mug on the table in front of her. A black-haired toddler sits on the kitchen floor, smashing two plastic cars together, dried snot flakes under his nose. Daisy's eyes flutter open and follow me as I move through the MDF kitchen towards the communal hallway. Daisy's shoulder-length hair is as mousy as Daisy. It hangs below her shoulders, framing a pale face which rotates between three expressions: wary, anxious and afraid.

'You scared me, I thought you were Leon for a second.' Daisy's voice is light. I pause.

'I didn't mean to scare you.' I stare at the baby. Annoyance dilutes the pity I feel for mothers. A screaming, shitting prison guard, holding you hostage in your own home, and yet, I marvel at the literal creation of another life. It baffles me that fleas have mothers; in my mind they crawl from nests, looking for someone to attach to. A part of me wants to snap Daisy's neck for starting another cycle. Miracle of life. Bullshit.

We both jump as the kitchen door swings open. Vivian, dressed in her self-imposed uniform of jeans and a polo shirt that is the same colour as her socks (today is pink), fills the doorway. Her hair is butchered short and bleached the colour of pale sand. Her year-long tan makes me wonder if her hair colour was inspired by the three foreign holidays she takes a year. Unlike us, Vivian gets to leave the refuge, because she isn't a resident, she is the senior welfare officer – whatever that means. Daisy sits straighter as Vivian appears and I find myself slumping into a chair.

'What are you doing?' Her words feel like a finger jabbing into my chest. I pause. Think of a lie, any lie, to get the wicked witch off my back. 'The curfew at the Misty Women's Refuge is for your safety.' I've heard words like this before. The sacrifices I must make for my own safety seem above and beyond those of other people. I run from one captor to another, gifting my freedom.

'Little one.' Daisy nods towards the toddler. 'He was making a racket, and Maddie was checking someone hadn't broken in.'

Vivian raises her overly groomed left eyebrow into an arch.

'In a coat and trainers?'

'In case I needed to run, Viv.'

She nods, lazily accepting my excuse. Vivian feeds off fear. She martyrs herself to horrific fantasy, spoon-feeding night terrors to the women who stay, their cold sweats bolstering her ego. Without fear, she'd be irrelevant. She is our self-appointed protector and that means more to her than it does to us.

'Maybe we are due a family meeting. I'm worried that stuff up in Manchester might be impacting some of the women here. Scaring them.'

'I hear another woman has gone missing,' I say, as my mind filters back to the students at the bus stop. Hoping one of the two women might provide more context.

'Yeah, did you see the news last night?' Daisy adds. 'They found her body. She's not the first and they think it might be a serial killer.' Daisy's face rotates to expression number three: fear.

A serial killer. It can't be. No. I mentally count my number of kills and swallow a laugh as I realize Daisy and Vivian are sitting next to a serial killer. Me.

'Yes,' Vivian says. 'Family meeting time. There is no harm in going over safety protocol again.'

Eurgh. Vivian's rules are like bricks being smashed into my face. She likes to think of the women in the refuge as family, a sugary sentiment that perhaps in the moment has value to its inhabitants. I think in Vivian's mind there is truth to it. She speaks of found family, as if it has biblical value. Really it's an excuse to lay down the law for us all.

'Quick word, Viv?' I say.

Viv glances at Daisy and back to me, nodding towards the hallway. We both shuffle into the hallway as Daisy's toddler whines.

'What's up?' Viv says, meeting my eyes.

'Did you get the permission to tell me where they buried Ben?'

Vivian looks towards her office and shakes her head no.

'It's an unmarked grave. No one is meant to know.'

Yet Vivian knows. Some gravediggers know. A priest knows. The police know. It appears that many people know the one thing I want to know. There's a moment of uncomfortable silence as I stare hard at Vivian, but she doesn't back down. She is slipping a noose around her own neck and I will kick the chair from under her. *FUCKING TELL ME.*

I smile.

'I understand, Vivian.'

Her returned smile is weak as she nods at me. Without explanation, she walks away in the direction of her office, and I return to Daisy. The toddler now on her lap and the baby in a bouncer.

'She's not even on nights,' Daisy says. 'She's been jumpy as anything lately. Do you think it's to do with Leon going missing?'

I shrug. Pick up Daisy's cold mug and flick the kettle on. Leon disappearing should be a source of joy for both Vivian and Daisy. The effect on Daisy is not happiness but a sense of impending dread; she has stopped sleeping and has taken on a watch, waiting for the return of her brutally violent husband.

'Two sugars?'

She nods. Since I moved to the Misty, I have learnt many things about polite society. Such as memorizing how someone takes their tea. This is a display of familiarity. After some experimentation, to Vivian's annoyance, I learnt I like it milky, with one heaped teaspoon of sugar. Every day is a school day when you don't know who you are.

The baby whimpers and points chubby fists towards Daisy. She struggles to pick him up with the toddler on her lap. The toddler looks like his father, and he stares at me as if he knows my secrets, as if he can smell smoke and is wondering where the fire is. Perhaps one day the boy will arrive in the night, asking if I remember him. I will say no, regardless of the truth.

The kettle whistles as I rinse Daisy's mug. I reach for the cheap teabags Vivian insists on keeping in the top cupboard, despite most of the women struggling to reach.

'Do you think he'll turn up?' Daisy says.

I look in her direction. 'Leon?'

I'm a clown spewing one-liners for jokes. Leon 'Teflon' Parker; nothing ever seems to stick. Regardless of how much evidence has marked Daisy's body, it never seems to be enough. I smile at the black-haired toddler. He cries.

The toddler curls up in the crook of Daisy's arm and both children sleep. I wonder if their weight makes her arms ache, or if the pain of motherhood was something Daisy was accustomed to, accepted, cherished.

'You wouldn't want that, would you?' I ask through narrow eyes.

She shakes her head.

'It's hard not knowing. I'm always on tenterhooks.'

I nod. It's tiring keeping up a facade of interest, but Leon's sudden disappearance has become a hot topic amongst the women in the household. Of all the ex-partners, he was the most persistent. He would flip-flop between flowers and threats. The night he went missing, they were discussing relocating Daisy and her children to another part of the country. She didn't want to go. Vivian insisted though: Daisy needed to go. Somewhere far, somewhere they could hide her. I don't understand why the onus is on Daisy. Can't they hide him instead? Somewhere far away. Maybe somewhere deep underground.

'No one has heard from him. He's vanished. It's been months. I spoke to his mum for the first time since I left, and she thinks something terrible has happened. She blamed me, of course, and said I should never have walked out on him. I shouldn't have called her, but part of me was hoping he had given up and moved on. I half thought it would be him who answered.'

Wanting answers is human. For a second, I wonder if she misses Leon's attention – so persistent, it was like clockwork – but the look in Daisy's eyes tells me otherwise. She wants to know if she can crack on with her life. Maybe, his disappearance hasn't presented her with a life free from Leon; maybe it's cast an endless doubt instead. Will Daisy be looking over her shoulder for decades to come?

Time passes as we both sit, the children on her lap and me in a coat, as if I am about to leave at any minute. We sip our tea in comfortable silence. The shadows dissolve as the sun rises. Beams of light flood into the kitchen, highlighting the hazel of Daisy's eyes. Vivian destroys the peace when she marches in, the fire door swinging behind her.

She flings a couple of packets of store-bought croissants onto the kitchen table. The sort that are always too dry but claim to be buttery.

'They're a treat for everyone. No more than one each.'

Sylvia, a bird-like woman and the only other resident without children, races into the kitchen.

'Another one of my T-shirts has gone missing, Viv.'

The hunt for Sylvia's missing royal family memorabilia T-shirt has been as thorough as any large-scale criminal investigation. The culprit has yet to be apprehended. I hand her my croissant, which she takes without question. As I leave the kitchen, I can hear Sylvia talking about how much they mean to her, and for a moment I feel great pity for her. Then a great pity for myself. How nice it would be to have a hobby that distracted me like Sylvia is distracted by her Tees.

The lock on the ugly brown fire door, which shields my room from the rest of the refuge, turns with a clunk. The laminated fire alarm procedures isn't the artwork I once imagined for my own space, nor the tacky cream walls, nor is the single bed or the scratchy chair that sits beside it. The bed squeaks as I fall into it, still in my coat and shoes. I rummage in the drawer of the white PDF bedside table until I find my small blue ball. I toss it towards the ceiling, watch it fall, catch it and repeat, until I fall into a meditation from the rhythm. The woman in the sequined dress fills my skull. I wonder who she has told about last night? The police? Doubtful. I can picture her typing long-winded social media posts and phone calls to friends. I wonder if she mentions me, her hero, or if I am omitted.

It doesn't matter. I am a hero. I've found my flea.

4

I should have come back sooner, but Viv has insisted upon a curfew to keep all the women at the refuge safe from some maniac a hundred miles away in Manchester. Days have festered since my last meeting with the flea. It's only tonight I have managed to give Viv the slip, as she snoozed away on her office sofa.

His house is average, even in the middle of the night. It could be anyone's house. I pick up discarded junk mail littering his front porch. It's sodden, and has half a footprint on it. I hold it up in the air between a finger and thumb. A name jumps out at me and I let it rest on my tongue for a second.

'Hello, Robert Jones?' I whisper.

I stare at the front door. I know he's not behind it. The house is plunged in darkness and devoid of noise. No footsteps, no television, no snoring. Robert Jones is elsewhere. I know he keeps his keys in the hanging basket.

I reach upwards and my fingers sift through soil. Bingo. The key glitters in the moonlight, as if it wants to be found.

I slip it into the lock and turn. The door swings open. I shuffle in, closing the door behind me, and switch on my phone's torch. In front of me is Robert Jones's life.

Downstairs is open plan. It appears average at first, pictures, a television, a leather sofa, but then oddities jump out – a riding whip leaning against the sofa, memorabilia from obscure splatterpunk movies on the walls, a small rodent's skull sits on the bookcase. I walk over to the back door. Barricaded. I pull at blocks of wood nailed over the frame of the door.

'Only one way in and out,' I mutter.

A familiar anxiety washes over me and I check the windows. Glued shut. I stand in the kitchen and I make excuses for him: maybe he is safety conscious; maybe he was recently burgled. That's what we do, we make excuses for men. I shake myself and remember not to fall into the trap of explaining away what I can clearly see, no matter how uncomfortable that might make me. I know Robert Jones is a dangerous man.

I slide open a drawer filled with old VHS tapes. My heart sinks. Ben had drawers like this, crammed full of plastic recordings. Your desires are of ill taste if you don't feel safe streaming them. I pull one out. The casing is thick, the plastic cover is torn at the side. Two young girls stare back at me from the cover, their wrists shackled. Both have black eyes and split lips. I take it to the freezer and hide it behind the frozen vegetables and potato waffles. I've seen enough. I close the door with a gentle touch on the way out.

The key hits the soft soil in the hanging basket with silence. The street is empty. Engulfed by the night. I spot a bus stop opposite his house and wander over to it as flecks of rain hit me. It's sheltered, unlike the one with the students during my first encounter with Robert the flea. I have a devilish thought of waiting inside for him. I know I wouldn't survive that. I have watched the fleas in action, and I have learnt there is no shame in tilting the stage. In fact, I will stab you in the back if it means you die and I live. I don't believe in honour. No, that's how you get yourself killed.

Every time I've murdered someone, I always tell myself afterwards that I will call the police next time I find a flea. I'm like a smoker who keeps telling themselves they'll quit. I mean it at the time. It's not a lie. Then another cigarette lands in my lap and I think, go on, just one more.

A group of men, drinking lager from cans, pass on the other side of the street, talking loudly. I'm told not all men are bad. Wouldn't it be easier if they were? If we could chuck that label at them and know we are lambs going to the fleas with our veins on display. Instead, we are forced to whittle them out. Playing a real-life game of Guess Who? Except everyone looks the same until a dagger slices across your throat.

I wait. I'm good at waiting. I have spent a lifetime waiting. Sometimes it's not even clear what I'm waiting for. The night becomes darker. Hours pass. I sit in silence.

Like magic he appears in the distance, the streetlamps illuminating his path. But he isn't walking like Robert Jones; there is a limp in his step as he approaches his house. He pauses, leaning against a streetlamp. Robert Jones stands in his very own spotlight. One hand on his hip and the other against the streetlamp. It is him. He looks gassed, deep gashes slice down his face.

'Someone has been in a scrap,' I mutter to myself.

Robert Jones and who? Whoever it was put up a fight, and they did not want to go down. Victim selection is instinctual for most predators. Myself included. Maybe he made a wrong choice. He did, after all, follow me, and look where that's led him.

He continues to limp until he is at his house. He struggles to reach up to his hanging basket, and when he opens his front door he stumbles and falls to his knees. Someone has had a bad night.

He is slow to get back onto his feet. They will talk about this, in the papers, word of mouth and the police officers themselves. They will praise the victim for fighting. What a distorted view of survival; sometimes the best play isn't direct confrontation.

The light flickers on in the front room. I watch him in his goldfish bowl. The scratches on his face look like fingernails dragging against his skin.

I open the plastic bag. Prince William stares back at me from a cotton T-shirt.

The TV flickers on in his living room, but not the same porn as last time. Instead cartoons flicker on the screen and I imagine him with a hot chocolate in hand. I know the episode. I mouth the words along with the characters. Ben loved *Scooby Doo*. He would put them on late at night when he needed to be soothed. Demand I stroke his hair as he chuckled.

The lights flicker off. I stare at my phone, giving myself a minute-by-minute countdown, ten minutes down to one. I pull my hood up and walk across the empty street to his front door.

The wise play would be to set the house on fire now, but I deserve a treat. The woman he attacked tonight deserves more. For the second time tonight, I unlock Robert's front door. I switch the downstairs light on. He is wounded and I don't care if he catches me. He is easy prey.

I pass the riding whip, the drawer of VHS tapes, the splatterpunk posters, and open his kitchen cupboard. I grab the table salt. I head to the staircase and spot a small torch. It's sticky to the touch and leaves red patches on my skin. Blood. His blood? His victim's blood? Both?

I flick the downstairs light off and the torch on. I'm gentle on the stairs. His breathing leads me to him. A musty smell hits me as I push his bedroom door open. His clothes are bloodied in the corner in a pile. I place my own bag down and pull out the T-shirt and drop it on the floor. Prince William's face is illuminated in the torch's spotlight. The T-shirt becomes saturated as I squeeze lighter fluid on it. The smell clings to my nostrils, burning my throat.

I wander over to his bed and I watch him sleep. He murmurs. The smell from the T-shirt rousing him. I shine the torch in his face. The cuts are worse than I thought. Deep welts pooled with blood. He raises his hands to his face as he wakes.

'Hello, Robert,' I say.

Before he can reply, I dump the table salt over his face. Granules cling to his open flesh. I inhale his screams. They are morphine for my soul.

The sodden T-shirt drips as I pick it up and place it over Robert's face. As he tries to rip it off, I light a match and flick it in his direction. The whoosh as the flames burst to life is the cherry on top of a delightful cake.

I take the stairs two at a time with the heat at my back. I'm not afraid of the fire. It's not hungry for me.

I close the front door behind me and make my way back to the bus stop. No point in running away. Very soon the whole neighbourhood will be standing watching the show.

The flames flicker behind the front door, and oranges, reds

and blue stalk the front room. I inhale the smoke on the air. Peace.

Sirens in the distance. Neighbours in dressing gowns and slippers spill into the street. Some have dogs on leads and others carry small children wrapped in blankets. It's the police first. They shout questions at people, but no one seems to know the answers. No one knows how many people live in this house, or who they are. Somewhere, someone utters my favourite phrase . . . *He kept himself to himself.* A loaded phrase. No, I didn't know the nutter next door, but not because I'm the unfriendly one, because he's a weirdo.

Firefighters arrive. Ten minutes later, all my favourite colours turn to black ash. One of them shouts something and an ambulance arrives. Some people on the street cry as the body bag is wheeled onto the street and into the ambulance on a gurney; some cover their children's eyes.

'That's four,' I whisper to myself.

5

2027 – HMP Bronzefield

'Have you ever listened to any of the podcasts, or read any of the books, or watched any of the documentaries about your crimes?'

I glance at the prison guard. Even if I have access to any of the material they are referencing, I wouldn't say yes. I'm not allowed. Even this book my guest is writing, I won't be able to read it. Not unless I'm freed. They will never free me. Like I said, they overestimate me. Even if I burnt this prison to the ground and wandered about the realms of Hell, they'd hunt me down, hose off the ashes and find me a new cage.

'No.'

'Most of them draw the same conclusion. Robert Jones was a turning point for you.'

At the time of my arrest, I sparked public imagination. I still receive letters. I don't open any of them. I am a woman who took it upon herself to save the world. A modern day Boudica. Except she dressed better than me.

I shrug.

They're right. I didn't see it through their lens at the time, but they are right. I've always questioned if three kills is enough for someone to be labelled a serial killer – surely that's a bare minimum. You're not excelling at three. It's a C minus at best. At worst, it's lacklustre.

'He was the . . .' They flick through their notes. Out of politeness, I think: they know the answer.

'He was,' I hold up four fingers. 'Number four.'

His cologne, sandalwood and patchouli, wafts past me, and for a second I wonder if the spirit of Robbie Jones will appear. Offer his two cents. Tell my guest he's an innocent man who didn't deserve what he had coming.

'I don't see how he's so special.'

My guest leans forward a little in their chair. They pause, as if they are mulling over what they're going to say.

'The previous men were all connected to you in some way. Robert Jones is different because you sought him out.'

'He found me as much as I found him. We were drawn to one another, and I am so glad we were.'

A reluctant smile. They want to correct me. I can feel it vibrating from them. Nineteen long years of people telling me who I am, how I behave, what triggers me. The police, the barrister, the prison guards, the therapists, the media. Their voices and opinions so loud they steal my oxygen and leave me suffocating.

'But you wanted to be found? You sought out the criminality.'

I can't quite tell if they're asking me a question or not. Of course, I didn't want to be found. I wanted to live in a world where I was safe to wander the streets at night. Feel the moonlight on my skin. Stare at the constellations in the sky. Smell petrol fumes as friends take late-night drives to spill their innermost secrets. I didn't want to be found by Robbie Jones. I didn't want him to exist. But if, hypothetically, a man like Robbie Jones was to exist, then yes, I want a man like that to find me before he finds someone else. Who would you prefer? A sister, mother, teacher, co-worker, lover? Or me?

'What's your point?'

'Prior to Robert Jones, you stumbled across your victims and, when they ran out, you sought more.'

Such a clever little duck. As if this is the first time this accusation has been levied at me. In fact, when the police interviewed me, they didn't send in the arresting officer, they sent in a woman. To sympathize. To pat my tears with soft tissues and whisper 'there, there'. She made that accusation first, and since then people have clung onto it, giving Robbie Jones more credit than he deserved.

'Well, rather him than me. Rather him than someone's daughter or mother or sister or wife. I think a lot of people, I think they secretly admire me. Do you admire me?'

'No.'

Their response is flat. Quicker than I'd like. A wave of tiredness hits me and the handcuffs become heavier, dragging my wrists further downwards. What does it take for them to see what I see? I'm not a villain.

'You exhaust me.' I stand and the prison guard opens the door. As I'm shuffling out, I hear their voice.

'Can I see you again, Maddie?'

I pause in the doorway. It's nice to have a guest, even if said guest needs some more persuasion to see what my mission was.

'Yes, we can discuss Leon Parker.'

6

2007 – Leicester

The fire demoted the brutal rape and assault of an eighteen-year-old woman to page eight of the local paper. The front cover had an image of the charred building in the daylight. I squint, turning my phone to an angle to get a better view.

'I hope the freezer survived,' I say to myself as I pull my duvet around me.

The headline reads: LOCAL MAN DIES IN ARSON ATTACK. At no point is the local man blamed for his role in the events; they say nothing about how he wasn't wearing flame-retardant clothing, or whether a fire alarm was fitted. It doesn't mention how hard the man fought against the flames. Nor does it mention the glued windows or the barricaded back door. It is almost as if the media does not blame this victim. I take a sip of my tea. One sugar. Milky.

I flick back to page eight. GIRL, 18, RAPED AT ABBEY PARK.

'That's the park he followed me and the woman in the sequined dress into,' I say to myself. 'He must have liked it there.'

The article says she had split from friends and was walking alone. We shouldn't need to be in gaggles to be safe; we should be able to walk home naked and alone if needs be. Then I notice, almost at the end of the article, the most important part of the story: she survived. My heart flickers. She survived. Interesting. If only I had been a bit quicker, gone the night before, I would have saved that lamb from a lifetime of nightmares.

The police have a funny way of knocking on a door. They visit the refuge often and, over my two years living here, I have learnt the policeman's knock. It's not a rat-ta-ta-tap, more a thud, thud, thud. A demand not a question. Viv's voice echoes throughout the house. She's on first-name terms with the local bobby, so I raise an eyebrow when she refers to whoever she is greeting as 'officer'. I swing my legs out of my bed and creep towards my door. The wood is cold against my ear as I press hard against it.

I wonder if they're here about the fire. I shouldn't have hung about afterwards, but I am drawn to those reds, oranges and blues. It was a thing of beauty. Art.

I should have considered my presence, the stranger in the crowd, might have led to me being noticed. If anything, I am the police, but far more effective – they should thank me. I picture myself in a uniform, and my body warms as my smile broadens. Maybe I should join. I imagine the camaraderie, the pats on the back for catching the bad guys. I bet my partner would be called Dave or Mike or Daz or Gaz or Baz. We'd have bacon butties at the start of every Sunday shift. He'd be salt of the earth and call me 'our kid'.

Still in my pyjamas, I creep out into the hallway, just in time to see Daisy flee from Vivian's office. I follow her silently. Tap at her door when she slams it shut. My knock is neither a demand or a question, more of a whisper.

Through a small crack, Daisy's red-eyed face appears. She opens the door wider when she sees it's me and ushers me in. The baby sleeps in a cot whilst the toddler pulls the head off a Smart Price Barbie. Our rooms are the same size, and it makes me feel gluttonous knowing the space I have, which is shared with no one, is the same size as her cluttered room.

'They found him,' her voice wobbles.

Careful now, a voice whispers in my head.

I picture Leon outside the refuge, looking up at Daisy's window. I can almost hear him screaming her name outside the front door. Tobacco lingers. I can feel Leon like he is in the room, but I know who she means. Even if I pretend I don't.

'Found who?' I raise an eyebrow and tilt my head as I wait for Daisy to tell me the police have found the third man I've murdered.

The toddler smashes the headless Barbie into the threadbare carpet, making grunting sounds as the plastic connects with the floor.

'Leon. They found Leon.'

She sits on the end of her bed and stares into empty space. I'm not sure if I should sit next to her and I question if it is rude to sit on someone else's bed. I play it safe and sit on a wooden nursing chair in the corner.

'Does that mean you have to move again?' I say, astounded at my ability to play dumb.

Just tell me he is dead, so I don't have to pretend not to know any more. Be a pal, and lift the weight from my shoulders, Daisy.

'No, you don't understand.'

I do understand.

'He's dead.'

I gasp. Race to her side and allow her to lean on me as her body heaves. Tears turn to dry retches as her body absorbs the news. When Ben died, part of me was sad. A very small part, granted. He was all I had known for so long, but Daisy has her children and her family. She can return to her hometown. See her old friends. She has her life back.

'I know I should be happy . . .'

Her sentence tails off. Yes, Daisy should be happy, and I am sure everyone agrees with that statement objectively. It's more complicated than that though, isn't it? Not everyone can understand the compassion we hold for those who abuse us; at its core, they are more damaged than we are, and though we are blessed to be rid of our chains, we understand that they were never unshackled from theirs. In different lives they could have been good people who cherished our love, not took advantage of it. In a different life, Leon Parker was the love of Daisy Parker's life.

'They think he was murdered.'

My body stiffens, just like Leon's did. Bodies do tend to be found, unless you have the time to hack them into little pieces. I have neither the time nor the fortitude to hack a cadaver into bits. I've never liked blood. Knocks me sick.

'The police?'

I can feel Daisy's head nodding in my chest where a damp patch has been formed. I pinch at the skin between my thumb and finger. This isn't my first rodeo. I'll be okay. If anything, all eyes should turn to Daisy.

'I'm sure they will catch whoever did it, Daisy,' I say.

A small scratch appears at the back of my brain, but disappears as quickly as it arrived. They'll never catch me.

7

The shower's water pressure is limp. I need it to be firm – assault my skin and bruise me. The temperature is tepid when I need it to make me scream. I pinch the skin between my thumb and forefinger. Hard. I scrub. I scrub until I am raw.

A knock on the bathroom door. Impatient.

'I'm in the shower.'

'I need everyone downstairs,' says Vivian. Her voice is hard. One moment this is a home for us all to be safe in, and the next a military camp run by Drill Sergeant Vivian.

'Why?'

My response is her footsteps stomping down the stairs and away from me. I switch the water off. Stand. Cold. Let goosebumps multiply over me.

I peek out of the window, a towel digging into my clean skin. A police car. Unoccupied. They're already inside. What a waste of everyone's time.

'Nobody thinks you murdered your husband.' There's a note of exasperation in Vivian's voice as I walk into the kitchen. She's right, though. Daisy is the type that catches spiders in glasses and chucks them out of the window. I'm glad Daisy is feeling a bit of heat, because it makes her look guilty. I swallow a laugh, imagining Daisy murdering her abusive husband. I'd buy front-row tickets for that show. The room is filled with women from the refuge. The lucky ones have grabbed chairs around the table and others have been forced to stand. There's never enough room at the refuge. Some nod along with Vivian, whilst others look irritated at the intrusion.

'The police asked for my whereabouts.' There is a hint of defensiveness in Daisy's voice. I look around the kitchen. Where are the Five-O?

'Maybe I should mention my stolen T-shirts,' Sylvia says, tapping her fingernails against the cheap MDF of the table. 'They might have something to do with Leon's murder,' Sylvia adds as an afterthought. There are visible eye-rolls, but no one replies. She's right though, her T-shirts are implicated in more than one murder. In this room there are two crimes, and I'm responsible for both.

'I'm sorry to hear about your Leon,' Sylvia ventures. Vivian moves around the women, collecting half-drunk brews. 'If they can catch the Manchester Maniac, though, I think they can catch whoever hurt your Leon.'

Sylvia holds up a phone and I lean in. MANCHESTER MANIAC finally caught.

'It was the landlord of the last victim.'

A face stares back at me: he's balding on top, with long hair at the sides and back. He sits hunched in the back of a police car, staring out at the camera. His bright orange shirt with ruffles appears odd in the context of his crime. Makes him appear circus-like. The article describes him as an oddball.

The same word used to describe Ben. Ben, Ben, Ben. How the figures in our past cast long shadows in our present.

Vivian looks over her shoulder.

'They haven't caught him. The landlord has been released.'

'Doesn't mean he didn't do it,' someone pipes up from the back. 'I've lost count of how many times they've released my ex-husband.' There's a murmur of agreement.

The landlord has been released. The women are correct, that doesn't mean he's not the man stalking the streets of Manchester. A small shiver. Excitement? A serial killer would be a king amongst the fleas. Now, that would be a crown worthy of snatching. Robert Jones is small fry compared to a flea with his very own moniker. I try to ignore the metaphorical cigarette that appears in my lap.

Daisy places her head in her hands. She is one of the fortunate ones to have nabbed a chair at the table. Daisy is jammy. A dead husband *and* a seat. Her toddler sits on her lap, smashing his fists into the table, whilst the baby sleeps in a pram.

'Is anyone going to tell me why we're all crammed in here like sardines?' My voice is louder than I intend. The room turns to stare at me. My hair is wet. It drips onto my jumper, creating damp patches. A woman in a suit appears at the kitchen door, her hair cropped at the shoulders. She gives the room a polite yet sombre smile.

'We'll start with you,' she says, pointing at a young woman who is new at the refuge. 'You don't all have to wait here. We know which rooms you are in. We'll send someone to let you know we're ready for you.' Another professional smile. New girl follows the woman in the suit. A quiet falls in the kitchen as the women look at Vivian, who has been undermined by the police officer. Vivian nods and all the women stand, leaving the kitchen and returning to their rooms one by one. Only Daisy remains, wide-eyed, at the table. I look at Vivian and she nods towards the hallway.

Vivian waits as the fire door closes at a snail's pace. She looks towards the kitchen and down the hallway to ensure we are alone.

'The police reckon it was one of us. I've told them there's no chance it's Daisy and they agree, but they seem to think it was someone in here, and the fact the CCTV was playing up that night hasn't helped,' she says in hushed tones.

A cold sweat breaks through my forehead.

'Clutching at straws,' I smile. 'Viv, while I've got you. I was thinking, there must be some way to appeal the decision.'

Viv raises her eyebrows.

'What decision?'

'About not telling me where Ben is buried.'

Viv shakes her head.

'No. Just drop it, Maddie. This isn't healthy.'

She walks back into the kitchen before I have time to reply, and I imagine daggers flying into her back. They should tell me. How can they justify not telling me?

The fire door feels heavier when I push it open. I plonk myself down next to Daisy. The thought of being arrested before I can find where Ben is buried makes me feel sick. What an injustice that would be. My eyes linger on Vivian, now collecting half-drunk mugs of tea. She is the world's best-paid washer-upper. I think about the ways I would like to kill Vivian:

A fall down some stairs?

She bites into a biscuit; crumbs tumble down her green polo shirt.

Poison?

I could strangle her with some Marigolds.

I'd cut her brakes. That's what I would do, I would cut her brakes. Vivian taught me how to drive, so that would feel full circle. Proper closure. I sigh. For what? For her replacement to also tell me no?

'I didn't kill him. Thinking about it, though, maybe I should have,' Daisy says, breaking my daydream.

I wipe a hair off her face and smile. Yes, maybe she should have killed him; perhaps she could have killed him more covertly than I had. Ground-up sleeping pills into a pie, and then send him on a midnight drive, push him down the stairs when he was drunk, leave the gas oven on one Sunday afternoon when he was snoozing on the sofa – you know, day-to-day 'accidents happen' stuff.

'I know, Daisy. Looks bad though, doesn't it? Do you have someone to look after the children if you go to prison?' I add a smile to the end of my sentence, as if I am offering helpful advice.

Her eyes widen. Big full moons stare back at me.

'You have an alibi, right?'

She shakes her head no, her mouth now a perfect O like her eyes.

'I've got an idea. I'll go in next, and you set the fire alarm off. When the police leave to see what is happening, I'll look in Viv's pad. She writes everything in there and I'll tell you what they've been saying about you.' My voice is low in Daisy's ear.

'You'd do that for me?'

'Yes,' I whisper. 'I'd do anything for a friend.'

Even murder her husband.

8

'Who's next?' The blonde police officer has a professional tone, like I'm here to audition for the role of Leon's murderer. Joke is on them, I already secured the part. Vivian opens her mouth, but I jump up before she has a chance to suggest we get someone hiding away in their room and ruin my plan. I smirk at Daisy, and she gives me a little nod.

I follow the officer into the drab hallway. A strand of her short blonde hair sticks out at the top of her head and bobs along as she walks.

'He deserved to die,' I whisper. She turns and looks at me. I'm playing with fire, my favourite element. It's true though – Leon deserved to die.

'Sorry, what did you say?' A confused look washes over her face.

'Nothing,' I avert my eyes towards the cheap grey carpet.

She presses down on the handle and we walk into Vivian's office. She takes a seat in the only expensive item in the entire refuge – a leather desk chair.

'Madeleine Reid?'

I nod.

The officer is tall for a woman, nearing six foot. I feel like a toddler in her shadow. She gestures to the seat in front of me. I sit down. The chair is on wheels and I can't help but swing a little to the left and right in it.

'Nervous?' she asks.

'No.'

On the wall, above an ugly grey filing cabinet, hang framed certificates of Vivian's diplomas. Vivian is keen on qualifications. She likes to add the letters BSc and MA at the end of her name. I've caught her admiring her own educational achievements on more than one occasion. The glass from the frames reflect sunlight onto the police officer, making her reflection look like she is glowing, radiant.

'DC Hancock.' She smiles for a moment, introducing herself, before returning to a solemn pose. 'And do you prefer Madeleine?'

'Maddie.'

She nods. The office door opens and a wiry man in a suit enters. Of course, what a fool I was to think a woman was running the show. I wonder how many female officers he has drained to get to his position. How many ideas stolen? How many times he has talked over a woman trying to be heard? I hate him.

'The toilet is the other end of the building,' he says with a note of irritation.

'This is Maddie.'

'DI Kennedy,' he says abruptly in my direction. The female officer shifts into a plastic chair and DI Kennedy takes the leather executive seat. Of course he does.

'We need to ask everyone a couple of questions. You're not under arrest, so you're not obligated, but I know you are as keen as us to clear this up.'

I nod. This is the problem with men like this; they like to pretend they are offering you options, giving you a way out, but really they are telling you what they want and how you'll help them.

The female officer pulls out a notebook. DI Kennedy takes a gulp of a fizzy orange drink in front of him and leans back in his chair. I'm disappointed. You'd think a man as busy as he should be would live on a diet of black coffee, not on fizzy drinks marketed at teenagers.

'Maddie.' He says my name as if it is a full sentence. 'Where were you on the night of Saturday the seventeenth of February between eight p.m. and two a.m.?'

Saturday? It's hard not to smile. I really have to fight the urge. Idiots. It was a Friday. I've murdered everyone on a Friday. If I was stupid and they were on to me, the media would nickname me the Friday Killer. The Friday Killer. A shiver runs through me and I think of the Manchester Maniac – a true adversary. Not Robert Jones. Not Leon Parker. Not the other two. That was like shooting fish in a barrel or – more appropriately – like killing stunned fleas. Easy.

'I was here,' I answer. And it's true, I was. I like to get a takeaway on a Saturday. 'I order fish and chips on the weekend.'

They both nod but don't ask for any further proof. Fish and chips is the least complicated order. I tried to have a Chinese once, but I didn't know where to start. I didn't even know about takeaway until I moved to the refuge and saw the other women salivate over pizza and curries. Sometimes, I have toyed with the idea of asking Sylvia what to order, but a voice always appears in my head telling me not to.

'Your,' DI Kennedy pauses, waves a hand in the air, 'manager? What did she describe herself as?' He looks at the female officer, who flicks through her notepad and shows him a page. 'Welfare officer, Viv. Welfare officer.' I'm watching him trying not to roll his eyes. 'She says you have a particular penchant for night-time walks, despite the refuge having a curfew.' I have a penchant for little freedoms.

'It's noisy in here at night-time. A lot of crying; the walls are too thin.'

The female officer looks at me and nods, as if she understands the burden of female turmoil. Perhaps she does. The male officer coughs into his hand. Uncomfortable?

I steady my focus on the bookcase on the far wall. Dusty academic texts sit next to well-thumbed paperback memoirs: *Lucky* by Alice Sebold, *Ugly* by Constance Briscoe, *Damaged* by Cathy Glass, to name a few.

'Doesn't seem safe,' he shrugs, as if the safety of the community has nothing to do with him. No reflection upon his profession. The female officer appears indifferent to his statement.

My lips begin to move, but the only sound is the whirr of the fire alarm. Well done, Daisy. I'm half surprised my meek-and-mild friend has followed through. DI Kennedy is first to get up.

'Is this a practice?' the female officer asks.

'No, they warn us about drills.'

DI Kennedy sighs without apology as he makes his way out of the office. The female officer follows and looks over her shoulder at me. I stand as if I'm waiting for them to leave first. The polite thing to do. The door closes behind the officers and I am forgotten. This office is the engine room for the refuge, and I am now the captain as the alarm bell screams at everyone else to jump ship. I soak in the luxury of isolation.

For a flicker, I imagine I am Vivian. I sit in her leather chair and I spin and survey what in another life could be my kingdom. I catch my reflection in the computer monitor and picture myself with Vivian's cropped blonde hair – it doesn't suit me.

Pens make a pleasing rattling sound as I slide open the top drawer of her desk. Fat raindrops hit against the window and I laugh, picturing the entire refuge standing outside. The middle and bottom drawer yield no results. I hit the buttons on the computer keyboard at random, and a lock-screen picture appears of Vivian in sunglasses with another woman. Both are reclining on sunbeds whilst holding drinks with tiny umbrellas poking from them.

The leather chair groans as I stand and glance around the room. A filing cabinet stares at me with a key lodged in the top drawer. The alarm bell stops. The universe has given me mere minutes. I race to the filing cabinet. It wobbles as I pull it open and discover a file on each woman who has ever lived here. Footsteps outside. Multiple. I land on the letter R. The handle lowers. Murmurs from outside the door. I pull the file and stuff it into the waistband of my jeans. My oversized jumper hides a literal secret for once.

'What are you doing in here alone? You should never be in here alone,' Vivian says as she enters the room. She stares at the filing cabinet and then back at me.

'I was waiting for the police to return.' I nod towards her certificates. 'I didn't know you were so accomplished, Viv.'

She likes that. Vivian glows in the warmth of her wall-mounted trinkets, which remind everyone of her worth. An education must be a fine thing.

'Alarm was a mistake,' the female officer says as she re-enters the room.

I nod, returning to my seat. They both take theirs. Vivian lingers for a moment but takes the hint to leave when she is greeted by a wall of silence and stares. The folder burns red-hot against my skin.

'So,' I say. 'Do you mind me asking? How did Leon die?'

9

I find myself at Daisy's door. It seems not only am I a murderer, but I am also a messenger sent to bring Daisy to her fate. The male police officer sent me off to run his errands without hesitation, as if following his commands was the most natural thing in the world. I almost kicked my shoes off and asked for a baby to perch on my hip and an oven to cook him some dinner.

Sniffling comes from inside Daisy's room. And yes, I roll my eyes. I can't say I am sympathetic to her situation because I do not know who she is crying for . . . herself? The fear of being blamed for something she didn't do, or for Leon? All of the above?

My knock sparks a baby's cry from within, and Daisy opens the door. I nod in the direction of Vivian's office where the officers are holing up.

Daisy gestures me inside and closes the door behind me. The baby is strapped into a pram in an off-white baby-grow, and the toddler is smashing DUPLO blocks together on the floor. He looks up at me and his bottom lip curls. I can't tell whether he plans to cry or bite me.

'They want you next,' I say, thinking my nod had not been enough to instruct Daisy.

'No, I know,' she says, wringing her hands together. 'But before I go in, what did they ask you?'

How many times did Ben spot a guilty look wash over my face as he caught me thinking about caving his face in or climbing out of a window or chewing my way through the mesh barrier that kept me from the front door. I hadn't done it, I wasn't going to do it, but the desire was there. I wanted to do those things. What would I give to crawl inside Daisy's brain and have a front-row view of her fantasies? How would Daisy like to murder the father of her children? Poison? Strangulation? Or perhaps a good old-fashioned knife to the heart?

'Just asked where I was on Saturday the seventeenth of February and if I knew Leon and stuff. Wasn't that exciting, to be honest.'

'And did you read Vivian's notes?'

Her eyeballs bulge from their sockets as she stares at me. The toddler throws a DUPLO brick at my leg and it ricochets off my shin. There's something about the way the hair is standing up on her arms that makes me want to lie to her. Don a verbal armour. I could have given her an alibi but I'm not sure how well Daisy lies.

'Of course. I said I would and I did.' The lie is delicious in my mouth. I don't care if they suspect Daisy. No jury would ever convict the woman in front of me of murder. 'They don't suspect you but they have to rule you out, of course. You have a stronger motive than most.'

She nods. Her body collapses at the end of her bed and

she puts her head in her hands. Don't start crying, I think to myself. Anything but the crying.

'You need to speak to the police, Daisy.'

She takes a sharp breath in and stands.

'Yes,' she says. 'Thank you, Maddie. Could you keep an eye on them while I'm gone?'

She doesn't wait for a reply and leaves the room. The baby strapped in a pram doesn't stir from a deep sleep, but the toddler looks up at me.

'Dada,' he says.

I sit down cross-legged opposite him; the carpet is thin and the floor is hard on my arse. He stares at me through thick 'Leon Parker' eyelashes without a single blink.

'I know, you know,' I say.

He smashes a yellow brick into a red brick without breaking eye contact, and I wonder if this toddler is threatening me. If I have created a debt he will one day come to collect.

'Look kid, I was doing you a favour as much as anyone else.'

'Dada.'

'I,' I say in hushed tones, 'murdered Dada. Okay? Happy now?'

I swear Daisy's crotch gremlin can read my mind, as if he can detect all my secrets and collect my fears. *Fine*, I say internally. *I'll tell you how I murdered your father. If that's what you really want to know.* He continues to smash his toy bricks together, one eye on me, and I filter back to a cold February.

Leon had this way of appearing. As if he could detect the very second you had forgotten about him. You'd be sitting at the kitchen table sipping a brew and you'd feel eyes on you. You'd look up and he'd be there at the window. Staring. His face an inch from the glass, a passport-picture expression looking through you as if you were made of glass.

The other women would scream, jolting him from his Peeping Tom meditation like a runner's pistol, and he would turn and jump the six-foot back fence. I hope you inherit your father's agility, I'm sure it could be put to much better use than escaping a women's refuge whilst stalking someone you are meant to love.

I nearly took some advice from Ben's playbook and nailed all the curtains to the walls to keep his prying eyes out, but Vivian wouldn't tell me where she kept the hammer. Vivian likes to keep secrets from me. I tap my bulging stomach. The folder snug against me. *Your mother, Daisy, isn't like that. I hope you don't take advantage of that when you grow. Because at some point you will be bigger and stronger than your mother. You'll be bigger and stronger than most women, but don't let that tempt you into thinking you are superior. If you do, I promise, a woman like me will be waiting for you.*

The baby stirs from the pram, and a cry slips from her mouth. Unclipping her harness, I lift her and hold her at arm's length. Her legs kick.

'It's tough being a girl,' I say. The toddler looks up at me. 'It's much easier being a flea.'

The baby giggles as I spin in circles, holding her mid-air. Her chubby arms reach out for me as I pop her back into her pram, realizing Daisy doesn't have a cot or a bouncer. Perhaps she had one at some point, at another refuge, but it was left behind in their race to escape Leon.

A sharpness hits the back of my leg like a bee sting, and when I turn a piece of DUPLO brick is on the floor and the toddler is laughing. I crouch down and make eye contact.

'Don't do that,' I say. He chucks another brick at my face.

It hits my chin and drops to the floor. He laughs. I sit back down. He chucks another plastic brick, and it hits me in the chest. Glee fills his face. I pick the plastic brick from the floor and fling it at him. It misses his eye by an inch, a welt forms on his cheek and his chin drops.

'Now, be quiet,' I say. 'I was telling you how I murdered your father.'

I close my eyes. The toddler whimpers and I float back to an image of Leon standing at the kitchen window staring in. He was too thin and too tall. His long fingers poked through fingerless gloves. *Like I said, the other women would scream. Daisy would shake when he appeared. But Daisy wasn't there, the other women weren't there. It was just me and your dad.*

'You know what I did? I waved.' I laugh, louder than I intended, and the toddler stares blank-faced at me.

And Leon waved back.

Your father mistook my boldness for something else. He thought he saw something he could use, mould, manipulate; he thought he could see compassion. He thought my veins were open wide ready for him to feast. Silly flea.

Daisy gasps as she enters the room.

'What happened to his face?'

At the sight of his mother, the toddler lets out a monstrous cry as he raises his arms towards her. She swoops him into her arms and picks him up.

'I'm so sorry. The baby started crying and I turned my back for one second and he had fallen.'

She makes small soothing sounds into the toddler's ears.

'Don't worry,' she says. 'You need eyes everywhere when they're this age. He's clumsy too, bless him.'

Maybe he didn't inherit his father's agility.

'What did the police say?' I ask.

'They think it was an accident, but they needed to speak to us all. I think it's finally over, Maddie. I think I'm free.'

Of course, Vivian was stirring the pot. Overegging the situation and making everyone terrified. That's what she's good at. I walk towards the door and Daisy is holding her child a little too tight, his face poking over her shoulder.

'I'll give you your space,' I say.

As I leave, I smile at the toddler and press a finger against my lips.

10

2027 – HMP Bronzefield

'Leon was a right whiny twat. You do know that, yeah?' I say.

Unlike most serial killer victims, mine achieved some degree of notoriety. I always thought it was because of their own criminal histories, but it could be argued it was because they were men. Specifically, men murdered by a tiny woman. The humiliation of such emasculation providing a spotlight most victims don't get. The tabloids at the time appeared to enjoy deep dives into their lurid histories.

'Have you seen Daisy? She won't let me see my kids.' I ball my hands into fists and raise them to my eyes, turning them in and then out to gesture crying. 'What sort of woman won't let her children see their own dad?' My voice is high-pitched. The guard, an older woman, messy hair, smirks. 'You shouldn't use kids as weapons.'

My guest rifles through paperwork. So old-fashioned, but who am I to judge? I burnt people alive when I could have hired someone off the dark net to do the dirty work for me.

'I've not been the best husband, but I deserve a second chance.' I howl, my laughter echoing around the room. Leon was a character. Very animated. The handcuffs clink against one another as I shake. My guest scribbles notes at a frantic pace.

'Can I ask you a question?'

They look up at me with an intent stare.

'Of course,' they smile.

'Why is it, men like Leon always think they deserve a second chance? A third? A fourth?'

'A fifth?' they continue with a shrug.

I'm not sure why I think they have the answer.

'Leon Parker was murdered Saturday the seventeenth of February . . .'

I raise my hands to stop them. My shackles catch a stream of light breaking through a small gap in the blinds.

'I told them, I told them it was a Friday.' I slump back into my plastic chair. My hands fall into my lap. 'They never listen. I killed everyone on a Friday; not on purpose, but at the end of a stressful week one needs to do something to relax.' I laugh. No one joins me. 'In a parallel universe, they would have called me the Friday Killer.'

In this universe, they call me Madeleine Reid. My guest grabs their bag and pulls out another piece of paper. It feels as if they carry a library of my crimes on their back.

'Ah,' they shrug, 'a member of the public said they saw him on Saturday evening, and the postmortem time frame was wide enough to make that work. Looks like someone made an error and unknowingly helped you out. Okay, Friday the sixteenth of February. It must have been cold.'

It had been a cold February. The sort of cold that makes the ground and the trees glisten. Picture-perfect, but no good for the body or soul. Myself and Leon met under a bridge down the canal path. The ground crunched beneath my feet. It took me a couple of minutes to adjust my eyes to the pitch-perfect black the evening had become. I remember it all, like every bite from a delicious meal.

'Yeah,' I say. 'It was cold.'

I could smell him long before I could see him. Lager and vodka wafted up the canal bank. Whilst I shivered, he swayed. The water had a frozen layer on top and my friends, the stars, looked as if they were drowning in the icy darkness below.

'How did you get Leon to meet you without anyone finding out?'

I glance over my shoulder at the guard. She's still smirking. I like her a lot more than the last guard. This one has scuffed boots and a strand of hair flying free from her scruffy ponytail.

'How do you get a man to meet you without him telling anyone?' I say, looking upwards, as if I was thinking a little too hard. The guard coughs to cover her titter of laughter but fails. She knows the answer to this question. Naughty prison officer.

'You promise him something he shouldn't have.' I glance at the guard and her shoulders heave as she represses a laugh. 'In this instance I promised him Daisy. He smelt like roasting meat as he burnt. I think of Leon every Saturday morning when the whole prison smells of grilled bacon.'

The guard turns the same off-green as the walls. Her laughter now gone.

'He screamed her name. Over and over until it was a whisper.' I throw my head back and scream, 'DAISY. DAISY. DAISY.'

My guest waits for me to finish, stony-faced. It's lucky I'm not trying to impress because if I was, I don't think I would be succeeding.

'You do understand, in the eyes of the law, your acts are deemed worse than Leon's?' my guest asks, head tilted.

'I'm not perfect,' I say.

No, none of us are perfect, but I didn't leave blisters that bubbled all over my wife's back. Burns that had to be treated and retreated. I didn't carry on whilst she screamed for him to stop. Whilst she sobbed. I wasn't in the pub toilets with a key to my nose as she crawled on all fours, bits of rock and gravel pushing into her hands and knees, crying for help. I wasn't downing another shot, telling another joke when the police arrived, when the ambulance turned up with flashing lights. Leon was. Daisy didn't deserve that. There are hundreds of Daisys who don't deserve that. Leon had it coming. He was asking for it.

'You and Leon had some commonalities though, right?' My guest chews on the end of their pencil as what they are saying is as obvious as the sky is blue. Clever duck. I've lost count of the shrinks who think they're the first to point out both Leon and I like to burn shit.

When he realized he was on fire, it wasn't panic that stared back at me. It was disbelief. He jumped into the canal of his own accord.

'Do you regret killing Leon Parker?'

'No,' I say. When I struggle to sleep, I see his face sinking into the darkness of the water, disappearing with nothing but a blank expression. Staring at me, staring at him. There is a subtle justice that the last thing he smelt burning was himself, but that wasn't planned. It's the way his cards fell. 'The only regrettable thing about Leon is he left me thinking I might get caught if I lingered in Leicester for too long. He began a chain of events which made me realize I could leave.'

My guest nods and scribbles something down. I watch as their pencil moves in a circular motion, as if what they have written was important.

'I think that's called the butterfly effect,' they say.

'I didn't see any butterflies. Just fleas.'

11

2007 – Leicester

I let the file sweat in the back of my wardrobe for a couple of weeks, under a pile of dirty T-shirts, jumpers and jeans. I lie in my bed, throwing my ball against the ceiling and listen to them whisper to me. Sometimes I toy with the idea of sneaking them back into Vivian's office and pretending there wasn't a thick manila folder with my name scratched over it.

Watching slow panic rise in Vivian should be a pleasure. For the first time she has paid attention to Sylvia's whines about the missing T-shirts. Vivian has questioned if there is a thief in our midst, whilst throwing glances in my direction. She has knocked on my bedroom door time and time again. Each time I have opened it, she has greeted me with a look of disappointment whilst clutching a bunch of keys. Vivian's desperation has become a gnarled claw of anxiety inside me. I can't ignore the paperwork I snatched forever.

I am greeted by anticlimactic silence when I open the wardrobe door. No eerie creak. No drum roll. No fireworks. I chuck discarded clothes over my shoulder. The file sits on the floor staring at me. Madeline Reid scratched in black across the top.

I hold the file at the spine, and papers drop with a thud to the floor. A couple of notebooks tumble across the grey carpet. I grab them. The letters MR are on the front page. They're A7 size, like the ones police officers carry, and plastic bands are knotted around them. The elastic bands are tacky against my skin, and I open what appears to be the rattiest pad first. The first page is dated. A date I know well. My first day here at the Misty Refuge.

MR has finally arrived at the hostel. None of the other women or staff suspect who she really is. I thought a couple of them might have put two and two together but no, they are all too absorbed in their own problems. I've assigned her a family room despite her single occupancy. I expect she will appreciate the space. She hasn't brought much with her but appears to be attached to a small blue ball gifted to her by a nurse.

I flick forward a few months later.

MR has a few quirks, which is to be expected given her circumstances. I feel we've really bonded today as she attempted to make a cup of tea to her 'liking'. It took several attempts but, in the end, she settled on milky with one sugar. She has taken to ordering fish and chips on a Saturday night. I think she finds comfort in routine.

I continue to skim-read the pages, flicking through each notepad. Each page is filled with Vivian's handwriting, scribbled across the lined paper in inky blotches. I skip to the most recent notepad, which is almost already full. Six months earlier:

MR has taken to roaming the streets at night. I worry for her. It's as if she is looking for a repeat of what happened to her. Does she find comfort in danger? I've spoken to the legal team, and they say I have no grounds to lock her bedroom door at night to keep her safe. I've pleaded with them, but as far as they are concerned she is an adult, and I would be detaining her illegally. How can that be when it is for her own safety?

I crawl to the wastepaper basket near my bed. Vomit lands on a pile of dirty tissues, my throat burns from the acid, and I roll on to my back and stare at the ceiling. A deep breath in and I flick to the more recent entries.

The night-time walks continue, and MR grows obsessed with BS's burial site. I fear I am losing her trust as I refuse to reveal the location. For now, I have blamed whoever I think she might blame too – the police, probation, social work and the courts, saying 'they' won't let me reveal where he is buried but 'they' don't care if she knows, and one even suggested allowing her to visit the site may offer her some closure. How they can't see the potential damage this may cause her is beyond me. I need to think of a way to rebuild our trust, our bond. This book won't write itself and I'll be struggling for content if the topic of said book wanders off to find a grave in Manchester.

Manchester. Ben is buried in Manchester.

No, I sound callous. It's not just about the book. I genuinely feel protective of MR, more so than the other women, and I'm afraid if she flies the nest, not only will I never see her again, but she might be easy pickings for some unscrupulous character. She has a story the world needs to hear.

A book? Is she allowed to do that? What about my privacy? I scramble back to the wardrobe. The rest of my paperwork is scattered across the floor and I pick through it all and then I see it. A form. Completed in triplicate. It's crumpled when

I hold it up to the light. My eyes follow the text and it dawns on me – it's a consent form, allowing Vivian to publish details about my recovery at the refuge. I squint, staring at the signature. There is no way for me to know if it's forged or real. I trusted her. I've signed many forms she has thrust in front of me without question.

I hold still. Afraid a single movement will cause me to shatter, an inhale, a wiggle of a toe or a finger, a quiver of a lip. Betrayed. Again.

A bang on my bedroom door.

'Daisy's leaving,' Sylvia shouts, her voice fading as she moves away from the door.

My body gasps for breath. Seal barks emerge from my mouth as I attempt to inhale more oxygen. An acrid smell comes from my bed as I notice a bit of my vomit missed the bin and landed on the corner of my sheets. I empty the pockets of my dirty jeans, which are lying on the floor, looking for some chewing gum. I find an old packet with soft gum and use a T-shirt to wipe at my mouth.

My legs are jelly as I stand. This room, the one I have possessed for two years, looks different in the light of Vivian's thoughts. It's no longer my space. It's a potential prison, awaiting the green light from a stranger. As I approach the door, the room appears smaller, as if the walls have closed in by an inch or two. When I first came here I thought the room was huge, but now it's boxy. I open my door and women from the refuge are filtering outside. I follow.

Daisy stands outside the refuge with a double buggy. The women of the refuge congregate around her, including Sylvia who has no doubt cast her eyes over the bin bags of Daisy's belongings in case she spotted a royal family memorabilia T-shirt.

'It's always a proud moment when one of my women flies the nest.'

Vivian stands with her chest puffed out. She has the audacity to be taking credit for this one, despite the night before asking Daisy if it was a good idea for her to leave so soon. I never thought Daisy would leave like this. I always assumed it would be in a body bag or squirrelled away in the middle of the night, but here we are.

'So, where are you going?' I say, kicking a pebble across the road.

'Back to my house. My actual home. I can't believe it. I never thought I'd see it again. He never stopped paying the mortgage. Leon must have been convinced I would return one day and I guess he was right,' Daisy says. There is a note of smugness in her voice that makes me proud. Gone is meek and mild, and born is a proud woman who owns a semi-detached somewhere in Huddersfield. Roam free, little lamb.

It only takes one person to change you, the direction of your life. Ben changed everything for me, in a second – whoosh, my old life had gone, and a new regime began. A new keeper with new rules. Walking away, escaping people like Ben or Leon isn't straightforward, and if you think it is then consider yourself blessed. We are vessels for darkness. And if you think the light always wins out, then go and have a chat with the sun about the moon.

'I just don't know what to do with the car,' she shrugs.

'The car? I'll buy it.'

The women turn and stare. I know they're wondering how I can afford the car, even the shit tip Leon was living in.

'Seriously? I was going to scrap it.'

'You don't need a car here,' Vivian says.

Then the penny drops. Her face falls. A dark cloud moves

overhead. The first drops of rain hit my forehead, and Daisy's toddler catches them with his mouth wide open.

Vivian has been watching. She's been studying me. Now I feel her eyes wherever I go and I feel naked before her. She is a traitor. I could cut her car brakes or poison her tea. Both perhaps. Instead, I will do something worse and I will walk away from her. Never let her near me again.

'Maybe we should move inside,' Vivian says.

'My mum will be here in a minute.'

A few of the women's shoulders slump as they resign themselves to standing in a light rain until Daisy's mum turns up.

'I'll need the keys,' I say to Daisy, who is attempting to stop the toddler from smashing his legs into the footrest of the pram. A couple of teenage girls give the group a bewildered look as they walk on the road to pass us.

'You're not ready, Maddie,' Viv says.

'I've been here long enough to write a book.'

I pinch the skin between my thumb and forefinger. Our eyes meet and her face stiffens. She knows. I know. I wait for her excuses to tumble from her mouth, but she has nothing.

'You said I could leave when I wanted to?' I continue.

All the women look at her now. I've verbally pushed her onto a tightrope and now she has to find a balance between us being free women, whilst maintaining the rules and boundaries of the refuge. A dark shadow crosses her face.

'Your circumstances are very different.' There's a tremble in her voice.

Are they? Ben and Leon are probably shaking hands in hell right now. Tucking into some steak tartare and a bold shiraz.

All the women are looking at me now, an eyebrow raised here, a tilted head there. It's an unspoken rule to never ask a woman how she ended up at the refuge. It's almost a pointless question, because we all end up there for the same reasons or thereabouts. I think Vivian is wrong. I deserve my freedom as much as any other woman does. I deserve to forge my own path. Away from the Vivians and the Bens of the world. My eyes narrow.

'In what way?'

The smarter of the women smirk. They know Vivian isn't allowed to disclose anything about us to the other residents. For a moment it looks like Vivian is going to tumble from her tightrope with no netting beneath her, but a honk from a car saves her. The driver, a portly woman, gives a friendly wave.

'That's me,' Daisy says smiling. She returns the friendly wave to the woman; both their hands move left to right in unison. The woman groans as she gets out of the car. She runs to Daisy. This large woman jiggles all over as she does and it is a sight of beauty. She raises her hands to wipe away tears and they embrace.

'I've missed you, Daisy,' the woman says. Her eyes are red and her nose streams. 'I promised myself I wouldn't cry.' She bends down to the children. 'Hello, I'm you're grandma. You remember me, don't you?' she says to the toddler, and for the first time I see the little boy smile. He raises a chubby hand and places it on her face. There is no way the child remembers his grandma. Daisy has been on the run for half of his short life, but there is something within their interaction that would say otherwise. This is me. I created this reunion.

The women help Daisy with the black bin bags of her items, and put them in the boot of the car. They secure both the children in brand-new car seats. They're so in sync I would never have guessed their forced years apart. You see all the best prison guards keep you away from the ones you're closest to. In this case, Leon forced Daisy to run away from her mother, whilst his own mother excused his actions.

Is it sad Leon died? Now Daisy can go home, to an actual home, not a building with fire doors, welfare managers and weeping women. A home. The engine starts. I wonder if this is the last time I'll ever see her. The car moves away. It brakes and reverses back to the house. The passenger window whirrs down. Daisy chucks me a set of car keys.

'It's a heap of garbage, Maddie. Take it. It's yours.'

The rest of the women file back into the refuge, leaving me and Vivian standing alone in the rain.

'Where?' I say.

Vivian wrings her hands. She knows I want to know the location of Ben's grave.

'Maddie—'

'I know everything. I can make life very difficult for you. Where in Manchester?'

We stand in silence. It shouldn't have ended this way. As annoying as Vivian is, I trusted her. She is lucky I don't murder women, because right now, I'd like to watch her bleeding out.

'Southern cemetery. South Manchester. Through the main entrance, and under a large oak tree in the most southwest corner.'

I nod.

12

The car window whirrs as I wind it down. I chuck an empty McDonald's bag onto the motorway. It floats away down the central lane. I follow it with an empty can of full-fat Coke, some chocolate wrappers and an empty plastic bottle of vodka.

I burnt the notebooks and invited the other women to toast marshmallows over my mystery bonfire. Vivian watched from an upstairs window. She didn't attempt to retrieve her notebooks. I was disappointed by our lack of a showdown; she didn't even say goodbye.

The car stinks of Leon. Cheap vodka and cheaper aftershave. The ghost of Leon appears on the back seat, smiling.

'I'm surprised you can drive,' he shouts over the noise of cars passing us. I throw a pair of boxers and some old shoes out of the window. 'Women are terrible drivers. I wouldn't let Daisy behind the wheel, even after I'd had a couple of pints.' I shove a pillow through, which drops rather than floats, followed by a towel.

Vivian taught me. She sat in the back seat during the exam

whilst biting her bottom lip. She cheered when I passed. A loud cheer that must have carried across the whole of Leicester. She grabbed me by the shoulders and promised me this was the first step to independence, but these moments were quick to fade.

'Mind your own business,' I say. 'You couldn't even keep yourself alive.'

He shrugs.

'You got me.'

I hold up a porn magazine. The car swerves but I bring it back with my free hand.

'Not sure I should leave this one on the motorway. What if a child finds it?'

'On the motorway?' he says.

I shrug and pull a lighter from my pocket. My knees keep the steering wheel steady. The magazine catches quickly and I cough from the smoke. As it sails down the motorway, the flames flicker out.

'You like fire, don't you?' he says, rubbing his hands together.

I glance in the mirror.

'They'll never catch me, no one cares you're dead. You're pathetic.' The word 'pathetic' hurtles from my pursed lips. Leon smiles.

'I used to say similar things to Daisy.'

Leon vanishes from the back seat. I shiver, close the window, and spin the dial that controls the heating. For an old car filled with Leon's dirty belongings, it drives nicely and warms up. I press down on the accelerator.

I unscrew a bottle of water. I gulp it down whilst swerving into the middle lane to pass an HGV. Someone beeps and I flip my middle finger in the air.

'I'm thirsty,' I shout as I pass the lorry, and swerve back into the inside lane. I lower the window and, with a flick of a wrist, the empty bottle is gone. That was my third litre bottle. I should stop chucking things out of the window. I'm sure they have bins in Manchester. I've only been there once before, and it was at night. I sneaked away from the refuge. In and out on a £10 mega bus.

I switch on the radio. I sing along to a song, something from the Eighties, the synths crash against the drum. My voice is an octave too high, but I believe you don't need to be good at something to enjoy it.

'Ben liked this song,' I say out loud.

The music is drowned out by the sound of a radio DJ, his voice upbeat and verging on the annoying. He introduces the news. Another male voice, this time sombre.

'The hunt continues for the murderer of Emily Sykes. The murder bore resemblance to a number of attacks in the South Manchester area. Police initially arrested Brian Daniels, who was a person of interest in the Emily Sykes case; he was then released without charge. It is not known if police have linked him to a spate of murders in the city, with some claiming an active serial killer is at large . . .'

I reach over and switch the radio off.

'Poor little lamb. I wish I could have saved you. I can't save everyone,' I whisper.

And I can't. I am a lamb in a world filled with fleas. They hop from one supply to another, claiming every woman they have encountered is a crazy ex. Whilst protesting, *it's not me. It's not all men.*

Rain splashes against the windscreen. The wipers spring to action, pushing the water back and forth. I must be close. It always rains in Manchester. I try to remember if it was raining the night I killed the second man. I peel through my memories. Was it raining?

Stars reflect in the sky. When did the sun set? An hour ago? Did the day leave with Leon's dirty trainers as they bounced down the road? It was night when I killed the second man, just like the third and the fourth. Night favours such deeds. It was raining.

'A drizzle,' I whisper. 'Mingled with damp body odour.'

Sweat breaks through my forehead as the heaters warm me. I pull my jumper over my head, keeping one hand on the wheel to keep the car straight. The late Queen Elizabeth stares out from the T-shirt I'm wearing. I laugh. One hundred per cent pure cotton. No wonder Sylvia was pissed. From now on, I will be the type of person who wears 100 per cent cotton T-shirts. It feels great against my skin.

I leave the motorway to join dual carriageways, which fade to become suburbia. I reach my hand out and feel for my fourth water bottle. I inhale it. The empty water bottle sits in the well of the passenger seat. It rolls back and forth as the car shudders up to the cemetery. Looks like the people in here won't be the only dead things lurking about. Leon's car can now keep them company. It took me where I was needed.

The moon lights the way as I click shut the car doors, not wanting to make any noise. I pass the graves of people whose lives deserved to be marked by engraved stone, and head deeper into the graveyard. No sound apart from *my* footsteps. I reach the far corner. An empty patch, no neighbours. This is it. This is Ben's final resting place. Tree branches hang over the plot.

I squat on Ben's grave with my jeans around my ankles. I look downwards.

'If you're wondering what I'm doing, Ben, I'm pissing on your grave.'

13

2027 – HMP Bronzefield

Same green room. Blinds closed. Different guard. I'm first to arrive and I wonder what the holdup is.

'If they're not here in five minutes, we're off and you're back to your cell.'

They've graced me with a male prison officer. Rare. He's young. Has that swagger that you see in men who flex their muscles in gym mirrors. The sort who indulge themselves in weekly haircuts and manicures. You know the type. Fleas masquerading as peacocks.

'We'll wait until my guest has arrived,' I say with my back to him.

'You're not the one in charge,' he says.

I stand. With my leg I nudge my chair until it is facing him. I sit back down with my legs crossed at my ankles and my shackled wrists on my lap.

'You're not meant to be here. Who did you swap with?'

He's similar to my first guard; shiny boots, crisp shirt, pleat down his trousers. I prefer the weathered guards. The ones with a bit of life experience. The ones with lines on their faces and spines that creak. He raises an eyebrow.

'How do you know that? You fancy yourself as a psychic?' He sniggers at his own joke.

'Come closer and I'll tell you.'

As he saunters towards me, I pull at the shackles to test their strength. He crouches beside me. I move my face, ever so slowly, towards his ear, as if I was about to whisper something, when the room door bursts open. My guest.

'Sorry, I'm late,' they say as they take the room in. They look at the guard and then back to me. A different prison officer – one who has escorted my guest – stares wide-eyed. She nods towards the corridor and my male guard leaves, closing the door behind him. I'm alone with my guest. My skin tingles.

'I think we're alone,' I grin.

They look towards the door. Pause.

'Do you need help moving your chair back? Did the guard do something to you? To someone you know? Another inmate, perhaps?'

I stand and my guest lifts my chair and places it back down so it faces their chair. They're asking me if I think he is a flea.

'It wasn't what it looked like,' I say.

'What do you think it looked like?' they say.

The male prison officer re-enters the room, red-faced. It looks like he has received quite the dressing-down from his colleague. I smile at him but he refuses to meet my eyes.

'It probably looked like I was about to choke him out with my handcuffs.' I raise my wrists and pull. The handcuffs make a chinking sound.

'And were you?' I look over my shoulder. The guard stares at the floor, ashen-faced.

'Of course not.'

They overestimate me. They only see me in one dimension. Murderer. Maybe I was going to whisper in his ear. Ask him his star sign. Compliment his shiny blue eyes. I guess we will never know.

My guest sits opposite me.

'How come you're late?'

They pull a Tupperware box from their rucksack. I hadn't paid attention to the bag before; they arrive before me and leave after. It's nice, blue and black. Classic looking. The sort a hiker might have. Do they hike? At the weekends? With a dog, some friends, family?

'They wouldn't let me through with this at first, but don't worry, I persuaded them.'

I'm not worried. I don't know what's in the box. They pass it to me with a plastic spoon. As I peel back the lid, citrus hits me, and I realize what they have brought me.

'Lemon drizzle cake?'

They nod and I raise the plastic box to my nose and inhale. The scent is magic, and I am transported back twenty years. I hold it close to my face so I can eat it with the handcuffs on. The sugar explodes inside me.

'I love lemon drizzle cake,' I say between bites.

And I question if it is the cake I love, or the memory that appears whenever I smell lemon. I smile to myself. Close my eyes. In prison there aren't many moments you want to last, but this is one. I want this cake to never end. I want to stay in the moment. Feel the sun on my skin, a breeze through my hair, picture a butterfly landing on a flower. We don't realize we are living through happy memories until they have gone, but we get a second chance to treasure those seconds, minutes, hours, days, and hold them tight to us for ever.

'Thank you.' I hand back the Tupperware box with only crumbs remaining.

'You're welcome,' they smile.

They place it back within their sensible rucksack and take out their paperwork. There's more than usual.

'Can I show you something?' they ask.

I nod.

They hold up an image of Ben.

And now I feel silly. They were bribing me with cake. I look at the prison officer, too young to recognize the main man in my life. Too young to recognize the face that appeared on so many front pages, web blogs, and crime documentaries.

'Go on,' I say.

I hold myself still. I don't react. A flicker of anger.

'I can't tell your story without telling Ben's.'

Some people worm their way into your life and, like thread, weave themselves into the fabric of your soul. They lower the picture of Ben.

'I know. You didn't need to bring the cake to coax me into talking about Ben.'

They shake their head and raise their hand.

'No, Maddie. I brought you the cake because I know you like it. There was no motive.'

I shrug. There's always a motive.

'Maddie, in your own words, can you explain who Ben Starr is?'

I'm silent for a moment.

'Ben Starr is the man who abducted me when I was ten, and kept me prisoner for twelve years. Ben Starr is a flea, and the first man I murdered.'

14

2007 – Manchester

Emily Sykes. I roll her name around my tongue, feel my lips move as I whisper it. I swallow her name. Allow it to take seed inside of me, so she can grow and spread around my body. The last victim of the Manchester Maniac was called Emily Sykes. Now, I need his name. The king flea. Is it Brian Daniels: the landlord?

It is no coincidence Ben Starr is buried here, that he has drawn me to Manchester where a flea is slaughtering women; there may as well be a big MR emblazoned in the sky like a bat signal. The women of Manchester need me. Emily needs me. If Vivian has taught me anything, if someone needs you, you get close to them. How can I get close to a woman who no longer walks the mortal realm? I can't, but I can get close to her landlord.

It's not been hard finding Brian. It's never hard to find a landlord, particularly one who might be short of tenants because he's been accused of murdering one of them. I struck lucky and found an advert buried deep on Gumtree: three bedrooms available in a shared house in Withington. Far enough away from the ghost of Ben, but close enough to make sure his zombie corpse doesn't come scrambling through the dirt.

I dragged my bin bag filled with all my worldly goods two miles to the house. It's large, at least three floors; the type of house that decades ago might have housed a family and a housekeeper. Maybe even a butler. Now, it houses young professionals, who can't afford a mortgage. A large tree, as tall as the house, sways in the front garden.

Outside is a small sign saying rooms for rent. Graffiti is scrawled across it, but I can't figure out what it says. Nor do I care. The spray paint has run, congealing at the ends of the sign. A man gets out of a car as I walk down the street with my bin bag in hand. He stands in front of the sign as if he's trying to conceal it.

Hello, Brian. He's clipped his hair short, his clothes are drab rather than colourful, but it is him. Emily Sykes's landlord. The man arrested and released for a young woman's murder. Will suspicion slide elsewhere now he has treated himself to a haircut and sombre clothing? He's fallen in line with society's expectations. He's conformed. Afraid the locals will label him a monster. Too late.

I catch my reflection as I pass a window. What does a murderer look like? Does a murderer look like me, or does it look like him? The clothes and haircut mean nothing. The little fleas seeking to slaughter the lambs look like your father, your brother, your friend, your work colleague, your landlord.

Finding him was easy. Too easy. They don't have to worry in the same way we do, even when they are accused of atrocities. Men don't have safety tips rammed down their throats; it is like they live in a different world, a safer one. I'm changing that. Little by little.

He smiles as I approach, glances at the bin bag but says nothing. His smile is tepid. As if being too happy or too sad would frighten me. He lives in an in-between place now, only allowed to exist. Has a flea been flushed from the pack, or is he one of the genuine *it's not me* men? He raises a hand to shake mine and then puts it back down again. A dancer performing out of step.

Maybe I should leave – the landlord was on bail for murdering a woman my very age – but go where? This is my best chance at getting close to Emily. To finding her killer. He doesn't scare me. I won't back down. There is a vulnerability to him and not in a Ted Bundy pretend way. I reach out my hand. He wipes his palm against his trousers before our hands intertwine in a limp shake.

'I saw you in the paper,' I say. His shoulders slump and he stands, awaiting some abuse, no doubt. 'Disgusting they can just put your face everywhere without any proof you've done anything.'

He tilts his head and raises an eyebrow.

'It's been a waking hell.'

I nod. I suspect it has. When I escaped Ben, I remember being in a paper suit, in a green room with cushions and soft furnishings. Everything was cosy and warm. A bright lady, with chubby, wholesome cheeks, came and sat next to me. I forget her name, but she asked me a question and told me whatever I decided would mould my life. Then she handed me a biscuit she called a cookie. She caught my interest because she said – *whatever I decided*. I had a choice. I had been waiting for choices. I'd seen on television how people choose their GCSEs or their university degree, how they choose their style, their music taste. or whether to be a vegan. I was eager, edge-of-my-seat for my first choice. She smiled at me and asked – do you want the world to know what happened to you, or do you want to make a go at a normal life?

'I'm guessing that's why you're the only landlord in Manchester with spare rooms.'

He sighs. It's a long sigh, because Mr It's-Not-Me knows I'm about to ask for a discount. He ambles up to the porch and opens the front door with his key. The door swings open, revealing a pitch-black hallway. He fumbles with a light switch until it flickers on.

'Half-price rent for six months, but only if you take the downstairs room.'

A discount? The room must have once belonged to Emily. Good. I want to be as close to her as possible. I follow him into the house. I leave my bin bag of belongings at the door, as if I'm not too bothered about the room. I am, of course, but I want the discount. Mr It's-Not-Me doesn't need to know I'm desperate. There's a musty smell, the sort that appears when somewhere has been unlived in. He nods in the direction of the first door we pass.

'That's my room.'

A live-in landlord. No wonder everyone abandoned this house. We keep going and take a corner. He points down to the bottom of the hallway. A dim bulb hangs naked and low.

'Kitchen and diner is down there, but I'm not sure who uses it these days; it's all Just Eat this and Just Eat that.' He pauses outside a wooden door and flicks through the keys on a large chain. 'Ten, fifteen years ago, we all used to eat dinner together. Like a family.' There's a distant look in his eye as he recalls a past he approves of. 'This would be your room, if you want the discount.'

I want the discount. He forces in the key and pushes the door open. The light from the hallway streams into the room. Again, he fumbles for a second to find the room's light switch. But from here in the hallway, the room is twice the size of the one I had at the refuge. Massive bay windows sit at the back, overlooking an overgrown garden. The ceilings are high and everything painted a glossy white, not the nasty cream colour Vivian always insisted on. The room looks like no one has ever lived there. Dead or alive.

'I'll take it,' I say. 'Today.'

He pauses for a second, looking like he is weighing up what to say, as if he may be able to push the rent up, but he soon concedes.

'Deal.'

He hands me the keys in exchange for less cash than the room is worth. Bargain. Mr It-Wasn't-Me disappears, leaving me standing alone. Was that man the Manchester Maniac?

'Do you want a hand?' Brian asks, nodding towards my black bin bag of belongings.

'I'm not sure it's a two-person job,' I say, gesturing to my bin bag.

Brian nods and looks towards the floor. My refusal of his help has left him lost as he moves his weight from one foot to another.

'You are safe here. I want you to know that. Believe it or not, I am one of the good guys.'

He follows me to my new room and I can feel his eyes on me.

'I've never hurt anyone. Especially a female.'

Brian spits the word 'female'. He forces each syllable to be hard – FE-MALE. He borders on defensive.

'How can I be so certain?' I say as I tilt my head and flash him a grin.

He laughs. My flippancy about my own safety has disarmed him. As if sacrificing my basic needs has made him comfortable.

'I suppose you can't.' He pauses.

More laughter. Mine. His eyes widen.

He comes into my room without invitation and sits on the corner of my bed. He places his hand to his eye to wipe away a tear that doesn't exist.

'This has been the worst few weeks of my life. All because Emily couldn't keep herself safe. I did everything I could to help that girl out, and this is what happens.'

He pats the bed at the side of him, gesturing for me to sit. I ignore him, forcing him to stand up.

'I hope you'll like it here,' he says as he stalks out of my room.

15

2027 – HMP Bronzefield

Same room. Same time. Same green walls. It's cold in here, the blinds blocking out the spring sunshine. My guest places a Dictaphone on the table.

'Do you mind?' they ask. 'I've been struggling to read all my notes and this way I can listen back when I need to.'

I shrug. I hate the thought of my voice being imprisoned by the recording; my words made permanent rather than a fleeting memory but at least this way my guest can't add their own interpretations. Over the years my story, my voice, has become twisted like a gnarled root.

'I've really struggled to identify how Ben Starr kidnapped you. There appears to be a gap in the timeline.'

It's there, if you look hard enough, amongst the police documentation and the transcripts. I sit and wait for them to ask me, and not assume what information they want, allowing an uncomfortable silence to gobble up the room. Even the assigned prison guard stares at her nails in an awkward attempt to avoid the uneasiness.

'Maddie,' they pause. 'How did Ben Starr kidnap you?'

I wish I could tell them that I was riding my bicycle, a red one with streamers attached to the handles, when I passed a white van with the engine still running, and Ben jumped out of the driver's side and bundled me into the back.

But it's not true.

Or perhaps, it was Christmas, I was shopping with my mum and I was distracted by sparkling lights adorning a twenty-foot fir tree. My hand slipped from hers, dazzled by the decorations, and in seconds I was lost. I wandered through the crowds, panicked, when Ben dressed as Santa Claus appeared. He knelt to meet my eyes and told me he knew where my mother was, took my hand and slipped me away.

But it's not true.

Or my favourite version of events – Ben entered my house in the middle of the night. He slaughtered everyone. My father and mother fought him until their last breath, my brother barricaded my bedroom door with his own body, their love for me keeping them alive, willing them to fight to protect me. Until, one by one, each of them was dead. Ben appeared at my bedside, blood dripping, grinning as he scooped me out of my bed. Stepping over my dead family as we left.

But it's not true. I have no father. I have no brother. No, my kidnap was a non-event. It barely happened. Life before Ben is hazy, my mother's face pixelated, always out of reach, blonde hair around a face I can't see. I don't remember the curve of her chin, how big her nose was, or how thin her lips. I don't know what colour her eyes were. I do remember she had one great love in her life. Drugs.

I was ten. Picture a ten-year-old who knew she was second best to a high. That was me. Second best. I didn't have a bike;

we didn't go shopping at Christmas and there was no family willing to put their lives on the line for my protection.

'Maddie, are you okay?'

I look up and my guest is staring at me. They hunt through their backpack and pull out a packet of tissues and offer me one. I raise my hand to my face. My cheek is damp. The tissue trembles in their hand and I can't quite take it from them.

'It's okay,' they say. Their voice is soft. Above a whisper. They take another tissue from the packet and stand up; they move around the table and lean on it in front of me and dab my eyes. Each pat tender.

'No,' the prison officer barks sharply enough to make me jump. 'No physical contact.'

We freeze.

'Sorry.' My guest raises their hands in the air and moves back to their chair. I notice how crisp their T-shirt is. Did they do that themselves, or is there someone at home who takes care of them? Who irons their clothes and pats their eyes dry when they cry.

'We can talk about this another time, Maddie. If you're not ready today.'

'It's fine.'

There was a drought. That's what druggies call it when there are no drugs. My mum had dragged me around all day, flat to flat, phone box to phone box. It was dark when we ended up at a house. She didn't knock on the door, we walked right in, and I remember there were no windows in the room my mum ushered me into. Broken glass was scattered on the floor. The walls vibrated from heavy bass music I didn't recognize. But nothing was as loud or as dirty as the smell. I was tired. Bone tired. I sat in the corner to begin the wait for my mum and I fell asleep.

'I'm not sure how Ben Starr kidnapped me. I fell asleep and when I woke up, Ben was there.'

I have a vague memory of waking up on the back seat of a moving car. A man telling me it was okay and I was safe. He kept repeating that phrase over and over. I was safe. I was safe now. Through sleep-crusted eyelashes, I saw a star flying across the sky and the moon huge above a canopy of trees. If I had known I wouldn't see the sky again for twelve years, I would have soaked it all in, but instead I fell back to sleep.

'That must have been scary, waking up somewhere unfamiliar.'

I want to tell my guest; I woke up and screamed my throat raw. Tell them, I begged for my mother. It wasn't unusual for me to wake up in different places. In the first moments, I thought I was dreaming. A pink bedroom, filled with clean furniture and toys. A four-poster bed with cushions and a heavy thick duvet, the sort a princess might have. Posters on the wall of ponies and bunnies and kittens. Everything was soft, clean and warm. Everything was just how I had always envisioned my perfect room. In the wardrobe was dress upon dress, with frills and laces and puffy sleeves. Tiny white socks and tiny shoes.

'Not really. You see, it wasn't unusual for my mum to leave me in the care of a friend here or there – all called "auntie" or "uncle", but none shared my DNA. It may have taken me a little longer than most to realize I'd been kidnapped.'

Years later, Ben told a couple of different stories of how I came into his custody. Once, in temper, he said my mother had sold me for £500 and a packet of cigarettes. I don't believe that story because I'm certain she would have asked for a bottle of vodka too. The second story came in bits as he vomited into a toilet after drinking too much. He said he had seen me with her; she was a crackhead with an unkempt child and, from time to time, he would follow us. The night he took me, she was outside some abandoned house overdosing. He went inside and found me asleep on a dirty mattress. He said if he hadn't taken me, then someone else would have and my fate would have been far worse in the hands of some addict looking for their next tenner. I think we will never know.

My guest removes a piece of paper from a folder and slides it across the table. I glance at it. My mother's death certificate. The woman with the cookies, the one who gave me choices, she told me my mother had died in hushed tones. Rambled about how people we love make mistakes.

'I was ten that year,' I say, nodding towards her date of death. 'It was early September. I remember her telling me I needed to memorize the route to my school.'

'Your mum died from an overdose on the same night Ben Starr took you, and you fell through the cracks and you were never reported missing.'

Ben loves this story. The one where he is my hero and saves me from my terrible mother.

'Say that again. The last bit.'

'You were never reported missing.'

I nod. It never fails to punch me in the gut. I press the skin between my finger and thumb. Hard.

16

2007 – Manchester

His knock trails like an ellipsis . . . Starting loud and brash, finishing with a quiet surrendering tap. I lie on the bed chucking a small blue ball in the air. The thin curtains allow the reds and oranges of dusk to filter into the room. I thought I would feel her in here. There's nothing; it is as if this room has always belonged to me, its past somehow erased.

It's Brian, dull Brian my landlord, not interesting Brian who was seated in the back of a police car in an orange shirt, I think, as the knocking begins again and my ball lands in my hands. I sit up. I knew he'd be back. He has a lonely stink about him. Do I stink like Brian?

I crack open the door an inch. Brian's face is too close to the gap, as if he is trying to will me invisible and catch clues about me and my life from the inside of the room. He takes a step back and holds up a bottle of red wine.

'I thought we could celebrate your first night in the crazy house . . .' He pauses. 'I mean crazy as in fun. Not in a bad way. Drink?'

It's not a question, more an assumption. I filter through excuses not to go. He must detect my unease and moves another step backwards and moves his arms in an open gesture. His belt is red, a throwback to the time he existed before he was accused of murder.

'I could do with the company; it's been difficult,' he says.

'I don't like wine.'

He shrugs.

'We can find you something else.'

I follow as Brian leads me into the kitchen. He grunts as he pulls the cork from the wine bottle. The scent knocks me like a fist to the face. Cheap red wine from the supermarket was Ben's Friday-night treat. It'd be my job to make sure his glass never emptied, a fool's quest because at some point in the evening the wine would always run out. I might be a saviour to the lambs but I can't turn water into wine.

The kitchen itself is large but sparse. An old dining table, wonky at one end, sits near a large bay window with no netting and drab brown curtains; at the other end is the kitchen area with white goods. Brian makes a cursory check of the room for other drinks.

'Water?' he shrugs.

Before I have time to reply, he fetches a glass from the cupboard and places it under the tap.

'It's definitely clean,' he says as I lift the glass to my lips. 'The police didn't take any of her crockery and Emily was house-proud. She was the perfect tenant.' I place the glass back on the counter. Something feels wrong about using a dead woman's belongings without her permission – would Emily allow me to drink from her cups? Eat from her plates? My gut instinct says yes, but without confirmation I'm hesitant. I move towards the bay window and perch on its ledge, imagining at another time someone sitting here basking in the afternoon sun.

'They emptied her room though. They put everything in bags. Labelled every item,' he says, his voice trailing off. 'That's why I gave you the discount. I'm not sure many people would be comfortable in Emily's old room.'

I remain still and refuse to allow any reaction to seep from me. My hunch was right. I am in Emily's old room. Good. I need to be close to her. Unlike Brian, who I am as far away from as possible, but it feels like he and his red wine gobble up all the space, forcing me closer and closer to the cold glass of the window.

'You already have work? Is that why you moved here?' he asks as he takes another gulp of his wine.

'No,' I say. 'I'm looking for a job.'

From the corner of my eye, I notice a dark shape sitting on a low garden wall opposite us. It doesn't move.

'Emily used to work at Queen of the Burgers. They always have vacancies.' His cheek indents, as if he is chewing on it. 'I'm more than just a landlord,' he lets out a forced laugh. 'I write wills on the side. Do you know much about the legalities of will writing?'

Will writing. That makes sense. He literally deals in death; he is one step away from undertaker in my mind. I nod and make a mental note of the name of the burger joint Emily worked at.

'Of course, we will have to sort you out a will too – never too young. I do it for everyone who moves in at a decent price. Mates' rates, if you like?' He's smiling. I notice a rip in the armpit of his jumper. 'What do you keep looking at?' he asks.

He moves closer to the window as I peer out at the shape across the road. Red swells in his cheeks.

'Her, again.'

He bangs his fist against the glass, and I move away, half afraid it will shatter. The form doesn't move and Brian storms out of the kitchen, his heelless slippers slapping against his bare feet as he stomps.

I follow in his shadow, darting into the night-time. The figure hangs back, away from streetlights. Brian marches across the street. I follow a few steps behind him. The cold air fills my nostrils. Brian raises his arms, and for a moment he looks bigger, meaner, as if he has unfurled into his true form. Is this the Brian Emily saw in her last moments?

'You need to bugger off. We're trying to move on with our lives and you're not helping.' His voice is filled with rage, red mist layering his thick flea tongue. His spittle flies across the street as he shouts.

A woman takes a step forward under the glow of a streetlamp, as if she is in her very own spotlight. She's willowy, almost lanky. Her coat is oversized and her beanie hat is pulled down to her eyebrows.

'You're not safe here,' she shouts in my direction. 'You need to leave. Do you need help? Are you being held against your will?'

Who is this woman? I take a couple of steps forward, impressed by her willingness to help me whilst an accused murderer is shouting at her.

Brian extends his arm to his side, creating a barrier between me and my new hero.

'I'll call the police.'

'Do what you want. I'm not afraid of you, Brian. Not today, not yesterday, and not tomorrow. I know what you are.'

She speaks with conviction. A part of me fights the urge

to slaughter Brian on the spot to impress her. Maybe I should. Her boldness is a far cry from the women at the refuge. Is she a flea hunter too?

'You know nothing about me.'

'I know everything I need to know,' she says, her hands on her hips. 'I'm going to be the thorn in your side until I know the truth.'

I stop myself from laughing. Again, who is this woman?

'Right, I'm calling the police. Maddie . . .' He glances over his shoulder at me. 'Maddie, call the police.'

'Maddie,' the woman says, 'you are not safe. Leave. Until next time, Brian.' She turns and walks away without glancing back to see if he is following her, or sneaking up with a hammer in hand.

'Come on,' he says to me as we both walk back to the house. As though I am his to command by default of my gender. I look back and the mysterious woman has disappeared. A half-shadow cast across Brian's face. He is back to the snivelling, smaller Brian of only ten minutes earlier.

'Who was that?'

'Don't listen to her. She's a nobody. You're safe here. I promise.' The shadow lengthens down his face and neck. Ben told me I was safe. Vivian told me I was safe. The second man I murdered told me I was safe. The only person who has told me to leave, to run, is that woman. She is at odds with everyone I have ever met.

A gust of wind causes the huge tree in the front garden to bow towards the house, leaves rustling. His cologne lingers. At odds with the rain-cleansed night.

'Tell me her name,' I say, making my voice soft and warm. The same way I'd soothe Ben when his foul moods would cast a cloud over my prison.

'I'd rather not, Maddie, she's just some ghoul,' he says with a sigh. 'Maybe we can discuss it another night, over a drink.'

Fucking tell me. Everything – it appears – has a price, even the truth. I run through a catalogue of ways to murder Brian and land on a slow death preceded by water-boarding using red wine.

'I'm going to bed,' I say.

'Don't listen to what she said, Maddie.'

His voice follows me into my bedroom and the front door closes with a slam.

The ghost of Robert Jones lies on my bed as I enter. An ethereal smile accompanied by empty eyes. My blue ball sits motionless on his chest. He sits up and my ball bounces off the bed and across the floor.

'Can I smell alcohol?' he asks.

'Robert, you need to leave.'

'You don't strike me as a drinker. And please, I insist you call me Robbie.'

I walk over to my bed, willing this figment of my imagination to evaporate.

'You know nothing about me.'

Robbie laughs as I perch at the end of the bed.

'So, why don't you tell me? What turned you into such a bitch? A man just like me, I bet. Look at the power we hold over you. Is that why you murdered me? Do you think killing me gets you revenge?'

Robbie slips his hand onto my knee and I look down at it. He's not here. He's not here.

'You were asking for it,' I say.

A cold wind blows between us. I feel his head nearing mine. Spittle on my ear as his lips move closer.

'I bet that's what you say to all the boys,' he whispers.

17

I pause outside Queen of the Burgers. The A4 piece of paper masquerading as my CV crinkles at the right-hand corner as my thumb and finger grips it. They're going to know I'm lying. They'll look at me and they will know. What was I meant to do? Hand it in empty? Or worse, tell the truth?

Viv didn't encourage any of the women to work. It was as if the refuge was a waiting room. It would be easy to assume we would be working on ourselves – picture meditation, yoga, massages, cold immersion dips, art therapy – but you would be wrong. Cheap milky tea and awkward group therapy led by Viv was the best we got and, even then, it was sporadic. A group of us staring at the ground in silence whilst Viv explained the difference between fight, flight, and fawn.

The front door is heavy, and I push my weight against it to enter the restaurant. Inside is busy: workmen, teenagers, families. Queen of the Burgers is popular. The walls are painted to look like old bricks and fireplaces. Replica oil paintings of burgers hang on the walls, as if they were aristocracy, with their names carved on gold plaques below. Cooking oil perfumes the air. People huddle around tables. The queue snakes to the front door.

Behind the counter is chaos. Teenagers wearing plastic crowns dodge one another as they pile fries on plastic trays and tap on registers. Coins rattling in tills add a rhythmic layer to the pop music playing in the background.

'There's a queue . . .' the teenager behind the counter pauses and then sighs. 'Your Majesty.'

'I was wondering if there are any jobs going?' My voice is barely audible and I struggle to maintain eye contact. I hold out my CV. The teenager looks at me like I have escaped the lunatic asylum. Their frown turns to a grin.

'Aaron,' she shouts towards the back of the kitchen. Her head turns to look back at me. 'Run while you can,' she says.

I stand to the side whilst she takes an order from a woman pushing a pram and a receipt buzzes from a machine behind her. Another woman wearing the same uniform but without the crown appears beside her behind the counter.

'Aaron isn't here,' she says.

A couple of the staff exchange looks between them. An awkwardness hangs in the air for a moment as everyone appears to avoid eye contact with the woman apart from me. She stares. I stare back. I outreach my arm again with my CV in hand.

'I'm looking for work.'

Without saying anything, she takes the CV.

'This you?'

I nod. She takes a cursory look over it and stuffs it in the bin.

'When can you start? There's only one correct answer.'

I look at the queues and the tables packed with people. Litter piles at the bins.

'Now?'

She raises the hatch and gestures me through. I dodge staff members, all of whom look at me for a second too long as I pass behind the counter and through the kitchen. A radio in the corner plays angry rap music and a man flipping burgers, with a cap on a little too low, jerks his head along to the tempo, as the lyrics talk about hoes and sex.

'I'm Karla by the way,' the woman says as a door swings open to reveal an undecorated stairwell. Her brown hair is pulled into a ponytail that bobs up and down as she takes the stairs two at a time. 'I take it you're Maddie.' Frown lines appear across her forehead each time she speaks. Her posture is slumped, as if the weight of the world is weighing her down. 'What size are you, Maddie?' she asks, looking over her shoulder for a moment.

'Don't know. Small?'

She takes me to a dressing room. Metal lockers line the wall. A full-length mirror is on another wall with a poster above it saying, 'Do you look like royalty?' Next to the mirror are faces in mock gold plastic frames under a banner saying 'Employee of the Month'. July, two months earlier, stares out at me, underneath the smiling face reads the name – Emily. Mousy-brown hair, brown eyes – we look similar. My mind rattles back to Brian giving me Emily's glass. I'm now standing where she once stood. I'd planned to find her work colleagues, they're pieces of the jigsaw, but instead I'm becoming one of them.

'I'm not going to lie and say they're new, but they're clean.'

Karla hands me burgundy trousers, a shirt and a plastic crown. I place the shirt and crown to one side and a name tag on the trousers pops out – Sykes. Emily Sykes. My thumb grazes over the name tag and I glance at Karla. She freezes and thaws in a microsecond. She places a hand on my knee.

'Look, we're a fast-food joint. People quit all the time. Even if . . .' She pauses, composes herself. 'Even if Emily were still,' she inhales and pauses again, 'here. We'd still need staff. You're not taking anyone's job.'

Karla takes the trousers and rips the name tag out of them with her teeth and passes them back to me. I stare at the number that remains. Six. I am a size six, like Emily. I picture us sharing clothes, brand-new clothes not hand-me-downs from the pile in Vivian's office, not the dresses Ben brought home. And not through pity, but as an act of friendship, sisterhood. I glance at her picture.

'I thought the tags had been taken out,' Karla says, jolting me from my daydream.

A thunderous knock comes from the dressing-room door. Karla gestures to me to stay where I am and gets up to cross the room. She holds the door half open, concealing most of her body.

'Aaron?'

She steps out of the room, closing the door behind her.

'You do not have the right to hire staff.' The voice is angry, male, slurred.

'The team are struggling. You can hit pause on your life, but you're making everyone else suffer. We've got people on double shifts. I caught Cody asleep behind the bins the other morning.'

I don't catch Aaron's reply but the irritation in Karla's voice rakes through me like a cat scratch.

'You smell of whisky, Aaron. Go sleep it off in the office before anyone else sees you.'

She comes back into the room ashen-faced.

'Did you hear any of that?'

I shake my head no, as a small tremble courses through me. Aaron. I scratch his name into my brain.

'It's not the easiest time for anyone. We're social, and people quickly become friends here . . .' She pauses. 'And I hope you do too. But I recommend you don't ask too many questions, okay?'

It doesn't feel like a request, more a warning. I don't know how much information I will get about Emily here. Karla looks up at a TV monitor in the corner behind me. Grainy CCTV plays. Her eyes open wide.

'Oh fuck, not her again. We've had to change the angle of the CCTV to catch her lurking about. It used to just cover the rear door, but now we need a view of the whole car park.'

We both stand watching the CCTV as another staff member chases someone out of the car park. A familiar shape slopes out between the cars at pace. I strip as I watch this unfold. It's the woman from last night. Who is she?

'Who are they chasing?'

'No one,' Karla says. She looks at me and I look back, wide-eyed. Butter wouldn't melt. 'She's from the local university. She's called Victoria Sloane, she's . . .' Karla raises her hands and makes quotation marks with her fingers. '"Investigating" Emily's death. She's causing a lot of upset. Thinks she can find the killer. She's an ambulance chaser. If the police can't, I don't know why some little undergrad thinks she can. I best go help in case it kicks off again.'

Karla races out of the room, leaving me standing in my underwear. Emily Sykes watches me from her photo as I put on her old uniform.

'I'm sorry, mate,' I say to her, as if we have known each

other for years. 'I know it must look like I am a cuckoo in your nest, but I am going to find the man who murdered you and I will punish him. An eye for an eye.'

I look at the CCTV footage, and Karla stands in the pouring rain, her arms waving about as if she is shouting at someone out of range of the camera. In isolation she looks crazy. What harm is Victoria Sloane doing? They should be more concerned about the serial killer roaming around.

The Manchester Maniac killed their friend.

I think of the men I have murdered. All of them less deserving than Emily's killer. How could I justify their murders whilst allowing him to carry on his campaign of terror? I can rectify that.

I stare at Emily's picture.

'I have some questions for this ambulance chaser.'

I look back at the CCTV, and rain pelts against the screen.

18

2027 – HMP Bronzefield

I still have the first grey tracksuit they issued me. It fits. I smile every time I slip it on. From what I understand, most people in prison gain weight, a bit like the freshman fifteen but with handcuffs, bars and shivs and no college degree at the end. The guard opens the meeting-room door and gestures to me to enter. They close it with a bang behind me. I'm alone. A familiar feeling. No doubt the prison guard sees no point in my company until my guest arrives. They're here for my guest's benefit, not mine.

I'm not waiting long. What novelty. They're seconds behind me and a warm feeling rushes through me as they enter the room. A quiet obsession is growing. I enjoy talking about myself, about my victories.

'Hello, how are you?' I ask too quickly, too eagerly. I'm not being polite. I want to know. How has their time been away from me? They need to know more about the many sacrifices I've made. Tell the world I'm a hero.

'Yeah, I'm alright ta, traffic was awful on the way in. How are you doing, Maddie?'

Traffic. The bus being late. Oversleeping. What I'd give for inconveniences.

'I'm good, thank you.'

I told myself I wouldn't lie when I began this. I haven't about any of the big things, the events, the people, my actions. It's the little things I find myself lying about: I'm good, thank you.

They rifle through their bag and pull out their papers and the Dictaphone. They place it on the table. Smile.

'By the time of your escape, you'd spent more than half your life with Ben. Were there any moments – when you look back – that might have come close to what you imagined was a normal life?'

No one has ever asked me that question before. No one. Perhaps they were afraid to offend, or maybe they think every moment was a living hell, but my time with Ben was littered with regular moments. Happy moments. I want to tell you every single second was filled with misery: that would make a compelling case for me murdering him. It wasn't so straightforward. I wish I could truthfully paint him as all bad, all wrong, a degenerate with no redeeming qualities. Wouldn't that be easy? If men like Ben were all bad we could spot them from the crowd with ease. Paint some light in with the dark and you never really know if it is day or night.

'Perhaps, for the first time, I felt an element of security and routine. I forgot what it felt like to be cold or hungry.'

I was happy watching films, eating three times a day, wearing clean clothes. I was happy not walking for miles in shoes that would become waterlogged from the holes in the soles. The sound follows me about from time to time when I walk, a squelch followed by another. That's not what I'm meant to say though, is it?

'Did you ever meet any of Ben's friends or family?'

I shake my head no. It was me and him for years. No one popped by for cups of tea and chats. There were no parties. There were no Sunday dinners with tucked-in elbows at the table. Ben, by his own admission, didn't fit in, and found himself on the outskirts of life. I was Ben's only friend. If you can call it that.

'No.'

They nod. I feel like I am being led down a path I might not like. My guest avoiding eye contact with me, is that a tell for them? Surely not. If anyone can handle an uncomfortable conversation, then it should be them.

'And never his mother?'

Ah. Mrs Starr. How do we define terrible people? People like me? Am I terrible? Or people like Ben? Or can someone awful cause harm in passive ways? Can loving too much make you terrible? Mrs Starr's love was akin to poison leaking through Ben's pores. He believed he was special. He thought he could take anything or anyone he wanted. Mrs Starr's love was a fog Ben was lost in. And even with all the love she smothered him with, there was someone Mrs Starr loved more: Mr Starr. Ben and I both had mothers who would turn a blind eye for the great loves of their lives.

'Never had the pleasure. Feel free to set up a date, though. I've heard she'd like fifteen minutes alone with me. Do you think she'll bring me cake?'

'I'm sorry to mention Mrs Starr, but she's never stopped defending Ben and I do think it's something we can't gloss over.'

'Is she not dead yet? She must be a hundred and five by now.'

I swear I detect a small smirk from my guest. Perhaps I'm

not the only person Mrs Starr irritates. The woman is cheap soap.

'She's eighty-six. I met with her last week. To interview her for the book.'

A knife to the heart. My guest looks away for a second. And so they should, meeting with Ben's mother. Allowing her to have an inch of column space is treason, with her muddled views and twisted recollections. Yet, I'm impressed they persuaded her to meet: she dropped the traditional media when she discovered the socials and created account after account to proclaim her son's innocence. Maybe she was impressed by my guest's CV. Most are.

'Did you ask her about Eric Starr?'

My guest nods. Eric was Ben's stepfather. They married when Ben was six.

'She denied everything and asked me to leave. I did manage to acquire Ben's medical records from when he was a child. There's nothing definitive but – on the balance of probability – your account is accurate.'

'It's not my account. It's Ben's.'

It feels like Ben lives on through me and I didn't murder him but inhaled him. His truths, his lies and, given everything he has done to me, they still want to know about him. What made him rot?

'Do you think that explains the dresses?'

I nod.

'I think that explains the dresses.'

19

2007 – Manchester

Brian said to use the bus stop at the end of the road to get to the university. He arched an eyebrow as I nodded in response to him, but I remained tight-lipped about my plan to find the woman he considers to be a ghoul, or who Karla considers to be an ambulance chaser. This woman Brian and Karla despise must have answers.

I considered walking, but I've promised myself no more meandering walks – day or night. If I'm going to catch the Manchester Maniac, I need to focus. On the way to the bus stop I pass an international food store, mangos and other fruit in boxes piled high outside. I slip an avocado into my pocket as I pass. A small Tesco and a kebab place are on the other side of the road. I keep walking. I pass a tram stop. Commuters mill about on the platform.

A huge pub sits on the corner, advertising Fizzy Fridays. Champagne and prosecco at cut prices and, for a second, I wonder what that would be like? Sitting with friends. Laughing. Knocking back our cheap champagne and prosecco. In the winters, one of us would get there early to secure a table by the fire, and in the summer a table outdoors. We'd talk about relationships, our jobs, we'd even talk about bland domesticity, like how to decorate our homes and the benefits of slow cookers. There'd be milestones too: engagements, weddings, babies and promotions. We'd celebrate each other with a raised glass on Fizz Fridays. And during the hard times, we'd drown our sorrows, with a choice of shoulders to cry on.

A shiver runs through me. If Ben hadn't kidnapped me, would my life be filled with Fridays that Fizz?

'You got any change?'

I shake my head at the woman who is cross-legged on the floor. Her clothes layered with filth, her teeth either missing or yellowed. No, perhaps not all are destined for Fizzy anything, let alone a whole friendship group.

The bus stop is a pole in the ground with a small sign displaying a number. A bin is near the pole. Cigarette ends overflow in the metal ashtray on the top. A few people linger. We all avoid eye contact with one another. Some stare into thin air, some at the ground. I feel my own eyes darting around, looking for something, someone who isn't there. A man with a walking stick looks at his watch and lets out a heavy sigh. He's old. His wrinkles deep-set. It would be easy to be fooled by a man like this, but not me. I wonder how many lambs he has fed on in his long life?

The bus appears at the end of the road, and a queue forms behind the old man, who I suspect wasn't there first. I linger near the bin until the queue disappears and then I jump on. The change hits the plastic well in the door, keeping the driver separated from the public. Lucky driver.

'Where to?' he says.

I was hoping I wouldn't have to speak to him.

'University,' I say.

He looks down at the shrapnel piled in the plastic well and scoops it up with a sigh. The ticket machine vibrates. My skin tingles as I rip my ticket from the metal teeth. Small freedoms.

The bus is moving as I make my way to the top floor, bouncing off the side as I climb the narrow flight of stairs. The top floor stinks of piss and cannabis. Explains why it's empty. I take a seat at the very front, the bit where the window is huge and it feels like you're in the driver's seat as you're travelling along.

The bus stops every three to five minutes as passengers embark and disembark. Rain hits the window, obscuring my view. Condensation clings to the glass and everything outside takes on an ethereal slant, as if I am watching a ghost town. The avocado in my pocket bulges through my trousers. Heavy footsteps echo from the stairwell and I turn as a man much larger than myself appears on the top deck. I'm no longer alone.

His footsteps become louder until they stop. In my periphery, he lingers. A shadow looming over me until he sits. Not on one of the many, many empty seats, but next to me. In the reflection of the foggy glass, the rest of the bus is empty and yet here he is. His legs spread, a millimetre at a time, until I am hunched into the corner with him taking my space.

Rage enters quietly. It does not knock or announce its arrival. It appears with a toothy grin.

'There's plenty of seats,' I say. My voice is quieter than I'd like. Above a whisper but only just.

'What?' His head snaps in my direction and he literally looks down at me.

His neck is thick and meaty. I doubt my hands would wrap around it entirely.

'I said,' and I take a deep breath, 'I said there are plenty of seats. Pick one not next to me.'

A curl in the side of his smile. A smirk? Likely. His head jerks towards me an inch.

'I'll sit where I want.'

Of course he will. Not content with taking our lives, they want our space too; they don't want us to feel safe. They like it when we're scared. When we take up the smallest spaces so they can expand, make themselves look bigger. Is this what Robbie Jones did before he had the courage to explore his desires? I bet Ben would look for the smallest girl on the bus to sit next to, to spread out and take what little space she already had.

He's sturdy. The way he sits, legs spread, arms crossed, his back pressed into the seat, and there is no way I could move him. He's smiling. He is enjoying this. I bet he would smell delicious as flames licked at his skin. I bet he would glow with intense reds and oranges. He stares forward as I find my head tilting in his direction, my eyeballs glued to his bloated, smug face. This flea is a waste of my time. He's barely larvae. I won't allow him to distract me.

I clamber over the back of the seat, struggling to keep balance, and his smile slips. It's too easy to escape his clutches. He doesn't say anything, but I know my reflection will be playing in the glass of the window as I walk down the aisle and I hope it's clear enough to watch the smile spread across my face as I stop at the top of the stairwell and turn. I reach into my pocket and feel the avocado, a little too soft, a little too ripe, and I launch it at the man. It flies through the air, a blur of green, its trajectory violently stopped by his skull. He shrieks. Unexpected, loud and sharp. It rings through me. A beautiful sound. The green mush spreads across the back of the man's head, worms its way into his hair as he touches it. It reminds me of when Daisy's baby had diarrhoea, and how

Daisy, no matter how hard she tried, could never quite get the baby clean. I grab a pole as the bus breaks to a harsh stop.

Change jangles as the driver's door slams and he appears at the foot of the stairwell. He takes the stairs two at a time and the man stands.

'She assaulted me,' the man shouts at the driver, as if I am not there.

The driver looks at me and then looks in the direction of the CCTV camera.

'He sat next to me,' I say.

Confusion spreads over the driver's face. 'So?'

There's a moment of metaphorical white noise as myself and the driver attempt to decipher one another. Then it dawns on me: he doesn't understand; they'll never understand. I bet he calls himself one of the good guys. One of the It's-Not-Me men.

'Get off my bus before I call the police.'

'Fucking psycho,' the man shouts towards me, his hand still at the back of his skull. 'If you won't call the police, I will.' He fumbles with a mobile phone.

'She's just a girl,' the driver shouts back. 'It can't have hurt that much.'

'It's my stop anyway,' I shout.

I race down the stairs, the driver in my shadow, but he makes no attempt to stop me. I jump off the bus as the driver pens himself in behind the wheel.

Up the street, the sign for the university is modern and bright. The bus comes back to life and leaves me, as if I am nothing but a memory.

The man is standing at the top-floor window, a phone to his ear. I stick my middle finger up to him. He'll never know how lucky he is.

20

The entrance is circular, made of grey stone; ivy climbs the walls. The signage is modern, the students are modern, but the building looks like something from a period drama. And the energy – it's alive. It's intimidating. People my age, some a touch younger and some a touch older, mill around, books tucked under their arms. They smile. They laugh. They drink coffee from small cardboard cups. They all have incredible posture. I pull my shoulders back, for a moment feeling exposed by the confidence of these people who surround me yet do not see me.

A small flock of young women stand in one corner. One gestures with her hands as she speaks; the others laugh. In another life they would be my friends. They'd have a nickname for me – maybe Mads instead of Maddie. I amble behind them as they enter the main building while scanning for my ghoul, my ambulance chaser, my hero who warned me Brian was a danger – Victoria Sloane.

A row of turnstiles click as my imagined friends venture

forth, leaving me standing alone as other students part around me. They swipe their passes, which hang like nooses around their necks. Maybe university isn't what it's cracked up to be. Fleas appear, the ones previously hidden behind coffee cups and books. Fleas. Dressed as students. Dressed as staff. Dressed as security. Everywhere. This university is infested.

Jump the turnstiles. They won't be able to catch up.

Students pass me, flooding into the university, and I don't know who or where the voice came from or who. I walk forward and, as I approach, I place my palms flat on the metal counters and jump. I'm over in seconds. Nobody shouts. Nobody runs. Nobody does anything as I walk down the corridors of this ivy-clad university.

Signs point me to where I want to go. I mentally tick off the places I don't – Geography, English, Drama, Physics. No thank you. A jolt of lightning runs through me when an arrow points in the direction of Criminology. My fantasy of being a student becomes three-dimensional. Criminology. That's me. That is where I would lurk. Maybe Victoria Sloane isn't a weirdo, an ambulance chaser, or a ghoul. Maybe I am. I wander in the direction the sign points towards. It's okay to treat myself and take a moment away from my mission, and bask in a life that might have been.

As I enter an auditorium accessed from the outside of the building via a small courtyard, I hide in the shadow of a man with long hair dressed in double denim. A whiff of cannabis mingles with his body odour. Other students, like him, are dotted about the room, but it is by and large empty. I count the bums on seats, including my own, and there are thirteen of us – unlucky for some.

A tired-looking flea with a creased shirt stands at the front. He asks someone to dim the lights as he turns on a projector –

THE DIFFERENCE BETWEEN SPREE, MASS AND SERIAL KILLERS flickers on a whiteboard. I raise an eyebrow. I am at home.

The flea stands stage right of the projector and reads the title. Everyone is listening. You could hear a pin drop. I bet it's not like this in Geography, a room of intent listeners waiting to hear the difference between sedimentary and metamorphic rock, or even Physics or English. What makes some people want to lurk in the dark? Explain away the depraved. Are they looking for answers for other people's bad deeds, or is it personal? Does something call to them in the small hours of the night, something strange and frightening? Something they'll spend their lives fighting. We can't all be good people.

A door squeaking open makes half the room jump, surprised at the unexpected intrusion. The lights flicker on. A tall, lean woman enters, a beanie hat pulled low, carrying a rucksack. It's her. She takes a seat in front of me without apology. She's only a desk away from me. I didn't need to find her because we are drawn to the same flickering darkness like moths. Myself and Victoria Sloane are kindred spirits.

'Victoria Sloane,' Mr Creased Shirt says. 'Late again.'

'I had a lead. I had to chase it up,' she shrugs.

Everyone rolls their eyes. One or two people accompany it with a long groan, but it is as if she hasn't noticed or doesn't care. The lights dim again. The words flicker on the whiteboard and the lecture begins. My eyes stray from the front of the room and settle on her. She rummages through her bag, emptying the contents on her desk. I reach out with a pen in hand. She nods. Mouths the words *thank you*. She's younger than I imagined. Twenty-one? Twenty-two?

So, this is her. Her lips move along with the lecturer in the front of the auditorium, as if he is delivering a film she has watched on repeat. The lecture no longer of interest to me as she becomes the sole object of my fascination. She stares intently at the front of the room, scribbling notes as she goes, nodding along, her mouth curling along to the word 'serial killer', and it dawns on me, I have found someone more interested in murder than myself.

Time passes. For the first time in my life, as I watch Victoria Sloane, I am not waiting. I am in the moment. So much so, as the lights flicker on, my eyes burn and I am loath to drag them away from her. Mr Creased Shirt bangs on about coursework and due dates before he releases everyone. I stand, steady myself to introduce myself to Victoria Sloane, my lips parted, when the same male voice that has taken up all the space for the last ninety minutes emerges again.

'Victoria Sloane. A minute please.'

She's like a newborn lamb descending the stairs of the auditorium, clumsy, her limbs gangly, and I hold my breath waiting for her to fall, but somehow she never does. The rest of the room trails out. Some look over their shoulder, curious about the obvious scolding my new friend is about to receive.

I trail behind them but linger at the external door. A cold wind hits me but I hold tight. I'm just out of sight but a long sigh travels in my direction.

'Victoria, I am compelled to ask you to stop this.' His voice.

'Stop what? Being late? It won't happen again.'

Some shuffling as if someone is attempting to walk away. My guess is she's trying to leave, get away from this flea who is using his power to hold her captive. Not all shackles are forged in steel. Some are mere glances, a threat, a gesture.

'I admire what you are doing, Victoria. You remind me of myself,' the male voice drones, never changing pitch. 'Ambition can be dangerous. Lead you to places you shouldn't go, and this investigative journalism? Let the police do their job. No more, okay?'

There's no response. A long pause unsettles me until her voice breaks the silence.

'Or you'll do what?'

'Victoria, I am telling you.'

'You're telling me to stand down. You're telling me because I'm a woman that I am automatically a potential victim. I can hear what you're saying, but I don't agree and I won't stop.'

Footsteps, hurried, come towards the door, and I picture Victoria Sloane racing away. She emerges from the auditorium and loses her footing on something I cannot see and flies into the air, her limbs tangling and spreading out as she hits the floor.

'Are you okay?'

I rush to her on the floor and she lies there. Her eyes water and yet she doesn't move. The skies part and bulbous raindrops fall, mixing with her tears.

'Are you okay?' I repeat.

No answer, she starfishes on the concrete. I don't know what to do, so I lie down next to her. The rain hits my face. She doesn't look at me. It's like we are sunbathing in the rain, on our own private patch of concrete.

'I heard your conversation with the professor,' I say. 'I was listening in.'

'It's rude to eavesdrop.'

Her voice is like honey. A cliché, I know, but it soothes me to hear her speak.

'I think what you're doing is incredible. I think you're brave and smart.'

She sits up. I follow suit and we're both staring at each other.

'Really?'

'Really.'

She becomes a little taller and her back a little straighter.

'We can't let some man go around murdering us. I've been looking into this since before Emily Sykes, and no one cared then but now they do. Now it's dangerous for women who aren't sex workers. His other victims were people too, but no one seems to care about them. They're allowing him to become a monster, something that goes bump in the night, but he, the Manchester Maniac, is just a man.'

He's a flea. A king flea, and he deserves to meet his fate at my hands. Victoria Sloane is a flea hunter and she won't allow anyone to stop her. Just like me.

'I know,' I say.

'You should hear the names they call me.'

I know the names they call her: ghoul, ambulance chaser. I've heard what they think of her and seen the way they chase her off. They don't see what I see. I don't see a morbid woman chasing after death. I see a hero. I see me.

I stand and she follows. She's taller than me by a good five inches but standing next to her it's as if we are equals. Being in her presence makes me taller, stronger, smarter. I can feel it. I need Victoria Sloane by my side to find the king flea and I will bring him to his knees.

'Maddie,' I say, looking up.

'I'm Vicky Sloane but all my mates call me Sloane. So, call me Sloane, yeah?'

I nod. Already we are fast friends. I think we were destined to meet. Ben told me I was destined to cross his path and enter his life and, maybe, this is the same.

'Do you like picnics? Can I take you on a picnic?'

I nod, although I have no idea if I do like picnics. I've never been on one.

'Excellent,' she smiles through the rain. 'I'm going to take you on a picnic.'

21

2027 – HMP Bronzefield

The door opens and my guest pops their head around it before entering.

'Traffic, again?' I say with a smile I like to imagine is warm. I forget how easy it is to slip on a new skin and pretend to be one of them.

They come in, nodding. Dressed in a pale grey jumper and dark blue jeans. The blue suits them.

'You look lost in thought,' my guest says as they take a seat.

'It's funny which memories stay and which ones leave. I wish my mind would let me choose.'

They put their backpack on the floor and take out a manila paper envelope I haven't seen before.

'I know that feeling,' my guest smiles. 'You're not alone in that sentiment. Are there any memories you're fond of and would like to share?'

'Will you put them in the book?'

'Maybe, if you'd like?'

Warmth inside me as I remember Sloane's flat. The taste of lemon drizzle cake. Listening to No Doubt. Slipping on a work uniform. Even Cody's cheap aftershave. All my happy memories are mundane. The type of daily occurrence someone like my guest would take for granted. I want to share them but I know they will laugh at me; maybe not to my face, but I fear they will take those cherished moments and spin them into dinner party anecdotes to amuse other ordinary folk.

'I'll think about it,' I say.

The prison guard coughs and I realize for a moment I didn't remember she was there. I thought I was alone, just me and my guest; that's been happening more and more. As if my escorts are fading into the background. They grow dimmer as my need to recount my story becomes brighter.

My guest opens the envelope and pulls photographs from them. The top image glares back at me – it's pictures of Ben's house, my cage, after the fire. The corner of a green sofa. A hollowed-out television. The stair banister, once white, now blackened. It's all too familiar.

'I have two regrets.'

'Go on,' they say.

Setting a house on fire is different to setting a person on fire. You set a person on fire and it doesn't matter if their entire body catches ablaze, they're going to die. A horrible, painful death. You set a house on fire – well, parts might survive. The kitchen. The bathroom. Upstairs. Downstairs. You get the gist. It's hard to destroy an entire house compared to destroying one measly flea.

'I regret that house didn't burn down into ashes.' I shrug and look away. 'And I regret I never went to the beach.'

My guest raises an eyebrow. Their lips curl.

'The beach?'

I've never felt sand between my toes. Or heard the ocean waves lapping or seagulls calling in the sky. Salt on my lips.

'Yeah, never got the chance.'

My guest takes another image from the manila folder and puts it on the table. I hold it up and stare. A pale pink dress with a white lace trim. The sleeves puff out and a white ribbon is tied in a bow at the waist. Next to the dress is a small piece of paper on which someone has written EXHIBIT 23. It's Tuesday's dress to me.

'I'd heard a rumour the dresses didn't burn.'

I struggled to believe it. The material was cheap: even a whiff of smoke might have set them alight. Yet, here they are. They survived. My guest flicks the other photographs face up so I can see them all. It's more of the same. I gravitate to one image. The dress I hated the most: it was white all over with an underskirt and a high neck, same lace trim as the pink dress. Ben would lose his shit if I spilt anything on the dress. My hands would tremble as I poured his drinks.

'Where are they now?' I say.

'I'm not sure.'

Lace from my memories scratches at my skin.

'That was Sunday,' I say, pointing at the white dress. I flick through the images and place them in order. I point to an olive dress. 'Monday.' My hands tremble as I point to the day of the week each dress symbolized to me. 'None of them fitted well.'

On a Sunday morning, he would return from taking his mother to church. I would already have the bath drawn. Goosebumps would cover my body as I shivered from the cold. I would stand at the bath until his return. *Okay, get in*, he would say with a smile. He would take a sponge and soap every part of my body, lingering at the inner thigh until he moved upwards. He'd towel me dry. Blow-dry my hair. He would tell me about the morning sermon and who his mother currently had a spat with as he combed my hair, and then I would climb into the white dress. *Just like an angel*, he would say.

I nod. All grown up, but inside is a girl with a dress for each day of the week. I pick up the final image and smirk. It's a pinafore dress in bright yellow and it remained hung in the wardrobe the entire time I was with Ben. I wish, as Ben lay screaming, I had asked him if that was the dress he muttered about in his sleep.

No Daddy, I don't want to wear the dress.

22

2007 – Manchester

She stares at me. Whenever I am in the locker room, I can feel her watching me like that painting, what's it called? The one with the woman whose eyes follow you. The *Mona Lisa*, that's it. She's just like the *Mona Lisa*. Smiling at me. Watching me. Willing me to bring justice to her killer. I've thought about tearing her from the wall. Censoring her memory and never thinking about her again, but she has burrowed into my brain.

'I've met someone who can help,' I whisper in her direction. 'She's called Sloane.'

I stand in the mirror and play with the plastic crown planted on my head. *Do you look like royalty?* the poster above the mirror asks me. In my reflection, I wonder if this burgundy uniform was always the final destination for me. In every timeline, behind every sliding door, is this it?

The locker door swings open, and Karla appears behind me. She plays with my collar at the back without asking if she can touch me. I freeze as she alters it.

'There. Just like a princess,' she laughs.

Her own uniform clashes with her ruddy complexion. I'm not sure this uniform was meant for Karla. She looks like she got lost once and ended up here and decided it was easier to stay than to find her way home.

'I'm glad I've found you. Sweeping-up duty is a thing of the past and you have been selected to work on the tills. Congratulations.' She says congratulations in a flat tone and it takes me a second to realize she's being sarcastic.

'I'd like to be in the kitchen,' I say.

'Wouldn't we all?' She's smiling at me, handing me a badge that says, *In training*. She gestures at me to follow her. I can feel Emily staring at us as we leave. Is this a replay of her first days here? Karla adjusting her uniform. Did she want to be in the kitchen too? I think Emily was born for the tills – all smiles and friendliness.

I follow Karla through the back corridors. The walls are bare apart from posters about food hygiene and washing our hands. Plaster flakes from them. Cardboard boxes are stacked in the corner. I think Queen of the Burgers is a lot like most people – fancy on the outside, not much to see when you go deeper.

The same rap music plays in the kitchen; as we approach the front of house, the restaurant's music and the kitchen's hip-hop merge, making a distorted, angry sound. A high-pitched teen pop singer duetting with a growling man.

'Okay,' Karla says, logging on to a till. 'You greet them . . . you know the greeting, right?' I nod. 'Then they order, and you press the picture of what they want. The price then comes up on the till and you take the money. And rinse and repeat. Okay, now your turn,' Karla says.

An overweight man approaches the counter; a button is bursting across his midriff. I envy his indulgence. I am a bag of bones inside this uniform.

'Good afternoon, Your Majesty,' I say. 'What would you like to feast on?'

'Good,' Karla whispers at my side.

The man looks at the menu displayed above my head in a series of flashing images.

'Tsar burger, extra onions' he pauses. 'Emperor size with Coke.'

I tap the pictures on the screen and an automated voice says the amount. The man inserts his card into the reader and takes his receipt with his number on and moves away.

'That was really good. Just keep up the pace and you'll be away. You'll be shadowing me for the first couple of weeks while I train you up.'

Karla moves to the till next to me and evicts a glum-looking teenager from the tills to sweeping-up duty. Karla's plastic crown looks tight across her skull. Her ponytail is flat against her neck, compressed by her plastic crown.

The entire shift is punctuated with me jabbing at brightly coloured pictures on the till screen. I wonder how Emily felt doing this day in, day out? Did she enjoy it? She worked here for long enough to suggest she didn't hate it. It's far too easy to turn your nose up at work that requires limited skill or thought, but Emily fed people. Most people's mothers do that; why would we devalue something so inherent to our survival?

The decorations in the restaurant become more and more garish as the big hand on the clock ticks over. The walls begin to morph as dusk enters through the windows and the customers thin out. The rap-loving burger flipper snakes out of the kitchen and behind the front desk.

'Hey, Karla,' he says, and smiles in her direction, looking at her briefly before looking away. 'So,' he says, sidling up to me. 'You're the new girl?' Unlike front of house, he wears a baseball cap. From beneath its rim, he looks at me through narrowed eyes framed by thick lashes.

'That would be me.'

'Cody,' he says, introducing himself. His eyes gleam, looking at me as if I was something shiny and he was a magpie. I know how he sees me. I'm an opportunity. He pauses for a second, awaiting my introduction, and I remain silent, wondering how long it takes to make a man like Cody uncomfortable. Seconds tick by and it's Karla who breaks our stalemate.

'She's called Maddie.'

'Maddie . . .' He draws out the *d*s in my name, making the sound longer than it ought to be. 'Cool name.' I bet he has said that to Karla, and to every woman who has crossed his path. 'I work all the late shifts except Fridays. Looks like you're going to be a late shifter too. We'll look after you. Lucky you.'

Karla lets out a laugh that may be more exasperated than humoured.

'Thanks,' I say.

'I'm DJ'ing at a club night in honour of one of our colleagues this Friday. Emily, she was called: you've probably read about her. She loved to party. It seems more fitting than a soggy sandwich in a function room. You should come.'

'Go back to the kitchen, Cody.' Karla's voice is flat.

'You should come,' he says again as he strolls back to the kitchen without an RSVP. That's the thing about confident boys. They never expect the inevitable, no. They live in a world where they can take, take, take and we're expected to give, give, give.

When I look over, a single tear is running down Karla's cheek.

'He's right – it is what she would've wanted.'

I suppose that doesn't stop it from feeling wrong. I wonder if Ben had moments when he felt something icky and unsettled inside him. Those wonky moments when the world shifts and the brightest light renders you blind, creating searing darkness for a moment. Blistering guilt scorching its way through your veins.

Karla pulls her sleeve over her hand and rubs at her eyes. Two men walk into the now nearly empty restaurant. Both in shirts with the top button undone and trousers, the older of the two is greying but handsome, in an old Hollywood-type way. Think Cary Grant or Charlton Heston and you wouldn't be far wrong. The eldest of the two takes a booth and stares out of the window. The younger approaches the till.

He doesn't have his companion's good genes. His right eye is slightly lower than his left, and for a moment I swear I detect the memory of a slight limp. Nonetheless, he gives me an easy smile as he approaches.

'You're new.'

'I am, Your Majesty.' The monotone in my voice is grating on me. 'What can I get you to feast on?'

He laughs, and I can't tell if it is at me or with me. He looks over at Karla, who greets him with a wide smile and adoring eyes.

'Please, I insist.' He raises his hands, as if gently batting something away. 'None of this "Your Majesty" stuff. It makes me uncomfortable.'

He orders food and I tap away at the screen and an automated voice rings out the total.

'No,' Karla says as he reaches into his pocket. Karla appears at my side like a whippet.

'Put that away,' she says to the man. 'Charlie and his colleague are police officers and we don't charge them to eat here.'

Charlie. It suits him. I wonder how many bad men Charlie has released into the wild because of lack of evidence? See, even the good guys make the world a worse place.

'Which is generous and unnecessary,' Charlie says. His smile is soft and genuine. Karla blushes as she walks into the kitchen to prepare his food. It leaves me in an awkward spot as I stand staring at him and he looks back.

'You look familiar,' he says.

'You arrested me once for skinny-dipping,' I whisper.

He blushes. I'm surprised as the pink enters his cheeks. He places both his hands on the counter; on his mobile phone lock-screen is an overweight ginger cat wearing a bow tie. I suspect it's called Marmalade or something equally unimaginative.

'No, I'm certain I'd remember that.' He tilts his head. A smile spreads across his face, and his lips purse as if he is suppressing a laugh. He leans across the counter and, in a whisper, he asks, 'Do you like avocados?'

This is what happens when you try to fight them. The oppressors call their buddies and do anything they can to keep you oppressed. How dare I expect to sit on a bus without a man squeezed up next to me, and when I said no, what does he do? He calls the cops.

Karla returns and hands him his food before I can reply. He doesn't look back as he walks over to his booth, but his colleague lets out a loud laugh and then glances in my direction. I shift my weight from one foot to another as I commit their faces to my memory. They don't look over again.

'Those gentlemen are our only defence against the Maniac,' Karla says.

I hate the idea of needing men to protect us against other men. Surely, we would be better with no men? And anyway, Karla is wrong. They're not our only defence. Even women have fists and fire.

23

2007 – Manchester

'The park is belting,' Sloane says. She has left the beanie hat at home and today she has donned an oversized yellow T-shirt and jeans. 'It's the perfect place for a picnic . . .' Her voice falters as we walk past the cemetery. I wonder if she is lying to me and if the park is far from belting. Every so often, she glances towards the gravestones, the sunlight catching her eyes. I spot Leon's old car abandoned in the small car park nearby and wonder when the council will drag it away.

'Yeah, I love a good park,' I say, and heat rises in my cheeks. My own awkwardness crippling me. 'I mean parks are good.'

'Mm,' she replies, again looking into the cemetery as if carried away in a memory. 'Sorry,' she says, snapping back to reality. 'I'm being rude. I just . . . it's just . . . I'm sure everybody knows someone in there.'

We pass row upon row of headstones. A metal fence keeping us out, or perhaps them in.

'Yeah, it's tough.'

She pauses. Her hands wrapped around her rucksack straps.

'Family member?' She nods towards the cemetery.

'No,' I say. 'But someone I grew up with. You?'

I feel a warm glow, picturing Ben's bones rattling in his unmarked grave. Next to Sloane, I welcome the thought of him crawling through the soil. Murdering him twice would be a gift.

'My mum. I miss her. She was a picnic connoisseur. What about the person you grew up with? Was it a friend? That must be tough.'

Words form in my mouth and press against my lips. I want to allow them to spill into the world and tell Sloane the truth about Ben and the prison I grew up in. About how this is my first picnic. I stop myself. I can't gauge how she would react – would I stop being a potential new friend and turn into a specimen to be interrogated and poked? A car speeds past us as we stare into the graveyard.

'I've got an idea,' I say and I grab her hand. Her skin is soft and warm. I pull her towards the wrought-iron gates that mark the entrance. 'Let's have a picnic with your mum.'

'No, I don't think you understand,' Sloane says, her voice breaking.

'I understand,' I say, gripping her hand tighter. 'I know we've only just met, but if having a picnic at your dead mother's grave helps you feel closer to her, then sign me up to the world's weirdest picnic.' Sunshine filters through the branches of old oak trees that scatter the grounds. 'Show me the way,' I say, gesturing with a sweep of my spare arm.

Her hand drops from mine and, for a second, I regret my words, and a creeping paranoia whispers in my ear that my suggestion is a neon sign making me out as a weirdo. She walks ahead and glances over her shoulder with a smile.

'Come on,' she says. 'I'll show you the way.'

I jog a few steps to catch up with her.

'Tell me about her,' I say.

'I get my strength from her. I watched her endure . . .' Sloane stops. 'She taught me to do what is right. She was funny, kind and smart.' Sloane's pace slows and she puts her hands on her hips. 'No, she was more than a bunch of adjectives. She used to comb my hair and had an infectious laugh. She loved Eighties films and grunge music.'

Grunge music? Cultural references are social grenades to me. I flick through my brain, trying to cling on to something I can reference or quote but I draw a blank. I nod along as Sloane talks gibberish to me about films, books and music.

Our walk grinds to a halt in front of a headstone. The flowers that lie in front of it are fresh, and I picture Sloane here alone, visiting her mum, and I fight an urge to wrap my arms around her. I read the inscription:

Diana Sloane
1965–2002

'Maddie,' she gestures her hand towards the headstone. 'This is my mum, Diana. Mum,' she sweeps a hand towards me, 'this is Maddie. My new friend who is going to help me.'

I've never been formally introduced to anybody's mum before, and I half wonder if a dead one counts. I chalk it up as a win.

'Nice to meet you, Mrs Sloane,' I say towards the grave.

We both sit down cross-legged on a patch of warm grass.

'Thanks for suggesting this. It's kind of you.'

Kind. The word glows in my stomach and warms my whole body. I'm kind.

'Do you spend a lot of time with your mum?'

'Overdose when I was ten,' I say, shaking my head no.

She pauses and I become aware of how still everything is around us. Not even a breeze strong enough to sway a blade of grass. She plucks an errant daisy from the ground and pulls on the petals.

'My mum's boyfriend.'

I wait for the rest of the sentence but Sloane stares towards the trees that pepper the cemetery. As I open my mouth to prompt her, I stop myself. That was the whole sentence. Cause of death: boyfriend.

I glance over my shoulder at Ben's grave and the urge to tell Sloane everything reappears. I open my mouth, hoping the words will appear.

'Ham or egg?' Her voice is high as she tries to shift the mood. A strained smile in my direction. 'I didn't know whether you were veggie or not so I made both and then on the way here it occurred to me you could be vegan and I thought, oh god, what if she's vegan and I brought only ham or egg?'

An awkward laugh from Sloane and the moment to reveal my secret leaves like daisy petals on the wind.

'Either is fine.'

Sloane unzips her rucksack and pulls a plastic bag from within. The same type I used to store my lighter fluid and my lighters when I killed Robbie Jones. A whiff of smoke and ash appears in my mind and I feel a cosy warmth through my veins.

'Let's share then,' she says, pulling clingfilm from both the sandwiches and handing me a triangle from each. 'Don't worry,' she says, pulling plastic plates from the bag. 'I've got us covered. Like I said,' she says, nodding towards the headstone, 'Mum was a picnic connoisseur.'

I place my sandwiches on the plastic plate which sits on

the ground. Sloane continues to remove Tupperware boxes from her bag and a bottle of lemonade. She pours us both a drink and I watch the liquid fizz to the top of red solo cups.

'So,' I tilt my head, trying to find the right way to ask where Sloane's mum's boyfriend is so I can slash his throat. 'Is he in prison?'

She shakes her head no and I force myself not to smile. What a gift for my new friend, when she discovers the man who took her mother met a grizzly fate.

'He killed himself straight afterwards,' she mumbles the words at the ground, as if she is ashamed. Her hand trembles as she reaches for her bag, and for a moment I think she is afraid, but I catch her eyes – hard, cold, defiant. She isn't afraid or ashamed. She's angry. The rage inside so consuming I can taste it on the air. 'What happened to your friend?'

'Similar story to yours.'

That's not a lie. It is a similar story, but the outcome was different for me, and because of my actions the outcome will be different for many women. If only I had met Sloane earlier, her mother would be alive, but five years ago I was fighting for my life too. There are many Maddies and Dianas.

'I have a confession to make,' she looks up at me through thick lashes. 'I know who you are.'

Ben's unmarked grave looms in my periphery. A handful of people know who I am, who I really am, and Victoria Sloane isn't one of them.

'I recognized you as soon as I walked into the lecture hall. You're the woman who has moved into Emily Sykes' old house, aren't you, Maddie?'

The stillness of the graveyard lifts. A bird sings, grass rustles, car engines pass, and in the distance a dog barks. I smile.

'I have a confession to make too.'

She arches an eyebrow.

'I know you're the woman who Brian was chasing off from the house. Who Karla was chasing away from Queen of the Burgers. You're the one they're calling a ghoul and an ambulance chaser . . .' I pause, unsure if I want to say the next part. 'I'm not a student, Sloane. I was looking for you.'

She tilts her head to the right until it is nuzzled to her shoulder, and a crack fills the grounds, echoing and returning. She shakes her head loose and her lips become thin.

'I know you're not a student and I was surprised to see you there. No, I was glad. I've been worried about you in that house with him.' She spits the word 'him' and I know she must mean Brian. 'And also, it's not like that,' she says, holding her hands up. 'I'm not an ambulance chaser. The police have messed up time and time again, letting a serial killer run free on our streets. They don't care if we die.' She bites into her sandwich as if we're discussing the weather. A drop of rain hits my forehead and grey clouds merge above, threatening rain.

'Maddie?'

'Yes?'

'How do you know the staff at Queen of the Burgers aren't cooperating with me?'

I guess I walked into that one. Sloane may have known I was living in Emily's old house, but she didn't know I had taken her job too. Will she peg me as some grim cuckoo invading a dead person's life?

'I needed work.'

And to get closer to Emily's old life. I've pulled her old uniform on, wedged a plastic crown on my skull and smiled at Cody. Ben whispers to me from his grave – *They don't understand you. Not like I do. You will never have friends.*

Sloane offers me a sausage roll from a Tupperware box and I take one. Pastry flakes down my top as I bite into it.

'I was looking for you,' Sloane says. 'You found me first. I knew, deep down in my gut you'd be able to help.'

'We need to find the killer . . .' Our words merge and we both meet each other's stares, our eyes locked together. A shiver passes through me.

'That reminds me,' Sloane says. She pulls out her phone and I wonder what she will show me. Instead she hands me the left piece of a pair of her earphones placing the right piece in her own ear. Upbeat funky guitars fill my left ear, followed by drums, and a woman's voice, upbeat yet protesting. The singer repeats into my brain that she is just a girl. Sloane grabs my arm and pulls us both to our feet. I look at Sloane. Her head moving back and forth, her arms in the air, her mouth moving along with the words. I find myself moving in sync with her.

'"Just a Girl" by No Doubt – my mum was partial to a bit of ska too,' she shouts at me, although we're both sitting cross-legged in the same position as minutes earlier. My hands move to my knees, tapping in rhythm with the drums as something – an energy I can't put a name to – courses through me, an urge to move and sing and shout. The lyrics are written for me.

Sloane jumps to her feet. Her hips sway left to right and I find myself on my feet, replicating her at her mother's grave. Sloane sings along to the words. No, she shouts along to the words, and I lose control, jumping up and down on the spot. Then it ends.

We both burst into laughter as an elderly lady with a walker passes us.

'This is a graveyard not a disco,' she says.

'Sorry, but we're listening to my dead mum's favourite song.'

Again, we're both laughing, and it's not forced. It's in tune. Sloane sighs and we both collapse to the floor.

'Do you want some more?' she asks, popping a grape in her mouth. I shake my head and she packs away the Tupperware boxes. 'At least I'll eat well tonight. I always overpack.'

Sloane stands, wiping crumbs from her clothing.

'Let's walk and talk. I need to get my steps in,' she says with a grin.

I jump up and, as promised, the grey clouds above open, releasing buckets of rain upon us. We both run with a squeal underneath the treeline, half laughing and half panting. We dawdle underneath the thick canopy, a stray raindrop occasionally making its way through the leaves. My heart races as we approach Ben's grave. Part terrified he will find a way to destroy my new friendship, part gleeful he might be able to see me having picnics with people who consider me a friend.

'Thanks for coming and meeting Mum with me,' Sloane says with a smile. 'I knew I was right about you.'

We inch closer to Ben's grave, and I spot the woman with the walker placing roses at the other side of the graveyard. I feel a small pang of guilt.

'We'll need to be careful,' Sloane says. 'Look out for each other. Until we know who the Manchester Maniac is, we are at risk. We can't become victims.'

Sloane's tone is dramatic, as if she is delivering her opinions to an audience of women and not just me. Why would I want to be a murder victim? I don't want to be any type of victim. I wonder if she sees it on me; whilst my skin may look clean, sometimes in the shower I cannot scrub away the invisible taint Ben has left on me.

We're nearly on top of Ben's grave. I can feel him. Like the oxygen is thinning around me, and if I don't run I will suffocate.

'I think they're hiding something at Queen of the Burgers,' I say.

'Yeah, they are.' She stares at me hard. 'They're hiding something, and the police are doing a terrible job. I've asked one too many questions, but I won't stop. I was looking into this before Emily Sykes. Prostitutes were disappearing and no one cared. It wasn't until she and the rest of the women were found that anyone started paying attention. And they were only found because they were looking for Emily.'

'How many prostitutes?'

Sloane raises a hand and then her second hand with one finger.

'Six. Six lives before Emily.'

'The Maniac has killed seven women?'

'And they only called him a maniac when the pretty young girl died.'

Seven women.

My mother had 'friends' who would disappear and reappear, they would come and go. A knock at the door. Another friend. Cartoons in the living room whilst music played loudly, and those were the better days – days when we didn't walk for miles or end up in strange places filled with smoke.

I look down and we have wandered on top of his grave. I look at the tree and I wonder if I should mark the bark to warn people what is beneath the ground. If an unmarked grave should be marked with a warning.

'Those women are daughters and mothers. I'm writing a

book about the crimes and how the police aren't catching him quick enough. No one wants to help. Not Brian. Not her ex-colleagues. No one. You have access to everything. Will you help me?'

I can smell fire. I look around but I see no flames, no smoke. 'What's the book called?'

'It's called,' she pauses for effect. '*How to Catch A Serial Killer.*'

I nod. A serial killer is stood in front of her – me.

'Yes.' I smile. 'I'll help you.'

I cast a quick grin at the ground. Did you hear that, Ben? I'm going to find me a king flea and burn that fucker alive. In my head I can hear guitars and drums and an upbeat woman protesting she is just a girl. My hips sway.

24

2007 – Manchester

Pickle juice leaks from the black bin bag as I drag it across the kitchen floor. Cody seems to have disappeared the moment someone suggested we should start cleaning for the night. Karla, however, appears to be relishing scrubbing the surfaces.

I push the back door open and the night air rushes in. It makes me feel clean. The night air smells different, feels different. It offers promises the daytime never could.

The outdoor bin is one of those large ones, and I struggle to open the lid due to its height. When I do manage to get enough momentum, it crashes against itself, creating a bang. I remain still for a moment, my icy breath lingering on the air. The bag is heavy as I lift it and fling it into the bin. I'm turning to go back, when in my periphery a figure appears.

'Ben?'

In every moment filled with stillness, I wait for him to collide with the silence and drag me to hell. I know Ben lurks. He lingers on the edges of my existence, waiting for his moment to swallow me whole. Death hasn't stopped that man. He lives on in men who still breathe.

'Hello?'

I creep forward on my toes. I'm ready to run.

'Who's Ben?' Sloane says as she enters the light from the building.

'No one. A friend.'

Sloane shrugs.

'What time do you knock off? I want to show you something.'

I look down at the imaginary watch on my wrist. A habit that knocks me sick every time I do it because I inherited it from Ben. I wonder how many more gestures I've never noticed that belong to him and not to me.

'In ten minutes, but you shouldn't be here.'

'I shouldn't be in a lot of places.' Her laugh is small. 'I'll meet you here, okay?'

'Maddie.' Karla's voice comes from within the kitchen, forcing Sloane to take a step back into the shadows.

'Meet here, yeah?' she whispers.

'Okay.'

Inside Cody has reappeared and is wiping down a large blade. Leaning on the counter next to him is a large man I haven't seen before; he glances in my direction and away again. His beard is unkempt and tattoos of flowers creep up his arms to biceps that bulge at his T-shirt sleeves. He says something to Cody who laughs loudly in response. The large man glances back at me.

'You must be Maddie. Welcome aboard.'

I can detect some sarcasm in his voice. It's faint but it's there.

'Nice to meet you,' I say.

'Is it?'

He laughs again and I walk out of the kitchen to the front of the restaurant. Karla is lifting chairs onto the tables. I help her.

'Who is the man talking to Cody?'

'Aaron,' Karla says, her tone hard and not inviting of further questions.

We make light work of the chairs and Karla hands me a brush as she drags out a mop and bucket.

'He's the guy in charge? The owner?'

'When it's convenient,' Karla says, mopping as I brush. She pauses for a second. 'I'm being unfair. Aaron has taken Emily's death hard. Too hard,' Karla's lips narrow. 'I've had to pick up a lot of the work he used to do.'

I keep sweeping, Karla returns to mopping.

'He was meant to give her a lift home. If you're wondering why he's been particularly impacted . . .' Karla fiddles with a gold band on her ring finger.

'But he didn't?'

She shakes her head no but doesn't meet my eyes.

'Like I said, you'll find it easier here if you don't ask too many questions. You can finish for the night.'

Cody's voice travels from the manager's office to me in the locker room – frantic, hushed tones. Cody and Aaron must be friends.

'Are they friends, Emily?'

I stare at her picture and await a response, but nothing comes. She stares at me silently.

Outside, pickle and ketchup stench clings to me, mixing with the night air. As I close the kitchen door behind me, I can detect her breathing – slow and heavy. Sloane emerges from amongst the bins. Her scarf is long and one end is thrown over her shoulder, her beanie hat pulled low. She points with her finger to a CCTV camera mounted over the kitchen door.

'That,' she says. 'Caught the last image of Emily Sykes alive. Walking into work. After that, nothing.'

I look up at it, a small black dome. Sloane walks along the perimeter, no doubt avoiding the CCTV camera. As we reach the edge of the car park, she stops.

'Here,' she says, looking around, 'is where it is alleged Emily waited. I've heard whisperings someone was meant to collect her but never showed up. Maybe they did show up and they don't want anyone to find out they were the last to see her alive. The CCTV didn't catch her final moments. The management claim the CCTV stopped working two hours before she left for the night. Very fishy, if you ask me.'

We walk down the pavement. I avoid the cracks and Sloane pretends not to notice.

'Aaron, the owner,' I say. 'He was meant to give her a lift, but I think he cancelled or something.'

'We should add him to our list of suspects.'

I nod. He is acting weird, and he could have been the last person to see her alive. He should be on our list of suspects.

'Do you think we should add the landlord?' I ask.

'Yeah, maybe she did make it home. I hear he has a connection to the other victims too, that's why the police were so quick to arrest him.'

'The six prostitutes?'

Sloane nods. The roads are empty and I relish walking again in the night. I've missed hearing my footsteps echo in the dark, and to my surprise two sets of footsteps sound better than one.

'So, what is it you want to show me?'

Sloane raises an eyebrow and gestures around her.

'This, what I've been showing you since we left Queen of the Burgers. This is the route Emily is believed to have walked on her last night. We're about to enter the red-light district. It's credible she was taken here like the others.'

We take a left and a right. The route back to my – and once Emily's house – is only twenty-five minutes, but it feels longer with Sloane, as if we are watching everything, both of us guarded and curious.

The red-light district is on the outskirts of an industrial estate. By day it is filled with tradies and HGVs, but at night women roam the streets and linger at corners. Sloane nods at some of the women as we pass. She waves at one and slows as we approach.

'Hiya, mate,' the woman says to Sloane.

Sloane hands her some loose cigarettes which she pockets.

'Ta, very much,' she replies. 'Who's your mate?' she says, nodding in my direction.

'I'm Maddie.' I smile.

'Mia,' she says.

I was expecting more vulnerability, but there is an unexpected hardness to her.

'She's helping with the investigation,' Sloane says, nodding towards Mia.

A car slows and a small woman gets into it. Mia studies my uniform.

'Queen of the Burgers?' she says. 'I used to babysit Cody when he was this high.' She gestures with her hand at waist height. 'That other girl worked there too, didn't she?'

Sloane nods to confirm Mia is right as she continues to talk. 'We're dying out here. We're being hunted, and nobody cared until that young girl got murdered, and I bet he mistook her for one of us. I feel like I'm on a ticking clock. I need the money, though.' Her eyes dart from left to right as she speaks to us. 'I thought it was over when they arrested the landlord.' She sighs, long and hard.

I look around and there are women of all shapes, sizes and ages. They're mostly standing in the shadows. If I was driving through here, would I notice them? I'm not sure I would. They all appear to fade into the background. In fact, seeing the bags under her eyes, the sharpness of her elbows, the woman in front of me is literally fading.

Sloane says her goodbyes and we keep walking through the estate.

'I don't think Emily was confused for a prostitute.'

'Me neither,' Sloane says.

I think the Manchester Maniac wanted us to think that. I think his intention was to grab a girl off the street who wasn't a prostitute. I think that was always his intention, but he knew as soon as he did, the police would be on to him. He knew he was taking a risk with Emily, but he couldn't resist.

A car slows and pulls up alongside me and Sloane.

'Oh shit, here we go,' Sloane says.

I look at the driver – Charlie the police officer from Queen of the Burgers.

'This isn't what I meant by take care of yourself,' he says. 'Jump in and I'll give you both a lift home or the Maniac will find you before I find him.'

'And how do we know you're not the Maniac?' Sloane is quick to reply.

'He's a cop who comes into my work,' I say.

He pulls out his badge.

'And you're everyone's favourite pain in the arse, Victoria Sloane. I've been getting a lot of nuisance complaints about you,' he says with a smirk. She smiles back, appearing thrilled Charlie knows who she is.

'I've got a few questions,' she says, jumping into the front passenger seat. I take the seat behind her. Sloane gives her address and I feel some relief knowing Charlie won't know I'm living at Emily's old house.

'Yes, I hear you're writing a book and upsetting plenty of people in the process.'

'The truth hurts,' Sloane says, with a note of seriousness that feels over the top.

Charlie laughs and his eyes scrunch up as he does.

'I bet it does,' his tone light. 'Almost as much as an avocado in the back of the skull. Don't you think so, Maddie?'

I can't see Sloane's face, but I imagine her confusion. I shrink into my seat. My and Charlie's eyes meet in the front mirror and he raises an eyebrow with a grin.

'I've always fancied writing a book,' Charlie says. 'I might when I retire.'

Sloane scoffs, but Charlie doesn't acknowledge her rebuttal.

'I always drive this route home just in case. Sometimes I'll pull over and walk a circuit through the woods at the back,' Charlie says. 'Keep your eyes out for anyone or anything suspicious.'

Sloane pulls her shoulders back; her spine becomes straight in the seat; she stares out of the window. I gaze out at the pathways, refusing to meet Charlie's eyes in the front mirror.

25

2027 – HMP Bronzefield

My cell walls are empty. Yellowing plaster peels at spots, revealing dirty bricks. The other inmates, even those here for short spells, have photographs pinned to their walls. Often of children, and sometimes of their mothers and of fleas they love. The old Maddie would have maybe stolen a picture. Perhaps a sweet one of a dead grandmother. I would have pretended it was mine. Imagined another lifetime, a different sequence of events in which I had a sweet grandmother. I'd have called her Nonna, in a nod to my imaginary heritage, and people would ask me questions about my culture. I wouldn't do that now. I've grown. I understand I have no Nonna, I have no heritage, I have no culture.

A knock at my cell door. Three bangs followed by a loud sigh. I don't move from my single bed. I know how a prison guard's knock sounds, but I don't need to. Only the guards visit the serial killer. The other inmates keep a distance. In my long stretch I have made no friends and I have made no enemies; the other women know what I did but do not seek revenge like they do with child killers. Some of them have scars from their own versions of Leon Parker, or they've felt safe around men like Robbie Jones only to discover, when it is too late, they were mice nibbling cheese laden on a trap. They're wary of me but they understand. They get why I did what I did. Some admire me, I suspect.

'I'm coming, ma'am,' I shout.

The grate in the door opens with a long whine followed by a bang.

'No need,' they shout back, 'your guest has cancelled. They must be fed up with you already, Reid.'

They've never cancelled before. I picture cars, piled into one another, my guest's face pale as firefighters race with the jaws of life. Glass littered across the motorway. A lightning bolt of pain strikes through my skull. I sway.

'Did they say why?'

'No . . . like I said, probably bored of you, Reid.' Laughter. Not mine. Footsteps moving away.

An armed robbery. My guest stopped at a corner shop on their way to visit me to buy me a small gift. They passed the baked beans, the bread; they passed the newspapers and sweets; as they approached the till, they saw the gun. They flung themselves at the attacker. One loud gunshot. The cashier's hooped earrings shake as she begs for help. The armed robber flees as my guest lies in an ever-increasing pool of their own blood. Nausea washes over me. They can't die before the world knows the truth about me.

I stagger to the door. Try the handle, knowing the metal door is locked, keeping me, a monster, from the outside world. I bang my fist against it. The noise swimming in my skull. At least my guest doesn't have to see me like this. I do not know if I could pretend to be fine, to be healthy. I have spent a lifetime swallowing my screams. I don't know if I could digest one more.

The grate opens again, a whine followed by a bang, the noise louder than it should be. Two eyes stare back at me.

'What now?'

'I need pain medication.'

A long sigh. Papers rustling.

'It's not been four hours. You'll have to wait.'

The grate slams shut, and the bang vibrates inside my skull as I crawl on all fours back to my bed. I drag myself into it. I count each deep breath I inhale.

I mentally comb through the letters we exchanged before I agreed to meet. There had been about ten. I had replied. I make it a rule never to write back to the many letters I receive. Be it from journalists or misplaced well-wishers, I never reply because they all want the same thing – answers. Their questions may vary but their demands never change. I replied this time, when I saw the name of my guest. It was the least I could do. The exchanges from both parties were short, courteous, and no telephone details had been swapped. If my guest decided to never return, that would be that. All I would have left would be some letters printed from the prison email system. How easy it would be to abandon me in here. How easy it would be for my chance to tell my side of the story to disappear.

I thought I would hate regurgitating the past, but it has reminded me why I did what needed to be done, the sacrifices. I'm on a ticking clock. My throat becomes clogged with panic. What if I run out of time?

Perhaps I will survive long enough to say goodbye. It's too much to expect visits after we are done. I wouldn't ask for that. But perhaps if they could offer me one memento, a picture to hang on my wall. And if the guards ever enquire who it is, I can tell them; it is a picture of my friend. One last lie.

Of course, I realize I might not make it that long. They have told me a priest will say a few words as I'm buried in an undisclosed location. I've asked them to burn me and scatter me at the beach. I hope someone grieves for me – a single tear would be enough. I just want someone in the world to notice I have gone, to notice for the second time in my life I am missing.

26

2007 – Manchester

Steam rises from the spout of the kettle in translucent clouds. I move my chin so the tail end of the heat hits me. It's euphoric to bathe in flames and smoke. I don't move away until the pain is too much. I don't want my skin to blister and welts to form. Would Robbie Jones reappear to pour salt in my wounds? I should stick to scrubbing myself clean in the shower.

I stare out across the kitchen and wonder if Emily spent much time here. Did she look out of the bay windows? Or was this where she would pre-game with glasses of vodka and energy drink. Shots of cheap spirits? I can't feel her here the same way I can feel her at Queen of the Burgers.

I've been standing here less than a couple of minutes when Brian walks in. He smiles, his mouth wide, his eyes vacant. He's in pyjamas. Harry Potter ones. The women in the refuge loved Harry Potter. The films were on near constant repeat in the refuge's common area as they discussed what house the Sorting Hat would pick for them. It was then I realized popular culture would be a black hole pointing me out as the anomaly.

'Let me guess,' I say pointing at his top. 'Hufflepuff.'

He laughs but it feels hollow.

'Ravenclaw. You?'

'Muggle,' I reply, and I feel like I have never spoken a truer word. I'm surrounded by magic, and yet I can't connect to this world I don't understand. To trust. To communicate. I am a muggle in a world of lambs and fleas.

He wanders out of the kitchen and I sigh in relief. I take out a mug from the cupboard and pop a tea bag in.

'Just milk for me.' Brian makes me jump as he reappears in the kitchen with a brown leather briefcase in hand. 'Didn't mean to scare you.' He has mischief in his eyes. This flea may not have intended to scare me, but the pleasure he has gained from it is plain to see across his face. He does not try to hide it. His smirk revealing his true nature. A knife sits in the sink, flaked with old food, and I wonder if I slit my throat would he drink from me?

I pull a second mug and place it on the counter with a forced smile. There's a part of me that wants to please. The part of me that stayed at the refuge for so long pleasing Vivian, it's the part of me Ben built. Brian sits at the table. His eyes follow as I move from the kettle to the fridge to the milk and back again.

'I'm starting to regret pointing you in the direction of Queen of the Burgers for a job. I never see you any more.'

A chill courses down my spine. What would Brian like? To keep me in this house and for me to never leave? To be available whenever he is lonely or wants a cup of tea – is this how Brian sees me? An object for his amusement. This one comment shows me he isn't many steps behind Ben. Does he realize he could pluck a woman from a bus stop, from a park, from an empty street, and keep her caged like a bird.

'They're keeping me busy,' I say.

I take a teaspoon and mix the tea, watching the mini typhoons I am creating inside the cup. This house feels too big with only me and Brian. I wonder how it felt to Emily when every room was rented, did it feel too big or claustrophobic?

I walk over and place Brian's drink on the table in front of him. He smiles at me as if he approves. As if he is my boss and I am his underling. As if his approval matters. The same way Ben would when I'd place a couple of custard creams on a saucer for him.

Brian places his chin on his hand as if he is thinking. I feel like he is mocking me. He should be more upset than this but it is as if he has lost a cat he didn't want in the first place.

Brian places his briefcase on the table. It opens with a click. Inside is a pile of papers and a gold pen. 'Let's get down to business,' he says, pointing to the chair next to him at the kitchen table. I hover for a second. I glance at his cup of tea. Remember that approving smile from a second ago and take the seat opposite. I can sit where I want. He looks up from shuffling papers but doesn't say anything. I smile. I approve.

'I've left something in my room,' he says. He scuffles away like a cockroach caught in the light. I move my chair out with care, hoping it won't scratch against the floor and make a noise. I tiptoe over to his side of the table; the briefcase is open and I peek in. Unremarkable. A stack of papers littered with legal terms. Boring. A gold pen rolls about at the side between the paper and the edge of the case. I pick it up, it's weighty. Inscribed are the words 'Dream Big'. I let out a little laugh. My eyes dart towards the door as I cover my mouth with my hand.

I pick up the papers. They're heavy and a little voice in my head tells me to fling them into the air. Provoke the flea. See what he will do, lure him to shed his mask and show his true colours. I stop myself. Perhaps I am as boring as the paperwork. I place them back into the briefcase when I notice something shiny poking out from amongst the dull A4 sheets. I pull on it carefully. I hold a strip of four old-fashioned photo-booth images up. They're of Brian and Emily. In black and white, he loses his odd quality and she is radiant. In the first, Emily sticks out her tongue at the camera, her hand behind Brian's head, her fingers creating a perfect V shape. Brian is grinning. Genuine joy. In the second, Brian pulls a face, his mouth and eyes wide. Emily leans away from him, mid-laughter. In the third, she is pecking Brian on the cheek. I stare at the last image, both faces in profile, their eyes locked. Emily's hand on the side of his face.

I lower the strip and place it on the table. I look up and Brian is standing in front of me, and I realize I was so absorbed in the pictures that I didn't notice him return to the room. He leans over the table and picks up the photos. His bottom lip quivers as he looks down at the images. My jaw lowers. Emily and this strange man. No.

'You weren't just her landlord, were you?'

He sits down and sighs. He places his head in his hands and his shoulders jerk up and down. I'm frozen to the spot, my body directed to the door I want to escape through. He looks up at me wiping his face with his hands.

'I cried rivers over Emily before she died,' he says through sniffles. 'I liked her.'

'You were her landlord.'

Did she want his attention, or did she feel obliged to play nice? Did Brian murder her because his desires were unrequited, or is this a show of true grief? Can both be true?

'I thought there was someone else but she denied it. I just, I'm a nice guy, and maybe if she liked me back then . . .' He trails off and grabs the gold pen from his briefcase. 'Wills,' he says. 'Business is slow. So mates' rates,' he mumbles. His eyes are red and his cheeks wet, but he is trying to smile at me. I sit down.

'Did you write Emily a will? At mates' rates?'

He leans back in his chair and I inch towards the edge of mine. I glance at the door.

'Yes, I wrote a will for Emily. I didn't kill her. I was in love with her.'

I nod. Like Diana Sloane's boyfriend probably loved her. Love. They use that to invalidate our fear.

'She was young. The probability of her . . .' He stops. 'I didn't kill her. Some fucked-up wacko did. Okay?' His face red. 'Okay?' His spittle lands on me. My mind scrambles, where is my lighter fluid, where are my matches? I feel naked without them as Brian stares at me. His face is a blank canvas not painted by any emotion. I stand trembling. I walk out of the kitchen without looking back and straight into my bedroom and lock the door, Brian apologizing as I go.

I take my lighter fluid and matches from my rucksack and place them on the bedside table. I'm calmer with them next to me. I lie on the bed and throw my small blue ball in the air. A knock comes at my bedroom door. It's one of Brian's desperate knocks. I throw the ball higher.

'Maddie, I'm sorry, okay?'

I throw the ball higher; it almost touches the ceiling. I

watch it as it falls back down towards my face. I remain silent.

'How do you grieve someone who left you heartbroken?' He sounds as if he's begging for an answer to his question.

A thud as I imagine him slumping into my door and sliding to the floor. My ball hits the ceiling. I hold my ground and remain silent. I am at no one's beck and call any more. I can do what I want and I do not want to talk to Brian.

'I'm going,' he shouts. 'You're overreacting. Talk to me when you've calmed down.'

He thinks I'm angry. What a nice life he must have led to assume that I am angry and not scared. What a privilege it must be for your rawest emotion to be rage and not fear. I glance at my bedside table, the lighter calling to me, and I wonder if I should kill him now? My ball smashes against the ceiling as I throw it too hard and a speck of plaster drifts towards me. I swear this place is falling apart if you look closely enough.

Brian wasn't just Emily's landlord. He might have liked her too much. I need to tell Sloane.

27

2007 – Manchester

Cody and Karla whisper in the corner of the kitchen. Every so often she nods along to whatever he's saying. Her hand moves to her face and she wipes at her eyes and I realize she's crying. Her body shakes. He pulls her into a large bear hug, her head resting on his shoulder; he tilts his head and his lips move millimetres away from her ears. She nods again. He breaks his hold. I shuffle back to the till, not wanting them to know I'm watching them in their moment of intimacy.

'You okay?' I ask, trying to course sunshine through my voice as Karla rejoins me at the counter. 'Slow shift, isn't it?'

'Emily hated working Sundays.'

Emily hated the Sunday shift. Emily liked to party. Emily was Employee of the Month and Brian liked her too much. Each thing I learn is like a jigsaw piece gluing together who Emily Sykes was beyond murder victim.

'I know we haven't known each other long, Karla, but you can talk to me, if you want.'

The soft Karla who Cody was hugging vanishes and the hard-faced Karla returns with a cold stare.

'There was a big article today in the paper about the Maniac. Did you see it? What they're saying about Emily?'

I shake my head no. I bet Sloane has read it and will give me the relevant bits. The last time I picked up a physical copy of a paper was when they were reporting Ben's death. Accuracy varied wildly.

'No.'

'Good,' she says, 'the fewer people who read that junk the better. It tried saying Emily was like the other victims. That's what happens when people like you ask too many questions.'

The prostitutes. The 'less than' victims. The ones whose images always appear grainy and faded. 'And that's why she was killed. That's what they're saying.'

Her eyes open wide followed by her mouth. Her face becomes pale. Her sobbing is loud and this time she doesn't wipe away her tears. Snot drips from her nose as she shakes. I move towards her to offer consolation, but Cody appears from the kitchen like a whippet in time to watch Karla push me away. He grabs her by her upper arms and crouches to meet her eyes.

'It's going to be okay.'

He guides her to the back of the restaurant. They both disappear and I wonder if it could be true? Was Emily mixed up with something darker? Was Emily a sex worker, and did she feel pressure to spend time with Brian because he was her landlord? Nothing I've learnt about her answers these questions.

Ten minutes and one customer later, I spy Karla in the parking lot walking towards her car in her day clothes. I pop my head in the kitchen and Cody is making the last order, rapping along to some horrendous lyrics about bitches. He looks up at me.

'I'm going to make you something to eat. You look hungry.'

He adds a couple of beef patties to the grill before I respond.

'If you move into the kitchen, you get a baseball cap instead. They're itchy, them, aren't they?' He points to the plastic crown on my head. I nod. He's right. They are itchy and uncomfortable and every shift all I want to do is throw it out of the window. I think I'd rather tolerate the crown than the bad music playing in the kitchen, though.

'I think they put women up front and men in the kitchen,' I say.

'Yeah, they do, normally,' Cody says, nodding along. 'There was one girl about three years ago that worked in the kitchen.'

I nod along as he gropes at other ways to keep our conversation going that don't involve talking about Karla. He flips my burgers and juices run from them, sizzling. He pulls a seeded bun from a clear bag and opens it on the chopping board.

'One day, I'm going to be a proper chef.' He looks towards me, smiling. 'In one of those restaurants in the city.' He adds ingredients to the bun – sauce, pickles, salad, and he then piles on the patties and adds cheese. 'Feeding people isn't the worst way to make a living.' He squashes the finished burger and hands it to me in a paper carton.

I open the box and he watches me. I pull the burger out; sauce drips down my wrist and I take a big bite. Wow. Salty and sweet. The lettuce cuts through the fat of the meat and it tastes good.

'This tastes amazing, Cody,' I say through mouthfuls. He grins in response, thrilled at my enjoyment, and I realize this is the first time a man has cooked for me. Made me something for my pleasure. I look at Cody. Is he different?

'That burger is on the employees' only secret menu,' he laughs. 'I used to make them for Emily and Karla all the time. After too many drinks in the basement,' he nods towards a wooden hatch in the ground outside the kitchen. 'Then I would come up here and cook up a storm for everyone. Aaron prefers nachos, which is funny considering he owns a burger joint. Good times. We haven't hung out in the basement for months.' He trails off and goes quiet. His gaze somewhere off in the distance.

'Were Emily and Karla close?'

Cody looks down at his fingernails, as if he is inspecting them for dirt.

'Yeah, I suppose,' he says. 'Emily always got on with the lads better. Me and Aaron. She was a fun girl to be around,' he glances away. 'If anyone should be going home early it should be me. I miss Ems, badly, but someone has to keep this place going and Karla has been putting in the hard yards of late. It's not like Karla to show her feelings like that.'

So, she's always hard-faced. I was beginning to think Karla was only interested in keeping Queen of the Burgers afloat whilst Aaron drank.

'She's – what's the word? – stoic. It's not like her to be dramatic,' he adds, as if reading my thoughts.

I don't think being upset about a friend being murdered is dramatic. I don't think getting upset about anyone being murdered is dramatic. I hate the way men do this: underplay the way we feel about things. As if we're too emotional about the things that matter. Maybe Cody is a flea after all.

'Hello?' A familiar voice shouts from the restaurant.

'Shit,' I mutter as I rush from the kitchen to the front of house.

Charlie is grinning at the counter. His colleague, Frank, is in the same booth he always sits at. Charlie wears the same shirt, open at the top button, and trousers.

'Hi,' he says.

'Hi,' I reply.

Charlie raises his hand to the side of his mouth, and it takes me a second to realize he means I have something on my face. I blush as I grab a napkin and wipe tomato sauce away. He laughs. I find myself laughing too. I take his order and I wander into the kitchen and relay it to Cody.

'Pigs?' he asks as he chops lettuce with a sharp knife.

'Yeah,' I say.

He nods as he keeps chopping.

Aaron walks out of the back office and I jump.

'Didn't mean to scare you.'

Cody places a hand on Aaron's forearm to stop him from walking through the kitchen to the restaurant and shakes his head.

'Police are out there, mate.'

Aaron scowls and Cody shrugs.

'Karla encourages it with the free food.'

'I'll speak to her,' Aaron says as he slinks back towards the side door of the kitchen. He pauses at the back door. 'It's a slap in the face, given they arrested me,' he hisses.

My body freezes in place. The landlord wasn't the only person who was arrested in connection with Emily's murder, but Aaron mustn't have made it to the media.

'He was the last to see her alive; they always arrest that person,' Cody says. 'He didn't do it, if that's what you're thinking.'

'I was thinking how long are you going to take making two burgers and fries.' I say with a shrug.

Through the window, I see Aaron open two wooden flaps

on the ground and descend a set of stairs into the darkness towards the basement Cody was talking about. He closes the wooden flaps behind him.

'On it,' he says.

'That's where you all used to hang out? Down in that basement?' I say, pointing outside.

'Back in the old days. I can't remember the last time we all hung out down there.'

I wander back to the front of house, where Charlie stands patiently.

'It won't be a minute,' I say. He looks tired. A large smartphone in his left hand reveals the same ginger cat on his lock-screen, this time in a superhero cape. 'And by the way, I think avocados taste like dirt.'

Those familiar wrinkles appear as Charlie's smile reaches his eyes. He's disarming. Which is terrifying.

'That's lucky. We're on the lookout for an avocado-wielding vigilante. Chucked one at some creep on a bus. Her aim. Spectacular.'

Now I find myself tilting my head. What does he want? Shouldn't he be arresting me for assault? Handcuffing me? Reading me my rights? His face returns to a tired expression, as if exhaustion is his normal mask and he dons a new one when speaking to me. I wonder if he is any closer to finding the Manchester Maniac. Did he read the newspaper article that Karla was talking about?

Cody appears from the kitchen with a stern look and nods at the sliding trays he puts the food in. He disappears again without a word.

'I'm not popular with everyone who works here, am I?' he says.

I shake my head. I don't know what to say to the man,

but if you're interested in winning popularity contests then becoming a police officer probably isn't the best way. He comes closer and lowers his voice.

'You won't be either if they find out you've been hanging out with Victoria Sloane.'

No, I won't be.

'Don't worry,' he says. 'Your secret . . .' He pauses. Smiles. 'Secrets,' he says exaggerating the plural, 'are safe with me.'

28

2027 – HMP Bronzefield

I'm early. I waited at the guards' station until they were bored of looking at my face and took me down to our meeting room. The blinds are closed. The walls are green. The plastic chair is uncomfortable. Each second that ticks by feels like an hour, a year. Since my guest cancelled, I have convinced myself they'll not return. Everyone leaves. I don't mean that in some self-pitying manner. It's a fact. Everyone, eventually, leaves.

I'm so convinced that I'm half surprised when my guest walks through the door. Jeans and jumper. Trainers instead of shoes. Smiling.

'Hi Maddie, how are you?'

Rage bubbles. Here they are, as if nothing has happened. What about my story? It's like they don't care about getting my words out to the people. And it dawns on me. Nothing has happened. In their world, life ticked on. It's my world which became static.

'Sorry about last time,' my guest says.

I raise an eyebrow, as if I'm not sure what they mean, and shrug. They take a seat in front of me.

'I knocked a tooth out.' They grin to reveal a gap at the back. 'I wasn't quick enough to save it.'

'Another life lost,' I say. They laugh, and warmness fills the room.

A dental emergency is an emergency. So, in a way I was right, and an emergency did happen to prevent their visit. It's not as if they couldn't be bothered. They wanted to be here but couldn't.

'Last time we met we talked about the dresses. And it seemed each one represented a different day of the week. I wondered what happened on special occasions – Christmas, New Year, birthdays?'

I was with Ben for twelve years and two months. No, I was held hostage by Ben for twelve years and two months. I was forced into a uniform of polyester dresses and I find myself thinking I was *with* Ben, not held *hostage*. Even now I slip into language which undermines my position. Language which apologizes for him. That infers the situation was consensual. It wasn't.

'There would've been markers. I don't know if he did it on purpose, but the only markers of time were the dresses and his Sunday visits to church and what I know now to be Valentine's cards. There were no clocks in the house. His morning alarm was on his phone which I didn't have access to.'

The weeks would blur. My only view was through a frosted bathroom window. It was small, too small for me to squeeze through, even if I could smash it open and even then, I was only allowed in the bathroom when Ben was at home. He'd lock it when he was away and leave a bucket outside. Whenever

I could, I would sit on lino floor and stare at that window. Sometimes I would make out the silhouette of a car parked on the street, or a shape walking past below me, but nothing more. It was a melting eternity. Monday through to Sunday and then back again. I did the math once – I spent six hundred and thirty-three repeating weeks there, give or take. No Christmas, no Easter, no summer holidays or New Year's Eve.

'That's what they were . . .' In my mind's eye, flashes of green, blue and red explode behind frosted glass. 'How did I not connect the dots before?'

My guest's eyebrows furrow as they lean forward.

'What were?'

'The only window not covered was the small, frosted bathroom window. Every so often, I thought the sky was on fire. Fireworks; they were fireworks for New Year's Eve.'

'That could have been bonfire night too.'

I nod. Halloween, bonfire night, Mother's Day. It's easy to forget the minor holidays when you've never even properly celebrated the major ones.

'Did he leave you alone often?'

'When he was at work. He'd return home late on a Friday due to picking up some shopping.'

After the escape, I was curious about Ben's outside world, but I couldn't identify any friends or work mates. I knew he visited his mother, but aside from that I think he was alone.

'I think I was his only friend.'

My guest nods. Is it a friendship if it is under duress, or if one party wants something?

'Are we friends?'

My question catches my guest off guard. They stop, their mouth parts as if they are going to say something and then slams shut. They blink, once then twice.

'I'm not sure it would be ethical if we were friends.' Comes an eventual answer.

'Fuck you.'

My words tumble out of my mouth without a second to think. Almost like an emergency ejection, I spit them out and my face reddens with warmth. Embarrassed not by what I have said, but because now they know I care and they can guess how alone I am. I stand and my handcuffs clink against each other in the otherwise silent room and I realize I am the anomaly here. Not the guard. Not my guest. I am the freak. I pinch the skin between my thumb and forefinger. Hard.

'You should be honoured to know me.' My words are louder than I want but I can't control the volume at which they are hurtling out of my mouth. 'Ethical? Everything you know about ethics is wrong. I wouldn't be in prison if the world's moral compass was better tuned.'

I'm not sure at what point I stood up, but I realize I am towering over the table, screaming at my guest. They gesture at the prison guard, who has made their way behind me without me noticing, that they are okay. They wait. Allow the silence to shrink-wrap me. They don't open their mouth again until I have sat down.

'I won't lie to you, Maddie,' they say, watching me. 'Not to make you feel better, not to save your feelings, not to gain your trust. I understand if you want to leave today, but I will be sitting here, same time, same place, next time I visit, hoping you still want to speak to me.'

I look at the guard. She nods along to my guest, as if they are giving the most incredible speech. But there is no cruelty in a trivial lie. I want to feel better, I want to be saved, I want to give my trust and I don't understand why it is so hard.

The prison feels bigger as I walk back to my cell. My

footsteps louder. My handcuffs tighter. I see faces move in slow motion as they watch me pass. The freak. The murderer. The serial killer. These labels are neon signs above my head. I've traded my youth, my freedom, my shot at living a good life, and for what? Some fading infamy?

Red marks circle my wrists. My cheeks are wet and I realize I'm crying. My skull vibrates sending lightning bolts of agony across my entire body, my brain trying to shatter its bone prison. I will die alone.

29

2007 – Manchester

Sloane's face is illuminated by the greenish back light of her laptop. The curtains are pulled shut, despite it being the middle of the day, and a small lamp on the table next to the double bed, which takes up most of the room, emits a dim light.

'I don't know where to start.'

She spins on her swivel chair so she is facing me. I'm lying on the bed. There's something comfortable about Sloane's flat that I can't put my finger on. Maybe it's the size. One large room with a kitchen at the rear end and a tiny boxroom for a bathroom. A corkboard stands in the only space remaining.

'From the start?' I shrug.

'I need to get my thoughts in order,' she says.

She shuffles, using her legs to push the chair she is sitting on towards the corkboard. In the middle are passport-sized images of the victims, all seven of them; strands of red strings loop out. It looks straight out of a 1970s cop show. From Emily a piece of red string loops into the right-hand corner. An image of my landlord is there.

I nod towards the image of Brian.

'He wasn't just her landlord. They were . . .' I pause, trying to find a way to explain their situation. 'He was infatuated by her. He also writes wills for a living, which is bizarre if you ask me.'

Sloane reaches for a notebook and scribbles everything down as I explain about the strip of photo-booth pictures I found in Brian's suitcase.

'Money and love. Both are big motives,' she says, nodding. 'Plus, he has connections to the other victims.' Sloane pauses and shakes her head. 'It seems unlikely he was in love with them all. Could he have written wills for them?' Her eyebrows rise, followed by a shake of her head. 'Seems unlikely, but I suppose it's a reasonable line of enquiry.'

I nod along as I scan the pictures of the other women. I wonder if one day there will be a board somewhere with my victims pinned to it? No. I doubt it. Those men deserved to die. I wish I could show Sloane what they looked like as the life drifted from their eyes. Beautiful.

'Aside from the location where the bodies have been found. What else did Emily have in common with the other women who were murdered?' I ask.

All the men I murdered were threats.

Sloane pulls out a journal and flicks through scrawled notes. Her eyebrows furrow as she is trying to piece together a challenging jigsaw.

'She was a woman,' Sloane shrugs. 'Anything suspicious at the Queen of the Burgers?'

'There's Aaron, the owner. Big guy with the tattoos. We said we would add him to the suspect list. He was arrested at the time and released. I've yet to see him sober.'

Sloane pulls up a social media website I don't recognize

and types *Aaron Queen of the Burgers* into the search bar. A result for *Aaron Queen* returns.

'This him? Right?' she says, showing me the screen.

He's pulling a face, an askew plastic crown on his head. I nod. That's him.

'We should add Aaron,' I say.

She opens a drawer and removes a picture of Aaron.

'Here's one I made earlier,' she says with a grin. 'I never liked his vibe, very off. Something not quite right there.'

'Anything else suspicious from her work?'

'Nothing obvious, but Cody, he's the cook, said she liked to party.'

Sloane shrugs.

'What twenty-two-year-old doesn't?' She pauses. 'Unless he meant she likes to party, party.'

She stares hard, as I try to understand the difference between party and party, party.

'You know,' Sloane says, 'hard drugs. If she was too deep into something, it might explain a few things we don't understand yet.' Her eyes flicker to the other women on the corkboard. Dead and they're still being judged.

'I know how I should start the book,' Sloane says. 'With the forgotten women.' I glance back up at the grainy photographs of the prostitutes – they're not forgotten women any more. 'Then the death of Emily Sykes changes everything. But first I should talk about us and how we want to stop this, about how women should be safe to live their lives.' There's a long pause. A moment of silence as we ponder on our goal – a safer world. 'But what happens next?' she shrugs. 'I guess I will wait and see.' She lets out an awkward laugh.

'Maybe we should meet with Mia again?' I say.

My mind flickers back to Mia fading away on a corner in

the red-light district. Sloane stands up from her chair and stretches out her arms with a groan.

'No,' Sloane says as she moves to the corkboard, with her back away from me, inspecting the images. 'I'm not sure how much more she can tell us.'

All the women were led somewhere. The bodies were found in the woods, scattered off the beaten paths, and weren't found until they were looking for Emily. I don't think the women were all taken. I think they followed someone willingly. Surely, someone would have noticed that many women being forced against their will to go somewhere? It doesn't make sense they were snatched.

'I mean, I'm not sure I agree. We should meet with her again,' I say. Sloane moves some of the images around the board.

'How many people do you trust implicitly?' She turns to face me, and she raises her hand and pops two fingers up. 'For me, it's three if you include my dead mother, but I suppose that doesn't really count, does it?' she says.

'No.'

Small mercies. I have enemies who are six foot deep; if the dead could earn our trust, then they could betray us too. My mind flickers to Ben's lonely grave. His words echo in my brain – *I am the only one you can trust, little lamb. The world is a bad place.*

'Are you saying you don't trust Mia? Because it makes sense for them to have been lured away by someone pretending to want to engage their services.'

Sloane shrugs.

'Posing as a customer makes sense for the first victims but not Emily. Maybe the Maniac is someone Emily trusted? Like her landlord? Or her boss?'

It feels like a riddle. Ben hated riddles; in his bleakest moments he would tell me I was a riddle he couldn't solve.

'The two people you trust? Who are they?' I say.

'My grandma,' she pauses as if unsure she should say the next thing. 'And you.' She trails off and looks away from me, as if she has confessed a dark secret.

'You?' she says.

No one. Everyone I have trusted has let me down, and that may sound clichéd, but it is true. Her eyes are dancing around my mouth now. No longer is she looking away, but she is waiting to see if the sentiment is returned.

'Blood freaks me out,' the words tumble out of my mouth. 'I hate the sight of blood. I've never told anyone that before.'

She nods but appears crestfallen, my confession not enough to sate her.

'I once chucked an avocado at a man on a bus because he sat next to me.'

She laughs at this, her head rolling backwards. She joins me on the bed and our shoulders touch, and wafts of coconuts and vanilla drift towards me.

'But the blood,' I say. 'Sometimes I have dreams about fleas attached to lambs.' Sloane turns to face me, with her head tilted a little and her eyes wide. 'The fleas suck the blood from the lambs but the lambs don't notice; it's as if they are used to them.'

She brushes a stray strand of hair from my face.

'That's a nightmare, Maddie.'

Her voice is soft and she places a hand on my knee.

'Do you really trust me?'

'Yes,' she whispers. She reaches out for my hand and our eyes lock.

'I trust you,' I say. 'I . . .' It's a sentence I can't finish. For a moment I want to tell her everything; tell her I'm a serial killer. I am the creature she loathes. 'I'd best hurry if I'm going to make it to this memorial club night Cody is holding for Emily,' I say, recovering.

'What are you going to wear? I wish I could come with you. Keep your eyes and ears peeled in case there's a clue,' she says, the mood turning in a heartbeat.

'I think I would rather chill here,' I say.

'No, you must attend Emily's memorial. If I could go I would, because you don't know who will be there and what will be said. You'll be my eyes and ears.'

Sloane stands and opens her wardrobe. It's stuffed with clothes, and a pile falls out as she opens the door.

'Most of my clothes might be a bit long for you,' she says, inspecting a red top on a hanger. 'I definitely have something in here you can wear,' she says, rummaging through. 'Ha, I found it. It's far too short for me, curse of being tall, but I think it would be a good fit for you.' From the back of the wardrobe she pulls out a black dress and holds it up. 'Nice, isn't it?'

Oxygen leaves the room. The dress is black, unlike all the dresses Ben would covet. It's missing the lace but it's still a dress. I swallow hard.

'Do you want to try it on?'

I look at the images of the Manchester Maniac's victims on the wall. Not one in a dress. Clothes don't get murdered or assaulted or mugged. People do. Ben would not have treated me any differently if I'd worn a tracksuit every day.

'Yes,' I say. 'I want to try it on.'

I swallow acid as she hands it to me with a smile. I get off the bed and take the three steps to the bathroom and lock the door behind me. The mirror reflects my image and then distorts to a ten-year-old me. I stare at the child I once was and then she disappears and I, twenty-four-year-old Maddie, reappear with tears in my eyes.

I'm shaking as I pull my clothes off, but I want to wear the dress, not for Ben or any man, but for myself. I want to put it on and know that Ben doesn't own me any more. I take my clothes off and place them folded on the toilet seat. I'm half afraid I will throw up, but as I pull the dress on, I feel different. No lace itches at my skin. I stare at myself in Sloane's full-length mirror, and I struggle to recognize the person who is reflected back. The dress is plain, but clings to my body, showing an hour-glass rather than a scrawny woman in an oversized shirt.

I don't look at Sloane when I re-enter the main room, but she gasps. I pinch the skin between my forefinger and thumb.

'You look amazing,' she says. 'You have to wear that dress every day for the rest of your life. I'm not even joking. Wear it to work, to the library, to the grocer's.' She laughs at herself. 'Here, I found this.' She holds up a gold necklace with a large pendant at the end. She walks over to me and gestures for me to raise my hair. I can feel her warm breath on my neck as she closes the clasp on the necklace.

'Sloane, this is really nice, but I think it's too formal.'

Sloane takes a step back and appraises me. She shakes her head. She doesn't agree. She is sincere in thinking I should wear the dress everywhere, at noon, at night, walking down the street, on the bus: because I should be able to wear what I want, when I want, where I want. I shouldn't fear a flea will become attached. No women should fear what the Bens in our worlds will think or say or how they will interpret our clothing choice.

Three bangs on the front door. A policeman's knock.

Demanding. Sloane and I look at one another; she raises her eyebrow before walking off to answer the front door. Charlie and Frank – their voices arrive before they do. They don't wait for an invitation. They walk in with Sloane at their rear. Her face is somewhere between confusion and anger. Frank walks over to the corkboard and examines it, his finger trailing the red cotton lines connecting the victims and suspects. Charlie looks around for somewhere to sit and settles on Sloane's swivel chair. His eyes linger on me for a second too long; he smiles and looks back to Sloane, who is still at her front door which leads to the shared hallway.

'Do you know why we're here, Victoria?'

'I prefer being called Sloane.'

'No one cares what you prefer,' Frank says, not looking away from the corkboard. His voice is grainy and deep and runs through me like a train.

Charlie pulls a mobile phone from his pocket and appears to load something.

'It'll take a second to buffer,' he says.

Sloane moves from her front door and stands in front of me. She half blocks my body, as if she is a human shield protecting me from Charlie and Frank. This situation is odd at best. Charlie holds up the phone.

'Where is that?'

'It's the path at the back of the industrial estate leading to the wooded area.'

Charlie nods. 'And who do you see walking along that path?'

Sloane casts her eyes downwards.

'Me,' she mumbles.

A flicker of mistrust ignites inside me. Sloane hasn't told me she had been scouting the areas around the industrial estate.

'Yes, you. Myself and Frank spot-check these areas during the day and at night. I'm here to tell you, you have no reason to be there.'

Sloane shrugs.

'I can go where I want.' She looks Charlie hard in the eye.

'If I catch you there, I will find a reason to arrest you. Do you understand? You're putting your life in danger and jeopardizing the police investigation.'

'Why? What's so special about the woods, officer?'

Charlie stands, pretending Sloane hasn't asked him a question she already knows the answer to. Blank-faced, he pulls out a notebook and takes her details. His scribbles are furious. His expression is hard. He looks to me.

'And your details, Maddie.' He looks up and his expression softens. 'The dress suits you, by the way.'

'You'd be prettier if you smiled,' Frank says, glancing at me for a second before returning to his inspection of the corkboard.

Under their eyes, I feel naked. It's as if I'm covered in lace and ants are crawling through my veins. I want to rip the dress off.

'Interesting list of suspects. The little girls want to find the bad man? I say we leave them to it,' Frank says as he approaches the door. 'I'll be in the car, Charlie.'

The door slams behind Frank, and Charlie stares at me and then down at his notebook.

'I live here.'

Sloane's head snaps in my direction but she doesn't correct me.

'And it's Reid.'

'It's a little tight for two,' Charlie says as his eyes shift to the right for a moment. 'Reid,' he mutters my name under his breath and looks up at me. 'I swear I know that name.'

There is a moment of silence. He snaps shut his notebook and leaves. Sloane breathes a sigh of relief.

'Let's get you to this club night,' she says.

Outside, a car engine starts, and I picture Charlie behind the wheel as Frank bitches about us.

'Yeah,' I say. 'Now, can we find this flea?'

'What?' Sloane's face scrunches up and she scratches her head. 'That does make sense,' she says nodding. 'They are like fleas, aren't they? Draining the life from us.'

I knew she would understand.

30

2027 – HMP Bronzefield

I'm going to make them wait. Both the prison guard assigned to accompany me, and my guest. I want my guest to sweat. To sit in that vomit-green room and question if I will ever return. They can wait. I've spent my life waiting. It's nice to turn the tables for once and have them wait for me.

Ever since our last meeting, I have gone back and forth about whether I wanted to continue. Every time I closed my eyes, I could hear the click of the Dictaphone as my guest hits record and the whirr of the tapes as they capture my words. It's like a mechanical grinder burrowing into my head. What if the book turns into a circus? And I am the star of the freakshow. My guest taking on the role of ringmaster. Line up! Line up!

'Reid, are you coming or not?' A guard's voice shouts through my cell.

The thought of spending my last few months staring at my cell wall in silence is enough to persuade me to keep going. I groan as I stand up from my bed. I walk over to the cell door and pull it open.

'Hang on,' the guard barks.

A clatter of keys, a whine, and a clunk. I pull again on the door and it opens to reveal a scowling guard. I hold out my wrists. A double click and I am secure. No longer an immediate threat. A muzzled dog. The guard gestures at me to walk ahead of her and I do so.

I pause as we reach the room off B wing. She opens the door and I walk in. My guest looks up and beams. I avoid their eyes and, as my glance darts off in another direction, I notice a slat missing from the blinds. Daylight streams in. I can see a sliver of the outside world. The room must be at the front of the prison. I can see a fence, cars streaming past, and opposite a wedged-open door – perhaps a corner shop?

'I'm glad you came, Maddie.'

I look away from my five-star view.

'Sorry I'm late, the traffic was bad,' I say with a smirk.

My guest glances at the guard as if they are my parent and I'm a naughty child.

'I was hoping we could talk more today about Ben and your time in captivity.'

I shake my head no. I'm bored of talking about Ben. I want to talk about the weather, if the trains are running on time and how to boil the perfect egg. I want five minutes of normality. I don't see why my breaks from this hellhole should be all work and no play.

'I know this must be difficult for you,' my guest tilts their head in a way I find patronizing. It's not difficult. It's boring, and I am sick to my back teeth talking about that man.

'Take me back to my cell,' I say, stifling a yawn.

'Did you hear that?' My guest jumps to their feet and looks around. Panic on their face. 'Did you hear that?' they repeat.

'Hear what?'

The guard takes a step towards my guest who is staring at me. There was no noise. I don't know what it is my guest thinks they heard because all around me is silence.

'A shout,' they say. 'Someone shouted help.'

'I didn't hear—'

I turn in my seat, interrupting the guard, and smile. 'Are you being serious?' I ask. 'You might want your hearing tested.'

The guard looks at me and then the door. This is an interesting turn of events, and I am intrigued enough to play along. I turn away. Footsteps. The door closing with a bang.

'We haven't got long, Maddie,' my guest says. 'We are allowed to meet in this room because our relationship is professional in nature. Any inkling of anything else and we would be in the visitors' room like the rest and, no doubt, many of those visitors would take a great interest in you and our conversations. I want you to know. I need you to know, I am your friend.'

Electricity runs through me. I shouldn't have doubted them. Then it dawns on me, maybe this is a response to my lateness; this could be a lie to appease me.

'How do I know this isn't an attempt to make me feel better? To save my feelings? To win my trust?' the words hurtle from me.

My guest picks up and opens their rucksack and moves their jumper to one side. Squashed at the bottom lies a single slat of a blind.

Our eyes meet. The guard bursts back into the room before I get the chance to thank my guest for the single kindest act anyone has ever done for me. The guard is red-faced, out of breath, their hands on their hips. They don't say anything. They close the door behind them and take watch.

'Okay,' I say. 'Let's talk.'

My guest leans back in their chair and reviews their notes.

'Last time we spoke, we talked about occasions that are special, but when I got home, I realized I'd assumed. I only mentioned occasions that are special to me. Holidays and the like. During your captivity, did you have any rituals or traditions?'

When they got home. House or apartment? Ha, maybe they have a caravan or one of those kitted-out vans. Maybe home is in the car park. No, I bet they have a wonderful home, picturesque. I bet it smells like fresh bread when you open the door. Do they have a dog who comes scuttling across wooden floors whenever they hear the key in the lock?

'No, not really. One thing did happen though?'

My guest gestures for me to continue.

'Ben and I. We aged. He got older and I got older. I entered as a ten-year-old girl and it was twelve long years before I walked out as a grown woman. I don't think he accounted for years passing. He planned for my arrival, soundproofed walls, and fitted locks upon locks, but I don't think he had thought much further than not getting caught.'

Puberty arrived late for me. I think in a normal life this would have bothered me, being the last girl to get her period, or to develop hips. I think this was a mercy. It gave me enough time to grow, to watch, and to realize the situation I was in was precarious. I stayed alive for so long because I looked like a child.

'Was there a defining moment when you realized Ben wasn't happy with you getting older?'

I nod. I can still remember his face. The way he sobbed, as if a loved one had died, with him blowing his nose in a large tissue. Him telling me he knew this day would eventually come.

My guest stares at me. I was seventeen when puberty kicked in, very late by all accounts, but the next five years became a battle of wits and one I don't think twelve-year-old me would have survived. I lean towards my guest.

'I got my first period.'

31

2007 – Manchester

The nightclub Cody told me about is down a side street and up a set of stairs. The first floor is illuminated with a sign which reads 'Be kee's' the C before the K darkened and dead. This is the first time I have been to a nightclub. I've had a lot of firsts recently. First landlord, first job . . . My phone vibrates in my pocket and the lock-screen flashes a message from Sloane: *Good luck*. First friend?

Smokers are gathered near the entrance. Their addiction makes the side street less lonely. Some of them raise coats above their heads as the first drops of rain strike. I've seen men stumbling alone, but women – it appears – come in flocks and pairs. I am an anomaly.

Head down, I approach the staircase. Loud music thrums from the top, luring partygoers inside. I pinch the skin between my forefinger and thumb. Hard. A hand the side of my head appears in front of me. I look up. A thick neck. Wide face. Each ear a wad of bumps. A crooked nose and hair shaved close to the head. His black suit a touch too small.

'We got a dress code. Sorry love.'

I feel good in my 100 per cent cotton T-shirt, jumper and jeans. My coat is practical and I don't see why I should go anywhere without it, given how much it rains. The dress was not practical. I look down at my outfit and back up at him.

'Like I said, dress code.' He shrugs.

A couple of women in tight dresses walk past me and straight up the stairs. Mr Too-Small-Suit's gaze follows them until they are out of sight. A couple of men approach. They, like me, are wearing jumpers and jeans. Likely fleas, and I move to one side to avoid being too close to them.

'ID?'

Both men pull driving licences out of their wallets. A brief inspection and they are both on their way towards the music.

'I thought you had a dress code?' I say.

'Look,' he says, 'we do. Not tonight okay.' He gestures in the direction away from the club and down the empty side street.

'They were wearing the same as me. Jeans and a jumper, but you let them in.'

His head turns back to where the men went, as if he might catch a glimpse of their shadows. Blank-faced for a second, he stares at me and blinks. It's as if he is glitching. I don't think for a moment he noticed I am dressed like the men he allowed into his little kingdom.

'That's different. It's different. I don't make the rules.'

Mr Too-Small-Suit is stationed at this door to protect the people inside, and even he cannot see his own audacity at holding me up to standards he does not apply to the fleas. I bet he is the first to label himself protector. To scream from his lungs – *it's not all men*. To offer anecdotes of his own heroism – this one time he saved a woman from this and another from that. Our hero failing to realize that all the lambs he claims to have saved from the slaughter were at the mercy of fleas. His own kind.

'Marty? Marty?'

A familiar voice comes from above, booming like God. My hood slips down as I look up. It takes a couple of seconds for my eyes to adjust from the neon and darkness of the club entrance to the moonlit night sky, but when I do, it's Cody grinning down at us. He leans out of a window. A cigarette in hand.

'You all right, Maddie?' he says with bounce in his tone, as if everything is okay in the world. 'She's all right, Marty. She's on the list.'

Mr Too-Small-Suit stands to one side and I take the stairs two at a time, half awaiting a hand to clamp on my shoulder. It doesn't come. I push darkened heavy doors and I am met by a wall of music as loud as it is thick. Something to swim through, not dance to. Bright, multicoloured strobe lights cut through the darkness. There's a crowd. A big one. Did they all know Emily? Could the king flea be here tonight? Is the Manchester Maniac watching me right now whilst waiting for the beat to drop?

Emily's face stares at me from every angle. Her image blown up and projected onto every wall. I remind myself she was living once, a human being with a job, friends, family, hobbies and interests.

I realize my victims had the same full lives. But the difference is a monster killed Emily, and I'm a hero, protecting every woman in my victims' orbits.

Wide-screen televisions play rotating slides of Emily. I stare at one picture, her tongue stuck out at the camera revealing a small stud, in her hand a bottle of blue-coloured drink.

She's in a nun's outfit and standing next to her is a woman in a banana suit and another in a school uniform. Blackpool Pier in the background.

In another, her face in profile as she downs a clear-coloured liquid in a shot glass. In nearly all the pictures she is standing in groups. Some all women, some mixed, and mostly in bars and pubs. In a rare solo picture, she looks up at the camera, head tilted, lips glossy and pouting. So, this is Emily. *Was* Emily.

I navigate my way through a crowd on springy wood – this must be the dance floor. Some sway, some shake, some laugh, and some have tears in their eyes meeting weak smiles. They all hold plastic cups.

Karla leans against the bar. Almost a slump. Her shoes have needle-thin heels. A thick gold chain around her neck makes her eyes sparkle, but appears to pull her down, as if it weighs too much.

She raises her head as I approach. Her face is flushed. Mascara has formed in the corner of her eyes. She puts her cup to her mouth and drinks steadily for three to four seconds. She wipes her mouth on the back of her hand, leaving a smear of red lipstick against her pale skin.

'I need another drink.' Her words slur together. She bangs her cup on the bar. 'Your round, new girl,' she says to me.

Karla leans over the bar and says something to the barman I cannot hear. He nods along. Two drinks arrive. She guzzles her drink and – unsteady on her feet – moves without a word through the crowd. She stumbles backwards into someone as I follow her across the dance floor; she raises her hands in apology. She turns to me as we pass, and I notice other girls queuing in the corner of the room.

'She wasn't perfect.'

'Who?'

Her hands gesture around the club at the projected images of Emily. Karla sways.

'Emily?' I say.

She shrugs and her gaze turns upwards. When I follow, I realize the club has a second floor, more like a balcony. Men hang over it, looking downwards at the dance floor. A shudder runs through me as single men look down at the people, mainly women, as they dance below them.

'Shut up,' Karla spits. 'You didn't even know her. You don't get to talk about her.'

Her mood shifts in a second as her face turns redder.

'Who wasn't perfect?' I shout back over the music.

'What?' She looks at me glassy-eyed. She takes a heavy gulp from her drink. 'I don't know,' she shrugs. 'Where's Cody? I need to find Cody.'

She staggers away and I'm compelled to follow her. She passes the women standing in a line against the wall. All of them dressed like Karla, but outfit colours vary. As she passes them, some of them mutter about there being a queue, but she snaps back at them with mumbled words about Emily. I can't decipher what she is saying but the other women look at the floor. She yanks me by the sleeve of my coat and we enter the toilets. The music fades.

The room is small and crammed. Perhaps half a dozen cubicles, not enough to accommodate the venue's capacity. I watch as one woman has her head under the hand-dryer, her fingers tousling her hair.

'Pissing down again,' she says to no one in particular. 'I should have brought a brolly but I've already lost three this year.'

Other women slather lipsticks in varying shades across their mouths and pucker their lips in the mirror.

'My fella is picking me up if you want a lift,' one woman says to another. 'He's got well jumpy with all this Maniac business.'

Her friend shrugs.

'Just another day in paradise if you ask me.'

Karla bounces off the walls and into a cubicle as a door opens.

'Watch the door for me, Maddie,' she says, and I find myself taking guard outside the toilet. The woman who left it washes her hands and removes a small jar of nail polish from her bag. She colours one nail, blows on it, and then places it back in her bag. She looks at me in the mirror and smiles as she slips her newly painted finger into her drink.

'If some fucker thinks he's spiking me then he's got another think coming,' she says.

Another woman holds out her drink and she repeats.

'You're fine; my polish will turn blue if there's anything in there.'

She does the same for a couple more women.

'What about you, love?'

I nod. Extend my drink, and again she slips the tip of her fingernail into my drink. She's trying to protect me. It's subtle. Not quite setting fire to people, but it works. What if I have missed a million subtle ways to protect the women around me? I spot a poster – Someone hassling you? Order an angel shot and we'll get you out of here safely.

'Do I look fat in this?' A slim woman examines herself in the mirror. A red sole on a black heel flashes towards us every time she changes her angle to look at the way her black dress clings to her. There's a collective eye-roll from the women in the room. Karla bursts out of the cubicle. The toilet flushes as she washes her hands and another woman goes in.

'Do you want me to test your drink?'

'Nah, I'll be all right,' Karla says.

There's always one who thinks they'll be all right. Odd behaviour for a woman mourning her murdered friend.

She splashes cold water on her face. Some of her colour returns. She reapplies makeup with haste. Smearing and layering as other women come and go.

'Come on,' she says. 'Let's go.'

Again, I am in her shadow as we leave the bathroom. The noise is again a wall to swim through as we enter the main room.

'Cody,' she says. She points upwards and I follow her hand.

Cody stands on the main balcony within a little booth. Cody has one headphone on his right ear and the other balances on his shoulder. He's dressed in a smart shirt and jeans. He gives us a wave. I sip my drink, and the strength makes me shudder.

'This one is a classic, but Emily loved Nineties retro,' he shouts, and the room turns into one merged voice shouting back at him a collective WOO. 'This is for you, Em.' The opening bars of N-Trance's 'Set You Free' kick in. Karla mouths along with the lyrics. A cold vice grips my heart. I can't move. I can almost feel the itch from the lacy hems of Friday's dress. Ben's slurred words in my ear.

I take another sip of my drink. The room blurs and spins before I return. The crowd shouts along to the chorus. I don't know the words to join in. I shouldn't have come here. This place is filled with fleas courting lambs.

'He looks great up there, doesn't he?' Karla says, looking away from Cody for only a second. 'He's wasted at our place.'

To me, Cody looks like a stranger without his Queen of the Burgers uniform on. He looks older, taller, his body looks wider, his smile magnetic, and many of the women in the room appear to have noticed this. Karla isn't the only woman watching him.

'Would Emily have liked this?' I shout into her ear.

'Liked it? An entire party dedicated to her? She would have loved it. She'll be looking down . . .' Karla's body freezes.

'Looking down,' I prompt her to finish the sentence.

'Looking down, wishing she was here. Front and centre.' She grabs my hand and drags me back to the bar and drinks from a glass which has been abandoned. Her body retches. She puts her hands to her mouth. 'I can't take this. The thought of her watching us.'

'It's okay,' I say.

Trails of vomit emerge from Karla's mouth and run down her chin. I look up at Cody; his body freezes as he watches this car crash unfold. As I steady Karla, he bounds over the hatch separating him and the crowd in one jump. He joins us at lightning-fast speed.

'Karla? This isn't like you,' he shouts over the music, his words filled with concern. He guides her away to a corner of the club, grabbing a wad of tissues from the bar and a glass of water.

I look around the room, wondering if I should join them, but looking after a drunk Karla was not on my bingo card.

Some would think this is inappropriate, but I understand what they are trying to do; they're separating her life from her death. They're remembering their friend as the woman who was fun, enjoyed a party and spending time with her friends, and not the woman who was murdered. Should young people be mourned like the old? A funeral sprinkled with peace lilies followed by a tame wake. It doesn't seem right.

She wasn't eighty, she hadn't lived a life, she hadn't even outgrown her partying stage.

She never married, she never got promoted, she never had children or grandchildren. She won't see another Christmas, eat another Easter egg, bask in the sun counting clouds. A flea took her for his own pleasure. How wasteful. Now I repay the favour.

I make my way through the club. In a corner, Cody holds a glass of water to Karla's mouth. Karla looks in my direction and straight through me. Cody waves me over to them.

'She doesn't normally drink so much. It's hard.'

I nod as if I understand but I don't. Not really. Why medicate yourself with booze when you could be out there looking for the Maniac. Seeking revenge.

'We need to get her out of here,' he says, nodding towards a closed door on the other side of the club. It's assumed I will help. I pinch the skin between my finger and thumb. Hard. I'm here to find the man I want to kill and not babysit a drunk. 'We can't leave her here.' He glances around the club. Does Cody know? Does he realize how dangerous it is to be a woman? I nod. Okay, fine. I'll help.

We both place one of Karla's arms over a shoulder and navigate her through the club. A couple of errant stares float our way, but nobody seems to care or be concerned. Cody lifts his leg and kicks at the door, which swings open. We walk into a labyrinth of corridors. Just like Queen of the Burgers, the back offices of the nightclub aren't much to rave about, the music becomes distant and is replaced by the odd murmur from Karla. Her arm is a dead weight and my shoulder aches. He pauses at a door. Plaster flakes from the wall next to it. He pulls a key from his pocket and with his spare hand unlocks the door, pushing it open.

Inside the room it's dark, but Cody doesn't switch the light on. He leads as we take Karla to a small grotty sofa and drop her into it. Out of instinct she curls up on it, and Cody moves her so she is on her side. I watch every part of her body he places his hands on, and he doesn't seem to notice me nodding in approval as he treats her with dignity and care.

'She needs fresh air,' he says.

I follow him over to a window, and he pulls open the curtains and slides the window up. A rush of cold air hits me. The room basks in an ethereal glow from the moon. Aside from the grotty sofa, there is a desk, a swivel chair and a couple of filing cabinets. The walls are bare. Not filled with inspirational posters or educational certificates like Vivian's.

Cody leans out of the window and I join him. He pulls a packet of cigarettes from his jeans pockets and offers me one. I shake my head no. Below is where I entered, but now Marty has been replaced by a woman with cropped hair and a tattoo of a swallow on the side of her neck. She looks up and Cody gives her a wave which is returned.

'Bad habit, I know,' he says as he lights a stick. The flame followed by the orange glow of the cigarette sends a buzz through me, as if my body is waking up. I watch the paper burn and turn to ash. Cody flicks it out of the window. 'You look nice, by the way.' I look down at my oversized jumper and jeans. I've not even taken my coat off. It's a far cry from the dress Sloane had picked out for me.

'I used to love standing here and looking at the stars. Feels different now, knowing I'm watching the same stars as the Maniac,' Cody says. A loud snore comes from Karla.

I look out from the window and Cody is right. We are staring at the same stars as the Maniac, the very stars I called friends and who are my audience as I hunt men down. They pay the Manchester Maniac the same privilege. Cody has a good view down a couple of side streets that all lead to the nightclub. Down one of them, a woman struggles on the cobbles in her heels, I smile as she gives in and takes them off, her bare feet now wet against the floor.

'I like looking at the stars, too,' I say. I lean out and tilt my head and point to a constellation in the sky. 'That's Orion's Belt. I always look for it if I'm feeling lost.'

Cody sticks his head out and looks up with wide eyes.

'That's cool. Did you learn that in school?'

I'm not sure if it's the alcohol or the night air, but part of me wants to tell Cody the truth. I didn't see the night sky for twelve long years, and my last memory of freedom was looking up at the stars. As soon as the night sky and I were reunited, I vowed to never take it for granted.

'Something like that,' I say.

A silhouette staggers along the ginnel at the back of the nightclub. I nudge him. Nod in the direction of the man. Cody lets out a long sigh.

'Aaron's here,' he says in Karla's direction. She stirs from her sleep.

'Is Emily with him?' comes a mumbled reply.

Cody pauses. His eyes well and for a moment I can hear his heart shattering into a thousand pieces. He swallows hard.

'Nah mate,' he says to her. He looks at me. 'She's out of it, isn't she?'

I place a hand on Cody's shoulder and nod as Aaron sways down the alleyway, his body bouncing between the walls as he approaches. The female bouncer takes a step forward and raises her hand.

'Not tonight. You're too drunk.'

Cody lowers his voice to a whisper. 'It's like the Maniac

knew which one of us would leave the biggest void. Cause the most collateral damage.' Is this his way of telling me Emily was the most popular, the most loved?

'Aaron,' Karla's voice echoes from the sofa, and she staggers to her feet. I look at Cody but he does nothing as she approaches the window and peers down. 'Aaron? Go home. You shouldn't be here,' she slurs.

'Go get me a beer, woman.'

Laughter. Hers. It's mocking, resentful and absent of joy. In her drunken stupor, her feelings towards Aaron are heightened not masked.

'Go home,' she repeats.

He attempts to walk straight past the bouncer but she has him on the floor in seconds. My chin almost touches the windowsill from shock. She stands over him.

'I said, not tonight.'

He lies on the ground not moving, and the bouncer laughs and takes a step back away from him. Aaron is no match for the woman bouncer. Not even head on. She does not have to sneak about to wield her power.

'You're embarrassing,' Karla says, leaning over the windowsill. Cody grabs her waist. The drop would be enough to break her back if she was to fall.

'Just leave him, Karla,' Cody whispers to her.

Karla looks at me and appears startled I'm by her side. Her face contorts as if I'm a Peeping Tom who has caught her getting undressed.

'What are you doing here?' She appears genuinely confused and Cody guides her back to the sofa. He gets out his phone and types out a message.

'I'll get someone to go get Aaron and take him home.'

'You guys do a lot to look after the boss,' I whisper with

a shrug. *Shouldn't it be the other way around?* I think to myself. *Shouldn't he be stepping up? Making sure you're all okay?*

'He's a mate.'

'Doesn't look like he's Karla's mate,' I say.

Karla tosses and turns on the sofa, murmuring about Aaron and Emily before she disappears into a deep sleep. A slow rage fills me as my time is stolen by these drunks.

'Nah,' Cody says. 'Karla's not his mate. She's his wife.'

32

Karla snores on the sofa as Cody lights another cigarette. Her wedding band glimmers in the moonlight. A twinge of sympathy runs through me for Cody because he should be celebrating his friend's life. Not sitting in here as Karla sleeps off the booze. From outside, Aaron sings a song I don't recognize about lost love, and the bouncer attempts to move him away from her club.

'I think she'll be fine sleeping it off in here.' Cody glances towards the exit. 'I'll lock the door just in case and leave a note, so she knows to give me a call if she wakes up.' Cody flicks his cigarette into the street below.

Does he sense the danger, or is he more aware because of what happened to Emily? Aaron is as drunk as Karla is, but Cody knows she's at more risk. I glance around the room, knowing my work here is done. I'm free.

Cody locks the door behind us and we walk in silence to the main club, parting ways as we enter, with Cody heading toward his DJ booth. I pass a woman in an identikit dress as

Karla, sitting on the floor crying as I race down the stairs and past the bouncer, who is now squaring up to Aaron. I almost run into two women wearing hi-vis jackets. They hand me a flyer and I stuff it into my coat pocket. The fresh air hits me. My drink was too strong. I regret the fuzzy edges the booze has left me with.

'Maddie,' Cody shouts as he comes sprinting outside. 'Where are you going?'

It dawns on me Cody assumed I would stay and fangirl over him playing a few records whilst his actual mates were too drunk to care.

'Home,' I say.

He glances back to the club, his headphones wrapped around his neck, and then back at me. I mean it too. I want to go home.

'I'll call you a taxi, yeah?'

I shake my head no. A couple of partygoers spill outside the club's entrance. Orange glows from cigarettes come and go.

'I can't let you walk, mate.'

'The Maniac could be a taxi driver – you ever think of that? It could be someone inside that club right now. It could be you, for all I know.'

His face hardens. He holds his hands up and takes a step back with a sigh.

'No, you're right. We don't know who the Maniac is, and I won't stand here and tell you who you should and shouldn't trust. I don't think I could live with myself if you walked home alone, though. I'll find another girl, that way we can all walk you home. That way you get home safely and you don't have to question my intentions. Deal?'

I'm nodding my head, like he does in the kitchen listening

to rap music, but the minute Cody turns his back, I fly into the night. In the distance, Aaron's voice, irritated and sharp, carries on the night breeze, becoming quieter and quieter until it fades to silence.

The centre of town is quiet, people either inside nightclubs or at home. Kebab meat sizzles, taxis honk their horns, garlic mayo lingers on the air mixing with exhaust fumes. I stand in the middle of an empty street, spinning on the spot: which way is home? My phone rumbles in my pocket and I half expect it to be Cody, but it's Sloane's name that flashes on the screen.

'Sloane—'

She stops me before I can say anything more. 'Maddie,' she whispers. 'Mia is missing. The woman I introduced you to in the red-light district.'

Mia told us she was on a ticking clock.

'She was last seen five days ago, Maddie. I think something has happened to her. I'm going to the industrial estate behind the red-light district to look for her. It's where she would take her punters.'

'Is that where you were going in the video Charlie was angry about? To meet Mia?'

Silence. A moment passes.

'Yes.'

'When I suggested we meet with her again and you told me no. It wasn't because you thought she wouldn't be able to assist us, but because you were already meeting her behind my back?'

More silence.

'Maddie. I'm sorry.'

She lied to me and then told me she trusted me. Was that a lie too?

'I'm coming,' I spit. 'Wait for me.'

The line cuts. She told me we were investigating together. A wave of paranoia washes over me. Can women be fleas too? Vivian was one.

I raise my hand and flag a black cab.

33

'Here?'

I can feel the taxi driver's eyes trained on me through the mirror, a crucifix dangles. I know what he's thinking, I'm too young, too meek; no righteous woman should be here in the city's red-light district.

'Please,' I say, slipping a ten-pound note through the small gap in the Perspex window. He takes the money, pauses for longer than a beat. A couple of women approach the vehicle and then take a step back when they see the driver isn't a punter.

'If you're short of money, love, I can take you anywhere. What about family? You must have a mum or dad nearby.'

I shake my head, he looks down, back, and turns his head. Our eyes meet. He opens his mouth but before he can say anything I open the door and get out. Rainwater splashes up my jeans and leaks into my trainers. A blast of wind hits me. I don't want to know what this man will suggest or say, what direction he will give in an attempt to save me. He thinks I'm like the other women here but I'm not for sale.

I pass the women haunting their corners. Some shiver, but not from the cold. In darkened shadows one man stands in a corner watching, his hands gesturing towards vehicles, encouraging slight women into the cars of strangers.

As I pass, their eyes follow me, and I remember the women in the high-visibility jackets. I reach into my pocket and pull out the leaflet one handed me. I squint in the darkness. A floodlight flashes on as I move past a garage. I linger for a moment, clutching onto the paper. WARNING, it reads, ACTIVE SERIAL KILLER AT LARGE. Large drops of rain reappear, hitting the leaflet. It disintegrates in my hand. Wet bits of paper fall to the floor and wash away, and I scurry away from the light like a cockroach. The rain stops. As if the weather wanted to hurry me along, distract me from what I am walking into.

I pause at the fringes of the red-light district. I've made my way through, and now I face the industrial estate that backs onto it. It's the wrong type of quiet. No birds, no insects, no cars in the distance.

The skies open and rain buckets down. Again. Tonight is wet and cold. The splash of the rain merges with my footsteps, with my heartbeat. I try ringing Sloane, but the entire area is a dead spot. Of course it is.

Maybe I should have gone home. I don't owe Sloane anything. Doubt wanders across my brain. Maybe I owe Sloane something but, as the woods loom at the perimeter of the industrial estate, I ask do I owe anyone anything? Daisy? Vivian? Sloane? Karla? What's the price of a smile, an opportunity, friendship? Yet, I feel a pull towards Sloane. It's different. Like we are connected by a cord that cannot be cut, and any harm to her is harm to me. Is this how Karla feels about Emily? The Maniac took Emily, but at the same time attacked everyone connected to her.

My clothes cling to me, hanging heavy from the rain. I'm soaked to my bones. A chill runs through me. Ahead the first guard of trees stands tall and proud, protecting whatever is inside the woods.

'Sloane?' I shout, but I can't hear my own voice over the rain as it hits the buildings and cars: a constant, hollow rumble. 'Sloane,' I shout again.

I'm at the perimeter of the woods, ahead only darkness. Behind me the industrial estate.

'Sloane?' I shout over the wind and the rain as my hair clings to my face.

I look back over my shoulder and, from the corner of my eye, a dark silhouette edges into my periphery. Crouched behind an overfilling industrial bin. I freeze. Hold still, as if this will make me invisible. It creeps forward, unfurling. The rain tapers like applause coming to an end.

'Maddie?'

'You've been keeping secrets from me.' The words scratch at my throat like needles as I speak.

'No, it's not like that. I've built trust with her. She wouldn't be open in front of strangers. I was meeting her to further our investigation. You believe me, right?'

A crack of lightning hits the tree canopy in the distance and the skies illuminate for a moment. A godly photographer taking a picture. Sloane, pale-faced, with trees towering behind her. Her hair sticks to her face too, and her sodden clothes hang from her frame. She's shaking. I believe her.

I approach her and we embrace. Both our bodies soggy from the weather, and we squelch as we cling onto one another. Her head snaps in the direction of the woods. 'Did you hear that?' she says, nodding towards the darkness between the trees. I stare out. I heard nothing. I pull away from her and shake my head.

'I think it was a woman. What if it's Mia?' There's a crack in her voice. Panic. Her eyes are moving around frantically, scanning the horizon for danger. 'We have to check.'

She pulls me towards the woods. 'This is the moment in my book when we will be brave. This will be the chapter people will talk about. This will set us apart from other journalists.'

My presence is awarding her bravery. Stupid, misguided bravery. I've always wondered what it would have been like if Ben had kidnapped another girl at the same time he took me. If there had been two of us the whole time. In all the trains of thought, the possible outcomes, the scenarios I have played out late at night, I always draw the same conclusion. I'd have killed Ben sooner.

Our feet slip in the mud as she pulls me into the woods.

'Let's stick to the path,' I say.

Our fingers interlock and my knuckles must be turning white. The canopy shields us from any light. The streetlights now dim in the background, small yellow dots becoming smaller as we go deeper into the woods. I think we've made a bad decision. This is not a level playing field if we come face to face with the Maniac.

We both pause. We don't know where we are going. We don't know where the noise Sloane thought she heard came from.

'This is creepy.' Her voice is a little too loud. It carries, bouncing off tree trunks. I turn and pull Sloane back the way we came.

'Let's go, Sloane.'

We both freeze when the crack of a tree branch comes from somewhere nearby.

'What was that?'

A rustle. Mud squelching. My heart races. I can't place where the noises are coming from. I want to run, but what if we run straight into the arms of the Maniac? But we can't stay here like startled deer.

'Let's run,' I shout, but Sloane is like a statue. I pull at her hand but she won't budge. The stars, my faithful friends, are hidden above the dense canopy. Footsteps approach us, becoming louder. I yank at Sloane but she doesn't move. I pray for another crack of lightning to gift us with sight and startle Sloane into movement.

'Sloane, we have to go.'

She breaks free from her paralysis but it's too late. A fallen branch snaps loud enough to know whoever is there is too close for us to run. I grab Sloane tight. I must protect her. Silence.

Torchlight blinds us.

34

2027 – HMP Bronzefield

He hated the blood. The way it dripped from me like a broken tap. He asked – with all seriousness, and on more than one occasion – if my period existed to punish him. As if my biology, my very being was designed to create disappointment. From birth, men are reliant on women's bodies. We create them, we feed them and as they grow, their parasitical needs grow hungrier, until we are nothing but carcasses for their pleasure and disposal.

'How did your period change your dynamic with Ben?' My guest leans forward in their chair. Their facial features soft. A box of tissues on the table for my assumed tears, but this is my greatest era. Not one I will cry about, because I survived, and he didn't. He died. Not me.

The years before Ben took a toll on my body. My mother didn't have much spare money and I don't remember eating much. I was small and I didn't seem to grow. I think Ben thought he had hit the jackpot and kidnapped an eternal child. A Peter Pan of sorts. His favourite film, by no coincidence.

'If you're a paedophile – and let's be clear, Ben was a paedophile – at some point the object of your desire will no longer be desirable.'

'Quite,' my guest says.

'If it wasn't for me, Ben would have been trapped in a lifetime loop of abusing vulnerable children, over and over. How long would it have taken the police to catch on? He would give me torn-up rags, and I didn't know better. I thought that was normal.'

'That's when the schemes began.'

'He yearned for eternal youth. Not for him but for me. He wanted me to stay forever young, trapped in his house available for his needs and an old pregnant Maddie did not suit his wants. I was never to have friends, a family, a career, a partner. The plan was not for me to go out into the world and become a whole person, but to keep me in his shadow, never learning what it was like to climb a tree, listen to No Doubt, eat lemon drizzle cake or confide in a friend. His plan was simple, but the execution difficult.

'The schemes?'

'To make my periods stop.'

My guest nods along, as if the situation was not absurd.

'First he tried to starve me.'

He bought locks for all the cupboards, the fridges, the freezer. Big, weighty, metal padlocks. In the morning before work, he would leave me an apple cut in half. One half for breakfast and one half for lunch. At dinner he would cry over his burger and chips whilst I sat with two rounds of dry toast. He liked food. He had a belly that tucked his penis away and he gorged on sweets, biscuits, pizza, and butter-smothered bacon barms.

'Did it work?'

'I lost weight, but my periods didn't stop.'

He'd come home to claw marks in the cupboard and he would gasp in horror. He'd tell me off, but it was half-hearted. As if he couldn't quite bring himself to chastise me. He kept it up, nonetheless, and weeks passed and I did become thinner.

'So, he gave up?'

'He came home one day and I had fainted and cracked my head on the coffee table. He found me in a pool of blood and assumed I was dead. Luckily on that day the gods decided not to let me die. He wept and apologized for over an hour when I came around. I was in shock, the room blurry from the concussion, but I remember an empty duffel bag sitting in the corner. The tags dangling from it. I never saw it again.

'What do you think Ben would have done if you'd died?'

'Chucked me out at sea, buried me deep in the forest, chopped me up and fed me to some pigs. Kidnapped another girl.'

My guest nods in agreement. I knew Ben for a long time, and I have no doubts this is what he would have done. I know the duffel bag was meant for me. It was to be my final prison if I didn't wake up.

'Next he tried over-exercise. He brought home an exercise bike. Rust flaked off it as I pedalled.'

He gave up on this quicker than starving me. There was no way to force me to cycle for eight hours a day, which had been his intention.

'Starvation and exercise didn't work?'

'No,' I shake my head. 'He moved on to more traditional means. Contraception pills.'

'Pills?'

Little white boxes. Inside blister packs of beige small pills, the day of the week above each tablet. On the front of the box was a label with an unfamiliar name and address. I would say the woman's name over and over in my head – Reeta Smith, Reeta Smith, Reeta Smith. It felt foreign in my mouth. This strange-tasting name gave me hope. There were other people out there, outside Ben's house, carrying on with their normal lives.

Seeing her name made me question who I was. Maddie Smith, or Jones or Brown or Singh? I hadn't used a surname for years; my last name was at my fingertips but just out of reach. My real name rotted away until it wasn't even a memory. A nurse told me after I escaped – *So, this must be Miss Reid*, she said. I don't know how they knew, but I played along.

'Did the contraception pills work?'

'Yes.'

The pills stopped my period, but they didn't stop me growing. All children are destined to become adults, that is the goal of being a child, to make it to adulthood. For some this will be easier than for others. The pills didn't stop black hairs sprouting from my body. A forest to remind Ben he was lost in the woods. All the locks and frilly dresses wouldn't stop me from becoming a woman.

'So, you took the pills for the remainder of your captivity?'

I shake my head no. The whole fiasco went on for what felt like for ever, the tree outside the bathroom's frosted window turned from orange, to green, and back to orange. One day, I opened the box. This time written across the cancer warnings was thick black biro. It read – *Hello?*

35

2007 – Manchester

My hands spread across my eyes. Palms out. The torchlight scorches. The darkness now a background to searing light. I reach out for her but I'm greeted by thin air. Sloane and I are separated by the night. I fumble until I find clammy skin and I cling to her. The light drops and I am ready to run. Ready to drag Sloane through the mud and trees.

'You two,' comes a male voice.

He raises the torch below his chin. Charlie.

'What did I tell you? Literally a few hours ago? I'm out here looking for a murderer and you're both wandering around in the dark like it's a sunny afternoon.'

'You can't tell me where to go, officer,' Sloane says.

Her hand goes limp in mine. I thought I afforded Sloane her bravery, but it appears Charlie's dramatic appearance has made Sloane revert to her combative ways. In the pitch-black woods with me she was brave, but with Charlie she's comfortable.

'I wasn't lying when I said I would arrest you. I'll find a reason. Damn it, I'll make one up.'

'You wouldn't,' Sloane says, her hand slipping from mine.

'I would,' Charlie says, pointing his torch back in our direction.

I'm the third wheel as they go back and forth about whether Charlie would or wouldn't make up a reason to arrest us. Charlie citing safety. Sloane citing personal freedom. Sloane verges on goading him. I know she would like to be arrested; it would make for an interesting chapter in her book.

'Okay, mystery solved,' I say. 'It was Charlie you heard and now we can leave.'

A pause amongst us. Charlie cocks an eyebrow in the light of the torch, but I can't see Sloane's face.

'Yeah,' Charlie swings out an arm, pointing in the direction we came from. 'I haven't been to that part of the woods yet. It was probably a squirrel . . .' Charlie trails off. 'I've not heard anything until Sloane announced how creepy everything in here is.'

I know she is loud, but I didn't expect her big mouth to land us in a literal run-in with Charlie. Perhaps Sloane did hear a squirrel, or maybe her imagination is in overdrive.

'What if the Maniac is here, tonight, now?' Sloane says.

The warning from the flyer given to me outside the nightclub plays over in my head: Warning. Active Serial Killer. This isn't a joke. This isn't another chapter in Sloane's book or a mystery for Charlie to solve. This man is worse than any other I have encountered, and I have to find him. I must kill him.

'Escorting you out of these woods will be a waste of my time, but I will do it anyway.'

There's a crackle of a police radio as Charlie advises unknown police officers in unknown places of the situation. Maybe Charlie is lucky tonight too; he was alone, roaming in a wooded void, waiting for a hand to clamp over his mouth. A whispered instruction in his ear.

The rain has stopped but the night is still missing the moon, the stars, or any semblance of natural light. I'm sinking into the mud as the seconds tick by. A click echoes around us as Charlie attaches his radio back on his belt.

'Can we go?' Sloane says.

'I'll walk you both out,' Charlie says.

Sloane lets out an exaggerated sigh, but I know she must be grateful. Part of me is. Every one of my kills has been planned, not a spontaneous head-on fight. I'm not daft. If the playing board was fair, I would've been killed, not the four men I've murdered. Tonight is not the night.

'I know a shortcut,' Charlie says, and he points his torch away from the path and towards the trees.

Sloane doesn't question him. She doesn't question if we are safe with him, assuming we are because he is a man who holds a badge. The badge, no doubt given to him by another man. When are we ever safe? Can a woman only be safe in a locked, padded cell? I don't want a world like that.

Branches slap across my face as I follow Charlie and Sloane, Sloane nattering about nonsense and trying to drum Charlie for information about his investigation. Charlie looking over his shoulder every couple of seconds to check I am behind him in the glow of his light. My feet slip and sink in the mud, making every step precarious.

'I thought this was a shortcut,' I say.

'It is. We're nearly there.'

In the distance, light filters through the tree branches. Something hard hits my foot as I step forward, my other foot loses its balance and I tumble. A small yelp leaves my mouth as I land hard on the ground. Mud covering my left side.

Charlie spins, the light following him. The noise from Sloane's mouth is one I recognize – fear and disgust.

'It's okay, I tripped,' I say.

'Oh my God,' Sloane says. 'Mia.'

Sloane gags. A gurgle from the back of her throat and the hairs on my arms stand alert. I follow the light. We're not alone. It's Mia, blue and wrinkled, lying naked at my feet. The heels of my hands push into the mud as I propel myself away, slack-jawed. Charlie drops the torch, pushing the base into the ground creating an umbrella of light. He races to the body and places two fingers on her neck. He then intertwines his hands and presses her chest over and over. He's wasting his time. She's dead. She looks like she has been sitting in the rain for days. My mind ticks to when Ben would force me to sit in a cold bath for hours, and the way my skin would turn from young to elderly. Mia met her own version of Ben. Sloane vomits as she caves to her body's natural response.

Water leaks from Mia's mouth. Charlie doesn't stop, his eyes wild.

'Charlie,' I whisper.

He doesn't look at me. His breathing is heavy, and he pants as he presses her chest. A crack comes when he presses too hard – a rib, no doubt. I reach over and place my arm on his forearm.

'Charlie? I'm sorry.'

Tears roll down his face, and all four of us are cocooned in the circle of light, but I know we are sitting in the presence of darkness. There is nothing natural about this death. Charlie looks at me and I shake my head. He nods. He understands we're too late. He stops, pulls out his radio, a crackle fills the air. His words are aggressive, harsh, and he barks down the receiver, demanding a doctor, forensics, more officers. Ben's words fill my head. *Sometimes I feel nothing, little lamb, but the world wants tears.* Was Charlie performing? Sloane has her back to us; her shoulders move up and down but her cries are silent.

'She could have been you,' Charlie says, unblinking.

The victim's eyes, now glassy, loll to the left. Towards the city. Did Mia watch her murderer leave? In her last moments, she would have been able to see how close she was to help. Close enough to be dazzled by streetlamps, but far enough to be swallowed by the night. His footsteps, walking away as she died will be the last sounds she heard. Her last breath would have been lonely. I wonder who she thought of. A child? A parent? A lover? I bet revenge never occurred to her. Women have always been good at forgiving. We must be.

People arrive. Some in uniforms. Some in white paper suits. They attach bright lights to the trees. Charlie commands them. He grabs a female officer and whispers instructions in her ear and points in our direction. She leads us away from the scene and out of the woods, all three of us in silence. Tears roll down Sloane's face. We slide into a police car and Sloane gives her address. I look down at myself; mud cakes my clothes. The engine comes to life as we drive away, a plain car arrives. In the mirror, Frank's reflection as he jumps out of the car and runs in the direction of where we left Charlie.

We're silent on the ride back to Sloane's. Silent as we sit on her bed. Silent as we stare at the wall. Silent as the sun rises. Sloane is first to crack when she slides off the bed and opens her laptop.

'I need to get this down while it's fresh,' she says.

36

It's a rare sunny day in Manchester, and light cascades through the canopy of a large oak tree. Images of Mia play on repeat in my head alongside Sloane's betrayal. I could have saved Mia if Sloane had been honest about visiting her. I'm sure of it. The cemetery is row upon row of headstones, but I stare down at an unmarked patch of soil. Untended. No flowers, no trinkets, no tears will ever spill on this ground.

'Can you hear me, Ben?'

No reply. I picture him listening. An ear pressed against a coffin as he struggles to breathe. It's harder to imagine the reality – bones rattling around in a rotting box. Ben wasn't superhuman, just a man, and he died and now he is no more, like all the dead men.

'Fuck you.'

I sit down and pound my feet against the soil. Clouds of dust spawn and dissipate at my shoes.

'I hate you, I hate you, I hate you.'

A butterfly, with wings so white they shimmer in the sun,

dances around my head. I don't bat it away. Transfixed with its freedom. It can choose to go where it likes, unbonded from anything. And with that choice it lands on my knee. Its body is thick and dark, like the body of a spider. It repulses me but, with a flick of its wing, I'm tricked again into believing it's beautiful. I bet Ben would like to take this butterfly and frame it. Front and centre of a glass box. Admire its beauty at his leisure. But Ben can't because Ben is dead. A little laugh leaves my mouth.

'Hello, again.' My head snaps upwards and Charlie is standing over me. 'I'd have thought you'd had enough of dead bodies.' His words are soft and gentle; in a harsher tone I'd consider him rude, flippant, but it's almost as if he's concerned. Such a tricky little flea. I say nothing. The butterfly dances away. I watch him watching it dance away. I bet he's already picked a frame for its glass box.

'I'm starting to think you're following me around,' Charlie says, leaning towards me.

I stand up and dust dirt off myself. He's in his work attire again, faded shirt and trousers. His body blocks the sun, and for a moment I am in his shadow, engulfed by a darkness he is unaware he has created.

'It concerns me that a police officer doesn't understand what constitutes stalking. I can't follow you if I'm here first.'

He blushes.

'That is true.'

In his hand is a large bouquet of flowers. Not just the same, sad limp roses I see scattered all around, but sunflowers and delphinium. He must see me looking at them because he glances down.

'For my girlfriend.'

And I wait for the end of the sentence. My girlfriend's

mother . . . father . . . cousin . . . dog. I half expect a pretty little woman to come running, half out of breath, around the corner, but nothing arrives. No person. No further words.

This lamb must have been young. Charlie himself is only early to mid-thirties. I wonder what flea took her. What flea wasn't crushed between my fingers? Was it Charlie? As if he is reading my mind, he answers my question.

'Cancer.'

Is he telling the truth? I want to doubt him. Call him a liar, but I know instinctively this is what happened. I half bet he gets drunk in bars and uses his tragic story to pick up women. He's looking at me and I know he's waiting for an explanation.

'It's quiet here and I like the butterflies.'

'So did Julia. She liked the butterflies but maybe not the quiet.'

He strolls ahead. And again, I spot the faint whisper of a limp in his leg. An injury echoing from the past. I keep in his shadow. Not knowing why, I want to accompany this man to the grave of his girlfriend.

'See, I told you,' he says over his shoulder. 'You are following me.' He chuckles to himself, and I find myself staring at him, blank-faced.

He stops at a gravestone. It's well-kept and adorned with flowers and a small teddy bear. I glance at the dates, and see she died two years ago – the same time the murders started. Her headstone is the type with a small image at the top of it. In the picture, her head is thrown back as if she has been caught mid-laughter, her eyes filled with pure joy. She's not looking into the camera but away. As if there is someone just out of my sight who is making her laugh, a moment not intended for the viewer, an eternal inside joke.

A single magpie lands a few graves ahead as a tear rolls down my face. And then another, and I'm standing next to Charlie with red eyes. I'm crying; I don't know how long it has been. When did I last cry?

'It's okay,' he says. 'She was in so much pain.'

He bites his bottom lip. A part of me wants to explain I'm not crying for her but I'm crying for all women. All the women who were stolen too soon. Who never had loving parents, went to university, had friends, attended Fizz Fridays, got married. Who missed out on normal, ordinary, decent lives. And Ben's voice echoes in my brain – *You don't deserve an ordinary life. You're safest here with me.* Lies. Please let it be lies.

'I'm sorry.' My voice sounds strange and garbled.

He takes a step towards me as if to embrace me, and I flinch. He moves back – two, three steps. His head tilts. There's something in his eyes I don't recognize. A penny dropping. Clever little duck.

'I should go,' he says. 'I'll walk you to the gate.'

I nod. Glad he doesn't intrude any further with a line of endless questions.

A small breeze blows against us as we make our way. I like to think it is Ben seeing me with another man. At the end of the graveyard sits Leon's car. It's not moved an inch.

'I saw that car here last time too. Do you think it's abandoned?' Charlie says.

I shrug.

'Did you know Ben Starr is buried in an unmarked grave in this cemetery,' he says. 'I shouldn't really know, but a pal worked the case and gave me a heads-up, with Julia being buried here.'

I glance at him. A young couple holding hands pass us.

'Ben Starr?'

I almost regret it as I say it. After I was found, Ben's face loomed everywhere, from the internet to television to newspapers and magazines. My identity was protected but his wasn't. The man murdered by the girl he abducted.

'He abducted a young girl and held her hostage for twelve years.'

'Oh yeah. I think I know who you mean.'

He opens a wooden gate at the front of the graveyard and gestures with his hand to let me through first. His eyes linger on me a moment too long.

'Of course, no one knows who or where she is or what she looks like. I hope wherever that woman may be . . .' Charlie says. He pauses for a second longer than is comfortable. 'She's staying safe and keeping out of trouble. She deserves a good life. A safe life. A boring one.'

I nod. Look at the ground. Does Charlie know who I am? No. He won't know but perhaps he suspects. I look up at him. His eyebrow rise.

'Yeah,' I say. 'I hope she's safe too.'

37

2027 – HMP Bronzefield

I'd trace my finger over the handwriting over and over. It was big and full of loops. *Hello?* The crepe-like paper crinkled underneath. I began to think more and more of the outside world.

'Reeta began sending messages written on the instruction leaflet in the box.'

'How did that make you feel?'

My guest drinks coffee from a small, beige plastic cup from the prison vending machine. Bags are under their eyes.

'It returned to me something I had lost: hope. I know that sounds silly, some words scribbled on an instruction leaflet, but I began to dream of a life outside of Ben and those four walls.'

'Being hopeful isn't silly.' Their voice is low and soft. They follow their words with a smile. 'Those words were your first taste of the outside world.'

The next three months were an agonizing wait. I couldn't write back. There was no way from my end to communicate.

I had to wait and see if another message would come in the pillbox.

'And over these months, how was Ben?'

'Restless.'

He began drinking more. Stayed out later. Some evenings he would be out for hours and return home, sometimes sullen and sometimes as if he had won the lottery. I have no idea what he was doing during this time. I was relieved. I had got to the point where I would rather be alone than around Ben. I was waiting for my messages from Reeta Smith.

'And was there a message in the next box?'

'There was,' I feel myself glow.

The same looped writing was all over the instruction sheet. This time Reeta told me to come to an address if I needed help. It was then I realized there was no way for me to do this. But I also realized if I did find a way, a way to leave, I would have somewhere to go. It was powerful. I returned to my memories as a child, walking with my mother, as I tried to locate the address in my mind's eye.

A shock of pain in my skull. For a moment I am dizzy; it's unclear where I am until I look up and see the green walls, the panel still missing from the blinds – my snapshot of the outside world. Over my shoulder, the guard leans against the wall, uninterested. My guest leans forward.

'Are you okay?'

'Yes, yes, I'm fine. The next box contained an address for me to go to if I needed help.'

'Which wasn't of any use to you in your circumstances.'

My guest always downplays their language – 'circumstances'. I think they're being kind. They don't want to pour salt into a wound that will never heal. Robbie Jones enters my brain, the way the salt clung to the gashes across his face, and a tingle of joy fizzles within me.

'No, I didn't have the keys to the many, many locks Ben had fitted. But now I had hope and a promise of help. Naïve of me, yes?'

My guest gulps and looks away for a second. This is how I repay people's kindness; I take it and squish it up into a little ball and throw it in their faces. I stare at the missing panel, watch as people walk in and out of the corner shop.

'I tried to find Reeta Smith,' my guest says.

My neck snaps in their direction. From time to time, my mind wandered to who was at the end of the biro. Who was trying to help me. Who came so close but didn't quite achieve their goal.

'And?'

'Reeta Smith doesn't exist. It was a fake name being used by a woman,' my guest rifles through some paperwork, 'called Andrea Holmes.'

'That name rings a bell,' the guard chimes in.

My guest nods.

'Andrea is in and out of prison. You may have even passed her once or twice, Maddie. Maybe you've even met her and never knew.'

The name doesn't ring a bell to me. Although, I spend zero hours and minutes getting to know the other inmates. My time for friendship is over. I want to be alone. What would this woman even say to me *I knew something was 'off', but I failed you.*

'I managed to track her down. Andrea, that is. Claims to be reformed but still asked me for fifty quid for thirty minutes of her time,' my guest laughs. 'I talked her down to thirty. Andrea was a prostitute back then and did some prescription fraud on the side. Ben asked her to get the contraceptive tablet for him. She didn't question it too much at the time but said Ben was creepy. She says it was a friend who thought he might be abusing someone underage and that's why the girl couldn't go to the doctor's herself. She had no idea.'

Who in their right mind thinks the man in front of them has a teenager locked in his house? No normal person should ever have to think that. That notion shouldn't exist. I was eliminating men who do these things and they had the audacity to stop me and accuse me of being the villain.

'Andrea said shortly after the last message, the police arrested her. She always suspected Ben had set her up, but not enough to tell them about her suspicions.'

Failed by another adult. I think a theme is beginning to emerge. A serial killer who had a horrific childhood and was let down by many adults. Again, I am nothing but a cliché.

'He found them under my pillow. I was wearing Thursday's dress.' Thursday's dress had a button on the back of the collar. It grew tighter as the years passed and my neck would bulge above the white lace that accented the emerald-green polyester. I slump into my chair. 'He made me read them aloud.' Over and over until the button on the back of the collar popped. 'Then he handed me a lighter to burn them.'

My guest looks at me wide-eyed. The same expression I had worn as I watched the flames flicker and destroy Reeta's messages. Ben made me stand in the bath so I didn't set the house alight, but I held on to those burning scraps of paper until the flames licked my skin. The pain was cleansing, but the tiny fires were enchanting. It was love at first sight.

'He never told me, but I could see in his eyes he was up to something. It didn't matter though, because I was formulating a plan of my own.'

38

2007 – Manchester

Sloane rots in bed. Taking solace in nothing but her writing. Her fingers hitting the keyboard being the backtrack to me attempting to lure her away. An invitation to where I live becomes the successful bait.

Sloane gasps as she crosses the threshold.

'So,' she says. 'This is where Emily lived.'

In the kitchen, Sloane is fascinated by the remains of Emily's belongings. Her pots and pans, plates, cutlery. Emily's averageness makes her extraordinary. She's no different from any young woman our age walking down the street. Perhaps Sloane passed her once or twice when she was alive. Maybe they sipped cocktails in the same bar, bought clothes from the same store, waited for the same bus. How often do I pass women who wake with bruises and broken bones? Whose stomachs drop as they put the key in the door? How many relive horrors in their sleep?

'Stop it, Sloane.'

She puts a simple white plate, the sort that can be bought

anywhere, back into the cupboard. Would Sloane be my friend if I didn't live here? I shake off the idea I am being used. I pass her a glass of water. A sly smile crosses her face.

'So,' she says, 'Creepy Brian has gone out? I wonder when he will be back?'

I shrug. 'No idea.'

'We should look in the rooms of the previous tenants.'

I watch her finger moving around the table in circles. We're not the only ones who have sat here; what about Emily's previous housemates? You don't have to dig too deep for dirt when you live with someone. What about the girls who used to live with Emily? I don't have time to reply as Sloane leaves the kitchen and I follow her up the stairs. Aside from the bathroom, three closed doors greet us. Sloane opens the first two and we are greeted with blank canvases. Just like my room when I moved in. Basic furniture and blank walls. Sloane tries the third door.

Sloane tuts. 'It's locked. Which surprises me because what could a landlord possibly have of such value that he feels the need to lock the door? I mean, surely the house is more valuable, and he lets you live in it.'

Sloane presses down on the handle. Then tries a second time, pushing her shoulder against the door.

She looks around the hallway. Her fingers trace the top of a cheap canvas painting, then she scurries to the edges of the carpets and tries to lift them without success.

'I don't think he has hidden the key,' I say.

'There must be something in that room,' Sloane says. 'We need to know where he was when Mia went missing.

'I'm trying his bedroom. You can't stop me. I bet the key is in there. Mr Will Writer – creepy job by the way – could be a murderer. You could be in danger here, Maddie.'

She stands, shoulders square, and races down the stairs. I follow. She plays the same game as she did outside the locked room. Checking under the corner of carpets, trailing her finger along cheap canvas prints on the walls. No key. She groans. Bangs a fist in mock anger against the cheap wood.

A memory bounces back of me trying to hide under a bed as Ben knocked once against a door to announce his arrival and a voice whispers to me – *You know the rules. Clever little duck.* That's what Ben said as he dragged me by the ankles from under the bed. He would mock me with a big smile and call me a clever little duck, as if my attempts were to be praised. This is how I learnt: never face your enemy head on, never assume they are stupider than you and, in the same breath, never assume they are smarter than you.

I reach across Sloane and press the handle down. The door swings open. She blushes. Laughs.

'Maybe we should have tried that first.'

Brian's room is dark despite the curtains being open. A large tree blocks any sunshine from entering the room. His bed is made. The room is tidy; his laptop blinks away in the corner. Sloane moves over to a bookshelf standing tall in the corner.

'What?' she says pointing at it. 'What grown man has the entire Harry Potter collection? I mean, honestly.'

She pulls at books randomly. As she grabs a copy of *The Silence of the Lambs*, an envelope falls to the floor. The envelope crinkles as she opens it. It's a card with a love heart on the front.

'Brian, thanks for everything, Emily,' Sloane reads aloud. 'Thanks for everything? That doesn't sound very romantic to me.'

On his bedside table is a picture of him and Emily. The

Eiffel Tower looms in the background. I slide open his bedside table and find more pictures of him and Emily. In one, Emily wears a small hat askew on her head and he is wearing a bow tie; in the distance is an awning adorned with white flowers. Did they attend a wedding together?

'Nope,' Sloane shook her head. 'I can't find anything connecting him to Mia.' Sloane swallows hard. 'His friendship with Emily is strange, though. I don't think we know the whole story there.'

I pick up a weighty black diary from his desk and flick through it. The edges of the pages are sharp and I stop on the date Emily went missing – the entire evening is blacked out.

'I can't find a key,' Sloane says.

'The night Emily went missing is blacked out,' I say, showing Sloane the diary. I hand it to her and she flicks to the nights the other women went missing. All blacked out.

'There are other nights blacked out too, and not just the nights the women went missing,' Sloane mumbles. 'It's not definitive. Do you think Charlie knows about this?'

Charlie must do. Charlie arrested him.

'Did you know Charlie's girlfriend died around the same time the murders began?' I say to Sloane. 'He must know. I get the impression he's thrown himself into his work.'

'That could have been a triggering event. Do you think we should add Charlie to my corkboard?'

I shrug, noncommittal. Did he snap? Charlie was roaming around the woods; what if we didn't *stumble* on a dead woman. What if Charlie took us there on purpose? What if he wanted to scare us? He's been trying to get rid of Sloane.

We close Brian's door behind us. Both our heads snap in the direction of the front door as a key scrapes against it. I gesture to Sloane to move into my room; she vanishes around the corner as Brian walks into the house; he carries plastic bags filled with food. He looks up at me.

'Food shop,' he says, rolling his eyes. He tries to walk past me and to the kitchen.

'Did you get anything nice?' I ask, trying to buy time for Sloane.

Brian's face scrunches up.

'Food, I just told you.' He barges past me just as my bedroom door closes. 'Did you see that?'

I shrug.

'Must be the wind.'

'Are you sure? Maybe I should check?'

'It's fine,' I say through gritted teeth.

He shrugs and walks past my room and into the kitchen. My heart beats through my chest. Brian would be livid if he knew how close he was to Sloane, and it feels too early in mine and Sloane's relationship to comfortably murder someone in front of her.

Sloane is sitting on my bed when I enter my room; her head is in her hands. Brian whistles in the kitchen and its upbeat melody travels to us. She smiles when she sees me, but it doesn't reach her eyes. She looks haunted. Something I haven't seen before.

'I know Mia's death must have impacted you.'

'I'm fine.'

She answers too quickly. I know she is lying, and it feels like an invisible fence being constructed between the two of us.

'It was pretty scary,' I venture.

'You have to be brave to be a true crime journalist,' she says. 'You can't be afraid.'

I'm not sure bravery is the absence of fear. To be brave is to feel fear, and continue in the face of it.

'We need to think of a way to get those keys,' she says, lying on my bed.

We should think of a way, or at least I should. Sloane acts without thinking. Her eyes are heavy and her lids close as her breathing becomes deeper. She jolts awake as a desperate knock comes from my bedroom door. Brian.

I tiptoe to the door and open it a crack.

'Brian? I was just napping,' I lie, hoping he will take the hint and leave. Brian's loneliness is more of a nuisance to me than it is him. My mind wanders to the second man I killed. It's funny where you find inspiration from. Even the darkest moments can shed light on a problem.

'Actually,' I say, 'I was wondering if you would like to have dinner with me? I've brought everything you'd need for a spag bol, and even a couple of nice bottles of red.'

Even he looks surprised. 'That sounds great.'

I close the door and creep back to the bed.

'What are you up to?' Sloane mumbles. Her voice is groggy.

I toy with telling her my plan, but I remember Sloane was meeting with Mia and she didn't tell me. I can have secrets too.

'Nothing,' I reply.

39

My uniform itches. I wonder if I remembered to use fabric softener when I washed it. I smile. I bet these are the sort of banal thoughts everyone has. I look over at Karla. She's serving a family who are struggling to decide what to order. Karla is straight faced as she punches in their final decision. The family move to the collection point, the children trailing behind the adults.

'Penny for your thoughts?' I say to Karla.

She screws her face up.

'What?'

'Penny for your thoughts,' I say again.

That is the expression, right? I roll through my mind, trying to latch on to where I had learnt it. Half hoping it wasn't one of those things Ben had made up.

'Oh, yeah right,' she says.

I'm hoping it's something dull like fabric conditioner, or what the weather will be like tomorrow. I get a real kick out of things that aren't interesting. What someone is having for dinner or how they take their tea. Milky with one sugar for me. No one cares. Not really.

'I was thinking about Emily's memorial. She was always telling me I needed to let my hair down and I guess I finally did.'

In my head, my body is pulled back to the locker room and I'm staring at her face again. Did she think Karla was uptight?

A single man with paint splashed across his work clothes comes into the restaurant and I gesture to him to come to my till.

'Good evening, Your Highness. What would you like to feast on?'

Karla taps against the counter board while I take the man's order. Her eyes stare off into the distance.

'Actually,' he says, 'can you take the cheese off the burger?'

I nod. Wander into the kitchen. Maybe he is one of those unicorns who don't like cheese. What a miserable life that must be. Cody is nodding along to his usual hip-hop.

'Hey, what's up Madddddddiiiieee!' He half shouts my name, as if I am a guest on a talk show. Cody would be a good talk-show host.

'Last order doesn't want cheese on his burger.'

Cody pulls a face of disgust.

'I know, right?'

Cody laughs and gestures me over to his workbench. He pulls a phone from his back pocket, and it lights up. An image of him, Karla, Emily and Aaron on his lock-screen. They've all got their arms around each other as they stare into the camera with grins on their faces.

'Photos from Saturday night,' he says as he opens the phone. He flicks through them. He's making new memories without Emily. This is how life works. 'Somehow you managed to avoid me,' he says, smiling. 'I think everyone had a good time, but mostly I think Em would have loved it. That's how she would have wanted to be remembered, you know what I mean?'

And I think I do know what he means. Why be remembered as the woman who was murdered when you can be remembered as the woman who was the most fun at the party. She was lucky to have a friend like Cody. He lets out a long sigh.

'It's not the same without her, you know?'

I nod. But I don't know. I don't know what it's like for Cody, Karla or Aaron to be missing one of their Scooby gang, to know that she will never return. I don't know what that is like. Because all the men I murdered deserved it. They deserved death. Emily didn't.

Cody doesn't mention me running away from the party, or how drunk Karla was, and I'm grateful he doesn't. Maybe that's what friends do. Overlook our flaws. Is Cody a friend? Could I be friends with a man? I take a step back from Cody, alarmed at how off guard he has caught me. From the kitchen window, I notice the basement doors open from the ground and Aaron walks out from them.

'Did Karla forgive Aaron?' I say.

Cody shrugs. He doesn't meet my eyes. He doesn't want to gossip about his friends. I understand, but it reminds me that I am not one of them.

'No cheese,' I shout over my shoulder as I leave the kitchen.

I freeze as Charlie walks through the front door. Karla straightens up the shiny name tag on her top and puts on a wide smile as he approaches the till. His older colleague Frank stalks to their usual booth.

'What can I get you?' Karla says, as Charlie glances in my direction, his fingers tapping against the countertop. She fiddles with her hair, giggling at everything he says. I'm so absorbed watching them, I don't notice the woman entering, pushing a pram, a toddler on reins pulling away to the side.

'Maddie,' she's almost shouting, 'is that you?'

I look away from Karla and Charlie. A woman waves at me. It takes me a second to recognize her, with glowing skin and hair, a wide smile on her face. Her clothes clean and new. Well fitting. Daisy Parker has never looked so alive. A flush of pride pings through me like a text message alert, which dissipates to be replaced by unease. Daisy connects me to Leon. To Leicester. Regardless of my suspicions about Charlie, he is a policeman; this is not good news for me. Daisy needs to go away. Now.

'I thought it was you. I can't believe it. Viv reckoned you'd be back begging for your room in no time. Goodbye, Leicester, hello, Manchester, eh?'

Both Charlie and Karla are watching. Karla appears to be irritated by the attention I'm drawing, but I'm sweating under the spotlight. Charlie is leaning towards us. His body not making any attempt to appear uninterested.

'Your uniform looks great on you,' Daisy says. 'I couldn't pull off that shade.' She picks up the toddler so he is at eye level with me. 'Say hello to Aunty Maddie.' The toddler kicks out his legs and wails. 'He's overtired and hungry,' Daisy says.

'What can I get you?'

Daisy looks up at the flashing screens overhead.

'Two children's meals, both with orange juice, and a Queen of the Burgers Meal Deal Two with a Diet Coke.' I nod along, tapping her order onto my screen. 'Takeout,' she says, to my relief.

'What are you doing in Manchester?' My voice is almost a whisper, knowing Charlie is enjoying his view into my life.

'Just a bit of shopping. I've been to the Trafford Centre

and then I popped to the Arndale. Manchester has great shopping. Then I saw this cute little burger restaurant when I was driving back and I thought I'd pop in.'

Charlie is grinning. Karla is scowling. My armpits are wet.

'Burger no cheese,' Cody shouts from the back. I grab it and place it on the counter for my previous customer.

'Isn't Manchester a bit far for you? What about the Maniac?'

Daisy shrugs. 'He doesn't do anything in the day and no, Manchester isn't too far.'

Oh, how brave Daisy has become. You're welcome.

'Didn't you hear? They ruled Leon's death an accident. I can't believe they thought he was murdered looking back.'

Charlie's head tilts at Daisy's revelation.

'Anyway, all his assets were transferred to me. His mum wouldn't let it go, though, coming around my house drunk and all sorts. Like mother like son, I suppose. So, me and my mum sold everything up and moved to Chester, which is only thirty minutes or so away. I've always liked the Roman walls there, so much history. Just like you, we've had a fresh start. Great minds, eh?'

My smile feels tepid on my face. A small sense of relief comes over me when Charlie's food arrives at the collection point. He's slow to take it, though, and slow to move away. He is milking everything he can get from Daisy. Is this how he looks when picking a victim? Or does he know something about me?

'I'll tell Vivian you said hi, we still talk. She's always asking about you. I think she misses you.'

I shrug. Fighting the urge to tell Daisy she can tell Vivian to do one.

'It was good seeing you, Daisy,' I say.

She takes her food and glances over her shoulder as she leaves. I give her toddler a small wave with a smile. The toddler cries. I glance up and both Charlie and Frank are looking in my direction.

Shit.

40

Brian doesn't let himself into the house. Despite having keys and despite living here. His usual knock is replaced by something musical – a rat-a-tap-tap – and when the door swings open, I am greeted by a smile and an armful of gifts.

'Something smells good,' he says, wiping his feet on the welcome mat. 'I thought I would play guest instead of landlord and knock on.'

It appears I'm not the only one who understands the importance of playing a role. I stand back and open the door wide and gesture for him to come in. He does so with a spring in his step. I follow him into the kitchen.

'I remember you said you're not much of a drinker, so I got you some chocolates instead.'

He hands over a box of something cheap from the corner store, and I pretend to admire them. He's dressed smarter than usual in slacks and a shirt, but he still a far cry from the man snapped sitting in the back of a police car. How easy it must be for him to tone down his appearance. That decision is a privilege. Men don't have to choose from many things. When I was with Ben, I was a caged animal with no decisions. Perhaps that is why society affords men so few choices – choices of clothing, life paths. Get a job. Get married. Pay the mortgage. Die. Instead of cages, we force men onto narrow paths and hope they behave.

Alongside the chocolates, Brian is, of course, carrying a bottle of red wine.

'I couldn't resist a cheeky little Malbec,' he says, holding the bottle up.

I knew he wouldn't be able to resist bringing something I find putrid. What a flea move. If Brian is happy, to hell with the rest of us. But I saw this coming, hence the spaghetti Bolognese cooking low and slow on the hob. Something to complement Brian's *cheeky little Malbec*.

He walks ahead of me and into the kitchen. I pause at the threshold and knock three times. His head snaps in my direction. We stare at each other for a moment, and I half expect the ghost of Ben to appear and instruct me as to whether I can enter or not. I walk in. Brian tilts his head. I wait for his questions but they don't come. An uneasy feeling enters me. I haven't knocked like that since I left Ben's house. I pinch the skin between my forefinger and thumb. Hard.

Brian takes a wine glass from the cupboard. His arm grazes mine as I reach for the spaghetti; he pauses and smiles at me as if he is my boyfriend and he is meeting my parents for the first time. As if this is a special moment we are sharing. In a sense, this is a special moment we are about to share but he doesn't know that.

Droplets of boiling water flash out of the saucepan as I drop the spaghetti in. I take a second to relish in the pain.

'Dinner should be ready in ten minutes,' I say, smiling.

The smile is genuine. All afternoon I have slaved over this minced meat and tomato sauce; I've added mushrooms, bacon, garlic, and a special ingredient just for Brian. Of course, I considered making a vegetarian portion so I don't have to eat the same food as him, but I didn't want to raise any suspicions. I am going to have to be careful.

'More wine?' I say, topping up Brian's glass.

Flashes of Ben slumped on the sofa enter my brain like unwelcome guests. I fight them off but they stay, refusing to leave. The smell, sour and sweet, pungent, hits me. I swallow the retching trying to claw through my throat.

'Did you hear they are planning to reopen some of the tram stops in South Manchester? I hope they open the Burton Road one. Do you know much about trams?'

'No,' I say, not feigning interest.

He continues at length about trams. How they're built. How the tracks are laid. The different models. Tram-related crime. I sieve the spaghetti, boiling water draining into the sink as he monologues about how his father was a tram driver and he has been fascinated by them since childhood. Ben sometimes would tell me he had returned home late because of the tram. Those extra moments without him were bliss – maybe I do like trams.

'Yeah, maybe trams are important,' I say loudly to no particular point.

He continues seamlessly, as if I haven't said anything, as I place spaghetti on both our plates. On one plate, I smother the Bolognese all over the spaghetti, not leaving a single white strand. On the final plate, I add the Bolognese on the side, not touching the spaghetti.

I place the first plate in front of Brian. The second I place in front of myself with a glass of water. I glance at the other bottles of wine on the countertop and realize the curtains are open and anyone could be watching us in our illuminated goldfish bowl.

'This is delicious,' says Brian. 'Thanks for suggesting this.'

'Shall I close the curtains? You know, just in case anyone is lurking.'

Brian stands up and pulls the curtains shut. The fabric is brown and scratchy, more sewn-together potato bags than curtains. I wonder when Brian last replaced them.

'Good shout, Maddie,' Brian says. 'We don't want that ghoul spoiling our night. She's not been bothering you, has she?'

He means Sloane. I shake my head no with a grin. She's not been bothering me because Sloane is my best friend and he doesn't want her spoiling the night. She wouldn't ruin it. She'd make it better. I toyed with the idea of letting her in on my plan, but she's taught me it's okay to have secrets.

'There's a grainy quality to this I can't put my finger on,' he says.

It's the crushed-up sleeping pills. I put more than I required in and, to be honest, I hope he makes the night, but I'm not sure I can guarantee that. There's enough to kill him. Oh well.

'There is?'

I take a spoonful of the Bolognese, I blow on it, and then I put it in my mouth. I knew I'd have to have some. I take the smallest mouthful and dilute it with a large gulp of tap water.

'Yes, I see what you mean,' I say. Brian watches intently, but the way he is scoffing down his food, it's obvious he doesn't care. 'Garlic granules instead of fresh,' I say with a shrug. 'I should've used fresh.'

'Always,' adds Brian, through mouthfuls of food. Some red Bolognese sauce lands on his chin and snakes towards his neck, trailing like blood. A fed flea.

For a moment I wonder if I should just kill him whilst he's knocked out. It might be easier that way. As he sips on wine and tells me dull anecdotes, I realize how disappointed I would be if he is the Manchester Maniac. I flick through my brain; all the men I have met in Manchester have been, in some way or another, disappointing. I extend my mental search to every man I have ever met and draw the same conclusion. Are my expectations too high, or are they the worst humans?

I top up his wine glass. Brian puts his hand over the glass to try and stop me.

'Don't be daft, Bri,' I say. 'Have another glass.'

'I'm not feeling too clever.'

I clear away the plates. Scraping the remaining food into the bin as Brian quietens. His eyelids become heavy. Brian slumps forward in his chair. His head bangs against the table. I dip my fingers into his wine, and flick specks across the table and onto his clothes. Then I empty out all three bottles. The smell is much better when it is going down the sink; in fact, it almost smells nice as it disappears down the plughole. I take the empty bottles and arrange them on the table.

I could have done something to the wine, but what if one decided they didn't want to drink or they spotted something floating. It was too obvious. And putting something in someone's drink is such a flea move. I could never replicate them. I'm far too clever for that.

Brian's neck is at an awkward angle, his top collar now looking too tight; drool runs from the corner of his mouth. Is this what it is like for men? When they drug us? When they find us drunk? Do they like these human vegetables? Incapable of even the smallest acts of defence. Is this how the fleas like the lambs? Malleable.

I take a deep breath and rifle in Brian's pockets, pulling

out a wallet and a bunch of keys. I return the wallet. The keys glimmer and chink. A jailer's bunch.

I leave the kitchen. I don't know how long I have until Brian wakes – an hour? A night? I have no idea. Maybe he won't. Maybe he will forever stay in an eternal slumber until a handsome prince comes and rescues him. He'll be waiting a while.

I go into my bedroom. For the first time I feel her with me in the room. This is where Emily peeled her Queen of the Burgers uniform off after a hard day's work. Where she sat in a towel after a bath. When she was on the phone chatting to friends. Did Brian have an ear to the door listening to her every move? Drinking her in?

I close my bedroom door behind me with a gentle touch. Half afraid Brian may wake. The light bulb in the hallway hangs naked, buzzing. I reach the stairs and take them two by two. A bang on the door stops me mid-flight. I freeze. Wait for them to leave. The banging starts again, a chatty knock reluctant to end.

'Go away,' I whisper.

I strain to hear any rumblings from the kitchen. A clue Brian might have awoken from his slumber, but nothing. It doesn't stop a slow panic trickling through my veins. Did the fourth man I murdered feel like this? On the precipice of being caught.

The banging stops but the letter box squeaks as it opens. Eyes peer through.

'Maddie,' Sloane hisses through the letter box.

My heart drops. No. Ignorance is bliss, my darling Sloane, and this is for me and not her. I can get into the landlord's office. She knocks again. The letter box snaps shut and footsteps disappear away from the house.

I don't wait for any more interruptions and race to Brian's office. I jam key after key into the lock until one turns. The door opens. I walk into the room, dark now, filled with shadows. Outside a figure looms near the bus stop opposite my house and I question if I should close the curtains, but instead I let the light flicker on and stand by the window. I can't see her any more but I wave in Sloane's direction, my phone rumbles in my pocket. I answer.

'Why didn't you answer the door?' is Sloane's greeting. 'How did you get in the office? I have so many questions, Maddie. Are you going to let me in?'

'Brian's about. I don't think it's a good idea.'

A long pause. I draw the curtains.

'Maddie?' Her tone is irritated but I'm not sure I care. I thought we told each other everything. If she had told me about meeting with Mia, maybe she wouldn't be dead.

'Go home, Sloane.'

I hang up the phone. Brian's office is what I expected it to be: a desk, a couple of filing cabinets and not much else. I get down on my hands and knees to inspect where I think the hole would be, but the floor is wooden and old. There is no hole. I was wrong. Brian was not watching Emily from up here. I sigh. I've poisoned Brian for no reason. The laugh that leaves my body surprises me, and I clamp a hand firmly over my mouth.

I pull open the filing cabinets. Each file is recorded by address. Most of the manila folders are slim, barely anything inside, but when I come to the folder that documents this house, it's thick and weighty. I glance at the clock. Do I have time before Brian wakes? Do I care? I sit in his leather swivel chair and open the folder. Complaints. All about Emily. I flick through the first few – mainly trivial matters: hogging the bathroom, cooking smelly food, playing her music too loud. As I make my way through them, I realize there aren't one or two or even ten. There're hundreds. On occasions her housemates were complaining about her twice a day. Is this why Emily felt she had to be nice to Brian?

In the complaint, it states Emily kept coming home in the middle of the night, waking everyone; it specifies three a.m. every Tuesday and Thursday. Queen of the Burgers closes at eight p.m. She should be home, after clean-up, by ten at the latest. Was she partying? On a Tuesday? She was murdered in the early hours of Friday morning. Was this another late Thursday night? Where was Emily Sykes going? We need to meet with these women. They must know something about Emily. By all accounts they were monitoring her and writing rambling complaints.

My hands shake as I jot down the names of the complainants who were both Emily's previous housemates. I've never felt so close to the Manchester Maniac. I can almost smell his skin charring in flames. I take a picture on my phone of their numbers and forwarding addresses. They might just lead me to my next kill.

I clear everything away, locking the door behind me, and return to Brian who is fast asleep, his head on the kitchen table. I put the keys back in his pocket.

'You might be afraid when you wake up,' I whisper, moving a strand of hair from Brian's face. 'Confused even. You might try to piece fragments of the night together. Try to glue memories together as if they form a complete picture, but they don't. Tonight isn't a jigsaw for you to complete. So, feel the shame, try and shake off the feeling that something bad happened to you, and carry on as if nothing happened. The only important thing is I got what I want and that's all that matters.'

41

2027 – HMP Bronzefield

The door slams shut behind me. Same room. Same guard. Same guest. Same snippet of the outside world teasing me. A glimmer of the life I could be living through a missing slat in a set of blinds. Traffic blocks my view of the corner shop, and I wonder where the people behind the wheels of those cars are going and where they are coming from. Are they wishing for something more than domesticity?

'Hi Maddie, how are you?'

Pain clusters behind my right eye, the same pain kept me awake staring at the cracks in the plaster on my cell wall.

'I'm great, thanks. You? How's your tooth?'

My guest shifts in their chair. The price of my honesty is my impending death, and all I want from them is to tell me the truth. Tell me how they are. Their deepest feelings, the ones they hold tight, the ones they buried deep down for too long. I want someone to tell me they dream of slaughter, of blood dripping through the cracks of their floorboards. Make me feel normal.

'Much better, thanks.'

My guest gives me a friendly smile. What else can they do? A smile here, a smile there. Polite. Cordial. They don't reassure me. I don't think they see me as a hero; in my guest's story I am the villain. The cell walls aren't the punishment, it's Ben Starr's whispers: *This is what you deserve.*

'So, the contraceptive pills stopped?' they say, flicking through handwritten notes.

'Yeah, I was on them for a good while, though. Maybe even a few years. Time is hard for me: days, months and years blur.'

I spent more time in the bathroom – whenever I was afforded the opportunity. I remember warm sun penetrating the frosted glass and bathing in it as Ben shouted along to the football downstairs. The distorted leaves outside were green. Lying flat on the lino floor and soaking it in. As those afternoons crept past, my desire to go outside became stronger. I tried every window but none opened. Some painted shut. Some locked. My hope flickered like a flame, coming and going, and I prayed it wouldn't be extinguished.

'How did you feel when the pills stopped?'

Nothing about the pills. Warmth when I pictured the notes from Reeta aflame in my hands. Flickers of power. I would sunbathe on the bathroom floor. I needed to feel the heat up close again. It went on like this for a while, however long a while is.

Then a Friday rolled around. Friday dress scraped past my thighs. I couldn't do up the zip and the seams bulged under my arms. The last remnants of the second bottle of wine had been drunk. Ben was balancing a bowl of popcorn on his stomach when I brought in his topped-up glass. He patted the seat next to him.

'I didn't feel anything,' I lie.

I sat down. He pulled a phone from his trouser pocket. I had seen the phone a few times before, more than once but fewer than five. He didn't have it out in front of me often. He opened it and handed it to me, that's how confident he was I wouldn't do anything – he handed me his phone. He grabbed my finger and pressed on a thumbnail.

'He showed me a picture on his phone of a little girl.' I pinch the skin between my finger and thumb hard. 'She was much younger than me.'

In the first image she was in a dress, white with big sunflowers on it, sitting on a swing, her legs high in the air. Laughter on her face. Her mother was leaning against the bars, staring at her nails. The sun was shining. The grass was green. In the background, boys played football, boys about my age. What was my age? Intuitively I knew they were about my age.

'You saw the images of Katie Richardson?'

'I did.'

The second picture was of Katie bending down to pet a cat. Her mother, again distracted, with a mobile phone to her ear. As I tapped through the pictures, the same auburn hair would appear. The same spatter of freckles across her cheeks and nose. And he would stare dewy-eyed. He told me he had tried everything he could think of to bring the little girl to her rightful home. But her mother thwarted his every attempt. The final image, the girl in a uniform at a school gate, and I noticed something unusual about her mum. Her stomach stuck out in a perfect semi-circle. When I looked up, he was staring at me, head tilted. He told me he had a wonderful idea.

'She's an accountant now. Three children. Married and has a scruffy dog.'

We both sit there for a second and I absorb the present tense. Somewhere out there is a woman called Katie who made it from childhood unscathed. What fortune.

'What's a scruffy dog?'

The guard chuckles behind me.

'You know, unkempt, but in an adorable fashion.'

I pretend to know what they mean.

'The mother was pregnant when he was attempting to abduct Katie. I think in his head this made it okay to take one of her children because she would have one left over. As if she would be less bothered,' I say with a shrug.

My guest nods along and rifles through some paper. My mind filters back to the image on Ben's phone of her at the school gate with her pregnant mum. Me squeezed into a dress. That familiar dragging feeling in my stomach. Dampness between my legs. Jumping up. Ben's face was contorted with repulsion, his lips curled back, revealing his yellowing teeth, his nose scrunched up with black hairs poking through and his eyes on the red stain I had left on the sofa.

'It's not fair,' I say. 'It's not fair he got away with this. Why was he allowed to succeed?'

'The police would have caught up. They would have caught all the men you killed. What I'm trying to say . . .' They pause. 'Is that sacrifices were made that didn't need to be made.'

Are they trying to say Ben should be alive? Is that what they are getting at? Every person I killed got what was coming to them. A small tremble covers my body.

'Sacrifice.' I look around the room, at the locks on the door, at the prison guard. 'I *was* the sacrifice.'

42

2007 – Manchester

The tearoom is chintzy. Pink curtains with matching tiebacks. Floral wallpaper clashes with bright red carpet. The tables all have white linen draped across them. The room is filled with elderly women, and their porcelain teacups chink against their tea saucers between sips. Sloane was so thrilled we'd tracked down Emily's flatmates, it distracted her from asking any awkward questions about how I got the key to Brian's office.

I'm left with Emily's previous housemates whilst Sloane collects our tea and cakes. Once again, I was asked what rock I had been living under when I said I had never tried lemon drizzle cake. I swear I spotted a moment of second-hand embarrassment as she giggled with the other girls about my lack of cake knowledge.

'Have you ever had lemon drizzle cake?'

'Yeah,' they both reply in unison. One looks at her fingernails, which are far too long to be practical. Bored. They're bored.

I can picture them both with their own groups of friends,

enjoying Fizz Fridays and cocktails. Laughing over pizza. Tucking into their mum's own recipe lemon drizzle. *You'll never be one of them. You'll never fit in.*

Sloane comes clattering over. The tray wobbles and I'm fifty–fifty if Sloane will get everything to the table in one piece as she swerves between the other tables. She does make it, and I help her place cups of tea and slabs of cake in front of everyone.

'Thank you for coming.' Sloane looks serious as she pulls out her own chair and takes a seat. She places a hand on my knee under the table and squeezes. She gives me a faint smile. 'A little about me,' Sloane says. And I wonder why her tone is different with these women; it's as if she wants to impress them. 'I'm completing a degree in investigative journalism and criminology. I'm writing a book about the Manchester Maniac. I want that book to have a conclusion. My mother was murdered five years ago. I . . .' she places an open palm across her chest, 'understand.'

'We knew Mia too,' I add. 'You might have read about her. She is the latest victim of these crimes. Her funeral is next week and we'll be attending.' I copy Sloane and place an open palm across my chest.

Sloane frowns. This is far from the graveside disco I received or the casual threats Brian the landlord was subjected to. I plunge a strange-looking fork, which has two normal prongs and one thick prong, into my cake. Sloane gets out a tape recorder and places it on the table. Both girls look at each other, their eyes meeting for a second, and I swear I detect a small nod from the brunette to the blonde.

'This is a little delicate,' Sloane says. 'But I want to get this question done and dusted. I don't want it to be the elephant in the room, okay?'

I take a bite of the cake from the fork. Sharp and sweet. Sugary and moist. My brain fizzes as I swallow. This may be the best thing I have ever tasted.

'Okay,' they say again in unison, nodding.

I wonder if Emily and Karla would answer questions in unison. Allow themselves to merge. Is that friendship? Becoming one? I look at Sloane. She watches both the women like a hawk.

Sloane takes a deep breath, and her ribcage moves under her plain white T-shirt. I picture myself in a tight fitted white T-shirt, a plaid shirt over it and a reassuring smile.

'Was Emily a sex worker?'

I take another bite of my cake, whilst the brunette throws her head back with laughter. The blonde girl smirks and looks away. They both appear to remember they're talking about a murdered woman and compose themselves.

'If you were a sex worker, would you be working in that greasy burger joint? She used to stink, didn't she?' She looks at her blonde companion. I shrink into my seat. My skull aches from the memory of the plastic crown I don to work the job they sneer at.

'Yeah, reeked of grease,' the blonde one says, wrinkling her nose. 'I complained to Brian, but he didn't do anything about it. I feel bad now, given what has happened.'

I wonder if this was the first question Sloane needed to ask. There must be more important things about Emily. I think about how interested Sloane has been in 'Emily the person' versus 'Emily the murder victim'. I picture hazy faces of journalists, seated behind computer screens, writing articles that draw vague assumptions. Anything to link Emily directly to the Manchester Maniac. I thought Sloane was different. Sloane *is* different.

'This is the best cake I have ever had,' I say, filling an awkward silence.

Sloane and the two girls all look at each other.

'That's great, Maddie. Thanks for sharing,' says Sloane.

The blonde one smirks again. I bet she thinks she's smart, smarter than Emily Sykes and all the women who have been taken by fleas. These are stupid lambs. Mistaking their good fortune for talent.

The brunette one is still, her eyes glaze over, and she takes a tissue from her handbag. Dabs at her dry eyes. Her makeup still applied to perfection.

'Talking about Brian, the police were quick to arrest him.'

The brunette shakes her head, her curls shake too, making her head look like jelly.

'Wrong guy. Brian wasn't interested in anything but the rent being paid on time. He wouldn't kill anyone giving him money. Particularly Emily.'

'We only moved out when Brian, our landlord, was arrested,' the blonde one adds. Her sombre mask now in full force. 'We couldn't take the risk.'

'So, were Brian and Emily close?' I say through a mouthful of cake.

The brunette blows her nose into the tissue and discards it on an empty saucer on the table.

'Not that we know of.' Whatever attentions Brian paid Emily, they were kept hidden. She lowers her voice as she continues. 'They were arguing the night before she went missing.'

A waitress hovers nearby; seeing everyone else's full plates, she disappears again. Crumbs pile on my plate. Best cake of my life and no one cares. Viv used to make a dry sponge and I never understood what the fuss was about.

'Did you tell the police?' Sloane asks.

The blonde nods.

'Yeah, and they arrested him.' She stares at her brunette friend.

'What were they arguing about?' I say.

Sloane's neck snaps in my direction and she throws me a stern look.

'Yes,' Sloane says. 'What were they arguing about?'

They both shrug.

'She kept coming home really late. Said she was doing a stock-take at work, but who does a stock-take twice a week until three in the morning?'

Sloane continues to ask questions about Emily and her life. Emily could be any woman in this room and yet she ended up in the clutches of a serial killer. Emily liked to drink with her friends and served people food for a job. Emily was getting on with her life. I feel invisible next to the other women at the table. I feel invisible next to Emily. As they discuss her, it is clear she had a fuller life than me. I glance at Sloane as she nods and smiles at these women. Another flicker of doubt. Did Emily trust her friends: Karla? Cody? Aaron?

Outside the window, the rain has begun its daily Manchester march. Thin sleet comes down in angled fine lines. I feel it first, a set of eyes watching me, and then I notice the car and then my eyes drift to Charlie in the driver's seat. He gives me a wave. The attention he pays me, the way he keeps popping up, is he lining me up as his next victim? Could Charlie be the Manchester Maniac?

'Sloane?' I say.

She looks at me through narrow eyes.

'Maddie? Yes, the cake is good. If you want more, you can get some from the counter.'

I feel heat rush through my cheeks as both the blonde and brunette stare at me.

'I need some fresh air,' I say.

She nods and the three of them continue their conversation.

A bell tinkles as I exit the tearoom with my hood up. Flanking the tearoom is a pharmacy and bookmaker's. Charlie smiles as I approach his car. He looks amused. I tap on his window. It whirrs as it lowers. Spatters of rain land on Charlie's shirt, turning the red into a maroon. I want to throw a Molotov cocktail onto his lap.

'Are you stalking me?' I say.

He shrugs and rolls his eyes playfully.

'How do you know I wasn't here first?' A heavy clunk comes from the vehicle as he unlocks the doors. 'Jump in. It'll be less wet for both of us.'

I look back towards the tearoom. Through the window I see Sloane with the other two women. They look like a group of friends catching up. Average, normal friends having a brew whilst deep in conversation. What would that make me and Charlie? Two serial killers swapping trade craft? I want to say no to Charlie and run back inside the tearoom and convince Sloane I am normal. I don't. I run to the passenger side and jump in.

The heater is on full blast and the wipers are frantically going back and forth. He switches them off. Rain assaults the car. He lowers the heat. For a moment, all that is between us is the drum roll of water on metal.

'You know, those two girls hated Emily,' he says, nodding in the direction of the tearoom. 'All accounts suggest they made her life a bit of a misery.'

A silence appears for a second. I glance at Charlie and he is watching me. He is not a conventionally attractive man. If he lacked his charm and wit, I have no doubt, given the right set of circumstances, he too would be labelled an oddball.

'Which forced her to spend so much time with Brian?' I say.

'I wouldn't know for sure,' he says as he tilts his head. 'But probably. How do you know they were friendly? Emily kept that quite the secret, according to Brian.'

The windows of the car mist from our breath and it feels as if we are sitting in a cocoon. He taps his fingers against the steering wheel.

'It was a guess,' I lie. 'Why were you following me?'

He laughs, throwing his head back. He opens the glove compartment and leans over me to retrieve a pale green prescription. His aftershave a heady mixture of musk and bergamot. He nods in the direction of the chemist.

'I was waiting for the rain to stop.'

Cars pass us, splashing water onto the pavement. Passersby raise their arms to shield themselves with no luck. *I would never tell you to mind your own business, clever duck. Lying to you is too much fun.* I want to smack my head as Ben's voice appears in my skull.

'If you're not feeling silly then you probably should be,' he says with a smirk. 'I'll try not to judge you.'

Rain tapers out and the windscreen clears.

'Why Brian?'

He looks at me and pauses for a second more than is comfortable.

'I'll answer your question if you answer mine.'

I look out at Sloane, through the tearoom window, and she is still deep in conversation. Nodding along to words I can't hear. I know she would offer up a slice of her soul for the answer to my question.

'Go on,' I say.

'Brian has multiple kerb-crawling offences. He really has a thing for prostitutes – and not the fancy type, the street corner type. He also was a bit too interested in Emily. When we reviewed her tenancy agreement, he had stipulated monthly room inspections that were not in any other contract.' He looks out at the street. 'He appeared to be a strong contender. But we have DNA and it doesn't match. Plus, a couple of the street workers have actually told us he turns up with a flask of tea looking for a chat, and has never shown any signs of violence. I think Brian is just very lonely.'

I nod.

'DNA? Is that all you have? Is it you, Charlie? Are you the Manchester Maniac?'

My words come from nowhere. They feel like bullets speeding at Charlie. His face becomes hard, as if I am Medusa turning him to stone. My breath quickens, knowing I have played these cards wrong and I have broken my rule about facing a flea head-on.

'Do you think I murdered all those women? Are you nuts?' He's surprised, his voice bordering on high-pitched. It leaves me questioning myself.

'You can't be too careful,' I say.

He pulls out his phone and opens it to reveal images of him standing next to the Tower of Pisa. He has his hand out, as if he is keeping the tower from falling.

'I was on holiday when Emily was murdered. I was called back a week early.' He sighs. 'If you think you or anyone else is in danger. No matter how slight or serious that danger might be. You call me. You don't, you never, get into a car with that person. Do you understand?'

Who is this man? I don't understand him. I accuse him of heinous crimes and his only concern is my safety.

'My turn.' He rubs his hands together in an exaggerated manner and grins. 'How well did you know Leon Parker?'

My life feels like dandelion fluff blowing on the breeze. Vanishing. The world spins and I try to capture my footing back in reality as he studies my face. I raise an eyebrow. I learnt my lesson lying to Charlie in the graveyard about Ben, so I shrug.

'Everyone who knows Daisy knows Leon. He was always just outside of her shadow. Lurking about. That's how well I knew him.'

Charlie maintains eye contact and nods.

'Sure,' he says. 'Sure.'

43

2027 – HMP Bronzefield

The other inmates linger in the block, hanging over the railings watching those below them, or they sit with others in the common area at tables, chatting whilst one muted TV plays in the far-right corner; small cliques form in cells. They all stare when I appear. I only leave my cell when I'm forced. Three meals a day. Two showers a week. One meeting with my guest.

'Hurry up, Reid.' The nameless guard ushers me past the common room. The ladies watch me as I pass the large windows. I do not smile. I do not nod. I do not acknowledge their existence. The pain is under my eyes, behind my nose. It pushes against my skin and I want to take a razor blade and open up my face to release it.

The guard opens the door. I walk through and they follow me, close the door, and lean against the back wall. My guest stands to greet me.

'Hello Maddie.'

The blinds have been repaired. They're closed and we return

to a dim hue with the banishing of natural light. I stare at the tissues my guest has placed on the table. Sometimes I want to wrap my hands around their throat until they tell me I'm right. I'm the hero of this story.

'Hi . . .' I stop myself. There's a wobble in my voice, as if my mouth can't construct my words. My body is giving up on me: the same way everything gives up on me. Can my guest hear me dying?

'Last time.' They flick through their notes, which has become customary. I think they remember, but worry any overeagerness on their part might cause me hesitation. They'd be right. 'We were talking about Ben struggling with your aging.'

'Yeah, he was going to replace me.' Internal relief as my brain remembers how to construct sentences. The man who was too afraid to purchase me feminine hygiene products wasn't too afraid to kidnap another child. No, in fact, he appeared excited. Salivating almost. 'His sexual desires lay elsewhere.'

There's a look on my guest's face. Not quite horror. Something close to it, though. Perhaps if you take horror and mix it with sadness and disappointment, you end up with my guest's face. Ordinary folk love sex. Cherish it. When it's weaponized, particularly against a child, it does something to them, which I don't understand.

'Did he have a plan?' my guest asks, their voice almost a whisper.

'Plan A was Katie.' A wave of exhaustion. 'I want to talk about me. About my plan.'

'Your plan?'

I detect a smirk. It's faint but it's there. This isn't like my guest, the ever-sympathetic, tissue-giving listener I have come to know.

'All the best women have a plan. In fact, as soon as it came to me, my only question was: why hasn't this occurred to me before? Yeah, I've learned, fail to plan, plan to fail. How do you think I killed all those big men? They never saw it coming.'

My guest turns the same colour as the room they keep forcing us to use. I notice a slight sway. As if they are struggling to keep upright in their own chair.

'Are you okay?' I ask. Now, it's my smirk spreading across my face.

'I'm fine.'

I wonder how many times they've met people like me and have been told about crimes that turn their stomach. How many times they have wanted to throw up or shout or retaliate, but instead have forced themselves to keep it together. Not for their own benefit. But for the benefit of everyone around them. How many times have they wanted to be weak and were forced to be strong?

'If you want, if it makes you feel better, I'll let you get a punch in,' I turn to reveal my left cheek. Horror spreads across their face and they look worse than moments before. 'Go on. Hit me. Coward.'

'That wouldn't make me feel better, Maddie, and I should be asking if you're fine. Not the other way around.' Their smile is limp. Forced.

'Never better,' I say with forced brightness.

For a moment I juggle with the idea of telling them constant pain has become the theme tune to my life. I'm being eaten alive, devoured one piece at a time until I can no longer hold myself up, until I will no longer know my own name, and death is a favoured outcome to a drawn-out life. If I do, will they be more inclined to see me in the light I deserve?

'If I was fine, I'm not sure we would all be here,' I say,

waving my arms to gesture at the room. 'No, correction. If the world was fine, a good place filled with good people, then I wouldn't be here. What world imprisons their heroes?'

A quiet laugh from me and a small smile from them, perhaps from politeness.

'So, you had a plan?'

'To escape? Yes, I did. I took all the hope I had left, and I invested it into a promise. I was going to escape. I just needed the right time. I needed my period. I can't stand blood normally.'

Every four weeks my period came like clockwork. *Not today*, I would usually whisper. Blood would drip from me. So much blood, as if I was a vessel for nothing else. I waited with anticipation for that clawing feeling in my stomach.

My guest scribbles something; their hand moves in a circular motion, as if whatever they have written they have circled.

'What did you write?'

They shake their head.

'Nothing important,' they say.

I stretch my neck, first towards the left and then towards the right. I then roll my head, keeping my shoulders in place. A therapist said this was meant to calm me in moments of stress. I find it doesn't work but makes others feel uncomfortable. My guest stares. I stare back. They sigh.

'If it means that much to you, Maddie.'

'It does.'

My guest takes a long inhale, to the point where I feel I could legitimately accuse them of being dramatic. I stare through narrowed eyes, wondering if I can move quickly enough to snatch it from their hands.

'I wrote . . .' They pause. 'A serial killer with an aversion to blood. Ironic.'

'Which bit did you circle?'

'I circled ironic,' they say, looking at the paper in front of them. For a moment I feel as powerful as a schoolteacher considering handing out a detention. I shrug.

'There's more than one way to skin a cat.' I smile.

My guest shudders.

44

2007 – Manchester

'I'm surprised you haven't brought Emily's old flatmates, given how well you were getting on,' I say to Sloane.

A large glass bowl filled only with red Skittles sits in the middle of the table in front of us. This must be a direct instruction from Mia, and someone cared enough to fulfil it. A picture of her sits on either side. On the left she is a child, hair in pigtails, dressed in a school uniform, smiling for the camera, the background an internal living-room door. The second picture is hazier; she's much older, she smiles for the camera, a drink in one hand and a cigarette in the other, the smoke clouding her face, the sun at the back of her head.

'Maddie,' Sloane says. 'It's not like that. We have to present in a certain way when we are speaking to sources.' She looks through me, biting on her bottom lip. 'You can be a bit weird sometimes.'

You'll never be like them, Ben's voice whispers in my ear.

'Don't be angry with me. We have a shared goal.'

I nod. Maybe she is right. Maybe I am weird.

'And how did you know the deceased?' Charlie whispers into my ear. His head almost perched on my shoulder.

'The same way you do, I suspect.'

Charlie wanders away without reply and joins an uninterested Frank. He looks a little taller in his black suit. I cast an eye across the crowd. Thirty or so people. They all have a quiet acceptance on their faces, like this was the death of an old person who went to bed one night and was stolen away amongst a beautiful dream of their youth. Not a woman in her early thirties slaughtered. Someone here must be angry. Someone must want vengeance.

'What did Charlie say to you?' Sloane, her eyes following him and Frank around the room.

'Nothing.'

Sloane's sigh is exasperated.

'He just said hi,' I lie.

Charlie is working the crowd, apologizing for their loss, making promises he can't keep about justice. Frank doesn't attempt to hide his boredom. After Ben, I met police officers like this, who thought they were above it all: the messes the common people make. How they shift the blame onto the victims, an easy explanation. She was murdered because she led a high-risk lifestyle, because she was a junkie. When it should be: she was murdered because a cruel man chose to take her life.

Sloane and I take a seat with our drinks. I feel eyes settle on me. I look up expecting to see Charlie watching me; instead I see Cody. I smile and wave. He half smiles back before he notices Sloane sitting next to me. His face drops. He turns and leaves. I almost knock Sloane's drink over as I get up to follow.

'Where are you going?' Her voice fades as I walk away.

I find Cody outside, lighting a cigarette. He inhales sharply when he sees me. I struggle to reach him as I crunch across gravel. His suit is too big for him, making the usually too-cool-for-school Cody appear younger and childlike. No longer a man but a boy who has to borrow a blazer.

I pause, not knowing what to say, knowing I have broken some unspoken rule by associating with Sloane.

'Hi,' is the only word I find.

He looks at me, then away; takes another puff on his cigarette.

'You know what she is, don't you?'

I know he means Sloane. I know he thinks she is a ghoul chasing ambulances in the night, following the scent of blood for a story. Someone who profits from personal loss. A bus rumbles past us.

'Her mother met a similar fate to your friend. She was thirty-eight when she was murdered by her boyfriend. The person who was meant to love her.' I look away from Cody. 'I shouldn't be telling you this. It's not my story.'

He holds up a carboard package towards me, revealing cigarettes. A peace offering. I take one and put it in my mouth. He holds a lighter up, a flame towards the end. The nicotine rushes to my head, and for a moment I am hit by a nauseating taste whilst my head spins.

'I didn't know that about Vicky Sloane. Puts a different slant on it, I suppose.'

We both sit on a low wall, staring at the working men's club. A couple of men, dressed all in black, come outside to smoke.

'How did you know Mia?'

Cody glances at me. 'She used to babysit me when she was

a teenager. Before things went shit for her. I'd still see her sometimes – sort her out with a bit of food or cash.'

I nod. Cody's story matches with what Mia said the night I met her.

'Your mate? Sloane?'

'Yeah?'

'Do you think she stands a chance of figuring out who this guy is? The police seem clueless.'

I can't help but picture both Sloane and Charlie weighing up one another in a boxing ring. Their gloved hands raised to their faces.

'I think she can.' I'm unsure of my own words. 'No,' I say. 'She definitely can, with the right help. The fact no one at work will speak to her doesn't help things.'

He nods, dropping his cigarette into the gravel. He extinguishes it with his shoe, tiny sparks dancing over the small grey stones. I copy him with a cigarette that has burnt out rather than been smoked. If nothing else, I have learnt smoking makes me want to vomit.

'I know where Mia lived. She was there unofficial; maybe there are clues for you both. Grab your mate and I'll take you there.'

'Thank you,' I say.

I race through the door of the working men's club, and nearly bounce off Charlie, who is lingering by the exit. Frank sneers.

'Easy tiger,' Charlie says with a gentle laugh.

'What's the rush?' Frank's eyes narrow. He looks to Charlie. 'Maybe they've cracked the case. Have you figured out who the bad man is, little girl?' There's a faint whiff of wine on his breath. I half want to ask Frank if he likes to keep women locked up in his house, but I'm afraid I won't like the answer.

'Ignore him,' Charlie says. He pauses, bites his lip, then releases it, as if he has decided to say something he shouldn't. 'Every time we fail to catch this guy, someone dies. That isn't easy. Let's go, Frank.'

Charlie looks over his shoulder as they both walk away from me.

Sloane is still nursing a drink when I approach.

'Come with me. I think we've got a break.'

I hold my hand up as her mouth opens and I look around the room. I shake my head. She closes her mouth and stands.

'Let's go,' she says.

We both follow Cody through the estate. We pass a pub with punters smoking cigarettes in the doorway. Cody stops at a tower block. He takes a deep breath as he approaches the lift and pulls his sleeve over his hand as he hits the sticky button. There is a pungent whiff of cannabis on the air.

'She had this place but not many people know about it. Her last place was cuckooed.'

I look at Sloane with a raised eyebrow, but she puts a finger on her lips, telling me to stay quiet. The lift doors open. There is no mirror inside, just shiny sheets of metal with graffiti tags sprayed across them. I count five colours of the rainbow. Cody hits the top button and the lift feels clanky as it ascends. I look for a railing to hold but there is none.

'I'm sorry about your friend,' Sloane says to Cody.

'Yeah, me too.' Cody's voice is hard and he looks away from Sloane.

As we leave the lift on the top floor, young men get in with their heads down and eyes averted. Cody says nothing as we pass them. Once the doors have closed, Cody gestures at us both to come closer to him.

'Last flat on the left,' he says in a hushed voice, and points to the very end of the hallway.

'Are you not coming?' Sloane asks. 'It seems odd for you to come all this way and then not come in.'

He rolls his eyes. 'Listen, that's two I'm connected with. I'm going nowhere near that flat.'

I nod. It makes sense for him to keep some sort of distance, just in case the police do consider him as a culprit. Sloane looks at me as if this thought is running through her head, but I shake my head no.

'She keeps her key in a hole in the ceiling above her door.'

We both rush down the corridor, eager not to be seen by anyone. When I glance over my shoulder, Cody is gone. The ceiling is made up of cardboard tiles. Most have dents and holes in them and cables hanging loose from them. Sloane stands in front of a plain door and looks up; on her tiptoes she manages to knock a tile loose and reach inside. She fumbles for a second. A grin spreads across her face.

'Bingo,' she says, pulling a key from the ceiling and inserting it into the door. The door swings open.

'What's cuckooing?' I ask.

'This is what I mean about you being a bit weird. It's like you've been living on a different planet,' she says as we enter the flat. It's barren: A single bed frame with a bare mattress, a sofa and a TV. No carpet, no curtains, nothing in the fridge; the radiators are stone-cold, as if they have never been switched on.

'It's when a criminal takes control of the property of someone who is vulnerable, as a base to deal drugs, for sex work, whatever.' She sighs. 'Do you think we need to add Cody to the suspect list?'

I shake my head no. Not Cody.

'He was with me the entire night Mia went missing. If the Manchester Maniac killed Mia and Emily, it can't be Cody,' I say, looking around the empty flat. An unsettling anxiety rests in my stomach as I realize I am defending a man. Could it be true? Could it be that not all men are the enemy. No. 'I'm not sure what we'll find in here.'

We both collapse on the sofa with a long sigh. A bit of paper peeks up between the sofa arm and the cushion.

'What's this?' I say, pulling it out.

The paper is long and thin. Not like anything I have seen before. Sloane takes it and looks hard at it.

'It's a stop-and-search notification.'

I look at the dates. 'She was stopped six days before she was murdered; that's one day before she disappeared. Says it was a negative search.'

'I can't make out the signature,' Sloane says.

She passes it back to me. I fold the slip and place it into my pocket. Sloane stands, but I want to stay a while; sit in her home and be the guest she never had. She had nothing. But that doesn't make her nothing. I am tempted to tell Sloane I will catch up, but I know that would be weird and instead I join her walking to the door. Voices come from outside. Charlie and Frank's shadows loom from the window.

'Fuck,' Sloane hisses.

We scramble away from the front door.

'Under the bed.' I push Sloane towards the corner of the flat.

'It's too small,' she says as she looks around the room. Desperation lines her face.

'We have no choice,' I say, pleading with her. 'We can't be found here. Please.'

Sloane drops to the floor first and she shuffles under. She

presses herself hard against the wall. I follow. Our backs touch and I breathe in time with her. The slats of the bed skim my face and an earthy smell crawls into my lungs.

It's Frank's voice we hear first.

'This is a waste of time,' he shouts. 'Look around, Charlie boy. She didn't have a pot to piss in.'

'It's odd the door was unlocked. Do you think someone has been here?'

Sloane fidgets. I move my hand and grip hers. A sofa cushion slides across the floor, as if someone has removed it to look underneath.

'No, I don't. I hate to say this, Charlie,' Frank's voice booms in the room. The normally quiet officer is louder when he thinks he is alone amongst comrades. 'And I doubly hate repeating myself, but like I said, this is a waste of time.'

From under the bed, I have a view of Charlie and Frank's feet moving around the flat. Frank in shoes, the type you polish. Leather, and finishing at a point near the toes. Charlie in black Skechers. Comfortable. Practical. They're at odds with one another as I watch them navigate Mia's flat from the floor. Even their gait. Frank sure-footed, Charlie's a little off.

'Yeah,' Charlie says. 'Maybe you're right, Frank. There's nothing here.'

The shoes walk towards the door, and then the Skechers stop.

'One second,' Charlie says. 'Let me check under the bed in case she left anything.'

I freeze and grip Sloane's hand tighter. There is nowhere to run. Charlie lowers himself joint by joint – foot, knee, hand, and then his face appears. Our eyes meet. I'm about to explain, to lie, to reason, when he shouts, 'Yeah, nothing here.'

He looks at me. I look at him. Then he disappears upwards the same way he came, until he is nothing but a pair of comfortable Skechers walking away.

'Let's go, Frank,' he says.

I hold still, with the echo of Charlie's face in my mind. He saw me and I saw him.

The door closes behind them with a bang and their voices trail into the distance. I roll out from under the bed and Sloane follows. She takes short shallow breaths.

'Did he see us?'

'No,' I lie. 'He barely even looked.'

Sloane tuts and shakes her head at Charlie's inability to look under a bed. To me it's an obvious lie. To her it's a testament to the inadequacies of the police.

'This is why they can't be trusted to investigate.'

I nod, confused as to why we are not sitting in the back of a police car. As we lock the door and return the key to its hiding spot, I wonder how long it will take the landlord to realize – for her neighbours to realize – she's gone. Her wake has already taken place with a crowd, most of whom didn't even know where she lived, too afraid her only resource will be stolen.

'I think we deserve a takeaway after that.' Sloane's voice is warm.

'Sounds good,' I say.

45

2027 – HMP Bronzefield

When I die, I have instructed them to engrave my tombstone with, *This life was shit*. They said no. Similar requests referencing my heroic deeds have also been declined. They said I could have a service, but I fail to see how that benefits me when they plan to hide me in an unmarked grave. I'll find a way to crawl out of it. The insult of it.

Let that sink in – an unmarked grave. Do you know who else has an unmarked grave? Ben. Ben Starr. Everything in my life, all this shit, and I take it on the chin because I know I leave this world a better place. Yet look at them, they think we are the same. How? I don't think he would have managed to keep an adult captive. He was performing on a tilted stage. So was I. Except that stage was set up for men like him, not for women like me.

Decades on, I can hear him, whispering in my ear.
What will I do with you?
'It became his favourite phrase. On repeat – *What will I do with you?*' I say to my guest as they look up from their papers.

'Do you think he was intending to kill you?'

And of course, I forget, we should be mind-readers too. Anticipate their needs whilst forgetting our own. We should know what they want, what they desire and, if we don't, well, we are to blame. Let me pass you the noose, sir, whilst I stand on the chair.

'I think he didn't know what to do. I think his question was in many ways sincere. He didn't know what to do with me. I have no doubt he knew his options, but which one to choose.'

A) Keep the girl. B) Let her go. C) Kill her.

'Did you ask to leave?'

'No. I mean *what?* Do you not think that is a stupid fucking question? Oh, excuse me, Mr Starr, but perhaps our little abduction experience is over and maybe I can go out in the world now. I won't tell the police. Scout's honour. Stupid question.'

I lift my hands and they fall against the table, the metal of my shackles banging against the cheap wood. They always do this, I thought my guest was better than this; they shift the blame back to me. Did I ask to leave? No one has ever asked if any of my victims asked me to stop. Not a single person. One of them did. One of them begged. My guest looks at the floor. Are they ashamed? They should be.

'What I mean is, this was a time of change and I wanted to know how you were changing as well as Ben.'

'He asked me to sleep on the sofa.'

That was the first big change. He said he wanted the bedroom to be in perfect condition in case he had to look after other little girls and, after all, I wasn't little any more.

His phone. The one I barely knew existed was now glued to his hand as he flicked through images. When I peeked over his shoulder, there she was, the little red-headed girl, staring back at me. She was to take my bed, my room, my hideous dresses. I pictured his hands wandering across her body. At night, in my head, she would cry for her mother. The reality of my situation only began to dawn on me when I pictured another little girl in it and without a single breathing child, I knew what it was to be a mother.

'How did you feel about that? The sofa?' my guest asks. 'Was it a relief?'

'The sofa was uncomfortable. I'd lie awake. He gave me time to think.'

A rage crept into me at the thought of my sentence being passed down to another. Would she have to wear those stupid lace dresses? Would he tell her that her mother was sick? The questions would play through my mind like film credits. I was willing to be the finale if it stopped him from kidnapping the girl in the picture. That's when I learnt what it really is to be a woman. To be a woman is to sacrifice. I was willing to give my life for a little girl I had never seen in the flesh. I had been numb for so long, I needed to imagine my life happening to someone who I saw as pure and innocent to understand what had happened to me.

'He was either going to keep me or kill me. I'm almost ashamed at how long it took me to realize that.'

'You have nothing to be ashamed of.'

'That night my period began, and I took the blood and smeared it all over my neck. I screamed and screamed from my favourite room: the bathroom. Ben's feet pounded on the staircase as he raced to me. I had fallen and I would bleed to death if he didn't take me to hospital.'

This was my clever little plan. To trick Ben into taking me to the hospital, and as I lay there screaming, I remembered the black duffel bag and I realized: the only way he is taking me out of this house is in a bag.

'Ben shrugged and went downstairs. He came back, though. Knelt beside me, and on reflection he must have known I was faking it.'

He said to me, *I know you've been in a lot of pain lately. I'm going to make that better.* He sprinkled white powder into my glass and he mixed it. This is how he wanted it to end. He was going to drug me and then God knows what. Coward.

'Maddie? Maddie? Are you okay?'

I look up and my guest is staring at me. In their hand is a box of tissues. I pluck one from the box and dab at my tears as my guest watches on.

'He hand-fed me sleeping pills and forced them down me with stale wine. And then everything went black. When I awoke, a crying child was standing over me.'

46

2007 – Manchester

Sloane had again asked me which rock I had crawled out from under when I confessed to never having eaten a Chinese takeaway. I didn't have an answer. Now, we're walking down the road to her flat with a white plastic bag, the handles straining from the weight of the food we've ordered. As my life moves on, I find myself needing explanations less and less. I know I like lemon drizzle cake, I don't like pretending to smoke, and my destiny in life is not to work at Queen of the Burgers but to make the world a safer place.

I notice it first. Sloane keeps moving as I stop dead in the street. She's a couple of feet ahead of me when the bag of food drops to the floor. Noodles and rice spill from containers. A dark liquid seeps out and is absorbed by the concrete, forming a blood like stain. Trance-like, she moves closer to her flat.

Bright red graffiti spells out the word GHOUL across the walls. The windows are smashed in. I approach it. I wipe my finger against the L, still wet.

'They were just here,' I say, looking around, but Sloane is on the floor saving our dinner.

'Most of this will be okay, I'll just leave the bits that are on the floor,' she shouts over to me. 'You will still have the taste sensation that is a prawn cracker topped with chow mein.' Her words are friendly but she sounds robotic. Across the front door is what I hope is tomato sauce, B list horror-movie style, but as I get closer, I gag on the smell of metal. Blood.

'Sloane,' I shout. 'I think we need to call the police.'

Her eyes wander over the graffiti, the blood on the door and her smashed-in windows.

'After dinner,' she says, matter of fact. It's as if someone has littered her front yard, not destroyed the entire exterior of her flat.

Inside, glass is scattered all over her floor. My boots crunch as I walk over to her kitchen and scan for a brush. She stands and stares, not moving. I sweep away the glass, moving it to a central spot as she takes plates from the kitchen cupboard.

'I'll warm the plates in the oven for a minute or two,' she says, watching me attempt to sweep the glass into a dustpan.

'You'll have to board up these windows,' I say.

'I've already texted the landlord.'

She places all the containers onto the table and takes plates from her cupboards.

'What did your landlord say?'

'He said I have thirty days to leave.'

I walk over to the table and place the containers back in the bag. I get bin bags from under her sink and open her wardrobe. The clothes crinkle as I stuff them into bags.

'It'd be quicker if you helped,' I say.

'What are you doing?' Sloane is blank-faced. Robotic almost. As if she has not digested what has happened and is going through the motions.

'Packing, we're going to mine. Can I borrow your phone? I have no credit.'

'Credit? How old are you? Fourteen?'

She passes me her phone as I shrink into myself. Again, I've done something odd without realizing. Brian answers on the first ring and I ask for his help. He turns up five minutes later and I load up Sloane's belongings before he sees her. Thunder creases across his face when he does, but he doesn't say anything. I step over the congealing takeaway rotting in the sun.

'Do you like Chinese, Brian? We've got plenty,' Sloane says.

His fingers grip the steering wheel as he passes through an amber light. He glances in the front mirror.

'Emily wouldn't have liked you.'

There's a short silence filled with static. It was sunny a second ago.

'Did she like you?' Sloane asks.

The brakes screech as he slams down on them. The car behind honks its horn and overtakes. He moves the car to the side of the road and switches the engine off.

'Get out.' His voice is low and his face red. Spittle flies from his mouth. 'Get out.'

'Sloane,' I say.

'It's okay. I'll walk, it's only five minutes away.'

She smiles at Brian as she gets out of the car: a thick, smug smile. The car shakes as she slams the door. I want to follow but he speeds off and I'm not sure I should leave her belongings with him. There's a slight tremble in my hand and I pinch the skin between my thumb and finger.

'You need tenants, and she needs a place to live,' I say.

'She thinks I'm a murderer.'

We sit in silence and a woman pushing a pram passes us.

'Are you?'

He takes a deep breath and turns to face me. 'No.' His shoulders slump and he wraps his fingers around the steering wheel. 'I didn't mean to get angry. Your mate hit a sore spot,' he says. 'I'm not sure Emily did like me. Night before she died, I thought she was seeing someone else.'

My mind rolls back to the previous tenants, Blondie and Brunette. They said they heard arguing the night before and Emily was coming home late.

He stares ahead.

'I thought she liked me. I'm stupid,' he says, pressing the palm of his hand against his forehead. 'I get a bit lonely, sometimes.'

I know that feeling. Being on the outskirts, whilst everyone else moves along in their life without a hiccup. His bottom lip trembles.

'We met with the women who used to rent the other rooms,' I say.

He lets out a groan and rolls his eyes.

'Awful girls. I should have booted them out. They complained about Emily so much I had to put a clause in her contract that I would inspect her room each month to shut them up.' He glances away. 'They thought I was hassling her out, too. I'm such a coward.'

'So, you didn't actually inspect her room each month?'

He shakes his head no, as if I have said the most ridiculous thing.

'Nah, I never inspected Emily's room. Like I said, she was house-proud. She was so angry when her mate,' Brian's eyes roll to the side as he tries to remember something, 'Karen?'

'Karla,' I correct.

'Yeah, Karla,' he says. Brian turns the key in the ignition

and we pull back out into the road. 'She popped over to visit Emily. She used to come over for a brew every so often. Lovely woman. She looked after Emily.' We stop at a red light. 'Which is why I was confused when I caught them arguing. Emily left the room to make them a cuppa, but when she came back, Karla was rifling through her drawers. Happened about a week before she went missing.'

'What was she looking for?'

Brian shrugs, and we both sit in silence as confusion eats at us. I make a mental note. Maybe Cody would know?

When we pull up to the house, Sloane is walking down the street, her face lobster-coloured from the sun. Brian looks at her and then back to me.

'Rent is eighty quid every Friday. You can pick either of the empty rooms.'

Sloane opens the lid of a wheelie bin and drops our Chinese takeaway into it. I guess I'll have to wait a little longer to find out if I like spring rolls and sweet-and-sour chicken.

It doesn't take long to unpack Sloane's stuff. Four black bin bags, a suitcase and a laptop. She's quick to turn the room from blank canvas to something homely.

'Do you think we're safe here?' she asks.

'I don't think he did it,' I say.

Sloane perches on the corner of the bed as I stand. She places her head in her hands.

'No,' she says. 'Neither do I. We'll catch him, though. Whoever the Maniac is. We will catch him.'

She pulls her corkboard from a black bag. All the images are attached still, and she pulls on the one of Brian and chucks it in the bin.

'Yeah,' I say, looking at the faces staring at me from Sloane's corkboard. 'We're getting close. I can feel it.'

47

Cody snitched. I was planning to ask him about Karla and Emily's friendship, but no one will look me in the eye or say hello. Karla, hard-faced as ever, stands square shouldered at the till next to me but refuses to engage. It's official. I'm a villain in a maroon uniform.

'Shall I sweep up, Karla?'

She stares straight ahead as if I've said nothing. Talking to Sloane seems like a bigger deal than it should be around here. The only customers are sitting in a far corner. A couple who have barely spoken a word to each other. I dawdle into the kitchen. Cody's head is bobbing up and down to his music. He freezes when he sees me.

'What have you said, Cody?'

He cringes, his body turning inward.

'We don't keep secrets from each other. We're loyal.' He fist-bumps his own chest and blushes. 'Sorry, I was trying to persuade them to speak to Sloane but it backfired.' He shrugs, his hand rubbing the back of his neck. Karla appears in the kitchen and Cody looks away from me and chops an onion. Witnessing his silence, she leaves again.

'Cody?'

He says nothing as his eyes water from the onions. Outside, the basement doors open outwards from the ground and Aaron appears. He bends to lock the door but struggles to keep his balance. It takes him three, no four, attempts to close the padlock. He staggers into the kitchen and I scurry back to the tills.

I hear Cody and Aaron talking in frantic hisses, their voices carrying on a wave of caustic rage. Karla looks over her shoulder. Her eyes wide, as if she is on a rollercoaster and it has reached the top of the highest peak. The customers in the corner look over as the hisses turn to shouts. Karla races into the kitchen.

'Aaron,' she shouts, as if she is reprimanding a teenager.

Aaron stares at her with sheer insolence as he plays the role Karla has cast for him.

'My darling wife.' He opens his arms, but the gesture feels mocking. He turns his head and notices me in the entrance. 'I wish they'd give me the silent treatment. You don't know how lucky you are. These people,' he waves his arm at Cody and Karla, 'they will steal your joy and tell you it's for your own good.'

'Come on, mate.' Cody steps towards Aaron.

Karla waves Cody away. I stare at the sign above the stainless-steel basin telling me how to correctly wash my hands.

'You're a bunch of petty fucks. Enjoy the silence, Maddie, I'm sure it's better than the screaming in my head.'

'Aaron,' Karla scolds. 'Get upstairs and sleep it off in the office.' Karla turns to me with a lip curled. 'You get back to work,' she barks at me.

Aaron laughs.

'They don't like you, Maddie.'

'Aaron . . .' Karla's voice is almost a growl, certainly a warning.

'What?' he says. 'I'm not the one acting like I've got something to hide.'

Karla grabs Aaron by the sleeve and pulls him out of the kitchen; his boots are out of sync with hers on the stairway.

'We loved her,' Cody says, staring at the floor. 'We loved Emily. Your mate is turning her into a spectacle.'

I slink back to the tills; I have no response. It's been easy for me to sum up Sloane's activities as noble and for want of genuine justice. But to Sloane, Emily does boil down to a murder victim, her entire life irrelevant until that point. Does Sloane see her mother in the same way? Everything before her tragic death a blur, her murder shadowing everything else? I will give these people the justice they deserve.

Charlie walks in as the only other customers walk out. The scrape of bin bags against the floor comes from the kitchen and I look up at the clock.

'Fancy seeing you here,' he says, his eyes locking with mine. 'Just a coffee today.'

'No Frank?' I say.

Charlie shakes his head no. 'We have to go home sometimes . . . What time are you knocking off?' Charlie continues, maintaining steady eye contact with me as if he wants to gauge my reaction. I shrug. 'I'll wait down the road for you. I think we need a chat.' He leaves with a cardboard cup of coffee in his hand.

I look towards the ceiling as muffled shouting comes from above. Karla and Aaron. An older woman enters the store wearing leggings and an oversized jumper and approaches the till.

'Good evening, Your Majesty, what would you like to feast on?'

'Yeah, I'll have a viscount meal, extra pickles on the burger, Royal size.'

My plastic crown slips as I hit the order into the till. Karla is red in the face as she reappears and her eyes rest on me in an intense stare as I take the customer's money. They remain on me as the customer takes her food and walks out of the store.

'I can't bear the sight of you,' Karla hisses. 'Your voice goes through me and you're shit at your job. You're fired.'

Another first. I rip the plastic crown from my head and I toss it at her. The urge to grab a kitchen knife and pluck out Karla's eyes so she doesn't have to see me ripples under my skin.

'Good,' I shrug. 'Wouldn't want to waste my life here.'

For a moment I glimpse something other than anger on Karla's face. Does she think she's wasted her life here? Was Emily's life wasted here?

My shoulders slump as I enter the kitchen; I pinch the skin between my thumb and forefinger hard. Cody looks over his shoulder at me. His music is subdued. He offers me a meek smile, but I don't return it as I enter the stairwell and stomp up the stairs of Queen of the Burgers and into the locker room.

I stare at the picture of Emily. This entire time, she has sat in that frame as Employee of the Month grinning at me. I've learnt so much about her, I feel as if I know her. I don't. It's Karla, Cody and Aaron who really knew her. I have failed. Another fresh experience, but this is more like wanting to throw up from smoking than eating lemon drizzle cake.

I stare at Emily and she stares back. Then a knock on the

door, gentle taps like a whisper in the ear. The door opens without me saying anything and Cody pops his head around.

'I'm so sorry,' he says. 'I didn't think Karla would fire you.'

I shake my head as he enters the room, the door closing with nothing more than a tap. He pads across to me and takes a seat.

'It could be worse,' I say, nodding towards the picture of Emily. 'How do you get over losing a friend?'

He looks down at the cheap aubergine carpet and then back up at me. His eyes moisten. He shrugs. 'I don't think you do.'

I take the Employee of the Month image of Emily off the wall and hand it to him. He holds it with both hands as if he is afraid he'll drop it.

'I'm sorry about what happened to your friend,' I say.

'Me too. I wish I could've saved her.'

'It was nice meeting you, Cody,' I say as I leave the room. He doesn't reply, transfixed by Emily's smile. I'm down the stairs and out of the back door before the urge to turn Karla into burger meat becomes too strong.

My backpack is light and bounces against my back as I speed-walk down the road, passing metal shutters and overflowing bins. Parked on the street is Charlie's car. The passenger door pops open as I approach. I slide into the passenger seat and the door clunks as it closes.

Charlie is sipping on what must now be tepid coffee. He looks at me, his eyes above the black plastic lid.

'Your colleagues didn't look very happy with you.'

'I've been fired.'

I shrug as he lowers his coffee cup and gives me an easy-going smile, as if nothing is wrong with the world. As if we were friends. As if there wasn't a serial killer on the loose.

'Sloane, right?' Charlie continues.

'Yeah, I bet you have the same problems with Frank.'

He switches the key in the engine and the car comes to life. In the sky, the moon looks like a smooth bite has been taken out of it.

'Why didn't you arrest me?'

'I should have,' he says, glancing in my direction. 'And no, the opposite. Frank is actually very popular with our colleagues.' He glances in the wing mirror. In the distance the Queen of the Burgers sign flashes in neon. I watch until it fades into the distance.

'Frank's popular?'

'He is. Some might say charming.'

He taps his fingers against the steering wheel, lets out a little laugh, and an awkward moment sits between us.

The vehicle slows as we approach the red-light district, and from the outside we could appear as kerb crawlers. Or even the Manchester Maniac hunting our next victim.

'Do you think he could be here?' My heart quickens at the thought of my king flea stalking the red-light area.

'Probably not. Like I said, we all have to go home sometimes.'

Nonetheless, he doesn't slow the car. Women move towards the kerb with a smile, but Charlie keeps moving until we are clear of the area.

'So, Mia's flat was empty?'

The question comes from nowhere, abrupt like a falling brick in a forest. It stuns me. For a moment I feel naïve; for the first time since I can remember, I didn't question Charlie's motives and I got into his car without a qualm. Am I adjusting to an ordinary life? Is this how it feels to be Karla or even Sloane? Not constantly bartering with a devil that might not exist?

'Nothing. Like you said, it was empty.'

'You know.' The indicator ticks as he takes a breath. 'I thought you were going to say that. Tell you what. I'll tell you something if you tell me something.'

The car accelerates as a light turns from green to amber. I wouldn't have thought of Charlie as the amber gambler, or any type of risk taker, no matter how small. I look at him, his profile, a funny shiver runs through me that I don't recognize.

'You first.'

He shrugs.

'All the victims died of drowning, apart from Emily Sykes. Rainwater was found in their lungs.'

'But they were all found in the woods,' I say. 'Is he killing them somewhere else?'

Charlie shakes his head no.

'So how is he drowning them?'

We pause at a roundabout. Cars whizz, their headlights dazzle as they pass.

'Your guess is as good as mine,' he says almost in a whisper. 'Your turn.'

'Mia's flat was empty on the whole. Cold.'

He slows the car as we enter a residential area near my house. He drives slowly and steadily over the speed bumps.

'I suspected she might have somewhere to live and was keeping it secret.' He pauses. 'Given her past. So, on the whole, it was empty?'

Charlie emphasizes *on the whole*. I bite my tongue. Literally. My teeth clamping on the side, worried I will tell Charlie everything.

'Spill.'

I figure if she was stopped and searched by the police it

would be on their systems anyway. Maybe this is a good way to build some trust.

'We found a stop-and-search notification.'

His neck snaps in my direction, and we narrowly miss a cat racing across the road.

'Do you have it?'

I rummage in my backpack, looking for the scrap of paper we had found shoved down the sofa. He pulls the car over by my house but keeps the engine running. I pass him the notification, but he doesn't look down at it.

'I don't like him. Frank, that is. He's popular, but that doesn't mean he's a good person,' I say.

He laughs for a second, but a wary look falls over his face. He looks down at the notification and something appears in his eyes, not joy or anger. Something I don't recognize, something magic.

'Thanks for the lift,' I say.

'Anytime,' he mumbles, his eyes focused on the paper.

48

The TV blasts from Brian's room as I pass. A woman broadcaster asking if the Manchester Maniac will ever be caught? If the police are doing enough? I wonder how Charlie and Frank feel seeing such news items, a public critique on their abilities as detectives.

As I enter my room, I think how nice it is to have Sloane under the same roof as me. The drum roll of the shower makes me think she must be upstairs. I lie on the bed and grab my small blue ball and toss it in the air and watch it fall towards my face before catching and throwing it again. The rhythm relaxes me. The beating water of the shower stops and is replaced by footsteps on the stairs.

Sloane is wrapped in a towel when she bursts through my door without knocking. Her hair clings to her face and drops of water fall to the floor. I jump up and grab another towel.

'Wrap your hair,' I say, louder than I intend. I throw the towel at her and she wraps it around her sodden hair; when she looks up, I realize she's crying.

'What's wrong? Is it Mia? I know it's tough and unfair.'

She shakes and I try to figure out if she is cold or whatever has happened has literally shaken her up.

'Is it Brian? Has he done something?'

She shakes her head no.

'Maddie,' she says with a stutter, 'I'm so happy. I've never been so happy.' My mouth opens but no words appear as she falls to the floor and sobs tears of joy. Her fist clinging to the towel to keep herself covered up. She uses her other hand to hold her phone. On the screen is an email from a woman I haven't heard of.

'*How to Catch a Serial Killer* is going to be published,' she says through tears. 'A literary agent has signed me.'

I sit cross-legged facing her. 'Your mum would be so proud,' I say.

She nods, cries some more. Of course, her mum would be proud, because Sloane is an orphan who is writing a book about the very thing that orphaned her – a violent man. Soon her tears change to laughter, and she wipes at her face.

'I'm being so silly,' she says with a grin. 'I just can't believe it. I don't know if I will ever feel this happy again.'

She pulls me in for an embrace and I don't resist. She smells clean and soapy. Her skin soft.

'Let's celebrate,' I say.

I stand, damp from Sloane, and leave the room. In the kitchen I root around cupboards looking for something worthy of the occasion, but I'm quick to be defeated. I contemplate knocking on Brian's door but fear he'd want to join in the celebrations.

Sloane appears in the kitchen, dressed and fresh-looking.

'You won't find anything in here. I'll go to the shop at the end of the road and get something fizzy and special, okay?'

I nod, realizing that this is it: this is my Fizz Friday and Sloane is my friend. All my doubts were wrong. Together we would drink and toast Sloane's success. I'm beaming as she walks away and I go back to the room. I tidy up a bit, wondering if I should put on some music or light a candle. What was appropriate for celebrations with friends? After tonight, I would know.

I grab my little blue ball and lie on my bed. I throw it towards the ceiling and watch it fall towards my face and catch it again. I do this on repeat. Then I realize, I hadn't thought about Ben all day and maybe not even yesterday. I don't think time is healing me, but life is. Living one. Free. With friends. I might have been fired, but there'll be plenty of job offers once we find Emily's killer. Maybe I'll write a book too.

Sloane startles me as she re-enters the room with a bottle of what she calls *Bolly*. I think about how many complaints there were about Emily when she lived here. How Brian insisted on monthly room inspections. Plaster flakes from the wall. My mind flits to the empty apartment and the key in her ceiling. It flits to Robbie Jones and the way he kept his key in his hanging basket.

'Sloane, what if she was keeping something in there?' I gesture to the ceiling. 'Brian said he caught Karla snooping around Emily's room. What if Emily has hidden something?'

'I doubt it, but let's have a look.'

Sloane places the champagne on the floor and joins me on the bed. We both wobble. The mattress dipping whenever we try to get some height.

'This is no good,' Sloane says, moving the bed. She crouches down below the hole, and I climb on her shoulders. I sway as I touch the ceiling but, as I find my balance, my hand goes straight through. There was a hole. I feel around and my skin grazes against a metal box. It's jammed in tight and the tips of my fingers ache as I try to manoeuvre it out of its small home.

'There's something in here,' I say.

I pull, and plaster crumbles onto Sloane's face as she groans with the exertion of holding me up. She stumbles and, as we both fall, the box comes with me. We're entangled on the bed, laughing. I look up at the hole we have left in the ceiling.

'No way,' she says. 'What's in the box?'

It's small and decorated with grooves and curves. A small bird with its wings spread out is carved into the top. It flips open. Five rolled ten-pound notes, tied together with a hairband sit in the corner, a half-used lipstick, a tatty piece of paper with a recipe for nachos, and a cinema stub.

'Memory box,' Sloane shrugs. 'Might not even be Emily's.'

At the bottom is a photograph face down, with its corners sitting snugly within the box. I tug on it with care and it springs out at me.

Sloane grabs the photo. 'The box is Emily's,' she says with a hint of disappointment. She shakes her head. I lean over Sloane and look at the image. In the photograph, Emily beams at the camera, a white sheet up to her collarbone. A topless Aaron kisses her cheek, his arm raised to take the image.

'I think we know who the Manchester Maniac is,' I say. 'He has a padlocked basement at work.'

Sloane rummages through her bags and pulls out a pair of bolt cutters with a flourish. We step over my first bottle of fizz and I am safe in the knowledge it will taste even sweeter once I have murdered the Manchester Maniac.

49

2027 – HMP Bronzefield

I like to think my guest and I were always destined to meet. Each one of our timelines woven together. Today they look healthy, all white teeth, clean hair, and is that a tan I spot? They lean back in their chair. Over our meetings, they have become comfortable in this room, in this prison, with a guard standing at the door. I spent my weekend avoiding the inmates, avoiding the guards as I chomped down on painkillers. As many as I could trick the guards into giving me.

'Did you have a nice weekend?'

They look up from their rucksack as they pull a paper wallet from out of it.

'Lovely thank you, Maddie. I went to Devon. It's a bit of a drive but worth it for the coastal views.'

Bingo. They did go away for the weekend.

'I've never been to the beach.'

'I remember you saying,' they say, placing the paper wallet and the Dictaphone on the table.

I try to summon the echoes of seagulls squawking, salt on

my lips, the smell of doughnuts sprinkled in sugar, being blinded by the neon candyfloss and the flashing lights of the amusement arcade. Each time I'm just out of reach, the imagination train refusing to leave the station.

'Maybe, one day, I'll get there.'

They look at me for a moment, head tilted ever so slightly with their eyes soft. They smile.

'Maybe.'

They look away. They're a terrible liar. I found that endearing to start with, but over the years I've learnt terrible liars are walking weapons. They'll wound you, over and over, with their kind words and their good intentions. A thousand paper-cuts.

'Found it,' they say, raising a pen in the air from their backpack. They return to their seat and we look at each other for a moment. Them tanned from their weekend away and me pasty in a pair of handcuffs. In a different timeline, maybe I'm tanned too.

'Picking up where we left off.' My guest pauses. 'It must have been a shock waking up to realize it wasn't just you and Ben anymore? Did you recognize the crying girl?'

'It was Katie.'

I later learnt, as I lay dying on the lino floor of the bathroom, he had entered the local hospital dressed as a doctor. My little plan fed into his much bigger plan. Katie and her grandma were visiting her new sibling, and Ben Starr wandered up to them and offered to take Katie for fifteen minutes so they could focus on the baby. They didn't agree at first. Then a nurse insisted it might do them some good and so they smiled and their waking hell began.

'I remember when she went missing,' my guest says. 'It was everywhere. All over the papers. On the news.' My guest shakes their head as they say this, as if they still can't quite believe Ben's audacity.

My guest taps a pen against their folder, as if they are trying to run that scenario through their head.

'I remember her tears falling on my face. That's what woke me, and at first I thought it was a dream. Then I realized it was the little girl from the pictures.'

'What did she say?'

She was so scared. My hope – the very thing I had clung onto for so long – disappeared and was replaced by something I have never quite managed to shake. Rage.

'She wanted her mummy and she wanted to know where her little brother was.'

I told her the same lie Ben had told me. I told her they were sick, but we were going to find them together.

'I asked her to be brave and she nodded. She stayed in the bathroom and I made my way to the top of the stairs and peered down. He was asleep. Passed out.'

I went into his bedroom. It smelt musty and unkempt. I ripped the curtains from the windows, the stars stared back at me and they encouraged me. I launched myself into the glass, and I bounced off it. I repeated it in what had once been my bedroom. I couldn't break the glass, it was hard; reinforced.

'I tried breaking through the bedroom windows. They were big enough for us both to try and escape from. I couldn't leave her there with him. He would kill me, and she would never be found,' I say.

Then it dawned on me – my favourite room in the house, the only one that let the sun in. The bathroom window. The frosted glass wouldn't be the same as the other rooms and that was why he wouldn't let me in there when he wasn't at home. But the window was small, really small.

'He had locked up the bleach, the knives, the razor blades, and anything long enough to hang myself with years ago. Also the hammers, and anything either too blunt or too sharp.'

We wouldn't both be leaving that house. I went back into the bathroom and I put Katie in the empty bath and asked her to cover her eyes. I wrapped a towel around my arm and I smashed the glass. I thought he would come running, but nothing. He was passed out from red wine. The fresh air. It knocked me still for a moment when it hit me; it was as if my lungs had been starved.

'I remember asking if she was brave and she nodded. I told her when I dropped her she might injure herself, but whatever happened, whatever pain she was in, she had to be brave and drag herself to a phone box.'

My guest nods, he knows this story, the world does. Brave Katie.

'She broke a leg,' my guest says. 'But she managed to drag herself half a mile to a phone box and dial 999. Her mum had taught her to do that in an emergency.'

Her young voice alerted the police, who raced to her. Of course, I didn't know this, I didn't think help would ever come for me. It had been twelve years.

I thought the only way I was getting out of there was death, but as I watched Katie crawl away across a street I'd never seen, power surged through me. I remembered the flames licking my hands when Ben forced me to burn Reeta Smith's messages. I was never going to allow the monster sleeping downstairs to touch another girl. He made the decision to die at my hands. He signed his own death certificate. In the end, they always do.

A sharp beep knocks me out of my thoughts. On the table

in front of me, the Dictaphone flashes a red light. My guest reaches down and inspects it.

'I think the battery is running low.'

They look past me to the guard.

'You don't have any spare AA batteries, do you?'

The guard shakes their head no.

'In the entire prison, you don't have any spare batteries?' Their voice is sharp and exasperated. It tickles me, the guard receiving a taste of their own medicine.

'I'm not meant to leave you alone with the prisoner.'

They overestimate me. What good am I shackled and half dead? Who is it I am meant to murder? Do they think every person who has been in my life is now under soil? That I am not capable of love, empathy, friendship? Did they not hear the story of how I saved a six-year-old? So obsessed with the fleas I've murdered, they forget about the victims I've saved.

'I pass a clerical office, thirty seconds down the corridor, every time I come here. You'll be what? One minute? I think I'll be okay.'

'I-I don't think . . .'

My guest raises a hand to stop the guard. 'Go. I'll be okay.'

I can sense a moment of hesitation, their body unsure whether to come or go, and then the click of a door. Never have I been so grateful for dying batteries.

'Are you okay, Maddie? This must be tough.'

'My head hurts. The pain gets worse each day. But talking about those awful men is fine. I'm glad I killed them.'

My mind is desperate, trying to remember how I feel in the moments I take their lives so I can relive the power over and over. My guest frowns at me.

The door swings open and the guard throws a packet of batteries onto the table with a thud. My guest uses their teeth to rip open the packet. My mind wanders to places it shouldn't go, to places I wish I had been when I had the chance nineteen years earlier.

The red light disappears from the Dictaphone as my guest slips the fresh batteries in.

'There we go,' they say, placing it back on the table. 'Sorry about that . . . So, what happened next?'

50

2007 – Manchester

Despite her being inches taller than me, Sloane and I walk in tandem, with the sun setting at our backs. Our strides matching. We discussed getting a taxi, but we decided we'd make it quicker on foot. The basement Aaron keeps under lock and key is an obvious first port of call. Once a den for their friendship group, it's now a forbidden area; he must be hiding something in there. Something that will prove, once and for all, Aaron Queen is the Manchester Maniac.

As we approach, the Queen of the Burgers building looks sad, with chairs placed on tables. I put a hand on Sloane's arm to gesture to her to stop.

'Cameras. There's monitors everywhere and they'll still be locking up.'

She nods.

'Good thinking. There's a dark spot around the back.'

My mind drifts to when Sloane and I had first met, her being chased off by Brian and then Karla at the burger place. No one took her seriously, but here we are, this is our moment.

We are going to catch a serial killer. The man slaughtering women.

We walk the perimeter, the very fences meant to keep us out guide us to our destination, The ground squelches underfoot, my feet slip on small rocks and wet grass. I try not to stay in one spot for too long, aware my shoes are leaving impressions as I sink into the mud.

'Here,' Sloane whispers, shining the torch from her phone on a hole in the fence. 'This is how I used to get in without being spotted.'

Karla's voice comes from the kitchen area and Aaron steps outside. He bangs the kitchen door closed. Sloane and I stay behind the fence as the scene unfolds.

'Sleep at your parents' tonight,' he shouts. 'I want a divorce.'

Aaron marches to his car and reverses out of Queen of the Burgers at speed. Karla follows in tears. She is followed by Cody who hugs her. Cody guides her back into the kitchen and the clunk of the lock echoes around me and Sloane.

I duck through the hole, dodging empty cardboard boxes. The smell of rotting meat hangs on the air from the bins. I lead the way to the basement doors.

'Do you think we should come back later? After dark?' I whisper.

'No,' Sloane hisses. 'We need to know now. Aaron might be looking for other victims as we speak.'

We both crouch down and I hold the padlock still. A crack makes us both jump as the bolt cutters make light work of the metal. Instinctively we both look around, but no one is there to hear it, nor is anyone there to hear the creaky yawn of the doors as we open them.

Concrete steps lead down towards a vast blackness. Sloane focuses the light on our feet so we don't stumble.

'Do you smell that?'

A pungent metallic smell hits us like a wall. Sloane lifts her torch as we reach the bottom of the stairs, and her hand fumbles across the wall for a light switch. A piece of string hanging from the ceiling bounces against my head as I enter the room. I pull on it. The room illuminates. Sloane gasps.

On a table are jam jars filled with red liquid. Metallics waft towards me, the scent lining the inside of my mouth with a thin film. I don't need to inspect the jars further to know it's blood in them. Are these from the victims? Does one of these jars contain Emily? What sick trophy collection is this? An A4 piece of paper sits on the table. I pick it up: an invoice for cow's blood from a local butcher. Why would Aaron want cow's blood?

'It's animal blood . . .' I trail off as Sloane cuts me off.

'Don't touch anything; we can't contaminate anything.'

And the penny drops. Sloane and I have the same goal but want different outcomes. She wants a name and a face. I want justice. She's snapping images with her camera when I notice the shrine, a table, a red cloth draped over it, a candle no longer burning and pictures of Emily. Some framed. Some not. Newspaper clippings scattered between the photographs.

'I think it's time to call the police,' she says. 'Do we 'fess to breaking in here, or an anonymous tip-off?'

I want to feel heat from giant orange flames, hear the screams only fire can exorcise. I want the flea dead.

'Maybe we should sleep on this?'

She pauses for a second, an eyebrow raised, her jaw drops open and she appears half stunned from my suggestion.

'What? Are you being serious?' Her words spit like bullets. 'No, I have what I need for the book. We need to pass this over to the police so we can get justice. Not just for Emily but for every woman Aaron has murdered.'

I could call Aaron, tell him to meet me here. Let him drink until he has passed out drunk and set fire to the entire basement. Lock the doors with a new padlock and run. Aaron needs to be squashed. Sloane puts her phone to her ear. Raises her hand to silence me as I try to object.

'I'm ringing the police. I'll ask for Charlie.'

I try to tell her to stop but she waves me off and shushes me. I'm back to the beginning. All the choice being removed from me – stripped.

'Charlie,' Sloane says into the phone. 'No, I don't know his surname. It's about the Manchester Maniac. Tell him it's Victoria Sloane.' Her words swim around my head as she explains what we have found, where we are, what the conclusion is to the operator. I want to run. Instead, I walk. One foot after another, I'm at the bottom of the concrete steps when her hand lands on my shoulder.

'Where you going?' She steps in front of me, blocking my exit. Claustrophobia kicks in. One way in. One way out. No windows. I struggle for breath. 'You can't go now, this is it. This is everything we worked for.'

No, Sloane was a bystander in all of this. We are here because of me and I cannot deny, all this time, only one thought was ticking through my head, feeding away at the back of my thoughts. I want to kill the Manchester Maniac. Sloane is stopping that and taking credit for my work.

She yelps as I push her to one side and race up the stairs. I run home, under the stars, with the shadow of Ben Starr nipping at my heels.

51

2027 – HMP Bronzefield

When it's all over, I think I'll miss this green room. It's been nice to sit here away from the rest of the prison, even with a guard at the door. My guest hasn't arrived. I amble over to the blinds, the guard's gaze lingers on me, but I part two panels and look outside. I'm waiting for a reprimand. It doesn't come.

The corner shop has people coming and going. Cars whizz up and down the street. A bus stops outside the prison and people depart. A woman with a pushchair struggles to get off the bus and a man stops to help her.

'I think it's cruel. What harm can come from you seeing outside?' says the guard.

The blind panels snap shut as I move my hand. I turn and take my seat.

'A thousand paper-cuts.'

'Particularly given your situation,' they say. 'I don't know how you're getting the right treatment without us transporting you to the hospital once in a while. My uncle had the same thing and spent half of his final years being poked and prodded by a doctor.'

Because I refused. I refused to go to a hospital and see a consultant, I refused the scans and I have refused any treatment. I want this to be over. Why would I extend a life trapped behind four walls, tormented by my own memories.

My guest is smiling as they come through the door. They nod at the guard and take the seat opposite me. They're quick to organize themselves. We exchange pleasantries.

'Let's get cracking,' they say. 'You were meant to be dead. Ben had tried to kill you but instead you survived and helped Katie escape.'

Katie dropped like a stone through the bathroom window, but she was a trooper as she dragged one leg behind as she crawled away down a street I hadn't seen before. I went downstairs. It was anticlimactic. Ben was passed out during my greatest act of defiance, but I was sure he wasn't going to miss the next one. I went downstairs and took a tea towel. I rifled through his pocket and pulled out his lighter. The flames flickered as I hovered a blue and white checked tea towel over it. It caught in seconds. I shouted his name. He awoke. He looked like he had seen a ghost, and perhaps to him that is what he thought he was seeing. I dropped the tea towel on his lap. All that red wine. He was one giant fireball before he could scream, *What am I going to do with you?*

'I screamed from the top of my lungs – *you should have killed me properly. You can't do anything right, you fucking flea.*'

I went upstairs and I lay on my bed.

'You never considered help was coming?'

'No. I was drifting in and out of consciousness. The smoke was thick, fire crackled and everything was warm. The firefighter was a dark shadow amongst the smoke, his mask demonic, and I thought: This is it. This creature is here to take me to hell.'

My guest takes a sip of what smells like strong coffee from a flask they've managed to get through security. The coffee is as dark as the smoke from that night.

The firefighter swooped me up in his arms as floorboards gave way, creaking followed by bangs. Outside he handed me to a police officer who wrapped me up in a blanket. I looked up and I saw the stars. They twinkled as if they were pleased to see me again. I was pleased to see them.

The mass of people outside, staring at Ben's house, caused panic to creep into me. The police officer covered my face with the blanket and whispered in my ear it would be okay and paramedics were en route. I must have passed out. When my eyes flickered open, I was in a white room. I held still. Expecting Ben Starr or another version of him to walk in.

'I learnt what had happened to me through the whispers of nurses as they gossiped in corridors. Young girl. Held captive. Bad way.'

They were hesitant around me, as if at any minute I might lunge at them from the bed. They spoke softly, moved slowly, told me what they were about to do and sought permission before they touched me. I was assigned a chubby woman to advocate for me, I don't remember her name. She was more messenger than advocate. I feared for all these women. I feared for what they had seen in the world and for what they hadn't.

'I didn't have many answers so instead they told me things. I was twenty-two. My name was Madeleine Reid. My mother was dead and they apologized for taking so long to find me.'

'Did they tell you much about Ben Starr?'

I waited a while before I asked. I thought I was going to be in trouble for starting the fire and for not seeking help sooner. His street was filled with houses I never knew existed. Filled with neighbours who never knew I existed. The neighbours thought it was strange the curtains were always closed, but their imaginations could never quite carry them to the reason why. Imagine their horror. Sometimes I do. I wonder if they feel guilty their innocent minds couldn't do the maths to work out what was happening at Ben's place. Maybe it's capability that makes someone a terrible person – not acting on it, but knowing you could. Having the imagination to wander down dark roads.

'They told me Ben was dead. They told me I was brave. He wasn't known to police. Never once had he appeared on their radar. They said, they believed I had prevented my own death and the abduction of further children. They said they could access the photos and videos on his phone. They weren't too damaged because Ben had them hidden away. They told me I was a hero. They told me again I was brave.'

'You are brave,' my guest says with a smile. 'I remember when they found you. My jaw dropped when I heard you had set fire to the entire house.'

Another sip of their coffee. Do I detect a tremble in their hand?

I'm not sure how long I stayed in hospital for. They were very keen on telling me the month and the year. They placed a calendar in my room; each month had a different bunny rabbit. Even so, I struggled. One day, the chubby woman appeared and by her side was Vivian. Vivian's eyes were red. She said hello to me, and told me she had heard my story. If I was willing, she had a spare bed at her refuge in Leicester and she would like for me to join her there. Chubby woman said it might be better than living alone, at least until I got on my feet.

'Vivian came and took me to the refuge. She said I had a family now.'

'Vivian . . .' My guest pauses and flicks through some paperwork. 'She attended your trial every day to support you, didn't she? Gave you a character reference?'

I smile, thinking about Vivian in her cheap suit, elbowing journalists out of the way to get the best seat. Her smiling at me when I arrived. Her mouthing, *It'll be okay*, when we both knew it wouldn't. I was so quick to assume she wanted to control me, when really she wanted the best for me and to learn how to make it better for other women in my situation.

'This is the time you met the second man you killed?'

'Yes, he would travel from Manchester to Leicester to take witness statements and the like. I have no idea how he got placed on my case.'

'He had specialist training for circumstances like yours.'

I nod. I can see why that would appeal to a man like him. My guest and I sit in silence for a moment, staring at one another.

'Who was the second man you killed?'

'PC Ian Walker.'

My guest nods. Their face paler than it was when they walked into the room.

'Which is how you caught me? Isn't it, Charlie?'

My guest Charlie looks at me with that same old easy smile.

'Yes, that's how I caught you.'

52

2007 – Manchester

I slot my key into the front door of my house. It's never felt like a home, nor did the hostel, and Ben's house was a cage. The door swings open. I lock it behind me. The hallway is dark as I walk down it listening to Brian snoring. Life moves on.

I pause, resting my forehead against the door.

'Sorry, Emily,' I whisper. 'I didn't mean to step into your life. I wanted to help.'

I take a deep breath as I open the bedroom door. I pause at the threshold. A silhouette – darker than the night that fills my bedroom – sits on the edge of my bed.

You're meant to knock three times before you enter a room.

The ghost of Ben Starr turns and grins. He has the metal box that once belonged to Emily and holds it in the air inspecting it. I walk into the room, fighting the urge to knock first.

Hello, little lamb, clever duck. Oh, my sweet, sweet Maddie. Look how you have grown. You're almost an old maid.

Emily's metal box tumbles from his hand and rolls with a clatter. It stops at my feet. I stare down at it and press the skin between my forefinger and thumb until my fingernails burst the skin. Blood trickles down my hand.

'You're not real,' my words scratch at my throat. 'I'm not afraid of you. I killed you and I could do it again.'

Ben pats the side of the bed next to him. In death, he is the same man as he was in life – his hair is a little too long, his teeth are grey and his rotund stomach juts out. I sit. Out of habit I follow his instruction and I hate myself for it. He places a hand on my knee.

You didn't really kill me, though. It's a bit of a reach to suggest you murdered me. Smoke inhalation is not exactly a jagged rock to the head, is it? Setting fires, he looks at me and rolls his eyes, *very timid.*

Car headlights shine through my curtains and pass along the wall.

'You're dead,' I say.

Oh, I'm very much alive. He taps on the centre of my chest with an overgrown fingernail. *I live inside here.*

No. He doesn't. I'm nothing like Ben or any of the men I murdered. I'm different. I wish this thing on my bed wasn't a ghost so I could kill him again, and this time I would make it slow. I'd smash him in the skull with a jagged rock.

If you're so different, he says, reading my thoughts, *why have you just abandoned the only friend you have ever had?*

His laughter takes up every inch of the room and seeps through the windows and under the gap below the door. Sloane. I've left her. My hands tremble as I pull my phone from my jeans pocket and the time blinks at me – hours have passed. I'm unsure how long I have been sitting on this bed.

I dial Sloane. The phone rings. Endlessly. Her voice kicks in – *This is Sloane. Leave a message after the beep.* I hang up. The phone slips from my palms and slides along the floor.

Fetch, Ben barks as I get up to get the phone.

I ring her again. No answer.

Oh no, Ben says. *What will you do?*

My phone lights up and Sloane's name flashes on the screen. Ben shrugs.

'Sloane, I'm so sorry,' I say. 'I'm coming back right now.'

Silence. I glance up at Ben and he mouths the words – *too late* – at me.

'Sloane?'

'I've been waiting here for hours for Charlie to arrive. I want to capture the scene when he realizes we have caught the Manchester Maniac, Maddie. You need to get here.' Her voice is filled with glee.

Footsteps on the other side of the phone.

'Maddie. Someone has arrived,' Sloane says, followed by a long pause. 'Shit. I don't think it's Charlie.'

'Sloane. Hide.'

Silence. One way in. One way out. It must be Aaron and she can't escape. She's trapped.

The footsteps again. Sloane doesn't hang up and a loud bang comes through the phone as if she has dropped it.

'Stop,' Sloane shouts. 'Maddie. Help.'

'I'm coming, Sloane.'

The line goes dead. I grab my lighter fluid and my matches and within seconds I'm on the street and racing back to Queen of the Burgers. Sweat drips from my forehead as I sprint through the red-light district and find myself for the second time tonight staring at the basement of Queen of the Burgers. This time the sky is filled with stars. I descend, readying myself for a head-on confrontation. The light is on. Sloane's phone is in pieces across the floor, but I'm standing alone.

I told you it was too late, says the ghost of Ben Starr. *Your mate has been taken. You'd best find her before . . .* Ben makes slashing gestures across his throat.

I look around the room. Sloane has been taken and it's my fault.

53

It's the type of night I used to love. Footsteps echo. The stars shine bright. Aaron and Karla's house looks like any semi-detached, on any new-build estate in any part of the country. I press the door buzzer. It feels anticlimactic to turn up to a serial killer's house and ring the bell. There's a mat on the front door that reads WELCOME. Bland. I bet Karla chose it. I wait. Nothing. I press the button again and the shrillness runs through me. I wait. Nothing.

My hands cup my face as I look in through the lit living-room window. A half-drunk bottle of vodka sits on the coffee table. The house looks average, a Live, Laugh, Love poster hangs above the sofa. This could be anyone's house. It looks like a home, but so did Ben's house, and that wasn't a home. It was a prison straight from the pages of IKEA.

The side gate swings open to reveal a tended garden. I picture an irritated Karla watching Aaron pour a nightcap, but Karla isn't anywhere to be seen. So, she took Aaron's advice and went to her parents. Lucky for me. Lucky for her.

Where is Aaron? Is he with Sloane or has he tied her up in some hidden basement? Is he here? Drunk?

I pull my sleeve over my hand as I push down on the kitchen door handle. It's unlocked. The door swings open. With my plastic bag in hand, a casual observer might confuse me with someone dropping off groceries, and not someone planning to murder the occupant. I can almost feel the warmth from the flames. I can almost hear his screams. Almost.

The kitchen bin overflows with empty lager bottles. Someone started early. Stale alcohol hangs on the air. I pass the living room, the half-drunk bottle of vodka still on the coffee table. Has he left the house? A snore from upstairs. His nasal choke tells me otherwise.

Pictures of Aaron and Karla line the hallway as I ascend the stairs. A timeline of their relationship, they age with each step I take and finish with a white dress and top hat and tails. In every image they are smiling. They were happy. Once. What happened to Aaron to make him like this? To make him a murderer.

The plastic bag in my hand rustles and I freeze. He doesn't know I'm coming. I didn't know Ben was coming. All is fair. Us or them. I keep moving down their cream hallway. Karla has avoided all colour when decorating her home, perhaps subconsciously distancing herself from the garish colours that adorn Queen of the Burgers. I pass a spare bedroom and a bathroom – the toilet seat up. The only room left and the door is closed. Snoring comes from within. Aaron. It must be. An early night or a drunken stupor?

I push down on the handle and enter the room. The curtains are closed but a bedside lamp illuminates the room. Aaron lies on top of the bed. Fully clothed. I watch him. So many nights I awoke to Ben standing over my bed, watching me. I want Aaron to wake and see a shadowy figure standing at the end of his bed, watching him.

The mattress dips as I take a seat. He still has his boots on; the soles are dirty, mud in the crevices. Another bottle of vodka on the bedside table. I watch his chest moving up and down as he inhales and nosily exhales, and I ask myself what did Emily see in this man? What enchantment did he cast to enthral her? Snores come thick and mucus-ridden from the back of his throat. I shake the contents of my plastic bag onto the bed. Lighter fluid, matches, a lighter.

I get my wish as his eyes flicker open. He jerks, pushing himself back and onto his hands. A gasp. His eyes narrow.

'Maddie?'

His voice sounds strange without the slur I have become accustomed too. Surprise, confusion, it's all over his face as he tries to figure out why I'm there.

'Hello, Aaron.'

'Maddie?' His face screws up, as if he is trying to figure out a puzzle. 'Why are you here?'

I open the lighter fluid, pulling at the child safety seal. I squirt it all over Aaron. He chokes from the fumes.

'Maddie?' he barks at me.

'I'm here to murder you, Aaron.'

He laughs. The audacity. His eyes flicker from me to the lighter fluid that I'm squirting everywhere. It leaves a whiter-than-white stain, similar to bleach, on the pastel pink sheets that no doubt Karla picked out. I feel like an artist as the curves and lines meet and cross.

'You're being serious, aren't you? Is this because Karla fired you?'

His eyes are wide now. His thick lips separate as his jaw slackens. His beard is thick and matted.

'No,' I say.

I hold a single lit match in the air. The flames dance.

'Where is Victoria Sloane?'

His eyes widen. His shoulders stiffen, and I wonder for a second if the frozen statue in front of me will come alive and attack.

'Sloane? Is she missing? Fuck.'

He begins to cry. His head falls into his hands and he sobs. My match burns to the end and I blow it out. Is this remorse?

'It's too late for tears. Tell me where she is.'

His head tilts as he lifts it. His expression softens. He wipes his nose on his sleeve, revealing tattoos inked across his arm.

'Maddie, I don't know where Vicky Sloane is,' he says. 'Fuck. This is what I was afraid would happen. That monster is never going to stop, is he?'

'I'm going to stop you, Aaron.'

I am the hero and he is the villain. I brace myself for his confession.

'What? I didn't hurt Victoria Sloane, and I sure as hell didn't lay a finger on Emily.' He trembles as he reaches for the vodka bottle; he unscrews the cap and gulps. He shudders at the end. 'I was in love with her and we were having an affair. Before you ask – yeah, Karla knows.'

I squirt more lighter fluid on his bed and he stares at me, blank-faced.

'I was planning to hang myself anyway.'

Even in their own deaths, a man will choose violence. They don't stick their heads in the oven. They want to break their own necks as much as they want to break ours. Aaron is not mine for the taking.

'I don't believe you,' I say.

The bed creaks as he stands and I take a step back. He

pulls a length of rope from underneath the bed and walks past me, dragging a chair from the corner of the bedroom and into the hallway at the top of the stairs.

'Why do they assume the mistress is the mistake and not the wife?' Aaron says as he attaches the rope to the light fitting above him. A question mark hangs in the air. I look at his soft carpets, flowery curtains, his clean home that he dirties with his boots and behaviour. It dawns on me, nothing Karla does will ever be enough. She has created a perfect nest for a flea desperate to jump away. 'I want my vodka.'

I glance at the photographs carefully framed in his hallway. He smiles in each picture. By his own record-keeping, he had years to walk away and didn't.

'Please,' he says.

I nod. Fine. I walk back into the bedroom and grab Aaron's booze. On his bedside table is another frame. Inside a wedding invite – once it represented a new start, but now it's a memory. I wander over to it and pick it up. The only dusty item in the house, I remove the back and take the thick cardboard from the frame. I stare at the wedding invite. It's white embossed with gold lettering.

I hand Aaron his vodka back in the hallway and he's sitting on the chair. The rope hangs above him. Aaron's lips are thin and he squeezes his eyes shut. He laughs – not from joy; it leaves his mouth like an aggressive bark. Shakes his head, takes a nip of vodka from the bottle.

'Did Karla kill Emily?'

Aaron nods, downing more vodka.

'Text Karla and tell her to meet you in the Queen of the Burgers basement. Tell her what you want – hell, tell her the truth.'

He pulls out a phone and types away and then drops it. He nods at me to signify it's done and stands on the chair. I walk past him and down the stairs. I was wrong, Aaron isn't the Manchester Maniac. He's grieving harder than I thought was possible. Today it won't be me who takes Aaron from this world.

As I leave the house, I hear the clatter of a chair tumbling down the staircase.

54

2027 – HMP Bronzefield

'He was an usher at my wedding.'

I nod. I knew Charlie and Ian Walker were friends. Thinking back, I remember seeing a picture of Ian, in his apartment, at a wedding. Charlie was probably in it. And his police officers' Class of 1999 picture he hung in his hallway.

'I'm sorry your friend was a flea.'

Charlie rolls his eyes. I'm not sorry I killed him. I'm not going to lie now because it'd be convenient for me. I suspect it must be hard, learning your friend isn't such a nice guy after all. The It's-Not-Me and Not-All-Men crowds are the worst.

'He loved coffee. Drank far too much of it. Was the life of the party.'

I know what Charlie is trying to do. He is trying to humanize my victim, and if he thinks it will work, he is wrong. I've lost count of the therapists who have tried.

'I wonder how many women and girls he assaulted before me.'

'None.'

Of course that is what the police claim. It's not a good look for them, is it? A woman who is held captive for twelve years by a predator is assaulted by the police officer who is meant to be her liaison officer.

'The police aren't going to admit to more, are they?'

Charlie taps a pen against the clipboard he is holding, as if he is considering what I am saying. He looks at me.

'What if it was a mistake? A one-off. Maybe he could have reformed. He should have known better, and yes, you would have been well within your rights to report the incident to the police. But setting his house on fire?'

I look down at the floor. It's been a while since I have been forced to listen to the justification of flea behaviour. I thought Charlie was coming round. Walker was a danger.

'You don't know what happened.'

I throw my words like a dart, hoping to get a bullseye and for Charlie to back down.

'Tell me,' he says.

It was Daisy who noticed him first, or at least the way he would have to duck when he came in the front door. This, according to Daisy, was attractive. Whenever a policeman's knock came from the front door, Daisy would poke her head out in case it was Walker. Some of the other women agreed, even Sylvia, and they would start appearing whenever he was about – *Cup of tea, officer?*

'What's the point? You've made up your mind. You're like all the other women in the hostel. Ian this, Ian that. Did you fancy him too?' I spit.

'He was popular with the ladies. Which makes it even harder . . .' Charlie shakes his head.

Vivian became fed up with the attention PC Ian Walker was getting. She was the only woman in the household who didn't succumb to his charm. She felt he was a distraction. The ladies in the house needed to focus on their healing, not lusting after a police officer. More than once had Vivian caught him giving a cheeky wink to Daisy, or one of his hands gently resting on the shoulders of one of the residents.

'Vivian complained about his presence at the refuge, said his regular visits were becoming a distraction to the other women.'

Charlie nods his head.

'I read the complaint,' he says. 'It wasn't unreasonable.'

We began meeting at a local police station. Similar story there. We would be interrupted a dozen times in an hour. The admin woman wanting to know if we wanted any tea and biscuits. The female officer wanting to know how long we had the room booked out for.

'Ian attracted people. They were drawn to him.'

'What about you? Were you drawn to him?' Charlie asks.

'No,' I say. 'I was tired of everything. Talking about Ben. Being coached through all the developments. It was exhausting and I was certain he was dragging it out. Overegging the situation. I wanted to move on. Have a normal life.'

I glance down at my handcuffs. At the green room. At the guard. At the blinds hiding the outside world from me. At Charlie. Heat in my cheeks. I didn't succeed in achieving the easiest of desires – *a normal life*.

'I'll concede you had far more meetings than necessary.'

'He became so fed up with the intrusions. He suggested we meet at his apartment in Manchester. He gave me his address on a scrap of paper.'

I remember that look in his eye. I might have been locked up for twelve years, but that was a look I was very familiar with. The look of a flea sizing up a vein.

'I see no record of that,' Charlie says.

'How do you think I knew where he lived?'

Charlie looks at the guard and then back at me. He puts his head into his hands and I watch him. When he looks back up at me, he nods.

'I'm sorry. I'm being defensive.' He pauses for a second more than is comfortable. 'It's easier for me to believe that you are a liar and my friend was everything I knew him to be – kind, funny, charming.' Charlie places his hands palms down on the table. 'I know you're not lying.'

'How?'

Checkmate. This is the part when he tells me how the police knew I wasn't lying about Walker.

'Because you left the Rohypnol in the freezer. But that's also how I knew the fire wasn't an accident. I thought perhaps it was planted, but it was the same batch lifted on a job Ian knocked. He must have slipped some for himself.'

In the end we agreed to meet in a hotel room. I, in my naivety, thought this would be a safe place because lots of people would be in the immediate vicinity. I knew there was something wrong three sips into my drink. When I woke up, I was naked. So was he. He kissed me on the forehead and asked if I wanted some breakfast. I had an omelette. I didn't eat it. I went home as soon as I thought I could excuse myself, but not before I dipped into his bag when his back was turned and I found the remnants of what he used to make me pass out and I stashed it in my pocket. Once home, I showered. I planned.

'I then arrived at the address he gave me for his apartment a week later. He wasn't expecting me, but gave me a warm smile as I entered. He said I couldn't stay long because he was expecting a guest. For a man of his size, he passed out quickly. He wouldn't have felt a thing as the flames roared. So, go on,' I say. 'Tell me how you caught me. Tell me how *you* catch a serial killer.'

55

2007 – Manchester

I don't avoid the cameras as I pass Queen of the Burgers; in fact, I stop and give one a wave. No doubt this footage will be used on a true crime series. You know, for the bit before the crime. The door to the basement is busted from when Sloane and I broke it open, so I walk straight in and down. Each step echoes.

The lights are on when I reach the main room. The image of Emily on Aaron's shrine has been placed face down. Karla stares at me. Once upon a time, all four of them would have hung out down here, eating Cody's burgers, enjoying their own version of Fizz Friday. This room would have been filled with laughter. Now a cold silence sits in the air – an unwelcome guest to a party.

'You came. I wasn't sure if you would,' I say.

Pure fury dances on Karla's face. It contorts, making her look like an angry flea. She's in her Queen of the Burger uniform; the red in Karla's face clashes with the maroon. I drop my plastic bag at my feet.

'Who the hell do you think you are? Coming to my house, threatening my husband and then demanding I meet you? The police are on the way to my property right now.' Her words hurtle past her thin lips like missiles, but I feel myself dodging each one of them.

Who do I think I am? In my mind's eye, images of Ben, Ian, Leon and Robbie dance. I feel warm inside, like a fire has been lit. I'm a hero.

'Why would they go to your house and not here? I'm going to bet you failed to mention I was coming to meet you, and why would you do that?' I roll my eyes. Enjoying my moment. 'Because I know your secret. Why don't you call the police and tell them I'm here.'

I pull my phone out and hold it towards Karla. I allow my sarcasm to take every inch of space in the room until it is suffocating.

'No?' I say. 'Well, if you change your mind, let me know.'

This is not how it was meant to be. This is not the world I imagined from inside Ben's four walls. For me there was a sanctuary outside; other women like me who were waiting to be saved and I would be their saviour.

'I know about the affair,' I say.

'So?' Karla looks towards the shrine. 'That doesn't mean anything.'

She's right, but that doesn't make her innocent. From my inside pocket, I pull the picture I found from inside Emily's box. I look at it. What have I learnt? Vivian wanted to lock me up under the guise it was for my own safety, Emily's roommates made malicious complaints about her, and now, Karla killed Emily because she was sleeping with Aaron.

'You didn't know Emily,' Karla says, jumping to her feet.

I know Emily was someone who liked to have a good time

with her friends. She liked Cody's burgers. Two of her flatmates didn't like her and Brian liked her too much. Emily was an ordinary woman with the rest of her life in front of her.

'I know enough.'

'She was a homewrecker. She pretended to be my friend whilst she was chasing my husband. She wasn't a girls' girl.' Maybe not all women are victims. The Karlas of the world are as bad as the Bens, the Leons, the Robbies and Ians. Maybe they're worse. They know what we face every day and, even with this knowledge, they choose to be fleas. They choose to respond with violence and hatred against their own gender. Aaron was ten years older than Emily, and he was her boss. He was the married one. Not Emily. Yet, at the hands of the woman she called friend, she was vilified. Yet Karla thinks she can lecture me on 'girl code' or how to be a 'girls' girl', as if some imaginary rule permits her to murder a woman barely out of childhood. As if Aaron is a prize to be won. A man who can't stay sober, who cheats, who keeps his boots on when he lies on the bed.

'I'm going,' Karla says.

The whole world needs to burn: this basement, this woman, this murderer. She will not make me a fool or a hypocrite. I bend down, rummage in my bag and pull out my lighter fluid. I squirt a thick heavy line in front of me.

'You come within three feet of this line, and I set it on fire,' I say.

'You won't,' Karla says, shaking her head in defiance.

I strike a match and hold it in the air. The flame is magnificent, a small acorn willing to grow and destroy an oak. Karla holds her hands up.

'Okay,' she says her voice now soft. 'I can stay. You've got this wrong, though.'

Ian was a police officer who was meant to be looking after a victim, but that didn't stop him. Leon was meant to be a loving husband and father, but that didn't stop him. The roles we assign ourselves will never mask our true colours.

'I was giving the police free food, Maddie. Would I do that if I murdered Emily?'

Of course she would. She was building a narrative about her character whilst keeping an eye on them and their investigation.

I walk over to Aaron's shrine and put Emily's photograph back up so we can all see it, and then move back behind my line. Karla refuses to move her gaze.

'I wondered why he wouldn't let any of us down here after her death,' Karla says, looking at the shrine. 'I guess I have my answer.'

I throw the image of Aaron and Emily at Karla. It's light and doesn't quite make its way across the room. Instead, it falls at her feet. Zigzagging downwards like a feather. Karla reaches down and picks the photo up. She studies it without emotion and places it back on the floor.

'If you're going to call the police, just do it,' Karla says.

All this time, I thought she was grieving for Emily, but she was protecting herself. She's murdered a woman and destroyed her whole life over an affair. How is that comparable to what I have done – the kidnapper, the bent cop, the wife beater, the rapist – they all deserved what was coming. Emily didn't.

'Maddie,' Karla smirks. 'If you do this. You're as bad as me.'

'Shut up,' I bark.

Cat-like, Karla inches forward. I light a match and wave it over the visible line I have drawn. She retreats onto the sofa.

'How did you persuade her to meet you in the woods?'

'I didn't,' Karla says, her lips pursed. 'I was suspicious. She'd already caught me rifling through her drawers when I visited her house.' Karla looks away. 'I couldn't find any proof there. So I had to catch her, and I did down here. She was half naked waiting for my husband. We argued. And . . .' She pauses as her face pales. She takes a deep breath in. 'Things got out of hand. I put her in a suitcase and I took her to the woods.'

She nods to a suitcase sitting in the corner of the room and I remember the holdall Ben had bought for me. All this for Aaron? Rain pelts against the wood of the basement door, as if the skies want to give me a drum roll. And she made it look like the Manchester Maniac had killed her to cover her own tracks. Karla watched her own husband be arrested, Emily's landlord's life be turned upside down, and Karla may have caused carnage with the actual Maniac's investigation. Because she was jealous.

'Does Cody know?' I say.

For the first time I see something on Karla's face, a flicker of guilt. She shakes her head no, and I believe her. I bet he has no idea, about the affair, about Emily being murdered by her own friends. Sweet little Cody. Fooled by them all. Karla stares at the floor.

'No, he's going to take it hard,' Karla says. She looks up at me. 'You happy now? I confess. Now go on, call the police.'

I smile. Not for a single second does she consider she could meet the same fate as Emily. The whole world needs to burn, this basement, and Karla.

'I don't call the police.'

Karla furrows her eyebrows for a second. I don't murder women, but for Karla I will make an exception. Before she can ask me for clarity, I light a match and drop it on the line of lighter fluid. I swear there's an actual *whoosh* as a wall of flames appears. I run upstairs and I close the basement doors. I didn't have chance to grab a new padlock, so I stand on the door so Karla can't escape.

In the corner of my eye, a ghost appears. He's tall. Smart in his uniform and, of course, he is smiling. PC Ian Walker tilts his head and waves as he approaches.

Good detective work, Maddie.

Karla must have run through the flames because underfoot I feel thuds against the basement doors. She begs me to let her out of the basement. I ignore her. This will be the part they show after the crime.

The thuds are replaced by scratches as Karla claws at the door. Then it stops. Silence.

The heat warms my feet in the midnight air. I look up at the stars. The worst thing about Karla is she's stolen time looking for Sloane.

Just one thing. The ghost of PC Ian Walker raises an eyebrow. *If you murder lambs, does that make you a flea?*

56

How do you catch a serial killer? You lure them out.

A lamb doesn't seek the flea. The flea seeks the lamb. Of course, even in the final hours, Sloane wasn't seeking the Manchester Maniac in the flesh, just his identity, the paper-based form, not the actual man. She had no desire to come face to face with the Maniac, that's what I wanted; it was me who wanted the flea. She just wanted a name.

The stars. They're still ten-out-of-ten company. They don't judge me as I return to my night-time habit of pacing the streets. I've swapped the roads and alleys of Leicester for a cemetery in Manchester. It's quiet. Deathly. I manoeuvre between gravestones, making my way to an oak tree that casts a permanent shadow over an unmarked plot of land. I look down when I get there, I stare at the dirt.

'Ben?' my voice almost a whisper. 'Can you hear me? That little show you put on didn't scare me.'

A slight breeze wanders through the trees, through my hair. A sign?

'Why me? Why did you choose me? So many lives you could have destroyed but you picked mine.'

I can almost hear his reply, as if his lips are moving against my ear, but he is muted. I know his answer: *Because if I don't, little lamb, someone else will.*

I've pissed on his grave. I've danced on his grave. I take a step back and I spit. I spit hard.

'I hate you, Ben Starr. I hate you.'

I race through the tombstones, half afraid Ben will crawl through the soil to come and drag me down to his wooden prison and keep me for ever. I pass Diana Sloane, I pass Charlie's girlfriend – Julia – and I pass too many women taken too soon.

I'm in the car park in no time, standing at Leon's car in no time. I yank on the driver's handle and the door creaks open. I slide in and pull open the glove compartment. The key is where I left it. Nobody wanted to steal this heap of junk. I slide the key in.

'Come on, we don't have to go far,' I say.

The engine roars to life.

'Bingo.'

I switch the radio on and blast the music too loudly for the time of night. I lower the window. I hope Sloane can hear this music, wherever she is, I hope she can hear this music and know I am coming to get her. We will have our Fizz Friday and eat Chinese food. We have so many years left on the clock and we will be friends for ever.

As I enter the industrial estate, I slow the car. Women step forward and then step back again when they see my face. I pick a corner under a streetlamp and park the car. I can feel eyes on me as I get out. The hood pops and I prop it open with the black metal arm and lean against it. Look at me with my broken-down car in the dodgy part of the neighbourhood. It's like I'm asking for trouble.

I'm not alone here. Other women linger on corners and under streetlights. The Maniac used these women as a pool for his victims and yet somehow, in his story, in mine and Sloane's story, they have still ended up as background characters. Pixelated people.

Have Sloane and I failed them by fixating on Emily Sykes? I think we have. And in turn, I have failed Sloane. This small patch, hidden in a big city, is a separate world populated with vulnerable women, and the Manchester Maniac knew that. We focused on a victim who led what many may have seen as an ordinary life and shielded our own eyes. For what? To make the story digestible? I guess we aren't the first and won't be the last to make this mistake.

I watch the cars slow and speed up. In the distance I spot a familiar car. It slows when it spots me. The passenger side window whirs down and Frank ducks his head a little.

'You hit tough times?' he sneers.

'Car's busted.'

I stare hard at him. Willing him to carry on and not distract me from my goal.

'Charlie will kill me if I leave you out here. Particularly with your little friend missing.' His voice echoes on the night air.

'How do you know Sloane is missing?'

Frank stares at me hard and smirks. 'Oops,' he says, mischief dancing in his eyes. 'Hop in. She'll be dead in an hour. Tick-tock.'

In my head, Charlie's voice rattles, warning me to call him if I'm in danger and not to get into the cars of people who might hurt me. I pull on the handle of the car and I get in.

It stinks of bleach, and as I try to pull the door shut I notice the interior car handles are missing. Frank leans over me. He slams the car door shut, grabbing the edge of the open window.

'Frank?'

The car slows at a red light. This is the point when I should be banging on the windows and screaming for help. But this is it, isn't it? This is my big moment. This is what I have been waiting for.

'I got you a present.'

All this time, he was right under my and Charlie's nose.

'Does Charlie know you're the Manchester Maniac?'

Frank throws a thin white plastic bag into my lap. I strain to reach it. Inside is lighter fluid and a packet of matches.

'Does Charlie know about me?' Frank sighs. 'I can't say for certain. He watches me in a way I don't like. I've never been keen on Charlie.'

Outside we pass some houses, ordinary houses with ordinary cars filled with ordinary people. A ghost appears in the back passenger seat. I turn in my seat and he smiles – *Hello, clever duck*. I want to run; I want to lash out. Instead, I freeze. My body frozen solid to the seat. He's not there. He's not there. Ignore him.

Sounds like Charlie watches my pal Frank the same way you used to watch me. Beady little eyes – calculating, scheming, plotting.

The car flies over potholes, bouncing along the road as I reach for the white plastic bag Frank gifted me. I shake it out beside me, unscrewing the lid of the lighter fluid with one hand.

'Don't bother,' Frank says. 'You need me more than I need you.'

I let go of the lid, it ricochets off the passenger footwell.

The plastic bag, the matches, the lighter fluid – they're not gifts. They're confirmation. He's the serial killer I have been hunting and now he knows what I am. There goes the surprise. I suppose he lured me out into the open too.

Sloane's face appears in my mind's eye. Frank has Sloane, and he knows I won't kill him if there is a chance I can save her. That's what heroes do. They save people. I catch Frank glancing at me as a smirk dances on his face.

'Have you hurt her?'

'Yes.'

No explanation, no excuses. Just a yes, a simple yes, a plain yes. As if I had asked him if he wanted a cup of tea. The clouds break and rain pours from the skies. The windscreen wipers go back and forth furiously.

'Is she alive?'

Ben's laughter fills the car. *Is she alive? Look how you destroy everything around you, little lamb. She never would have even been on Frank's radar if it wasn't for you. You drag everyone to hell with you.*

Frank doesn't answer as I ignore Ben's ghost. Reminding myself he is dead and he is not there and he can no longer harm me. Frank hits the brakes. My body slams forward.

'Aaron Queen didn't manage to finish the job, by the way,' Frank laughs. 'Charlie cut him down. He was in quite the state when we found him. I take it the rope coiled around his neck was him and not you. The lighter fluid – that was you, right?'

It appears Frank has been searching for me as much as I've been searching for him.

We pass Queen of the Burgers. Frank slows. One gurney. One body bag. People in uniforms. The scene is chaos. At the centre of the hurricane, the eye of the storm, is Charlie, his arms waving as he directs people. For a second, I swear he freezes as the car passes.

Looks like your work, Ben's ghost says with a grin.

'Don't rubberneck,' Frank scolds.

'It is my work,' I say.

Frank raises an eyebrow and Ben gives me a mock round of applause. Ben leans back in the passenger seat with a glass of red wine. He sips on it.

'Does Charlie know about me, Frank?'

A twinge of disappointment. Is this how it feels to let someone down, to know they will think badly of you?

'Know about you?' Frank laughs. 'He figured it out. You're lucky I found you first.'

I swivel on the back seat and watch Queen of the Burgers become smaller as we drive further away, a plume of smoke marking its spot. Frank merges onto the motorway; a couple of junctions later and he is off again and onto a roundabout. He takes the third exit and straight past a large retail park. Shops advertise sofa sales, computers, clothes, and fried chicken. I wonder if this is the last journey his victims travel. If this dual carriageway is one of the last things they ever see.

He says nothing. Ben drinks his wine, and a bowl of popcorn appears balanced on his stomach. We pass houses, the tall, terraced types with steps leading up to the front doors. I wonder at what point Frank's victims realized something was wrong. When their spider senses kicked in.

Rain hammers against the windscreen and – as each drop hits the glass – it feels as if Frank is becoming lighter. Enjoying himself a bit more. The smile on his face creeping ever wider.

'I'm not sure this weather plays to your particular set of . . .' he pauses and then settles on a word, 'kinks. You don't meet many girls like you, Maddie. Men, there are plenty of men who are like me or want to be me. I said to Charlie, you're lucky to come across a single Maddie Reid in an entire career.'

I believe him. Give a man enough solitude, it will only be a matter of time before his thoughts wander to violence. It's like they're all on the same meandering path heading towards the same destination.

Gravel crunches under the tyres as Frank pulls into a jet-dark car park. Trees border the outskirts. In the distance are lights. Frank has driven me in a very large circle, returning to the rear of the industrial estate. The only thing between us and the industrial estate is the woods. The same woods in which bodies keep showing up.

'We're getting out here. No funny business, okay?' he says to me.

No funny business, little lamb, Ben says, getting out of the car with Frank.

He gets out, each footstep crunching against the gravel, and opens the passenger seat. I jump out of the car. We stare into each other's eyes for a moment. Witnessed from the outside, one might mistake us for forbidden lovers, not two serial killers preparing to trade blows. I step into a puddle. The rain hits me in the face.

'This is usually the point they start asking questions or requesting to go back,' Frank says as if he is a tour guide. 'It's predictable to the point of annoying. You probably know what I mean.'

Isn't he fun, little lamb? The yin to your yang.

The ghost of Ben Starr has disappeared, but his voice is here. Echoing from the trees. Frank takes off at pace. Not once does he look behind to see if I am following; perhaps he can hear my shoes squelching in thick mud, or maybe my shadow at his side. He's not concerned I will run away. Again, my mind flickers to all the women who have gone before me. Did they follow him willingly? Did Sloane trail him in the darkness? Something crawls on my shoulder and tells me to leave. To turn. To run. But I brush it off.

Wet leaves smack me in the face. The rain becomes heavier, the ground beneath me sinks with every step I take.

'Hurry up, we're going to miss it.' Frank reaches behind and grabs my wrist, pulling me along. He's strong. For a man of his age, I wouldn't expect his strength. They like to trick us like that, pretend they're maturing, becoming more fragile when secretly they're getting worse, sneakier. Frank was meant to protect us. Frank was killing us.

The trees surround us, but he knows which direction to take himself. This is a well-worn route for him. I slip as we tread downwards, but Frank grabs my arm and pulls me back on my feet before my arse hits the floor. He's rushing me. Is this a tactic? Something to throw me off guard?

He stops. Abrupt. In the darkness, I don't know how he can tell where we are. Rustling comes from near him; he must be rummaging through his backpack. I'm blinded as a light flickers on. A torch. He sticks it into the ground, and we are in a circle of light, the same thing Charlie did when we found one of Frank's victims. Did Frank teach Charlie that trick? A small, sloped clearing. A camp chair sits empty in the middle. At the periphery of the light, a familiar smile. Ben doesn't look like a ghost, more a demon.

I bet you think you're a clever little duck, but you're a tiny little lamb marching to the abattoir.

I stare at him.

'Ben?'

He vanishes. I shake my head. My clothes are drenched. My hair sticks to my face. The ground below me swallows my feet, as if the mud wants to keep me prisoner.

'Are you kidding me, Frank? You brought me all this way to look at a chair on a slope?'

'Maddie?!' Sloane's voice echoes amongst the trees, bouncing off the tree trunks. Her voice high-pitched. Raw. 'Run, Maddie. Run.'

She's alive. I knew she would be. I knew our story didn't end here. Frank grabs the torch and the light hovers on some scattered leaves. I squint. Even in the light I would struggle to see the hole. A plastic storage box. The lid screwed shut. Small holes are drilled across the top. I look to the skies and the water doesn't stop. This is how he is drowning them. He stuffs women into these tiny plastic boxes and lets the rain drip in, an inch at a time until there is no room left and they drown.

'Not long now,' Frank says in a bright voice. 'Tick-tock.'

He takes a seat in his camping chair. The light now in his hand, shining into the endless trees, and I wonder if it's always the same trench or if across this forest is a dozen holes. I pull my matches from my pocket. They're as wet as me. He knew they would be of no use.

'They call me a maniac but I'm not, Maddie. We're poets, artists.'

I picture Sloane cramped as her body is doubled up in the box. Screaming for help. Her skin turning blue and wrinkled. Praying Charlie would pass by and save her. How has no one heard her?

Hollow punches softened by water against sturdy plastic. I slide, struggling to keep my balance as I stumble towards the hole. The field beyond Frank's narrow torchlight is now darker. I fall onto all fours and reach out, one hand at a time, until I feel the plastic underneath me. Rain pelts.

My skin is soft from the rain. It slices open against the hard plastic, and I smell my blood mingling with the Manchester rain. Water thrashes inside the storage box as Sloane fights for air. I push my fingers through the holes, attempting to widen them and to tear the lid open.

Ben Starr reappears and sits cross-legged at the edge of the hole.

You are not going to get that box open in time. You're not strong enough. You're not smart enough. What am I going to do with you?

White-hot pain sears through my body. All I can see are the outlines of trees bending in the wind. A single overpowering beam of light from Frank and a dead Ben Starr.

'Let her out,' I yell over the rain which refuses to stop.

You know it doesn't work like that, Ben says.

Frank remains in his chair, silent, watching.

Do you want to borrow my phone? Ben says, his voice at one with the wind and water. He holds a phone up to my face. Flicks through images of a young girl being pulled along by a stick-thin woman. It's me. *Why don't we call your new friend Charlie?*

'Frank,' I say. I'm shouting but he doesn't move. He's silent.

I try to heave the plastic storage box from the ground, but the combined weight of the water and Sloane is too much, and mud covers my face as I collapse on the floor.

Just give up, Ben says.

Ben drifts away on the breeze.

'Let her out.' I stagger as I approach Frank, wiping sodden hair from my face. Rage building with every step. 'Let her out, she is my friend.'

The rain tapers to a slow patter. A reprieve. The clouds break and a waning crescent becomes our audience.

'Ben Starr's mum loved him, yes?' Frank looks down at his fingernails and then back up at me. He shrugs.

She did love him. Too much.

'Charlie, the good man, he was friends with PC Walker.'

He was.

'Leon Parker, another mummy's boy? And I bet even Robert Jones had a pal or two? Do you see what I'm saying? They all have people who love them.' He points at himself and then at me. 'WE DON'T CARE.'

The ghost of Ben appears, his head resting on my shoulder.

Not strictly true. No one loved you, Ben whispers in my ear.

'Maddie,' her voice is hollow and tired. 'Run. Please.'

The light shines on my face. I try to look away, but Frank's synthetic gaze follows me.

'She's not here for you, Sloane. She's here for me.'

Frank pulls a Zippo lighter from his pocket. The flint grates against his thumb and a flame dances at his fingertips. The lid closes with a click and the fire is extinguished. I'm hypnotized. My hand aches. Blood drips, turning pale pink as it dilutes with rainwater. Frank strikes the lighter again and I lunge at him. The lighter slips from Frank's hand and is swallowed by the darkness.

I have no choice. I can't save Sloane. I'm not strong enough or smart enough and maybe I'm not a good enough person.

Ben leans on a tree. He is darker than the night.

You're right little duck. Let's go home now. He reaches out a hand towards me. It's a black swirling shadow. *Come on, let's go. You'll be safe with me. You don't even have to decide what to wear.*

The rain returns. Heavy. It's a downpour. I must save Sloane. I slide back to the box, and I squeeze into one of the holes drilled into the top. The plastic frays and becomes weaker. I yank the lid off.

Frank steadies his light over Sloane's pale, wrinkled body. She's curled in the foetal position. The water is above her head. She looks like a doll floating in a bath. I pull her onto the dirt.

'Is she dead? She should be dead. I hate it when they take too long to die,' Frank says with his lips curled with disgust.

My fingers on her neck. A pulse. Faint. I pull at my own clothes, tearing them from my body and wrapping her up in them. My feet slip as I attempt to pick her up. She's too heavy. I grab her ankles and pull her.

A loud crack. At first, I think a tree branch has given way in the weather. Then the left side of my jaw, I raise my hand to it instinctively. A sharp burst of pain followed by a pulsating ache. I look up. The moon is above Frank's head. His fist clenched. He's broken my jaw.

He crouches down and with one big push, Sloane goes toppling down the slope into the void.

'She'll die.'

'That's the point,' Frank says.

He turns and sprints away. Ben appears.

Decision time, little lamb. Do you want to save the lamb, or do you want to kill the flea?

Panting comes from somewhere amongst the trees to my left. Frank is still here.

There's no time. Save the lamb or kill the flea?

Decision made. I race towards the panting and Frank's laughter echoes around the forest.

I knew it. I knew you couldn't resist, says the ghost of Ben, running alongside me. *I knew you couldn't say goodbye to me. I'm a part of you, and forever you'll be running with me.*

He vanishes and I keep racing, slipping and sliding uphill in the mud. Wet branches slap me in the face. From a bush, low down, moonlight twinkles in a set of glimmering eyes. I dart towards them. A dark Frank-shaped body springs from the undergrowth and changes direction, descending the slope.

I hold still as he extends his arms, losing balance as he trips over something in the void. I take my chance. He's lying on his back. Disorientated. I use my knees to pin him down at the biceps.

'Clever little duck,' I whisper in Frank's ear as he struggles beneath me. 'You didn't stand a chance.'

I pick up a jagged rock nearby. I hold it high above my head and smash it into Frank's face. His nose flattens. I repeat. His blood sprays over my face as the stars watch. I repeat, again and again and again. I don't stop until a hand lands on my shoulder. I look up.

The moon hangs low behind Charlie's head, and it's as if he has a halo. I smile.

'The fleas and the lambs bleed the same, Charlie. They bleed the same.'

57

2027 – HMP Bronzefield

'I won't lie, Reid,' the prison officer says. 'But I'll be glad when these meetings are over. They have been a resource nightmare.' The officer opens the room, and my eyes burn with the light from the day. 'Looks like someone forgot to close the blinds,' she says, closing the door behind us. 'I won't tell if you don't,' she sniggers, and for a moment I remember the governor of the prison is the guard's boss and it's shit having a boss. I hated the way Karla would throw her weight about. The way Aaron spent all his time avoiding us, as if his employees were children that he never wanted or planned for. Maybe it was different before Emily died.

I stand at the window and breathe everything in. The people passing on foot, the cars, the bus at the bus stop, the corner shop. In all these years, nothing has really changed. Technology may have moved forward, but out there is a boss falling in love with someone who isn't his wife. There are men and women both good and bad.

A click as the door opens.

'Bright in here,' Charlie says.

'Room with a view,' I say.

Charlie stands next to me and we both watch the world go by. I look up at him and he is smiling.

'I've been speaking with a solicitor, Maddie. I think we can get your sentence shortened. With everything you went through and all the time you served . . . Plus, how long do you have left, Maddie? You can go to the beach.'

I would love to go to the beach. I would love to go anywhere. I would relive my past over and over, face every cruelty again and again, until I hit the right set of decisions that lead me to a different set of circumstances. To a raise a glass with friends on a Fizz Friday.

'I'm sorry, Charlie,' I say, shaking my head.

'It's okay, you think about it.'

It's not that I need time to adjust to the idea Charlie is proposing. I have spent seasons dreaming of this very scenario, but a dull ache behind my eye suggests it's too late. I take a seat and Charlie follows me, his limp more distinct now.

'Why a book, Charlie?'

'I've always fancied writing one. I had to retire early because of an old knee injury, and I thought, why not write a book? I hear that catching you and Frank in one night is quite the accomplishment.'

'I hope your arrests after me were a bit quicker.'

Charlie blushes.

'So, go on. How did you catch me?'

'Gut instinct and detective work.'

I nod. I knew Charlie would say something like 'gut instinct'. I think it'd be easier to call him a liar, but I think of all the fleas I found, that found me too; they were drawn to me like I was drawn to them. Maybe Charlie is a beacon for bad guys too.

'Gut instinct?'

'It's like an alarm ringing in your brain and no one else can hear it.'

I laugh. 'No, I know what it is, but Frank? Me?'

A sly smile crosses Charlie's face. 'I was moved to work with Frank because there were suspicions. No one knew how bad it was, but the minute I shook his hand, an alarm was ringing loud and clear. The night you found him, I was planning to arrest him. In fact, he would have been arrested sooner but there was an arson attack at Queen of the Burgers.'

He looks at me through narrowed eyes.

'But let's start from the beginning. You burn Ben Starr's house down and nobody blames you for that. You were being held hostage. You had no other choices. With the other men, you had a choice, and each time you chose the wrong one.'

I'm not sure I agree. No, maybe I would let them live, if it meant an ordinary life. I stop myself from gasping when that thought runs through my head, but I have failed to experience so many of life's moments because of these men. I'm not even sure who it was I have saved. I didn't save myself.

'When Ian died, I was surprised. I won't wax lyrical about him being a careful or sensible man because that would be bullshit. He was impulsive. A fire, at least at first, seemed like a very Ian way to die. Until I found out about the Rohypnol. He would not have left that out in the open; it would have been hidden – under floorboards, a toilet tank, but not in the freezer. He had too many police officer friends.'

Killing them wasn't enough. It was the same with Robbie Jones, I wanted to expose them too. I wanted the world to know what a monster these men were. If I hadn't put anything in the freezer, then maybe I wouldn't have been caught.

'Then I heard about Leon Parker in Leicester. You remember when I was in Queen of the Burgers and Daisy walked in.'

I nod. I knew at the time she was bad news.

'I looked it up. Another bizarre fire. Only this time they claim he accidentally set himself on fire and then jumped into a canal.'

'He did jump into the canal of his own accord,' I shrug.

'I looked up Ian's vehicle movements on the night he died. He went nowhere near Leicester. Which makes sense now you say he wasn't expecting you, so I looked up coach ticket manifests. There was your name. If you'd got the train, I'd have no evidence you were in Manchester that night.'

The coaches ran throughout the night, unlike the trains. I thought I'd been smart. Maybe I should have set up camp in the train station and waited for the first train.

'I knew you were guilty of Ben Starr's death. You were in Manchester on the night Ian died and you were personally connected to him. I went to the refuge. Vivian chucked me out a couple of times, but I met a lovely woman called Sylvia.'

I let out a long sigh.

'She told me she had some royal family memorabilia T-shirts going missing.' Charlie raises an eyebrow. 'That led me to Robbert Jones. The specialist team who investigated the arson attack on his house found a fragment of a T-shirt label, and when they traced it back . . .'

'Royal family memorabilia T-shirt.'

'Plus, you left a clue in the freezer, just like you did with Ian.'

I smirk remembering the obnoxious pornography I had left in Robbie Jones' freezer. It all sounds circumstantial to me, but I know a jury would have found me guilty based on those circumstances. They'd have been right too. I was guilty.

'How did you know where Frank was that night?'

'I had everything I needed on Frank. We had a tracker in his shoe. We were slowed down because of the fire. Frank was as desperate to find you as you were him. I'd let him in on my investigation on you to win his trust and distract him from covering his own tracks. I regret that, because it was clear he was fascinated by the idea of a female version of him. With regards to Sloane—'

I hold my hand up to stop him. Nausea hits me abruptly. The world becomes blurred and I'm aware I am swaying in my chair. Charlie rushes to me, followed by the guard.

'Is she okay?' Charlie asks.

'I don't know,' says the guard.

I feel them both lift me under my arms, one either side, and move me out of the room. I look at Charlie. He's concerned for me.

'Slow-growing brain tumour,' the guard says. 'Probably been there for decades.'

'Charlie,' I say. 'Even though you arrested me, I think you're a good guy.'

My eyelids become heavy. When I come around, I am back in my cell and a guard is watching over me.

'We have a doctor on the way, Reid.'

'Charlie?'

I wish he was here. I want to tell him the truth now, I want to tell him how sick I am and how I want him to forgive me for all the things I have done because I understand now. I understand that not all people are bad. Men or otherwise. And Charlie, he makes the world better, and there aren't many men and women who can claim that with honesty.

'He left a message saying he will see you next time. And

something about a Sloane? I don't know what a Sloane is.' The guard laughs.

I smile and the ghost of Victoria Sloane appears in the corner of the room.

'Sloane. Noun: a powerful woman who is tenacious in her quest for justice.' Laughter. Mine and hers. The guard looks to the corner of the room. I can hear the guard calling for someone. In the periphery, her uniformed body leaves my cell, shouting something for someone, but all I can concentrate is on Sloane.

'You owe me a bottle of fizz and a Chinese takeaway,' I say, smiling.

'I hear you've been getting visits from DI Charlie Hart. I always knew you fancied him, but I was too embarrassed for you to say anything.'

'I don't fancy him.'

Sloane climbs into my bed and kisses me on the forehead.

'I forgive you,' she whispers in my ear. Because that's what friends do. They forgive.

Sloane is warm against my skin, and she strokes my head. At the corner of my cell, guards huddle; one runs towards me in a panic.

'Sloane? I only have one meeting left with Charlie. Do you think he will continue to visit me as a friend?'

Sloane squeezes me. 'I think, maybe, when he strolls along the beach, you'll visit him.'

All around me, guards voices are raised and panicked, but I feel okay, I feel fine. I close my eyes and for the first time, I don't see Ben, Ian, Leon, Robbie, Karla or Frank. I see my mother, Sloane, Cody, Vivian and Charlie. I smile. I see the stars.

Godfrey – I hope this novel makes its way to the library upstairs.

Joe – thank you for listening to me repeat varying iterations of the same sentence a million times, only for me to decide it was fine how it was.

Last, but not least, the wonderful Freddie Gillan. You believed in me before I believed in me. Thank you.

Acknowledgements

It appears dreams can indeed come true. I want to thank the below for all their help and support in making my dream come true.

My agent Hannah Todd. Thank you for all your insight, editorial expertise and for believing in me. I am truly blessed to have you in my corner.

A huge thanks to Elinor Davies for all your support with early drafts.

Anna Nightingale and Rachel Hart – your editorial wisdom has been beyond excellent. Thank you for all your notes. Working with you both has been a privilege, and I have grown as a writer from your insightful edits.

All the Avon team who have supported me in the creation of this novel.

All my fellow writers who have given me support and encouragement. Emma Steele for answering my endless questions. My writing group: Melissa, Joely, Ravi and Daragh. An incredibly bittersweet thank you to Gill Darling and Mark